BY HELEN SCHEUERER

The Legends of Thezmarr
Blood & Steel
Vows & Ruins
Fate & Furies
Shadow & Storms

The Ashes of Thezmarr
Iron & Embers
Thorns & Fire

HELEN SCHEUERER

THE ASHES OF THEZMARR
BOOK TWO

BRAMBLE

First published 2025 by Tor Bramble
an imprint of Pan Macmillan
The Smithson, 6 Briset Street, London ECIM 5NR
EU representative: Macmillan Publishers Ireland Ltd, 1st Floor,
The Liffey Trust Centre, 117–126 Sheriff Street Upper,
Dublin 1 DOI YC43
Associated companies throughout the world

ISBN 978-1-03506-731-2 HB
ISBN 978-1-0350-6732-9 TPB

Copyright © Helen Scheuerer 2025

The right of Helen Scheuerer to be identified as the
author of this work has been asserted in accordance
with the Copyright, Designs and Patents Act 1988.

All rights reserved. No part of this publication may be reproduced,
stored in a retrieval system, or transmitted, in any form, or by any means
(including, without limitation, electronic, mechanical, photocopying, recording or otherwise)
without the prior written permission of the publisher.

Pan Macmillan does not have any control over, or any responsibility for,
any author or third-party websites (including, without limitation, URLs,
emails and QR codes) referred to in or on this book.

1 3 5 7 9 8 6 4 2

A CIP catalogue record for this book is available from the British Library.

Midrealms map by Alec McKinley
Drevenor map by Melissa Nash

Typeset in Portrait Text by Palimpsest Book Production Ltd, Falkirk, Stirlingshire
Printed and bound in the UK using 100% Renewable Electricity by CPI Group (UK) Ltd

This book is sold subject to the condition that it shall not, by way of
trade or otherwise, be lent, hired out, or otherwise circulated without
the publisher's prior consent in any form of binding or cover other than
that in which it is published and without a similar condition including this
condition being imposed on the subsequent purchaser. The publisher does not
authorize the use or reproduction of any part of this book in any manner
for the purpose of training artificial intelligence technologies or systems.
The publisher expressly reserves this book from the Text and Data Mining
exception in accordance with Article 4(3) of the European Union
Digital Single Market Directive 2019/790.

Visit **www.panmacmillan.com** to read more about all
our books and to buy them.

*To every woman who was told to make herself
smaller and chose to burn brighter instead.
Your fire can light up the world.
This one's for you.*

REGARDING REFERENCES TO PLANTS AND POISONS

*Some are true, some are not.
It's safest not to guess which is which.
Don't try this at home.*

PROPHECY

'Gold will turn to silver in a blaze of iron and embers, giving rise to ancient power long forgotten'

– PROPHECY FROM
THE SEER QUEEN OF AVEUM

Map

- Delmira
- Dorinth
- Thezmarr
- The Mourner's Trail
- The Bloodwoods
- Hailford
- Harenth
- The Chained Islands
- The Broken Isles
- Ciraun
- Naarva
- The Scarlet Tower
- The Veil

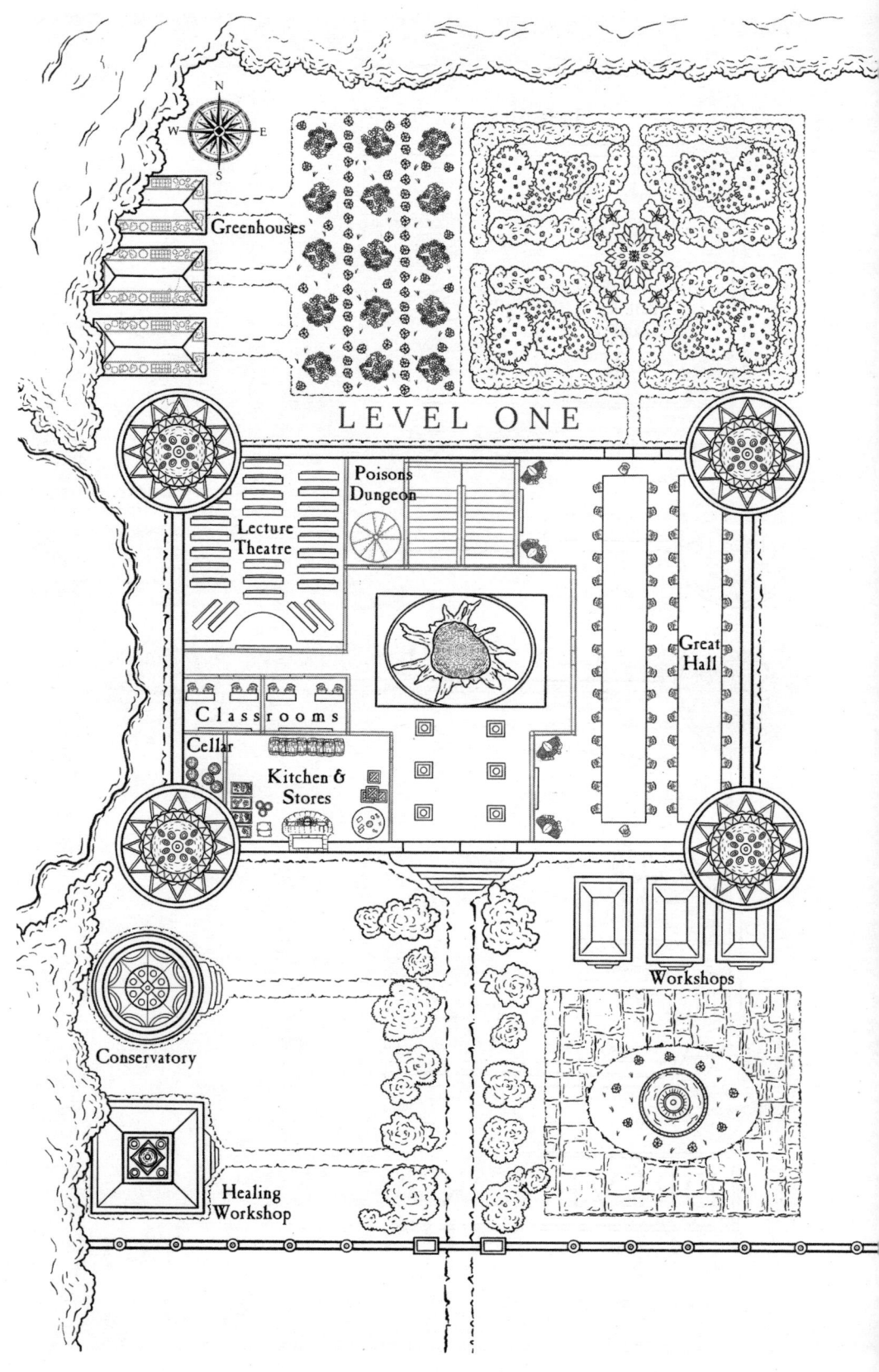

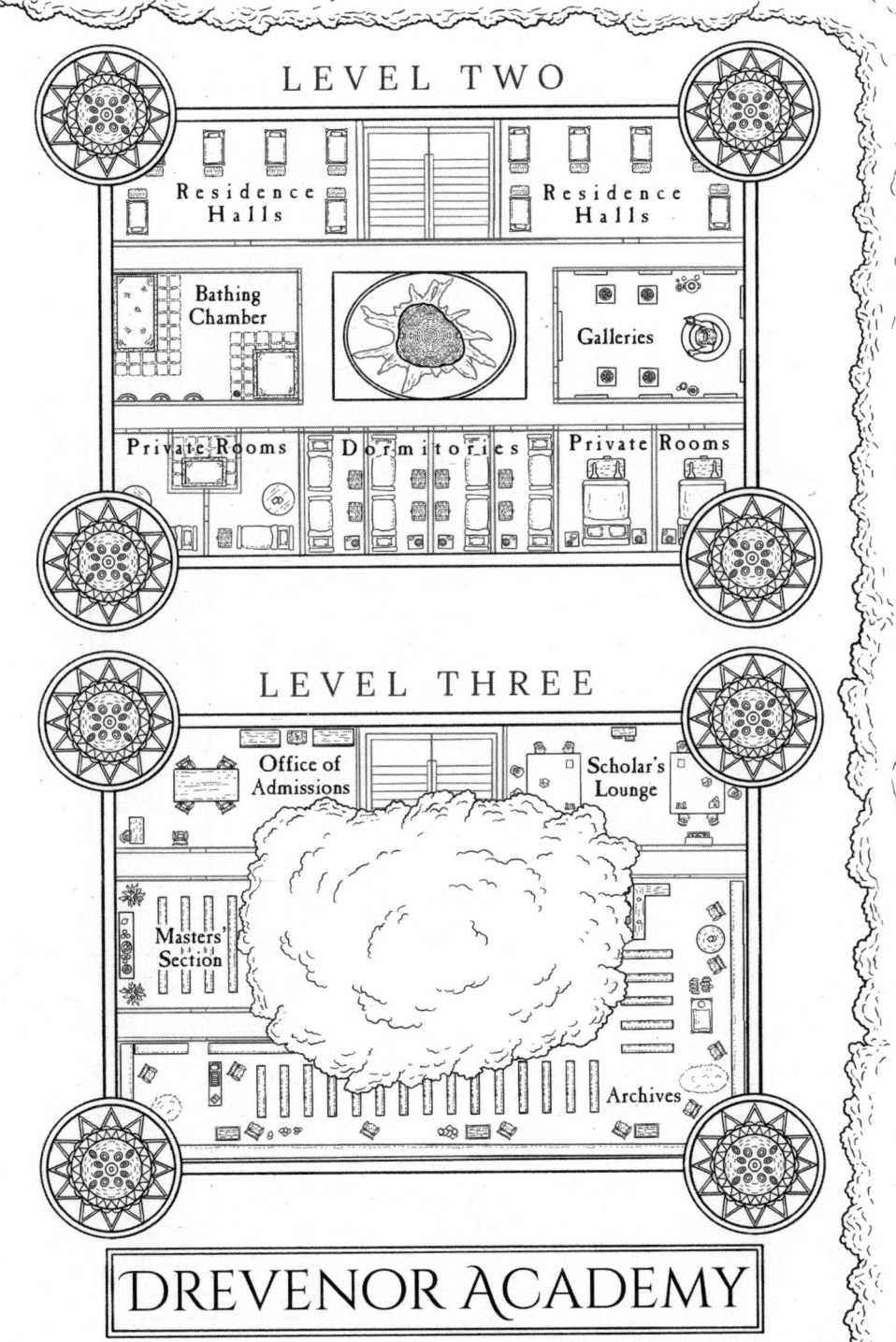

CHAPTER 1

Torj

'When the midrealms descended into the core conflict of the shadow war, there were only three Warswords in existence: Vernich Warner, Torj Elderbrock and Wilder Hawthorne. The Bloodletter, the Bear Slayer and the Hand of Death fought valiantly against tyranny and emerged triumphant from the harrowing final battle'

– *A History of Thezmarr*

THE AGONY OF it was blinding. The very fibres of Torj's soul were fraying apart, his bones catching alight, the flames devouring him from within. On and on it went, like nothing he'd ever endured.

And it wasn't his pain alone.

It was *Wren's*.

A golden thread joined them, a bond that went deeper than love, and it was now the very thing that was killing her.

Wren was dying.

Torj could feel the life leaving her through the tether between them.

'I love you,' he whispered, before, with all his strength, he tore the soul bond in two—

The slice of a blade through his skin brought him back to the present. A skirmish with a band of rebels, where he savoured the familiar dance of combat and the way his body leaned into the violence like the embrace of an old friend.

There was nothing like ending a life with his war hammer. Nothing like the impact vibrating up his arm as he swung and swung again.

Three dozen traitors.

Two Warswords.

And the clash of steel to drown out Torj's regrets.

'I thought there were only supposed to be five of them,' grunted his friend, Wilder, as he sliced the heel tendon of an opponent, blood spraying.

Torj brought his hammer down on another assailant. 'That's what our source said. Apparently, they were wrong.' He didn't care. Brushing a lock of silver hair from his eyes, he pivoted and struck out with his gore-streaked weapon again.

For two weeks, Torj and Wilder had tracked what they believed to be a small unit of the traitor organization, the People's Vanguard, across the midrealms. They were in search of Queen Reyna, who had been taken hostage during the recent attack on Drevenor Academy. But now, in an abandoned underground temple in Tver, there was no sign of her. Instead, flickering torchlight cast writhing shadows on the moss-covered walls, revealing that the enemy numbers far exceeded the details the Warswords had been given.

'On your left!' Torj shouted at his brother-in-arms as an assailant leapt from behind a statue. There was a flash of silver – steel gifted by the Furies – as the warrior known as the Hand of Death swung his swords.

The look of surprise was frozen on the enemy's face as his severed head flew, landing with a thud in a pool of someone else's blood.

'You're welcome,' Torj muttered.

Wilder launched himself into another attack. 'I knew he was there.'

Torj relished the battle-calm that settled over him as time slowed. His hammer became an extension of him, a blur of iron connecting with a knee, the joint giving way beneath the blow. Torj's momentum carried the weapon in an arc, catching another rebel in the side, ribs cracking beneath it. The thrill of the fight, the rhythm of combat – it was all he needed, all he *wanted*, or so he told himself as more bones and bodies broke around him. But it didn't matter how much damage he inflicted, or how much enemy blood he spilled . . .

There was no forgetting what he'd done.

To her.

His hand drifted to the web of scars beneath his shirt and a part of him reached out into the dark nothing before him, searching for something it would never find. Something that he had destroyed.

'It's the last piece of me you'll ever have.'

He'd hurt her, hurt her to save her, and now . . . he'd never have her.

With each swing of his hammer, he banished a memory of her from his mind. Wren's gaze softening as she showed him how to harvest lavender from Drevenor's gardens. The gentle weight of her hand on his chest. The taste of her on his lips.

'I'm yours as well.'

As more blood stained the tiles of the temple, he cast away the fantasies he'd had. Of one day showing her Tver, just the two of them; of building her a greenhouse of her own; of attending a gala, a name day – *anything*, proudly hand in hand.

Wilder's voice cut through the chaos. 'Queen Reyna's not with them.'

'I can see that,' Torj grunted as the flat of a blade hit his shoulder and he sent its wielder's head through a wall of tile. 'No hostages down here. Doesn't mean they don't know where she's being held.'

Torj's muscles burned as he hefted the massive war hammer, its weight a familiar comfort in his calloused hands. A line of rebels charged at him, shields raised high. He couldn't help the sense of satisfaction that washed over him as he swung low and the hammer's head whistled through the air. It connected with a resounding crack, splintering the shields and sending wooden shards flying. The rebels stumbled, off-balance, and Torj seized the opportunity. He pivoted, bringing the hammer up, catching the first man square in the chest. Ribs crunched beneath the blow, and the rebel flew backwards, crashing into his comrades.

'How have they recruited so many, so quickly?' Wilder called out.

'Why? Losing your touch, Hawthorne?' Torj shouted back, pushing forwards and using his Furies-given strength to throw another rebel off him. In one fluid motion, he reversed his grip and swung the hammer's spike end. It found its mark in the man's shoulder, puncturing armour and flesh alike. The rebel's scream was cut short as Torj wrenched the weapon free, bringing it down once more on the man's helm. The metal caved with a sickening crunch, and the rebel dropped like a stone.

'Hardly,' Wilder replied, thrusting his blade through an exposed neck. 'But it's not their numbers I'm worried about.'

Frowning, Torj whirled around, following his friend's gaze. A fresh group of rebels appeared in a passageway, glass vials in their hands.

'Shit,' he muttered, slitting another attacker's throat with his dagger, blood gushing across the tops of his boots. 'Hawthorne! Pull your mask up!' From around his neck, Torj drew a piece of fabric up over his mouth and nose—

Glass shattered at his feet.

A strange vapour coiled around his boots, attempting to creep up his leathers. Torj darted away, lifting rebels bodily from his path and hurling them across the temple, their shrieks echoing in the cavernous space.

Standing shoulder to shoulder with Wilder, Torj took in the vials exploding around them. 'There's no knowing how effective these masks are . . .' He brought his hammer down with all his might, aiming for the juncture of a nearby soldier's neck and shoulder. The squelch of ruined flesh and bone followed.

THORNS & FIRE

'They've been tested against the alchemy used at Drevenor during the battle.' Wilder threw a dagger across the temple, pinning a rebel through his shoulder to the wall by the entrance. 'Farissa warned that they'd only buy us time, if anything.'

'Great.' Torj scanned the advancing unit. Their vials glinted in the candlelight, more glass shattering around them. The acrid scent of chemicals and fumes filled the air. 'Then it's time to get the fuck out of here.'

'Agreed,' Wilder replied, thrusting his blade into an incoming rebel's ribs.

'But I'm not leaving empty-handed,' Torj growled. He started for the exit, pointing to where the lone rebel was still immobilized by Wilder's dagger. An emblem signalling a rank of leadership was clear on his chest. 'We fight our way out and take that bastard with us.'

Torj didn't wait to see if Wilder followed his order. With plumes of another chemical concoction billowing through the temple, he took on three attackers, the thrill of the fight still singing in his veins. This dance of life and death – this was what he was made for. Alchemy and alchemists be damned.

The Warswords battled their way through the ranks closing in, dodging potions and powders and all manner of horrors that had been born in a crucible. The temple was a flurry of chaos. Enemies screamed upon exposure to their own concoctions. Many clearly weren't trained in combat, which was something, but it made the creations they hurled at the warriors no less dangerous.

Ducking and weaving through the madness, Torj ripped Wilder's dagger free from the man, his scream near deafening. Lifting him by the back of his jerkin, Torj sprinted for the exit, where Wilder was carving his way through the last line of rebels.

Sunlight kissed Torj's face as he burst from the temple, passing beneath three towering stone statues of the great goddesses, the Furies.

'Hawthorne!' he shouted, glancing back at the angry mob still rushing towards them. Torj flung aside his captive, who scrambled back and cowered in the dust. With a deep breath, the Bear Slayer reached for the first stone likeness of the deities and pushed.

With all his Furies-given strength, he pressed his shoulder against the statue and bore down, meaning to block the passage entirely. The ancient monument creaked and protested beneath the force, but he could feel the leverage tipping in his favour—

'Now!' Wilder yelled from nearby.

A roar escaped Torj as he sank everything he had into a final drive of his body against the stone.

The statue gave way.

Torj sprang back as it crashed to the ground, a second monument following in its wake at the hands of Wilder, the sound booming through the surrounding valley, muffling the screams from within. Clouds of white dust poured from the site, rubble and ruins blocking the entrance to the temple entirely.

Only one of the Furies' likenesses remained standing.

Beside Torj, Wilder wiped the sweat from his brow and shook his head. 'How much bad luck did we just saddle ourselves with?'

Torj spat a mouthful of dust on the ground, surveying the damage. 'I don't want to know.' He turned to the rebel, who whimpered at the sight of him. 'Let's get this over with.'

His captive's eyes were wide with fear, but he remained stubbornly silent.

'I'm not against getting creative,' Torj warned the pitiful bastard, drawing his dagger from his belt menacingly. Without Wren, his purpose was singular now: to find and rescue the queen by whatever means necessary. When the job was done, he could leave everything behind.

Wilder approached, sheathing his swords with a tired sigh. 'Allow me,' he said, pulling out a small vial filled with a deep violet syrup. 'Our friend here is about to become very talkative.'

Torj's eyes narrowed at the potion. 'What is it?'

'A gift from your poisoner,' Wilder replied, uncorking the vial.

'She's not *my* anything,' Torj bit out.

Wilder simply snorted and forced the concoction to the rebel's mouth, pouring it down his throat as he thrashed against their hold. 'Wren called it a truth serum of sorts,' he explained, ramming his hand across the lower half of the man's face so he couldn't spit it out.

Torj faltered. Her name spoken aloud sent a bolt of lightning through his chest, had the scent of spring rain and jasmine unfurling impossibly around him.

'She said it would make our jobs easier without resorting to . . . Well, more traditional methods,' Wilder continued.

'When?'

'Around the same time she dismissed you as her guard . . . which you *still* haven't talked about.'

Torj clenched his jaw. It certainly wasn't the first time his friend had tried to wrangle an explanation from him or rile him up. 'There's nothing to say.'

'No?' Wilder raised a brow as the rebel kicked out, his eyes widening as the potion took effect. 'Because one minute you were kissing her for all the world to see, and the next . . . Well, look around, Bear Slayer. You obviously fucked up.'

'You would know. You've made more than your fair share of mistakes.'

'Exactly, which is why—'

'Enough,' Torj growled, thrusting his chin towards their captive. 'There are more pressing matters at hand.'

Wilder gave a grunt of reluctant agreement and removed his hand from the rebel's mouth.

Torj noted the telltale signs of poisoning in his dilated pupils and shallow breaths; he was no longer thrashing against them, but seemed be experiencing an internal struggle.

A calculated and powerful concoction was at work. It was Wren's creation alright.

'Where is the Queen of Aveum?' Torj asked. 'Where is Queen Reyna?'

The rebel seemed to fight against the words escaping him, but they broke from his lips all the same: 'There's a shipping yard . . . A few days' ride from here . . .'

Torj gaped at him. He knew better than to question what exactly was in the potion. Wren was as deadly as a viper when she wanted to be. Though he knew well enough by now that there were no limits to what she could achieve, it was another thing entirely to see a man's willpower altered so quickly before his very eyes. Still, he had an interrogation to conduct.

'Be more specific,' he snapped. 'Where is the shipping yard? Is Queen Reyna there now? How many hold her?'

'Three days' ride at most, south-west as the crow flies. There's a map with it marked in my pocket,' he rasped. 'Your queen is there. And will be until the end of the week. A band of the People's Vanguard holds her. Some of our very best. More than you found here.'

'Have they harmed her?' he demanded.

'Not that I know of,' the rebel replied. 'But things happen on the road . . .'

Torj glared at their captive, jabbing a finger into the emblem on his chest. 'What are you, a captain? How is your leader recruiting? From where?'

'A captain, yes.' The rebel sighed, blinking slowly and sagging in defeat against the effects of the serum. 'He targets the worst-affected villages from each of the kingdoms, the ones still not recovered from the shadow war. He arms them with potions and poisons, with alchemy . . . He chooses people to spread word of the cause and to root out anyone who still believes in the old ways.'

'Old ways?' Wilder barked. 'What the fuck does that mean?'

'The ways of kings and queens.' The fervour in the man's eyes made Torj uneasy. 'Where we commoners are forced to bow to magic wielders. Rulers and Warswords are relics now, brought down by humble potions . . .'

Torj's hand found its way around their captive's throat. 'Thezmarr won't stand for it.'

The traitor spoke his final words with a bitter smile. 'Every reign has its end.'

CHAPTER 2

Wren

'Repetition and failure are the backbones of alchemy'

– *Alchemy Unbound*

'For Furies' sake,' Wren cursed, watching as yet another experiment failed in the shallow dish before her.

Her sister Thea glanced up from where she was poring over several maps on Wren's bed, twirling her dagger between her fingers. 'What is it?'

The war hero hadn't objected to being appointed Wren's temporary guard after the Bear Slayer had been sent away. She hadn't even complained about being separated from Wilder, nor had she pushed Wren to divulge what had happened between her and the Bear Slayer after the battle. But seeing her sister where *he* had sat cleaning his hammer struck a raw nerve in Wren every time.

'We were fooling ourselves, thinking this could work.'

'You made me someone I'm not. I'm a fucking Warsword, Embervale. I'll always *be a Warsword.'*

'I'm exactly *the man you thought I was.'*

His absence made her feel how she'd felt in those early months after the war had ended – when she was bone-weary, when all hope seemed to have been sucked out of the world around her, even though it was finally free of darkness. Worse, now a new darkness had taken hold of the world, taken hold of *her*, and she couldn't seem to defeat it.

'I don't understand,' she told her sister, staring into the alchemy samples that had been the bane of her existence for a fortnight. 'The solution I gave Zavier *worked*. It saved his life! Yet two weeks later, I still can't replicate it . . . *What am I missing?*'

'Have you considered that what you're missing might be *sleep*?' Thea grumbled.

'No one else at Drevenor is sleeping, Thea,' Wren replied sharply. 'Everyone here is doing what they can to understand the threat, to prepare us for what's to come. Every adept and sage in this academy is working as we speak, perfecting advanced forms of alchemy that will aid us in any conflict.'

As an adept, Wren would not be competing in another Gauntlet, but rather contributing to the field of alchemy itself. An opus. Each adept was to work on one – a major project within their particular area of interest, which they would present to the masters at the end of the semester in order to graduate to the rank of sage.

With Farissa's guidance, Wren had chosen to recreate the counter-alchemy she had invented as a novice – the potion that had saved Zavier Terling, the long-lost Prince of Naarva, who was currently being crowned on the far side of the kingdom.

'Wren,' Thea said evenly, swinging her legs over the side of the bed and pinning her with a pointed look. 'All I'm saying is that you can't work yourself to death. You're the one who solved this puzzle last time. You will be the one to solve it again.'

Wren braced herself against her workbench with a huff of frustration. 'I'm not sure that I can . . .' It was the first time she'd admitted it out loud, but over the past fortnight, she'd questioned if the first time had been a fluke. Her doubts only continued to fester, particularly as more was revealed about the substances the so-called People's Vanguard had weaponized.

In the aftermath, the academy masters had studied each and every trace of enemy alchemy left behind on weapons and bodies. It was the largest sample they'd had to work with, which meant Wren and Farissa had been able to analyse its properties in a way they hadn't before.

What they'd found had terrified them.

Darkness. Shadow. Remnants of the previous war, laced with poison and chemicals, their deadliest elements combined. A fusion that explained the enemy's ability to mute the magic of royals and Warswords alike.

Power like this had swept across the midrealms before, and they had barely survived. Were men so hungry for dominion that they would burn the world to ash around them to achieve it? Was history doomed to repeat itself?

A bitter taste filled Wren's mouth. She knew the answer to that. And she was partly to blame. It had been her work from the previous war that had led the enemy's discoveries . . . The manacles flashed in her mind. They were her invention, something she'd prided herself on – a unique form of alchemy designed to target specific properties in the blood, specific people. Now, magic wielders like her were those targets.

Wren wasn't sure if she was imagining it, but the triggering scent of burnt hair tickled her nostrils. The smell brought bile to the back of her throat, and she gripped the edge of her workbench as a cold sweat broke out across her skin.

Breathe, she told herself. *You're at Drevenor. In your room.* Her gaze swept the bench for something to ground her. *Mortar and pestle. Crucible. Harvesting knife.* She listed the objects she saw, and slowly, air began to fill her lungs once more.

Taking a sip of water to soothe her dry throat, Wren peered out the window. The ivy-clad iron gates and the academy motto – *Knowledge is the victor over fate. The mind is a blade* – seemed to mock her. She dropped her head into her hands. 'I'm failing.'

'Wren,' Thea scoffed. 'What a load of horseshit. You did it before.

You'll do it again. But for the love of Thezmarr, eat something. Rest. And for all our sakes, take a fucking bath.'

'I'm not that bad.' That was a lie. She passed a hand over her face, knowing exactly what she looked like. Dark smudges loomed beneath her eyes; her bronze hair was even more unkempt than usual in its messy knot. Black ink stained her fingers and was splattered across her apron and gown.

Thea snorted. 'It's like you've never heard of soap. Or a hairbrush. And that's saying something, coming from me.'

Wren pushed the loose, dishevelled hair from her eyes and glanced around at the pile of unopened letters by the door, the half-eaten bowl of stew and stale bread sitting atop her trunk of supplies . . . Guttering candles and a smoky oil lamp illuminated the medallion she'd won by passing the Gauntlet, discarded on the windowsill by her box of poisoner's trinkets, long forgotten. Gods, there were even cobwebs in the corners of the room. She supposed she had let things get out of hand.

Thea wrinkled her nose at the vials of blood on her work surface. 'It's probably not helping that you're bloodletting yourself so regularly for these experiments. I've offered a million times.'

'I'm fine, Thea.' Wren flipped through her notes again, agitated. 'For now, all I need is to get back to work.'

Wren could feel her sister's eyes on her as she sorted through her concoctions, as she spilled more ink on her apron and as she swore under her breath . . .

'It's alright to miss him, you know,' Thea began cautiously.

Wren's gaze snapped up to hers. She opened her mouth—

'Don't you dare say "who,"' Thea warned.

Sparks crackled at Wren's fingertips without warning, and she fought to keep her already broken magic within the confines of her body. Now more than ever, it was a living thing inside her, as restless and chaotic as she felt, always clawing to be let loose.

'I can feel it, you know,' Thea commented, pinning her with a knowing look. 'The lightning singing in your veins.'

'Of course you can feel it,' Wren bit back. 'We're family. We share the same blood, the same power.'

Thea raised a sceptical brow. 'Tell me you have it under control.'

'I have it under control,' Wren replied flatly.

'Then why haven't you talked about the Bear Slayer? Asked about him?' Thea pressed, her face lined with concern. 'There's more to this than either of you are letting on, but every time he's mentioned I can feel a storm gathering around you . . .'

'Then it's a good thing he's far away.' Wren hated how raw her voice sounded, how vulnerable. She gestured to the potions on her bench, determined to return her focus to her work and her desperation to succeed. 'What am I supposed to do, Thea? If I can't do this, then *why am I here*? What's the point? How many people will suffer?'

Thea stood, moving forwards to grip her shoulder firmly. 'The devastation will pass. I promise. I have felt those things before, and I came out the other side. You will too. You're far from worthless. We've all watched you go from strength to strength. You're allowed to wobble. You're allowed to have a gloomy day. But this is not your *forever*. This is not the day to base all other days on.'

Her sister's words were of little comfort when Wren found herself in what remained of the great hall the next day, waiting for Farissa. Sunlight filtered through the shattered stained-glass windows, casting broken rainbows across the floor. The debris had been swept away in the wake of the battle, but the deep gouges and scorch marks remained. The hair on Wren's nape stood on end as she anticipated the scent of smoke, only to find that it had at last cleared. But something more sinister lingered in its place: spilled blood and the potent chemical tang of a darker kind of alchemy.

I hereby pledge myself to Drevenor.

The oath danced on the tip of her tongue as she took in the torn tapestries hanging above the dais where she had graduated from novice alchemist to adept only weeks before. For a moment, she wondered if she was destined to walk among the ruins for ever. Heir to a fallen kingdom, survivor of a war-torn fortress, student of a ravaged academy . . . Perhaps she was cursed.

When Farissa approached, she was sure of it. 'I cannot hold them off any longer, Elwren. The masters want answers. Thezmarr and the rulers want answers. How soon until the elixir is ready to replicate?'

Wren tried not to let her shoulders cave in. She fought desperately to keep her throat from closing as she met her former mentor's gaze. 'Farissa, I—'

But her voice cracked. Horror filled her as burning tears blurred her vision and her storm magic surged, as though it sensed the fracture in her armour. She felt lightning beneath her skin, a current she could surrender to so that the maelstrom of the past, her failings of the present, couldn't drag her down, couldn't break her apart.

Of all things, it was *his* voice that came to her, that filled her mind.

'We survived. You and me. Together.'

A gentle hand guided her by her elbow. 'Come with me, Elwren.'

In the more intimate setting of Farissa's private quarters, seated at the small table by the bookshelves, the older woman said with unflinching frankness, 'You've been unable to replicate it, haven't you?'

Steeling herself against any further emotional breakdown, Wren gave a single nod of confirmation, shame flaming her cheeks.

If Farissa was shocked or angry, she didn't show it. Instead, she sighed. 'Drevenor demands a lot from its students. You more than most. Alchemy is all about transformation, knowledge and learning, and somewhere along the way, I have failed to guide you.'

'Farissa, it's not your fault—'

The older woman silenced her with a look. 'You have been treated like a sage here, when you are but a newly graduated adept. I think because of the war I forget how young you are.'

'I'm thirty—'

Farissa gave a wry smile. 'And so? You think you should have all the answers? You think that every facet of this complicated world is your responsibility alone to bear? That you can stop a war on your own?'

'I can try.'

'Yes, you can try, Elwren . . . But you can *also* ask for help.' The Master Alchemist leaned back in her chair. 'The midrealms as we know them are changing. Kings and queens can be stripped of their magic . . . Warswords who were once the ultimate beacons of strength can be felled by a potion. And at the heart of it all is this.'

Farissa held up a familiar glass vial of iridescent liquid.

'The mind is a blade, Elwren. Let's see what ours can do together.'

Wren brought her research to Farissa's quarters, and hours later, the two alchemists had reviewed every page of notes, every sample, every ingredient Wren had trialled. The robust bookshelves were almost bare, with countless volumes pulled from their stacks only to be rifled through and set aside on the floor.

Looking more than a little unhinged, grey fly-aways framing her face, Farissa surveyed the assorted vials. 'You're *certain* this is everything you used?'

'Yes. I've checked everything to the point of madness,' Wren told her, eyes gritty as she stared into the fire. The crackling hearth failed to soothe the sinking despair in her chest.

But Farissa paced around the table, picking items up, reading their labels and placing them back down, clicking her tongue in frustration, as though the answer were staring them right in the face.

'We've been over it a hundred times,' Wren said gently.

'And we'll review it a hundred more if necessary.' Farissa picked up an empty jar. 'Remind me what was in this?'

'The binding agent,' Wren replied. 'The powdered leaves of that plant from Delmira. I discovered later that it was actually a common silvertide rose. They're a hardy climber; they grow all over the midrealms.'

Farissa nodded. 'Master Norlander would be pleased with you. Isolating the leaves is a well-established use for such a plant in lifelore.'

Wren made a noise of agreement, reaching for another book—

'Wait,' Farissa said suddenly, tipping the jar to dislodge any remnants. Only a fine dust remained. 'You brought these leaves from Delmira?'

Wren's brow furrowed as she slowly turned back to the older woman. 'Yes, originally. And then once I identified what the plant was, I sourced it from the greenhouses here . . .' She trailed off.

Farissa chewed her lip. 'And you harvested the original leaves yourself?'

'Yes, though the academy's crop was in a far healthier state.'

'What was the original growing site like?' Farissa pressed.

'Like everywhere else in Delmira: barren, poisoned land . . . Just a small patch of weeds in the cracked earth near my cottage. Honestly, I was surprised anything was growing there at all.'

'And yet . . . you used it in your work.'

Wren folded her arms over her chest defensively. 'And it was effective. Is it wrong to hypothesize that the same species of rose grown in far more nourishing conditions would serve as an even better binding agent?'

'It's not wrong,' Farissa allowed with a small smile. 'But did it do as hypothesized?'

Wren approached the table, taking the empty jar and the one containing her new supply from the greenhouse. At what point had she switched from one to the other? 'I . . .'

'I should have asked you this sooner.' Farissa heaved an enormous tome from her shelves and set it down on the table, flipping to the table of contents, scanning it intensely. Biting her lip, Wren's former master turned to a page full of botanical drawings, pointing to one of them. 'Was this the flower?'

Wren stared at the page, scrutinizing the likeness. 'The leaves are identical, yes, but the bush wasn't blooming when I harvested, so the petals . . . I'm not sure.'

Not taking her eyes from the page, the older woman rubbed her temples. 'I think one of two things has happened here . . . Either you misidentified the species – an easy thing to do when you're not at the original site and don't have the full plant available for observation – or there was something particular about the conditions there that affected your supplies from Delmira.'

Wren's stomach bottomed out. She had never even considered that she might have misidentified the plant, or that the ruins of her homeland might have properties that could somehow *favourably* impact the plant life there.

'I was arrogant,' she murmured, hanging her head. 'I didn't question myself. I didn't interrogate—'

'You made a mistake,' Farissa cut in.

'A mistake that cost the midrealms weeks of time,' Wren argued. 'Time that could have been spent putting an end to this madness, had I not been so *stupid*—'

'Stop.' Farissa's gaze was sharp as it met hers. 'I will not watch you descend into the endless pit of what could have been. We need to look forward to what *can* be done.'

Wren searched Farissa's eyes for the same hopelessness she herself felt, but she found none.

'From here, there's only one path left for you, Elwren.'

The air around Wren rippled, and tiny arcs of lightning danced between her fingers. She felt its current through her whole body as she breathed, 'And that is?'

Farissa placed a hand on her shoulder, her grip firm, fierce determination burning in the depths of her eyes. 'You must return to Delmira.'

CHAPTER 3

Torj

'Do you want our kingdoms to be a place of peace?
Join us in our fight for a better world'

— *The People's Vanguard*

WITH THE TRAITOR'S words still ringing in their ears, Torj and Wilder travelled swiftly across the golden plains of Tver towards the south-west coast. Both Warswords hid the telltale symbols of rank on their arms. Torj wore a cloak and hood, concealing his silver hair. His war hammer was wrapped in canvas and strapped to his saddle. There was not much to be done about the impressive stallions they rode but to dull their gleaming black coats with dust from the road. There could be no reports back to the People's Vanguard about their approach, not if they meant to extract Queen Reyna safely.

Riding beside Torj, Wilder patted the twin swords he'd tied to his own bags rather than wearing them across his back as he usually did. 'Just two average men taking in the sights, eh, Bear Slayer?'

'Speak for yourself. Nothing average about me, Hawthorne.'

Around them, dusk had fallen, and Torj couldn't stop his gaze from lingering on the gilded hillsides and sweeping valleys. The last time he'd set foot in this kingdom had been in the war years, during the battle for the castle in the capital of Notos. It had hurt to see the lands drenched in darkness and swarming with shadow wraiths; the conflict was bloody and brutal, leaving their victory bittersweet. The time before that had been to continue his search for his missing grandmother, and before that, when he had faced the cursed bears that had earned him his moniker.

It hadn't been all that long ago that he'd imagined bringing Wren here, just the two of them, showing her where the great teerah panthers roamed and where fields of wild thyme bloomed as far as the eye could see. He'd always thought she'd like to see it. He was hit with a wave of anguish at the thought that now she never would – not by his side, anyway.

They rode through the night and into the next morning. The long grass was kissed with dew in the golden dawn rays. A cool breeze carried the scent of salt from the distant coast, mingling with the earthy smell of damp soil and sending a shiver across the stretches of untamed fields. The creaking of leather beneath Torj brought another flash of Wren to his mind – flush against him in this very saddle, her backside rubbing over the hard length of him, causing a burst of pleasure that was over all too soon.

A melodic laugh had followed. *'Challenge me to a game, Bear Slayer, and you'd best prepare to lose.'*

The longing hit him like a physical blow, leaving him breathless for a moment.

The delicate, infectious notes of her laugh, the softness of her skin, the storm in her eyes when she was irritated . . . All of which made him want to fuck her senseless. But those moments were now replaced by the sound of her scream as his own wound had seared itself into her flesh, her cries of agony as he'd severed the soul bond between them . . . And then the sight of the confusion and hurt on her beautiful face when he'd ended things between them without so much as an explanation.

He'd done it for her.

To save her.

But it ached no less for that fact. He knew in his bones that, bond or no, it would never end.

He would be cursed to want the poisoner until the end of his days.

⁂

After another day's ride, Torj found himself staking out the derelict Tverrian coastline. The Warswords had left their horses at a nearby village and now crouched on the outskirts of a strange place, scanning the site for any sign of the People's Vanguard and the queen they had taken captive.

Dotted along the city waterfront were three abandoned dry docks – rectangular basins carved into the shore, the walls lined with rough-hewn stone. In the one just below Torj and Wilder, a half-built ship rested on a cradle of enormous timber beams, its hull exposed to the air, covered in algae, slowly being reclaimed by nature.

Torj could smell decay. 'Must have gone out of business after the war,' he murmured, his gaze falling to the seaward end of the dock, where a massive wooden gate held back the lapping waves. Pools of stagnant water had gathered in the dips of the uneven ground regardless, and from where the warriors hid up on the side wall, they could see remnants of old scaffolding leaning precariously, the timber bleached by sun and salt, while rusted chains and corroded equipment lay scattered about the dock floor.

'Perfect place to hold someone hostage,' Wilder observed. 'I'll wager no one can hear the screams for miles.'

'All the better for us when we deal with them.' Torj gripped his hammer as he spotted two guards patrolling below. 'There must be a way into their headquarters there. Did you see where they came from?'

Wilder pointed. 'There looks to be an entrance by those blocks over there. See the wall?'

'I see it.' Torj shouldered his hammer, taking the lead.

Together, the Warswords descended into the dry dock in silence, using the yard's clutter and shadows to their advantage. They had to be fast and silent. Queen Reyna's life would depend on it.

'No blades,' Torj instructed his friend in a low voice. 'Don't want to alert whoever's inside that we're coming.'

Wilder simply nodded.

They crouched behind the cover of a crumbling facade. Torj's gaze fixed on the four visible guards walking the length of the wall in pairs. He held up three fingers, then two, then one. On his signal, the warriors sprang into action.

Torj darted towards the two guards on the left, his footfalls softened by the damp silt. The first guard barely had time to turn before Torj's arm snaked around his throat, cutting off his air and, with a single jerk, snapping his neck.

To his right, Wilder had already taken down one guard and was silencing the next. Torj's second target reached for his sword, a shout of warning on his lips, but Torj was faster, lunging and clapping a hand over his opponent's mouth. The man's eyes bulged, his fingers clawing uselessly at Torj's iron grip before he went limp.

With all four guards taken care of swiftly, Torj and Wilder exchanged a look of grim satisfaction. Neither had broken a sweat. They dragged the bodies behind several stacked pallets, concealing them from view before turning to a rusted side door in the towering wall.

'We take them out quickly and at a distance where possible. They might have those strength-muting manacles,' Torj reminded Wilder.

'And if the manacles are on the queen?' Wilder asked.

'We take her anyway. Someone at Drevenor will find a way to remove them.'

'Someone?' Wilder prodded with mock innocence.

'Time and place, Hawthorne,' Torj growled in warning.

'Right.'

Torj rummaged through his pockets. 'Masks,' he said, thrusting a fresh piece of material at Wilder.

'Thanks,' his friend replied, placing the material over his nose and mouth and tying it at the back of his head.

With his own mask in place, Torj rose to his feet, hammer at the ready. 'Let's go.'

To his surprise, the rusted door made no sound as it swung inwards, revealing more of the vast dock beyond. They met no resistance at the immediate entrance. The only sound was the dripping water that ran down the walls. Skeletal shadows of hanging tools danced in the weak afternoon sun and the air hung heavy with the stench of rot.

Peering around the corner, Torj loosed a breath. 'It's empty,' he murmured.

'Then why the guards outside?' Wilder's eyes narrowed as they followed Torj's gaze across the neglected space. He pointed. 'There's a tunnel.'

'Then that's where we go.'

The Warswords followed the perimeter until they heard voices drifting towards them and the distant sound of waves crashing. Daylight filtered in from further down.

'The dry dock was just a holding area,' Torj guessed as he saw movement. 'A place to store supplies, to hide hostages until they were ready . . .'

Sticking to the shadows of the walls, the two warriors crept closer, at last able to make out the scene before them.

Boats.

And a unit of traitors preparing them.

'We can take them,' Wilder said.

'Not before we find the queen,' Torj murmured, scanning the cavern. A group of rebels bustled about, piling crates, coils of rope and sheets of canvas into vessels bobbing on the water just below. Torj counted two dozen men, but his view of whatever platform sat beneath was obscured, and there was no telling how many could be down there.

Amid the clutter, he saw something that made his blood run cold. 'Do you see that?'

Beside him, Wilder squinted. 'Is that . . .'

A few yards away, a crate lay on its side, an array of what looked like bones spilling out across the wet ground.

'It's been a long time, but I'd never forget the sight of shadow wraith horns and talons,' Torj murmured. 'What the fuck are they doing here?'

Wilder's answer was grim. 'My guess? We don't want to know . . .'

Torj nodded. 'Something tells me they're not being collected for fun. We need to take one back to the academy.'

'Be my guest, Bear Slayer.'

Using the shifting shadows as cover, Torj approached the crate, snatching up a talon and a horn for good measure, pocketing them with a grimace.

When he returned to his brother-in-arms, Wilder nodded towards the far end of the tunnel. 'She's there,' he whispered.

Queen Reyna was slumped against a broken beam of timber, her wrists and ankles bound, the same regal dress she'd worn to the novice graduation ceremony weeks ago now tattered and stained.

'No one's guarding her . . .' Torj gauged the distance between the traitor unit and Aveum's queen. 'But there's no way we won't be seen.'

'Then we go in swinging,' Wilder replied, slowly unsheathing his swords.

Torj scanned the men, noting that none had belts of potions and most were occupied with the task at hand. He nodded, gripping his hammer. 'Fuck it.'

As one, they burst from the shadows, launching themselves at the nearest rebels, who barely had time to scream.

Torj's hammer carved its arc, and once more he found himself relishing the song of violence, the keen blows of retribution. He pivoted, avoiding the kiss of a rusted cutlass, bringing his hammer around in a powerful swing. It connected with a rebel's side, sending him flying backwards into his comrades.

The clash of steel rang out as, nearby, Wilder's twin swords met incoming blades. Out of the corner of his eye, Torj saw the queen stir. And still no one went to her. No one tried to protect their prize.

He carved a line through a unit of rebels, closing the gap between him and their captive. But a particularly brave – or foolish – rebel attempted to flank him. Torj reversed his grip, driving the hammer's spike into the man's thigh. As the rebel howled in agony, Torj wrenched the weapon free and brought it down on the man's skull with a wet thud. Beneath rune-marked iron and Furies-given strength, armour crumpled like parchment.

Before Torj could move on, a small vial flew through the air, shattering at his feet. Green smoke billowed up, forcing him back as he clutched the material of his mask to his face.

'Torj!'

Wilder's voice sounded distant. Through watering eyes, Torj saw his friend swaying. His mask had slipped in the fighting, and he was clearly being affected by whatever vapour now drifted in the air around them.

Disposing of another rebel, Torj reached for the pouch at his belt – for the antidote kit Wren had prepared a lifetime ago. 'Hawthorne!' he called. 'Catch! There's iruseed in there—'

He was cut off by a glancing blow to the shoulder, but he regained his footing and unleashed a whirlwind of devastating strikes, blood splattering in his wake.

'Furies save us,' he heard one rebel gasp.

'Who do you think made us?' Torj said, and snapped the man's neck with his bare hands—

'*Enough.*'

The voice was calm, and it cut through the chaos like a hot blade, strange enough that the fighting paused.

Torj's gaze snapped up. He recognized the mask instantly – it was different from all the rest. A monster rendered in blackened metal; eyeholes elongated in a menacing design. The mask of the man who'd stabbed him at Drevenor, who'd nearly killed Wren.

With a roar, Torj surged for him, ready to shed blood, ready to crush—

'Not yet, Warsword.' The enemy's voice carried a gentle amusement as he raised a small vial, its contents catching the sunlight streaming in behind him. 'One drop of this could strip you of all that Furies-given power you hold so dear . . .'

Torj faltered. There was something strangely familiar about that voice, a lilt he couldn't quite place. Beside him, he heard Wilder curse under his breath.

'Who are you?' Torj demanded, keeping his eyes locked on the enemy leader even as his soldiers closed ranks around them. Many now held potions they hadn't had before, their synchronized movements too practised to be spontaneous.

'Lord Silas, leader of the people.' That delicate hint of an accent slipped through again. 'Liberator of the midrealms.'

Torj twirled his hammer with a dark laugh. 'What kind of *liberator* poisons an innocent woman?'

Though the man's face wasn't visible, Torj heard the smile in his voice, noted the satisfaction radiating from his stance. 'Innocent? Hardly, Warsword. And poison? What flows through her veins is far more . . . *interesting* than mere poison. You will see.'

Behind him, the queen's laboured breathing suddenly seemed more ominous.

'We won't let you take her,' Wilder said fiercely.

'Take her?' Silas's laugh held genuine amusement. 'Why would I want to do that? She's exactly where she needs to be.'

Torj took a step forward, hammer raised. 'If you think—'

'I don't think, Warsword. I *know*.' Silas reached into his cloak. 'Time will prove me right.'

Torj took another step forward. He had no intention of allowing the bastard to leave—

The masked alchemist laughed again, the sound chilling. 'Consider this a parting gift.'

With a flick of his wrist, he threw a small box, which opened in mid-air. An array of darts exploded from its confines. Torj threw himself not at Silas but at Queen Reyna, using his body to shield her. He felt the sting of tiny, sharp pinpricks at his back, but a strangled cry from the queen snatched his attention.

Scanning her quickly, he realized she wasn't hurt, but was watching in terror as Silas's men moved with practised efficiency, one smashing a vial beneath his boot. Blue-grey smoke billowed out, rapidly expanding to engulf the entire area. Through the haze, Torj heard the enemy's voice again.

'Healing is such a fascinating branch of alchemy.' Silas's words drifted back to them, the vapour parting to reveal him and his boats already moving out to sea.

Torj stared after the leader, mind racing. Around him, the smoke dissipated too quickly to be natural, leaving him alive, armed and with a sinking realization: they weren't just witnesses to an attack. There was a much bigger game at play here, and they had all just become pawns in whatever came next.

'Check the queen,' Wilder coughed from nearby, kicking shattered glass away.

With a stiff nod, Torj turned back to the ruler still in his grasp. 'Your Majesty, are you hurt?' he asked softly, as he sliced through her bonds with a quick flick of his dagger.

Queen Reyna's eyes were unfocused, her movements sluggish. 'Bear Slayer?'

'Yes, it's me, Your Majesty,' he soothed, checking her over for any wounds. Why would the rebels leave her – or any of them – alive? He forced down the worst of his thoughts and tried to help Reyna up.

The queen reached out, her fingers brushing Torj's hair softly. 'Gold . . .' she muttered. 'Gold will turn to silver.'

A knot of unease tightened in Torj's stomach, and he exchanged a worried glance with Wilder. Whatever drug the rebels had given her was strong.

'Yes,' he murmured. 'My hair changed during the shadow war, Your Majesty. You've seen me like this before. It's alright. You're alright. We'll get you cleaned up.'

'Speaking of,' Wilder said warily, sheathing his swords as he approached Torj and reached for his back. Three sharp stings followed.

'What the fuck?' Torj turned in time to see Wilder casting a handful of darts aside.

His friend's brow furrowed. 'You alright?'

'I'm fine,' Torj replied, the sting already gone.

Wilder looked like he wanted to say more, but he gave a stiff nod instead. 'Let's get out of here. There could be more forces on the way . . . Or we could be standing in some sort of trap . . .'

'Agreed,' Torj nodded, helping the queen to her feet. 'And let's flood the dock on the way out. Leave no trace of them here.'

Beside him, the queen swayed and blinked up at him, mesmerized. She reached for his hair again. 'Gold will turn to silver in a blaze of iron and embers, giving rise to ancient power long forgotten . . .'

A breath shuddered out of Torj, his skin prickling. 'What did you say?'

But the queen fainted in his arms.

CHAPTER 4

Wren

'Untamed sovereign magic has always been a threat
to the common folk of the midrealms'

— The Midrealms Chronicles

'WHAT DID YOU say?'

The words rang through Wren – a surreal ripple, tying her to another place. For a moment, she was not aboard the *Sea Serpent's Destiny* on her way to Delmira, but somewhere else entirely. The scent of black cedar and oakmoss surrounded her, consuming her senses, and she could feel the echo of a familiar spark in her chest.

'When I'm nothing but ash among the embers, I'll still be yours . . .'

It hit her like a bolt of lightning to the heart: the rush of his impassioned words against her skin, the slide of him deep inside her, that piercing storm-blue gaze that saw right into her soul—

'Wren?' Thea nudged her. 'What did you say?'

Wren blinked, coming back to herself as the crisp, briny sea air swept away any trace of what she thought she'd smelled in the wind. 'I . . . I was saying that for the first time since we discovered our heritage, we're . . .'

'Together? Going home?' Thea finished for her.

Home. It should have stirred something within her – excitement, relief, perhaps a piece of some long-forgotten puzzle falling into place. Instead, it left an ache in her chest, a void she couldn't name.

Thezmarr. Delmira. Drevenor. Each place had meant something to her.

But none of them had ever been *home*.

For a whisper of time, home had smelled of black cedar and oakmoss, had tasted of dark promises and desire . . . had sounded like a husky laugh dancing along her skin.

'It's bittersweet, isn't it?' Thea asked, leaning on the weathered railing beside her, and for a moment Wren thought her sister had read her mind. But Thea sighed. 'The last time we travelled together, Anya was with us.'

Wren stared at the waves on the horizon. 'She was.'

'We don't talk much about her,' her sister observed.

'It hurts to talk about her. About Sam and Ida, too.' Wren picked at the skin around her nails, bracing herself against the rush of grief flooding her chest.

'I miss them,' Thea said.

'Me too. Every day. It feels so unfair that we lost them. And Anya . . . We had only just got her back. We were only just getting to know her.'

'I know.' Thea reached out and stilled Wren's fingers. 'But it's not just them you're sad about.'

'I don't—'

'Want to talk about it, I know. But you can listen,' Thea snapped. 'I've tried to give you your space. I've tried to ask how you are. I've tried *everything* I can think of, and I still don't understand what happened between you and Torj.'

'That makes two of us, then,' Wren muttered, wincing at the sound of his name.

'Then why in the name of the Furies aren't you figuring it out?' Thea cried. 'For someone whose head is always buried in a book and questioning everything, you've left this mystery unsolved. Why?'

Wren bit her lip hard to stop it from quivering. She had practically begged him to stay. She'd told him that she *loved* him. She would not cry, not over him. Not any more.

'Because it's not a fucking mystery, Thee. He ended things—'

'But *why*? That man is *head over heels* in love with you. Has been for years, Wren.' Thea threw her hands up, clearly exasperated. 'We found something while you were in the Gauntlet.'

Wren's narrowed gaze slid to her sister. 'What do you mean, "found something"?'

Thea sighed. 'A book. Wilder and I don't know what it meant exactly, but it meant *something*.'

'What book?' Wren demanded.

'*Tethers and Magical Bonds Throughout History.*'

Wren stared at her sister. She knew there were magical bonds in existence, of course – she, Thea and Anya had shared one through their sovereign magic, through *family*. From what she'd seen of the Warswords and their Tverrian stallions over the years, she'd assumed there was a magical connection there as well . . . The midrealms and the lands beyond were full of unknown powers; she just didn't understand what any of that had to do with Torj.

'What?' she said at last.

'During the Gauntlet, when he was going mad with worry for you, he kept saying he could *feel* you – your emotions, your magic . . .'

A shiver ran down Wren's spine. 'We thought there was a sliver of my power trapped in his scars . . .'

'It wasn't his scars,' Thea replied. 'He'd been looking into magical wounds with Farissa.'

Wren loosed a tense breath. 'I knew I had hurt him. I knew—'

Thea shook her head. 'When he talked to me and Wilder, he wasn't describing pain . . .'

'What, then?'

'Connection. A *bond*,' Thea answered, stressing the last word. 'I'd seen that book in Kipp's room, so I brought it to Torj. Next thing we know, he was storming off to find Audra. Then you returned from the trials, and you were hurt . . . He didn't leave your side for weeks. And I didn't see the book again.'

'That was the last you heard of it?'

Thea nodded.

Wren turned back to the waves, resting against the ship's railing, shaking her head. 'What the fuck does any of that mean?'

Thea nudged her with her elbow. 'It means there's a *reason* the Bear Slayer did what he did.'

'Keep your fists up,' Thea barked at Wren across the deck of the ship. 'Remember, you need to protect your face, be ready to strike.'

Though Wren wanted to snap right back at her sister, she clenched her jaw instead and did as instructed, ensuring that her elbows didn't drop. The physical exertion offered a reprieve from the onslaught of questions pummelling her mind. After her conversation with Thea the day before, she had thought of little else but that mysterious book. She had asked Kipp about it, but he'd insisted that Thea had taken it from his rooms before he'd had a chance to read it. The irony was not lost on her that the one time she needed vital information, she was as far away from a library as she could be. And so she had combed her memories of every past moment with the Bear Slayer instead, searching for traces of magic beyond her storm powers and his Furies-given abilities, finding nothing.

In the little time she'd known of the book's existence, it had become her new obsession, Thea's words echoing constantly in her mind. But it made no sense to her. She had *always* felt connected to the Warsword.

Thea's swinging fist brought her abruptly back to the present.

Light on the balls of her feet as she'd been taught, Wren watched Thea circle her. They had started training together after the battle at Drevenor; it had been the only thing that got her out of her quarters each day. A minimum of one hour of daily sparring, as ordered by Audra, the Guild Master of Thezmarr. Truth be told, Wren would have attended with or without orders – never again did she want to feel helpless or rely upon the strength of a man.

Now, even aboard the *Sea Serpent's Destiny*, Thea was a relentless trainer. Wren hated to admit that it was paying off. She was getting stronger, faster, *better*. She knew she'd never match Thea's skill as a Warsword, but she was no longer weak.

She swung her fist, hard, landing another blow to the padding Thea held up.

'Good!' Her sister beamed. 'Really good, Wren. Just imagine it's Torj's face.'

Heat bloomed across Wren's cheeks as she hit again. 'Shut up, Thee.'

'Make me.' Suddenly, Thea lunged forwards, her right fist shooting out in a swift jab. Wren jerked her head back, the punch whistling past her cheek. She countered with a quick left hook, which Thea easily blocked with her forearm.

But Wren launched herself into a combination, sweat beading at her brow – jab, cross, hook, each punch met by Thea's solid guards. The sharp smack of Wren's knuckles against the padding had Kipp and Dessa cheering from the sidelines.

'You're doing well. Anya would be proud,' Thea said warmly, clapping her on the shoulder.

For once, the mention of their sister's name didn't hurt; rather, it soothed something inside her. Wren returned Thea's smile, the exercise having relieved her of that tension she constantly carried with her.

She waved to Dessa. 'Your turn!'

Wren gave her friend an encouraging smile as they swapped places. When she settled beside Kipp, she saw that he was grinning.

'You'll be the deadliest of us all before long, Your Queenliness,' he quipped.

Wren rolled her eyes. 'You're not sparring today?'

'It never was the best use of my talents,' he replied with a wink.

'Speaking of . . . How *did* you wrangle your attendance on this expedition? Don't you have lectures to give?' Wren asked him with a quirk of her brow. During her previous semester, Kipp had caused quite a stir as a supposed visiting academic, delivering talks on strategy and how alchemy had been employed during the war.

He offered a roguish grin. 'I'm always in high demand, but there's nowhere I'd rather be than at your side during your time of need.'

Wren snorted. 'So it has nothing to do with the fact that we'll be within a few hours' ride of the Laughing Fox at some point?' she asked, naming his favourite tavern.

'No idea what you mean,' he replied with a straight face.

'And where's Cal? You usually like to rope him into all the trouble you make.'

Kipp gave a wistful sigh. 'Off doing important Warsword things. He was assigned to be Zavier's guard for his return to Naarva.'

'And you didn't want to pester him instead? Swing by the Dancing Badger?'

'I hear it's been restored to its former glory, but no . . . I'd rather scope out your homeland. For when you need to come good on our deal.'

Wren cringed, cursing her past drunken self for calling in a favour with Kipp in the early hours at the Mortar and Pestle. Sliding her hand into her pocket, she found the scrap of parchment she'd torn from the scroll her friend had given her after the battle at Drevenor. How many times had she considered tossing it in the hearth? How many more had she considered giving it over to Audra to send to the Bear Slayer, wherever he was in the midrealms?

'Have you decided if you want me to take further action?' Kipp asked her now, eyes bright. 'I'll remind you that it's a deal regardless of what happens next . . .'

She'd known for years that the Son of the Fox loved to collect favours like they were going out of style, and yet she'd gladly put herself in his debt.

For Torj.

'Is she still alive? Your grandmother?' she had asked the Bear Slayer, watching the emotion ripple across his painfully handsome face at the mention of the woman who'd sent him to Thezmarr, who'd saved him from himself all those years ago.

'She went missing a long time ago, presumed dead. I searched for her for years, but never found anything.'

'Well?' Kipp prompted eventually, brow furrowed.

Wren didn't know why she said it, but she said it all the same. 'I want you to keep digging.'

If Kipp was surprised by her answer, he didn't show it. Instead, he saluted her. 'My investigative services are yours as long as you require them.'

A message was waiting for them the next morning, delivered by raven in the night.

'Apparently Audra has found a suitable Warsword replacement for me,' Thea mused over the curling parchment. 'We're to meet Cahira on Trader's Road, at the Harenth turnoff.'

'Oh.' Disappointment soured in Wren's gut. 'I guess this means we won't be visiting Delmira together after all.'

'I guess not,' Thea replied glumly. 'But Audra doesn't like the idea of us together for extended periods – she says that two magic wielders together, one of them a Warsword, is too much of a prize for the enemy to resist.'

Wren knew the Guild Master had a point, but it didn't mean she had to like it.

'Cahira's nice, though,' Thea offered. 'You'll like her.'

Wren gave her sister a reassuring nod. Their arrangement had always been temporary while Audra found someone else, but that didn't stop the ache from forming. Thea had been her distraction from it all, her connection to a life long-gone. They had both said how they missed Anya, Sam and Ida, but Wren hadn't told Thea that she missed *her* as well.

Making her excuses, Wren wandered the ship, weaving through the other passengers, catching a glimpse of the midrealms' mainland on the horizon.

The closer they got to shore, the more restless her magic became.

CHAPTER 5

Torj

'Every war that has ever come to pass in the
midrealms was first foretold by a seer'

— *A History of Thezmarr*

Queen Reyna's condition hadn't worsened, but nor had it improved.

'Either she's dead and doesn't know it yet, or they want us to have whatever information she's gleaned in the past few weeks,' Torj wagered to Wilder after they had located rooms at a local inn. 'Whatever the reason, it's not good.'

'No shit,' Wilder huffed.

The Warswords stood by the door inside the queen's room while the healer they'd requested tended to her. Torj was driving himself insane with all manner of theories. In the brief time they'd been away, they'd seen first hand the influence Lord Silas had garnered over the common people, and now this?

'You can ask, you know.' Queen Reyna's voice floated towards them as the healer took the coin they'd left and bid them a silent farewell.

Torj glanced up to see the queen settled against a pile of pillows, the quilts tucked in around her waist. The colour had returned to her cheeks, but she still looked frail and weak. He wanted to ask her about what she'd said earlier, about the blaze of iron and embers . . .

'How are you feeling?' he asked instead.

'As well as can be expected,' she sighed. 'I presume you want to discuss the events while they're still fresh?'

'It would help,' Torj replied.

'I don't know how long I've been gone,' Queen Reyna began. 'But I know we travelled nearly every day, moving from camp to camp. I was blindfolded for a lot of it . . . but I heard enough.'

Hope soared in Torj's chest. 'Do you know where they were headed? I could get word to Audra to rally the other Warswords.'

'Lord Silas had planned to remain in the dry docks until you caught up. He wanted to make examples of you both. To show how his dark alchemy can eliminate your kind. But an hour or so before you arrived, he received word from another base. They had something he wanted. Apparently, he wanted it badly enough to abandon two Warswords and a ruler . . . The very things he says he's most intent on destroying.'

Torj shifted, knots tightening uncomfortably in his stomach. 'Did they harm you?'

'They . . . they held me down and forced some sort of tonic down my throat. I fought, but there was no use. As soon as that substance touched my tongue, a numbness spread through me. Like my magic was being leached away, drawn out by something . . .'

'Fuck,' Torj muttered. 'So they took whatever they put on those blades and made it into something consumable?'

'Seems that way.' She closed her eyes, as though bracing herself against something. 'My magic . . . I can't feel it at all. On an ordinary day, I can always feel its presence. But not now. Not after they gave me that tonic. I think . . . I think it might be permanent.'

'Only an alchemist or healer can confirm that,' Torj tried to reassure her. 'It might just take time to fade from your system, or perhaps it was designed to stay there and do something else. I don't know . . . but we can take you back to Drevenor. Have the masters look you over. Have—' He cut himself off.

'Wren make a cure?' Wilder finished for him.

Torj didn't look at his friend. 'If need be, yes.'

'I won't go back to the academy,' Queen Reyna said. 'I wish to return to Aveum as soon as I am able.'

'Your Majesty,' Torj protested. 'If you do indeed need treatment—'

The queen shook her head sharply. 'In captivity, I was privy to a lot of their conversations concerning their forces. Lord Silas draws more followers to his side every day. They're more organized than we thought. They have a recruitment process. They hold at least three villages between here and Naarva. We would have to pass through them all or take four times as long to return. They will not expect us to go back to my homeland, and that is where I wish to go.'

Torj exchanged a look with Wilder, who had started to pace the worn carpet before the hearth. 'Perhaps you only heard what they wanted you to, Your Majesty.'

'Why would they leave me behind, only to recapture me on the way to Aveum?' she asked.

'I don't know,' Torj admitted. 'But that's the problem. At the moment, we can't predict their actions. And whatever you've heard could be false information they wanted you to report back to us—'

'They captured a Warsword,' Queen Reyna interrupted.

Wilder turned to face her slowly. 'What?'

'They thought I was unconscious,' she told them. 'But I heard them . . . Lord Silas – he was instructing some of his underlings on how to keep the Warsword contained, what dose of the alchemy to ply her with.'

'Her?' Wilder's voice rose. 'Did you hear a name?'

A resigned sigh escaped her. 'No.'

'Fuck,' Wilder muttered.

'It's not Thea,' Torj told him. 'They'd be shouting that from the rooftops.'

'If they've got Thea, they've got Wren,' Wilder said bluntly, searching Torj's face.

Torj had already made the connection and he was using every ounce of willpower to hide it from his friend as images of the poisoner flooded his mind.

'You look like you're going to kiss me.'

'Tell me you don't want me, Bear Slayer.'

Torj turned to face the hearth. 'It's not her, Hawthorne. They're safe.'

The queen was shivering. 'They call him by another name as well . . .' she said quietly. 'Lord Silas, I mean.'

Torj took a blanket and wrapped it around her shoulders. 'And what is this other name, Your Majesty?'

Her teeth were chattering now. 'Silas the Kingsbane . . . For all the royal blood he intends to spill.'

A wave of goosebumps rushed across Torj's arms.

'I'm sending a raven to Audra,' Wilder declared abruptly before leaving the room, the door slamming behind him.

When Wilder was gone, Torj faced the queen once more. 'It's going to be alright, Your Majesty.'

'Is it?' she whispered.

'You're safe with us. But I do need to ask you something else,' he ventured.

Queen Reyna dipped her head, giving him permission.

'That was a premonition you said earlier?' he said, fighting to keep his voice even. 'Before you fainted?'

She looked up at him, brow furrowed, as though she were surprised, as though it were something he should already know. 'It was . . .'

A moment of stunned silence followed before Torj spoke again. 'And that's not the first time you've said it . . . ?'

Queen Reyna rubbed her temples. 'No, it's not. I had a vision, during the final days of the war, before the penultimate battle. It was why I requested that you lead my forces. I saw your potential.'

Torj distantly remembered the request coming to him, but the battle had been so chaotic, so brutal, that he hadn't led the Aveum forces for very long. All the Warswords had united in the fray, using their joint Furies-given powers to drive the enemy back, and Wren . . . Wren had saved them time and time again with her exploding potions, a warrior in her own right.

'What exactly did you see?' Torj pressed, his shoulders bunching.

Queen Reyna's eyes widened in surprise. 'I thought you'd know . . . I told the Embervale sisters.'

He wasn't sure he was breathing. 'Told them what?'

The queen met his eyes, lifting her chin. 'What I saw in my vision . . . That gold would turn to silver in a blaze of iron and embers. That it would give rise to ancient power long forgotten.'

A chill raked down Torj's spine as he came back to himself, the queen's words washing over him, a piece of the past falling into place with brutal clarity. He gripped his hair by the roots, formalities forgotten. 'You saw this? You knew this was going to happen?'

Queen Reyna's attention was not on his silver locks, but on the centre of his chest, as though she knew the very scars that marred the skin over his heart. 'Yes.'

Torj dropped his trembling hands to his sides, biting his tongue so he didn't spill all manner of frustrations to the queen. It wasn't her fault that Wren, Thea and Anya hadn't thought to share this information with him. It wasn't her fault that in the days, weeks and months after the battle in Thezmarr's courtyard, Wren hadn't sought him out to tell him what she'd learned from the winter queen.

For the past six months they'd spent together, she'd withheld that piece of information. That the moment between them before the vortex of darkness had been foretold . . . Torj felt as though the ground had disappeared beneath him, as though he were freefalling into a dark abyss.

'I didn't name anyone in the prophecy,' Queen Reyna told him as she watched him pace the worn carpet before the fire.

'And yet you knew to ask for me to lead your forces.'

'I did.'

Gold will turn to silver in a blaze of iron and embers, giving rise to ancient power long forgotten.

He had seen the power of a different prophecy come to life before his very eyes during the war, only to learn that he himself was part of one . . .

And that Wren hadn't told him.

'You love her,' Queen Reyna said quietly, studying him. 'The youngest of the Embervale sisters.'

Torj struggled to swallow the lump in his throat, not meeting her gaze. 'That doesn't matter now.'

The queen gave a sad smile. 'You loved her then as you love her today and will for all the days that come after. You will always love her. That is the *only* thing that matters, Bear Slayer.'

'You're bleeding,' Torj said to Wilder as they threw their packs into the adjoining room. He pointed to where blood was dripping from his friend's sleeve onto the floorboards.

'A scratch.'

Torj sighed. 'It's never just a fucking scratch.'

Wilder waved him off. 'I'll take first watch. You get some rest. You look like shit.'

Torj snorted. 'Cheers.'

'If I feel old, you must feel fucking ancient,' his friend added with a wry grin.

'Oh, fuck off, Hawthorne.'

When the door clicked closed behind Wilder, Torj surveyed the room. There were two narrow beds, certainly not designed for men of their stature, but the sheets were clean and the fire was crackling in the hearth, a luxury they hadn't had for the two weeks they'd been on the road.

The thought of trekking to the winter kingdom of Aveum was not appealing. The ride south-east would be treacherous and – with the queen in tow – long. He knew he would need his strength and wits, but when it came time to sleep, Torj resisted. There would be no dreamless slumber for him, only nightmares, regrets and dreams of Wren.

So he sat on the edge of his mattress and rested his hammer across his thighs. Without thinking, he reached for the cleaning aid she had made him. As he worked out the red stains with a rag, he let his thoughts stray – not to recent memories as they were usually wont to do, but to the very first . . .

He was injured, and she was brandishing a knife at him. A fucking *knife.*

Her bronze hair was piled atop her head, held messily in place by a pin, and her skirts were stained dark with dirt. Wide willow-green eyes met his.

'Who are you?' she demanded, her voice surprisingly steady.

Torj couldn't help the twitch in his lips, even as he struggled to remain upright. 'I usually don't need an introduction.'

The woman's eyes narrowed, taking in his bloodied state. 'Someone thinks highly of himself,' she retorted, stepping closer. Her gaze swept over him, assessing critically. 'Sit down before you fall down,' she ordered, sheathing her blade and reaching for a kit at her belt.

Torj raised an eyebrow, amused despite himself. 'You know, most people wouldn't dare talk to me like that.'

It was true. He could scarcely remember a time where the answer to anything he said hadn't simply been, 'Yes, Warsword Elderbrock.' There was always an element of awe and fear when people dealt with him now.

He gaped at the woman as she grabbed his arm without preamble and pushed him to the ground.

'Most people don't know their head from their arse,' she said bluntly.

A laugh bubbled from Torj at that. Then he was wincing again as she adjusted his position on the forest floor, apparently having no qualms with laying hands on an injured warrior all alone in the woods. Who was this storm of a woman?

He watched her as she tended to his wound, watched as the realization of who he was dawned on her face . . .

'You're a Warsword,' she said quietly, surveying the armband around his bicep: three crossed swords that marked him as one of the most elite warriors in the midrealms.

'Did the giant war hammer not give it away?' he mused, nodding towards his weapon lying on the ground nearby.

'The arrogance should have,' she replied, not bothering to look up as she cleaned his wound.

A surprised laugh burst from him. 'I suppose we deserve that reputation.'

'Among others.' The woman did look up then, her gaze shifting from his golden hair to his war hammer on the ground. Her expression was guarded. He saw none of the awe that usually accompanied the recognition of who he was.

'You're the one they call the Bear Slayer,' she surmised.

'Guilty.' He gave her a winning smile. 'Or Torj, if we're friendly.'

'We're not.'

Oh, he liked her. He liked her a lot. Finally, a sparring partner worthy of a round or two. Still smiling, he waited until she locked eyes with him once more. 'And what do they call you?'

It had been a slow cascade of feeling, even then, one that he'd forced away, knowing that she was so much younger than him. But every time he'd glimpsed the fiery alchemist since that first meeting, his breath had caught. He'd found excuses to visit the workshops, hoping to run into her, fascinated by her no-nonsense attitude, by her sharp tongue and, yes, by her beauty.

He'd learned that she was one of the orphans of Thezmarr, the younger sister to another alchemist who was often found in the infirmary, dubbed a troublemaker among the women. Back then,

Torj had made a passing comment to Audra that perhaps she had the sisters mixed up. The librarian had simply stared at him.

Now, Torj finished with the cleaning aid and rested his hammer against the bedside table with a sigh. He was forever living in the past, it seemed. *Soul bonded.*

He'd had someone – *the* one – who fate itself had chosen for him, and he'd had to let her go. The agony went beyond the wound that had sealed over his chest, beyond the moment of tearing the thread between them in two. No, the pain was a part of him now, and he knew in his bones that it always would be.

Already dreading the dawn, he turned to the window, opening it so the crisp air could hit his face. Only the glow of the tavern's torches spilled onto the street below, leaving the rest of the world dark – dark but for the lone strike of lightning that illuminated the horizon, calling out to him like a song.

CHAPTER 6

Wren

'Healing isn't an act – it's an essence. It flows not
from what we do, but from who we are'

– *Alchemy of Afflictions*

THE STORM ROLLED in as they disembarked from the *Sea Serpent's Destiny* and Wren shifted uneasily as her magic tried to respond in kind. Sparks of lightning formed at her fingertips, and she shoved her hands in her pockets to hide them from the others.

The south-east dock of Settler's Port was bustling. The evening markets were already in full swing, with a variety of stalls lined up along the shore front despite the conditions. Wren pulled her hood up over her hair and squinted through the rain.

Thea nudged her. 'Stop it,' she hissed, jutting her chin towards the dark clouds closing in.

'I *can't*,' Wren shot back, her magic crackling unhelpfully beneath her skin.

'That's a problem. You know that, right?' Thea made a noise of frustration, then shouldered her pack with a grimace.

Wren clenched her jaw before biting back, 'Add it to the list, Thee.'

As their feet touched solid ground for the first time in days, Kipp squeezed between Wren and Thea, throwing his long arms around their shoulders. He winked at Dessa, who was overseeing the unloading of their horses. 'I'd say we've got time for a tipple at the Fox, right?'

Wren laughed hoarsely; she'd anticipated this exact moment. 'Sorry to disappoint, Kristopher, but we're on a tight schedule. By the time we get the horses—'

'We can wait at the Fox!' he interjected.

Thea also shook her head. 'Not tonight. We need to stock up on supplies before heading out.'

'The Laughing Fox has *plenty* of supplies,' he countered.

Wren rolled her eyes. 'We can't survive on sour mead for a week—'

Kipp looked genuinely shocked. 'Speak for yourself.'

Wren folded her arms over her chest. 'By all means, Kipp. You stay at the Fox while Thea, Dessa and I do the real work.'

Kipp gave a dramatic sigh. 'Perhaps on the way back, then . . . ?'

'You and Dessa wait here for the horses. Thea and I will get rations for the road.' Wren didn't wait to hear more of his protests; she simply nodded to Thea, who instantly fell into step beside her. 'Do you think there will ever come a day where he's not a menace?' she asked her sister, with a backwards glance at their friend.

Thea laughed. 'Gods, I hope not.'

As dusk fell, Wren and Thea made their way through the port town market. Despite the rain and the claps of thunder, the vendors lit lanterns that bathed the rows of stalls in a warm, flickering glow. The air was thick with an array of scents – spices, leather, roasting meats and the salt of the nearby sea. Wren's eyes darted from stall to stall, taking in the vibrant tapestry of colours and textures. Bolts of silk in jewel tones caught the lantern light, while baskets overflowed with fruits and vegetables. The calls of merchants hawking their wares mingled with the low hum of conversation and the occasional burst of laughter.

Thea pointed to a stall laden with hard cheese and dried meats. 'We should start there.'

While Thea haggled over their provisions, Wren spotted a trader selling liquor. She purchased a small flagon of sour mead for Kipp.

'He'll be insufferable now, you realize?' Thea said over her shoulder with a note of amusement.

'I know. Perhaps I'll keep it hidden until I need to bribe him for something.'

'Genius.'

But Wren's skin prickled. 'Does this place feel different to you?' she whispered, glancing around and realizing that they were being watched.

'Yes.' Thea drew her cloak around her, hiding the Warsword totem around her arm.

'Bit late for that,' Wren muttered, noticing the suspicious looks being thrown their way, the whispering behind cupped hands. 'What's going on here?'

Thea surveyed the market with a furrowed brow. 'I haven't been back here in a long time, but this was always a friendly place . . .'

'They don't like outsiders,' came a voice from the shadows.

A herbalist stood behind a booth with bundles of dried plants hanging from the awning, the fragrance sharp and medicinal. Wren and Thea approached him.

'We're not outsiders,' Wren told him, admiring his wares and wondering if she should stock up on her own supplies. 'We're from Thezmarr originally.'

The man scrutinized them. 'I'm not sure that means what you think it does these days . . .'

Wren ignored the crawling sensation along her skin. 'Well, that's where we're headed now,' she lied.

Thea didn't so much as blink at the falsehood. Instead, she tugged Wren's arm in the direction of the docks. 'We don't want to be late for the Guild Master.'

The stall owner continued to study them. 'A word of warning,' he offered, glancing around distrustfully. 'If you've not been in these parts for a while, you're outsiders now . . . I've seen folks abducted right off the street for standing out less than the Shadow of Death.'

Wren's gaze shot to Thea. Her sister's eyes were full of rage as she said, 'I didn't realize those who defended the midrealms in the war weren't welcome in Harenth.'

Wren remembered her own fiery words to the Bear Slayer not all that long ago . . . *'I didn't fight in the fucking shadow war so a man could tell me where my place is.'* Had they already lost the very thing they'd been fighting for?

She tugged on Thea's cloak, the nape of her neck prickling again. 'We should go.'

The man shrugged. 'Only trying to help. Things are not as they once were.'

Wren pulled Thea away from the stall, a wave of goosebumps rushing across her skin as they started back towards the dock. Her unease grew, and she could have sworn she saw a glimpse of a cloaked figure darting through the crowd at the edge of her vision.

'Thee . . .' she said softly, hands drifting to the belt of potions at her waist. 'We're being followed.'

Thea gave a subtle nod. 'I know.'

Wren, Thea, Kipp and Dessa rode well into the night, the road before them illuminated by the moon as the rain eased at last. Wren could feel their pursuer watching, their gaze boring a hole in her back as they followed at a distance.

'We're just going to let them trail us?' she murmured to Thea.

Thea scoffed. 'I was waiting until we were far enough away from the city in case it turned ugly. Wait here.'

Wren laughed darkly. 'No.'

Her sister considered her, matching celadon eyes pausing at the belt of potions around Wren's waist. 'Fair enough,' Thea said with a shrug, turning her stallion and urging it into a canter to confront their follower.

'Wait here,' Wren told the others, and went after her.

When she reached her sister, Thea had already leapt from her saddle and dragged the man from his horse. She had him pinned to the ground, a sword on either side of his neck, a black bruise already blooming around his left eye.

'Who are you?' the Warsword demanded.

'No one,' the man spluttered. 'Just a commoner from Harenth.'

'Then why are you following us?' Wren asked over Thea's shoulder.

'They offered to pay—'

'Who?' Thea spat, pressing the blades harder against his throat. A fine stream of blood trickled down from where one sword had nicked his skin. 'Who offered to pay?' Thea repeated, her voice deadly calm.

Wren recognized herself in her sister then. The cold, unflinching tone that suggested there would be pain, that silence was not an option.

Thea cast her swords aside and grabbed a fistful of his shirt instead – a shirt that was in tatters. Wren heard it rip beyond repair as Thea hauled him to his feet, her face contorted in a snarl.

'I won't ask you again,' said the Shadow of Death.

Wren recognized the wide-eyed fear on the man's face; she had seen it many times before. But his was not the look of an evil man, for she had seen plenty of those as well. Dirt lined his hands and face, and he was barefoot. His cheeks were hollow, his eyes sunken. She glanced back to his horse to find that it wore no saddle, only a bridle.

'Thea,' she called gently.

'If you didn't want to see it, you shouldn't have come with me,' Thea snapped.

'I can stomach as much violence as you, sister, but it's not needed here,' Wren told her. She motioned to the man's appearance. 'He's not a traitor. He's desperate.'

Thea let go instantly, and the man staggered back, panting.

Wren reached for her coin purse. 'You were paid to follow us. How about you tell us why, and we pay you instead?'

The man stared at both sisters for a moment, catching his breath, glancing between them and his horse. But when Wren held out the coin, he took it.

'The People's Vanguard are offering rewards for information,' he told them, voice trembling. 'If new folk arrive in town, if neighbours start acting different . . . They're giving out gold and silver for almost anything.'

'And you intended to collect at our expense?' Thea said, raising a brow that promised more brute force.

'I wasn't going to hurt you. J-just see where you were going,' he stammered. 'I just wanted to help my family. My daughter is sick, you see . . .' He passed a hand across his weary face. 'I need to get her to a healer. I need—'

'What ails her?' Wren asked, unable to help herself.

The man's brow furrowed in confusion. 'She . . . she hasn't stopped coughing. Not for weeks.'

'Is there blood when she coughs?'

The man shook his head. 'But she is skin and bones and pale as the moon. She cries all night from the aches and pain, and we've got nothing to give her.'

'Buy a pot of honey with that coin. It will soothe the irritation in her throat.' Ignoring Thea's stare, Wren reached for her belt and rummaged through its pouches until she found what she was looking for. One by one, she placed the supplies in the man's outstretched hand. 'Ginger and feverfew,' she explained. 'Make a tea with these extracts to give her some relief. And this?' She produced a vial. 'The oil from a string bark tree. Put five drops in boiling water and have your daughter inhale the steam. It should ease the symptoms so she can rest and recover.'

The man blinked at her, cupping the supplies in his hands. 'You're a healer?'

'Not a healer. I just have a decent knowledge of herbs.' Wren didn't reveal that she was an alchemist, knowing there was still a chance he'd report their movements for more coin back in the city. 'What happens to "outsiders" who get sold out to the People's Vanguard?' she asked evenly. 'Once you receive your reward, what becomes of them?'

'I . . .' He looked between her and Thea, visibly shaking. 'I don't know.'

Thea scoffed, sheathing her swords and shoving her own coin purse into his chest. 'Whoever these traitors are, they don't care about you and your family.'

'Until now, what choice did I have?' he asked, voice raw as he pocketed the items Wren had given him.

'Well, you have a choice now,' Wren told him.

The man sighed. 'For how long? I am grateful for your help, truly. But . . .'

'But it's a short-term solution?' Wren finished for him.

He nodded. 'I'm sorry.'

Thea studied him. 'What's your name?'

'Paden.'

'Well, Paden of Harenth,' Thea said, mounting her horse. 'I trust you won't forget this?'

'No, my lady.'

Wren followed her sister's lead, fitting her boot to her stirrup and mounting her mare. 'We're heading to Thezmarr,' she told him. 'I trust that information will stay with you as well.'

'Yes, my lady. Thank you.'

'We wish you and your family well, Paden.' She motioned for him to leave.

Wren and her sister watched him ride back towards Harenth, disappearing over the horizon.

'Should have killed him,' Thea observed as they steered their horses in the opposite direction. 'He'll report straight back to whoever he wanted coin from.'

'I'm not so sure,' Wren replied. 'There are far greater currencies than gold and silver to some people.'

Thea made a noncommittal noise. 'Either way, this isn't good.'

'No, it's not.'

They urged their horses into a gallop. 'The sooner we meet with Cahira,' Thea called out to Wren, 'the sooner we can figure out just how fucked we are.'

The next day, as another sunset kissed the horizon, Wren admired the vast expanse of land before them. A sea of silver-green blades swayed gently in the cool afternoon breeze, with dew clinging to every stem, catching the light and transforming the field into a glittering tapestry.

Crossing the open fields should have felt like freedom, but Wren only felt exposed and vulnerable out here. Every rustling blade of grass seemed to whisper of hidden dangers, turning the once-inspiring landscape into a reminder of the strange undercurrent now sweeping through the midrealms.

Lost in thought, she almost didn't hear the approach of hoofbeats. But she twisted in her saddle to see a lone warrior riding towards them.

Her new bodyguard.

Wren straightened, curiosity piqued. She had only met a handful of the newer Warswords over the years, though Thea had done nothing but sing their praises. If having a guard was mandatory, she needed someone strong, disciplined, able to put duty above all else, someone detached—

A familiar figure dipped their head in greeting.

It was no woman Warsword.

Silver hair peeked out from beneath a hooded cloak, and broad shoulders bore the weight of a war hammer across his back.

'You . . .' The word slipped from Wren's lips while her fingernails cut half-moons into her palms.

As he reached them, Torj Elderbrock blocked out the sun. 'Me.'

CHAPTER 7

Torj

'The bond between guard and ward strengthens
with time'

– Mastering the Craft of Close Protection

*G*ODS, *I'VE MISSED you.*
 The words bloomed in his mind and formed on the tip of his tongue, aching inside him. He'd missed the freckles scattered across her nose, the storm in her eyes, the way her hand drifted to the belt of potions he knew was beneath her grey travelling cloak. He moved towards her without deciding to do so, drawn to her as though in a trance.

Wren Embervale was more beautiful than she'd ever been, and Torj could hardly breathe as he drank in the sight of her: a freshwater stream in the middle of a desert. Her bronze hair was swept up in a dishevelled bun, damp tendrils curling at her nape. As he drew closer, the scent of spring rain and jasmine enveloped him, and it was all he could do not to come apart at the seams. She was devastating.

Despite the disastrous events that had brought him back to her, despite how bad things had become with Silas and the People's Vanguard . . . he couldn't help but feel grateful to have the chance to see her again. A part of him had hoped that with the bond between them torn her effect on him would be lessened, or at least bearable. But even without an otherworldly connection to one another, he was utterly overpowered by her.

Her gaze traced over him in return, seeming to catalogue his cuts and bruises, her breasts rising and falling with each laboured breath.

'Well,' she said at last, her throat bobbing. 'This ought to be good.'

'Wren—'

But she was already signalling to the others to set up camp for the night.

Kipp greeted him with a clap on his shoulder, a gesture that felt a little harder than necessary. 'I assume you have much to tell us, Bear Slayer?'

Torj had forgotten the others were there. He had followed the lure of the current right to her, the rest of the world fading away around him. For him, there had only ever been Wren. And from the way she was looking at him . . . The cloud of rage parted briefly as those green eyes tried to peer into his soul, to understand.

'I do,' he told Kipp. 'And it's not good.' *Isn't that the understatement of the century,* he thought. The state of the midrealms had gone from bad to worse, and Audra's orders had left no room for debate. It was at her bidding that he'd raced across the kingdoms to rejoin his former charge as her protector once more.

'Right. I won't be listening on an empty stomach,' Kipp replied, glancing between the Warsword and poisoner before heading for their saddlebags.

As Torj built the fire, he stole glances at Wren. Her expression was unreadable. In the flickering firelight, she was transformed – a gilded goddess, so beautiful that it hurt to look at her. She had belonged to him once. For that fleeting moment, he'd been able to freely tuck her hair behind her ear, rest his hand on her thigh, press his lips to hers . . . Now, the chasm between them was greater than ever.

He could feel their eyes on him, waiting for the news he brought, or for him to implode. Suddenly he couldn't bear it a moment longer. He muttered an excuse and stepped away, standing on the edge of camp as night closed in around him. The need for her burned so fiercely that he didn't feel the chill in the air. He ached to touch her, to talk to her, and he fought every raging instinct to go to her, to take her pain as his own. But that was what had got them here. She'd taken *his* pain and nearly died for it. It was only that stark reminder that had him standing guard alone, rooted to the spot.

Only he was not alone.

Grass rustled behind him.

Wren. He knew it was her before he turned, could somehow feel the world shift in her presence – that familiar electric charge in the air that made the fine hairs on his arms rise. And there she was, the faint glow of the distant fire behind her painting gold across her skin, the moon illuminating the determined gleam in her eyes, like a lightning strike over dark water. In a handful of strides, she closed the gap between them, staring up at him.

She was everywhere all at once, and he breathed in deeply, as though she were the air he desperately needed filling his lungs. His whole body was too tight, a canvas stretched taut across a frame that was bound to snap. Her stare was mesmerizing, so consuming that he couldn't look away even if the world went up in flames. He trembled with restraint as Wren's hand came up between them, slipping between the V of his half-buttoned shirt.

'What are you doing?' he whispered hoarsely, barely breathing, his heart nearly bursting through his chest.

Mine, a voice whispered within him. *Mine.* The word came with memories of a different time – her laugh tickling his neck, her fingers tracing his tattoo in all of its ruined glory . . .

But she's not yours, he argued with himself. *You severed the bond. The beautiful thing between you is gone.*

Wren's fingertips brushed the lightning-shaped scars over his heart, sending a rush of desire through him that left him trembling. The ink seemed to pulse beneath her touch; his skin aflame at her command.

'I wanted to see,' she said, peering at the marred flesh, the ruined tattoo.

'See what?' he croaked.

She peered up at him through thick, dark lashes. 'If it was real. If you still felt it . . .' She trailed off.

Torj tipped his head to the stars, silently praying to the Furies to grant him mercy. He could deny it until he was blue in the face, but his body's reaction to her? The way he looked at her? There was no hiding that. He'd been a fool to think he could.

'You ended it with me,' she said. 'Why?'

'I told you why.'

'No,' Wren replied. 'You didn't.'

'It was never going to work—'

'Do we have some sort of magical bond?' she cut him off. 'Beyond when we shared my power during the war?'

It was the last thing he had expected her to say, but clearly Thea had mentioned the damn book. How could she not?

He didn't recover well. 'Not any more.'

'But we did?' she pressed, searching his face, her eyes lined with silver.

'It doesn't matter now—'

A bolt of brilliant white lightning split the sky and, on instinct, Torj grabbed Wren, shielding her body with his – until he realized the storm closing in above was her doing, her magic singing beneath him.

For the first time in a long while, Wren looked scared.

'You didn't mean to do that?' he murmured.

Thunder clapped overhead and he flinched, the realization

dawning. *He* had done this. Because of him, Wren's magic was out of control . . . Unbeknownst to her, their severed bond had left her power jagged and wild. The tempest threatening to break around them was a mirror to the pain swimming in her gaze, pain he had caused.

'Embers . . .' Torj's chest was tight as he cupped her face without thinking.

Those willow-green eyes flashed in anger, and she shoved him away with enough force to make him stumble. Her words were charged with all the power of the storm above. 'You don't get to call me that any more.'

CHAPTER 8

Wren

'The kingdom of Delmira was once ruled by the Embervales, a family of lightning wielders who held the most prosperous lands in the midrealms, until it fell to the shadow wraiths during the reign of King Soren and Queen Brigh'

– *The Midrealms Chronicles*

HE HAD *FLINCHED*. Flinched at her magic. In all their years of knowing each other and fighting together, Torj had never done that. He had never feared her, or her power. Until now.

Was that why he'd ended things? Despite all that had come to pass between them, she *had* earned that fear. She could still feel the rough texture of his scars at her fingertips. She'd marked him for ever, and she supposed he had done the same to her, only her scars were on the inside.

'Embers . . .'

The nickname sparked something painful within her. There had been a bond between them of some kind, he'd admitted as much . . . but what? Something to do with sharing her power during the war? Something that he wanted no part in?

With the ghost of his touch still lingering on her skin, Wren walked away from the Warsword before she fell apart. A sob lodged itself in her throat and familiar panic rose in her chest ... but she would not break. Not now. Not because of him.

Forcing down the wave of grief that threatened to knock her legs from beneath her, she returned to the camp that had been set up in her absence. She felt eyes on her instantly, and though she knew there was only concern in her friends' stares, she resented them. The fact that people knew she was hurting made her feel all the more vulnerable, and it made her sick to the stomach.

As she joined Thea at the fire, her sister studied her. 'You alright?' she asked.

Wren sighed, glancing back at the lone figure at the edge of camp. 'Let's just find out why he's here.'

Thea knocked her hip against Wren's. 'You want him dead, say the word.'

Wren's answering laugh was hollow. 'I'll keep that in mind. But I could probably do a better job.'

'No arguments here,' Thea quipped.

The group settled around the fire for bread and roast hare, and Wren tensed as the Bear Slayer returned. He seated himself on the ground, putting much-needed distance between them, and looked to Thea expectantly. 'Well?' he prompted.

'What happened to Cahira?' she asked without hesitation. 'We were told it was her we were meeting.'

'Cahira's dead,' Torj said bluntly.

Thea stared at him. '*What?*'

'Dead,' he repeated. 'She was captured by the People's Vanguard not long ago. And handed over to the enemy who's calling himself Silas the Kingsbane. What he did to her ... She didn't recover. She's gone.'

'Silas the Kingsbane ... ?' The name tasted bitter on Wren's tongue. 'That's the bastard's name? The same coward who attacked Drevenor?'

'So Queen Reyna told us. A moniker fit for all the royal blood he intends to spill, apparently,' Torj replied.

'Let him fucking try,' Thea muttered, shaking her head. 'Poor Cahira. She was one of the first to pass the Great Rite after the war . . .'

'She was a fucking *Warsword* . . .' Kipp said slowly. 'When was the last time a Warsword was *slain*? How did this happen? What did they do to her?'

'Dark alchemy,' Wren ventured, more desperate now than ever to set foot back on Delmirian soil. 'That's what they used in the attack at Drevenor.'

'Yes.' Torj pushed his food around. 'And now there's another Warsword missing.'

Thea looked to Wren, disbelief clear in her eyes. 'So this is it . . . Silas the fucking Kingsbane and the People's Vanguard really have the power to wipe Warswords from the midrealms?'

'We already suspected that,' Wren reminded her gently, not looking at Torj. 'The world is changing.'

Thea was tracing the scars on the backs of her hands. 'There was a time where only three Warswords roamed the world . . . We can't go back to that.'

'We won't,' Torj interjected. 'Even with Cahira gone, there are far more Warswords than we had back then.'

'You're forgetting that Vernich is *retired*, out in the middle of nowhere – fishing, of all things,' Thea countered. 'And with another missing, our numbers are sliding.'

'There's more,' the Bear Slayer said quietly, reaching for his pocket. He retrieved two items and tossed them onto the ground between them, the fire illuminating the strange pieces of curved bone.

Wren's chest constricted, and the acrid burning scent surrounded her suddenly. 'Tell me those aren't what I think they are.'

A horn and talon of a monster. The very kind that had threatened to consume the midrealms with shadow.

'I wish I could,' Torj replied. 'I retrieved them from Silas's stronghold. From a crate full of them.'

Wren was going to be sick. She was going to hurl all over her boots—

Boots. Hammer. Saddle. Flask. Buttons. She focused on each object until her vision stopped blurring.

'So that's how they're doing it,' she said eventually. 'They're extracting whatever magic lingers in these remains and infusing it with their own alchemy, corrupting it even further . . .'

A shocked noise escaped Thea. 'They're insane. Don't they remember what it was like? Don't they remember that we nearly *lost?*'

'That's why we're here.' Wren reached out and squeezed her hand. 'It's why getting to Delmira and finding that plant is so important. So we can stop them.'

Torj grimaced. 'Thea, the guild has asked you to escort Queen Reyna to Aveum. She's refusing to return to Drevenor and Audra seems to think you might be able to persuade her otherwise.'

Thea flung an arm in Wren's direction. 'But Wren—'

'Will be safe with me, until Audra can find an alternative replacement as she promised,' Torj replied. Wren tried to suppress a snort from across the fire and failed. He ignored her, pressing on. 'And you should know – Wilder's been injured.'

'*What?* Why didn't you lead with *that?*' Thea snapped, eyes wide as she leapt to her feet.

'Because he's fine.'

Thea looked ready to strangle the Bear Slayer. 'Tell me. How bad?'

'He'll be *fine*, Thea. Just keep an eye on him when you get there. You know how stubborn he gets.'

'What happened?' Her eyes were bright with worry.

'We've been in several ambushes over the past few days. Stupid bastard failed to mention that he was hurt until I saw the blood dripping onto the floorboards.'

'Ambushes?' Wren blurted the word before she could stop herself, her stomach suddenly roiling with concern. She had noted the cuts and bruises on the Bear Slayer the moment he'd arrived, but it was another thing to know he'd been in true danger.

Torj simply nodded before continuing to reassure Thea. 'I'll let him explain the rest. He told me to tell you not to worry. I told him you would anyway.'

'Imagine the state he'd be in if our positions were reversed. I'll worry as much as I damn well please.' Thea turned to Wren, her face lined with anguish. 'I didn't want to leave you just yet—'

Wren forced a smile and waved her off. 'Go. You belong at his side.'

'I really did want to see it with you this time,' Thea said quietly, her gaze drifting north, to where their homeland lay beyond the borders.

'One day,' Wren told her gently. 'Now go. There's a Warsword who needs fussing over.'

Thea nodded and got to her feet. 'I'll leave now.'

Wren walked her sister over to her stallion and hugged her. 'Be careful.'

'Careful's my middle name,' Thea grinned as she broke away from the embrace.

Wren huffed a laugh. Noting the Bear Slayer lingering in the shadows, clearly wanting a final word with his fellow warrior, she bid her sister farewell.

Without looking at Torj, Wren passed him, but as soon as he reached Thea, she slowed her steps and ducked into the nearby underbrush. She knew she shouldn't eavesdrop, that it was a childish solution, but if Torj wouldn't talk to her, he'd left her no choice. She spared little guilt for Thea, knowing her sister would have done exactly the same in her shoes.

Wren watched as Thea checked over her tack, speaking to the Bear Slayer in a low voice, her words drifting through the night.

'After this expedition, Audra will keep her word to replace you,' she warned. 'The Guild Master is many things, but her word is her bond.'

'I know,' Torj replied hoarsely.

'So don't fuck it up.'

'Thea, I can't—'

'You need to fix this, Elderbrock. And you'll have no chance of doing that if you're not by her side. Don't leave her again. *Don't fuck it up,*' she repeated firmly, before setting her gaze in the opposite direction. 'As for being on the road? Keep a watchful eye. We were followed from Settler's Port. There are bounties on all of our heads, and plenty of hungry villagers keen to claim them.'

'You dealt with them? Whoever followed?' he asked.

Thea mounted her horse. 'Wren did.'

'Of course she did.' His words were warm and rich with pride, and from her hiding spot, Wren felt them wash over her in a wave. It contradicted the way he'd flinched at her magic . . . It made no sense.

'You need to tell her,' Thea said gently.

Wren stiffened, her heart suddenly hammering. But a smile tugged at her lips. Thea clearly knew she was there in the shadows and was trying to get Torj to explain himself. If Wren hadn't been so desperate for answers, she would have laughed. It was typical of her sister. Gnawing at the inside of her cheek, she peered through the underbrush, studying the warrior, waiting.

'There's nothing to tell,' Torj said at last.

Wren's stomach bottomed out. The Bear Slayer was lying. He was lying to all of them. *Why?* What was so bad that he couldn't bear to tell them? To tell *her*?

'You know where you're going?' he asked Thea, changing tack.

Thea scoffed. 'I always know where I'm going, Bear Slayer.'

Torj gave a hollow laugh. 'Then stay safe.'

'And you, Bear Slayer. Keep *her* safe.'

Torj started back towards the camp and Wren scrambled to hide her presence, but not before she heard his parting words to her sister . . .

'I'd die before I let anything happen to her.'

CHAPTER 9

Torj

'During any conflict between ruling powers, it's always the common folk who suffer the most and pay the dearest price'

— *A History of Thezmarr*

As they rode north the next day with Wren and Dessa in the lead, Torj tried to focus on the bird calls through the trees and the earthy aroma of the decaying leaves around him, but his gaze tracked Wren constantly—

'Subtle,' Kipp commented from beside him.

Torj looked away. 'Shut up.'

To his dismay, Kipp did no such thing. 'No one knows what happened between you,' the strategist said quietly. 'She won't even say your name.'

'Do you ever mind your own business, Kipp?'

'Not if I can help it,' he replied. 'But for the record, Wren *is* my business. She's my friend. We've been through a lot together, and I hate to see her hurting.'

Torj sighed, brushing the hair from his brow. 'I never wanted that.'

'And yet, you *promised* it wouldn't happen. Remember? You told me and Cal you'd never—'

'You think this is necessary, Kipp? You think I don't hate myself enough already?' Torj drew a sharp breath. 'If she wants to tell you, that's up to her.'

'And you? Who have you confided in? You're my friend too, Bear Slayer.'

'I gave up that right. She deserves you more. It was me who . . .' Torj trailed off before giving a sad laugh. 'Sometimes it feels like yesterday that you and Cal came to me as scrawny shieldbearers. You could barely lift a sword. And you called me *sir*.'

'Those days are long behind us,' Kipp told him.

'I'll say. Now you're just a regular pain in my arse.'

'You wound me.'

'A likely tale.'

Kipp stared at him long and hard. 'When you're ready to talk, Bear Slayer, we're here for you too.'

Torj shook his head. 'Just look after her, alright?'

'You never have to ask me that,' Kipp replied.

Torj admired how easily Wren navigated the sprawling lands and kept them off the main routes. But then, she *had* spent five years after the war tracking down nobles all over the midrealms and delivering the Poisoner's justice – that was more than enough reason to know her way around, to know the roads less travelled.

Still within the kingdom of Harenth, they followed a wide, rushing river north, passing by several smaller towns but not entering them. Torj ensured that his hood covered his silver hair and that his hammer was wrapped in canvas, but they saw no one on the road.

Torj was keenly aware of the others' presence the further they rode and the less they talked. He stole glances at Wren, wanting nothing more than to get her alone again. But for what? To say sorry? Sorry for tearing apart that sacred thing between them? Sorry wasn't enough – not nearly enough . . .

A horrified gasp escaped Dessa, drawing Torj out of his spiralling thoughts.

'Shit . . .' Kipp murmured, looking green.

Torj instantly saw why.

On a hill up ahead, three bodies swung from a roadside tree, hung by the neck, left to rot. A violent warning to anyone who passed.

Wren tensed in her saddle, but said nothing, only giving a slight shake of her head. Torj wanted to hold her hand, to reassure her, but there was no reassurance for something like this. They had rid the midrealms of monsters years ago, only to find there was so little humanity left . . .

As they approached, it became clear the bodies had been dead for a while. Eyes plucked out by crows, flies buzzing around open wounds, and the stench . . . It was foul enough to make Torj want to retch.

'*Little rats, hanging for all to see,*' Wren read aloud, pointing to a sign propped against the foot of the tree.

'These poor people,' Dessa whispered, her gaze dropping to the tools lying discarded in the dirt. 'They were just farmers by the looks of things. Just regular men . . .'

Torj made himself look upon their corpses. He marked their wounds and what remained of their faces, before he decided he would be the last to do so. 'I'm going to cut them down.'

He made quick work of the task, wary of the need to press on towards Delmira. There wasn't time for a proper burial, so he stacked the bodies as respectfully as he could, surrounding them with branches.

Without looking at him, Wren stepped forwards and uncorked one of her many vials, tipping the substance over the gathered brush. When Torj struck his flint, flames roared to life, flickering blue as whatever Wren had used took hold.

'Everyone should ride with their hoods up,' Torj declared as they continued north. 'Hide any notable weapons or possessions. There are spies everywhere.'

After a while, they could no longer see the plumes of smoke from the pyre. They entered a forest of towering oak trees. Gnarled branches and lobed leaves danced in the breeze, and beams of sunlight filtered through the canopy.

'We'll ride until dusk,' Wren told them, not bothering to look back to make sure they were listening. She had always been her own woman, but now Torj saw her as something else – a leader. There was no uncertainty in her voice, no droop to her shoulders; she carried herself straight in the saddle. He'd always thought fury became her, and the new scar across her cheek from the Gauntlet's loyalty test made her look all the fiercer.

Their soul bond was lost to the wind, as Wren herself was to him. And it was all his fault. But if it was the only decent thing he'd ever do, he'd protect her from himself.

Feeling as though he were drowning, Torj grasped at the only lifeline he could find – he forced himself to look away, to pretend her presence didn't still set his soul ablaze.

CHAPTER 10

Torj

'A true bodyguard is not merely one who protects –
they become the shield itself, flesh and bone
becoming rampart when battle demands'

*– Vigilance and Valour: Tactical Training for
Professional Bodyguards*

'THERE'S NO VILLAGE mapped here,' Wren said as they halted on the other side of the forest. 'Nor was this here the last time I came through . . .'

Torj followed her gaze to a towering wooden palisade, the likes of which he hadn't seen since the shadow war. It surrounded an encampment; a timber sign had been hammered into the ground before its gates. *Elmridge*, it read.

'It's new,' Torj offered, noting the mud surrounding the fence. 'They use paling like this to protect a site until a more permanent stone wall can be built.'

'Do you think they're responsible for the hangings?' Dessa asked, glancing over her shoulder.

'There's a good chance,' Torj replied, surveying the settlement. They'd been there long enough to erect walls around it. 'We need to steer clear of this place regardless. There are posters all over the midrealms calling for information on outsiders . . . That's exactly what we'd be here.'

Wren shook her head. 'We need to stock up on supplies,' she said reluctantly, her eyes fixed on the gates ahead. 'I assure you, Delmira has *nothing* to offer in the way of living off the land.'

'No,' Torj told her.

Only then did she look at him, her expression cold and hard, so far removed from the woman he'd declared his love to only a fortnight ago. 'You are here in a guard capacity only,' she said. 'You are not the commander of this trip.'

'I am when it comes to your safety,' he countered, voice low. 'You're my responsibility—'

'I'm not *your* anything, Warsword.'

They had had this fight before, but this time it was like a lance to the heart.

'Dessa and I will go,' Kipp blurted. 'We're less recognizable than you or the Bear Slayer. And I can charm the pants off just about anyone.'

Wren started to protest. 'But—'

'He's right,' Torj told her. 'As much as you loathe my company, there's no way I'm letting you go into a camp likely full of traitors to the kingdoms. If you want supplies, Kipp and Dessa will get them for us.'

Wren's glare could have melted skin off bones. 'I can handle myself.'

'Not the point,' he argued, reaching across for her reins.

'Don't you dare—'

'Too late, Embervale.' Torj started to guide their horses away from the settlement. 'We'll water the horses and wait for Kipp and Dessa.'

A stream of curses followed as Wren jumped down from her saddle. She turned to Kipp. 'Be quick,' she warned.

'If you're not back in thirty minutes, we'll meet you at the turn-off for the Mourner's Trail,' Torj added.

As Kipp and Dessa approached the gates, Torj guided an unhappy Wren around the fringes of the forest, looking for water.

'We could get all sorts of information if we went inside,' she muttered.

'We could also get ourselves killed,' Torj replied through clenched teeth.

'That's true no matter where in the midrealms we are,' she bit back, twisting around to keep the gates in view. 'Look!'

Torj followed her pointed finger back to the entrance, where the larger gates had swung inwards. He tugged Wren close, behind the cover of a thick oak tree, her back flush against him as they watched a band of men emerge from the camp on horseback.

'How many?' Wren asked, unmoving in his arms.

'Twenty, maybe thirty...' Torj muttered, hoping that she couldn't feel the hammering of his heart against her spine.

'So basically, their entire defence force is leaving?' Wren guessed as the unit rode out through the forest without fanfare.

'We can't know that.'

Torj's skin crawled as his gaze fell to something else: a long piece of parchment nailed to the outer wall. Spotting it, Wren darted from where they were hidden, tearing it free.

'Embervale,' Torj hissed, at her side again in a matter of strides. 'What the fuck are you thinking?'

But Wren's eyes were transfixed on the text. Torj peered over her shoulder.

> *On the fourteenth day of the month, Lord Silas*
> *invites you to a gathering of like minds at noon.*
> *Learn how you can assist the People's*
> *Vanguard with its noble cause.*
> *It's time for liberation.*

'That's today,' Wren murmured. 'We have to see it. We have to know what they're planning.'

'No.'

'Torj, put all our bullshit aside and *think*. Whatever is going on, we'll need to report back to Audra when we return. We need *as much* information as possible to have a chance of stopping an all-out war.'

Torj wanted to shake her by the shoulders. Didn't she know what she was asking of him? What she wanted him to risk? He could feel the phantom echo of the bond between them, humming in her presence. But there was no bond. Not any more.

That hardly mattered in their current predicament. He started his protest anew. 'There's no way—'

'If you were with Thea or Wilder, you wouldn't hesitate,' she said, unflinching.

'They're *Warswords*.'

'Warswords aren't as infallible as they once were,' Wren argued. 'Whereas I am an *alchemist*, a storm wielder—'

'I know what you are,' Torj countered.

'I think you've forgotten, Bear Slayer,' she challenged.

'I don't forget.'

Her eyes were green flames. '*Nor do I.*'

Torj speared his fingers through his hair, a noise of frustration escaping him. He hated that she had a point. He *would* infiltrate the camp if it were anyone else with him. Any information from the inside was vital given the current state of the midrealms.

'We stake out the perimeter, see if there's a smaller, unguarded entrance. We look, *that's all*,' he said at last, already wishing he hadn't. He unsheathed his dagger and pushed the grip into Wren's hands. 'Take this.'

'I have a knife—'

She fell silent as his hands closed over hers. 'It's not weighted or sized right for you,' he told her. 'But along with your throwing poisons, it will serve you better than that needle you have in your boot, or the hairpin you're so fond of. It's Naarvian steel.'

She glanced back to where his hammer was strapped to his saddle, hidden beneath a sheet of canvas. 'What about you?'

'It's too recognizable,' he explained. 'My fists are weapon enough.'

Wren scoffed. 'Warsword arrogance never ceases to amaze me.'

Torj almost smiled at that. 'Stay close.'

After ensuring there were no lookouts atop the wall, they followed the line of the palisade, searching for a side entrance. They were in luck. A smaller gate was open, a cart of supplies abandoned beneath its arch, its owner clearly called away to whatever was happening further inside the encampment. Torj could hear the rallying cries already.

Dozens of tents had been erected beyond the paling, while work had started on more lasting stone structures – a town in progress, by the looks of things, clearly unsanctioned by any ruler of the midrealms. They crept deeper into the stronghold, where permanent buildings stood and the voices grew louder. Torj memorized as many details as he could. Audra would demand specifics upon his return.

They pressed themselves into a recess between two towering walls, the stones rough at their backs, but keeping them hidden. From there, they could see a sliver of the makeshift town square beyond, where a crowd had indeed gathered.

But Wren wasn't looking at the scene before them. She was looking at her feet, where a small, furry creature was weaving itself between her boots, purring so loudly that Torj was convinced it would give their position away.

Wren did not, as he expected, shoo the feral cat away. Instead, she reached down and scratched behind its ears, a sad smile on her face.

'I never took you for an animal lover,' Torj said, wrinkling his nose at the stray. The thing was probably riddled with fleas.

Wren didn't look up from where she was stroking the creature's long ginger fur. 'I've actually always wanted a cat . . . Someone to keep me company during the late hours in the workshop.'

'Ever thought of a person instead?'

'You might have noticed this, but most people annoy me.'

Torj snorted. 'I prefer dogs,' he told her flatly.

'Then I suppose you were right,' Wren quipped, not missing a beat. 'It would never have worked between us, Warsword.'

He blinked at her for a moment, not knowing whether to laugh or be offended. He nudged the cat away and returned his attention to the assembly.

Torj didn't like what he saw. The rally's fervour seemed to grow with each passing moment. A speaker's voice rose above the crowd, words indistinct but tone clear – passionate, angry.

'Did you see much of this during your travels?' Wren asked quietly, not taking her eyes off the eager mob.

'Beyond the work of tracking the traitors? We saw traces of it.' Torj tried to ignore the heat radiating from her body, tried not to breathe in her heady scent. 'Posters on noticeboards, conversations in taverns, reports of missing people . . . but not a full-blown gathering. Not like this.'

Wren tensed beside him. 'It's an age-old tactic, though, isn't it? Target the poorer populations on the outskirts and work your way in, amassing followers as you go with promises of a better world . . .'

'Something like that,' Torj muttered, still scanning the square. As they waited, the anticipation only grew thicker. Something was building, a powder keg ready for a spark. The heightened tension only made Torj more aware of his thigh brushing against Wren's, of her breath dancing along his heated skin.

The energy of the crowd shifted, like a storm gathering strength. The speaker's voice grew louder, his words clearer now: 'The good common folk of the midrealms have been collateral in the rulers' wars for centuries. But no more! Lord Silas has liberated us!'

A roar of approval shook the air. Torj tensed, his hand instinctively moving to Wren's arm. It was a testament to her own horror that she didn't pull away. Instead, they watched the surging crowd grow more and more agitated.

'Who here fought in the shadow war?' the speaker called.

A wave of raised hands rippled across the townsfolk.

'Who here lost people they loved?'

Another rush of hands, and several jeers.

'And yet who reaped the rewards for your sacrifice? Are they with us today? Are they working alongside you now?'

'No!' the crowd shouted back.

'Of course not! They're in their castles, fortresses, palaces. Hosting balls and feasts while you struggle to feed your children!'

A unified roar of anger echoed across the square.

'Shit . . .' Torj positioned himself in front of Wren, shielding her completely from prying eyes. This was so much worse than he'd realized. How long could they remain unnoticed in this tinderbox of an encampment?

There was a flurry of movement beyond their hiding spot. The sounds of doors being pounded, shutters thrown open, angry voices growing closer.

'We need to go,' Torj murmured, pulling Wren back towards the alley.

'But Kipp and Dessa—'

'Will meet us by the Mourner's Trail turn-off as agreed. We can't stay here.' He'd damn well carry her if he had to. It wasn't safe here.

'Lord Silas implores you to do your part for the cause! We received word that some folk among us have taken bribes to hide noble families of the kingdoms . . . Should you notice anyone acting suspicious, report it. Should your neighbours host guests you don't recognize, report it. The crowns of the midrealms will be sending people here to break our spirit and our unity, and we have rooted out many an outsider threatening our liberation since—'

Suddenly, a commotion erupted near the edge of the square. A man was dragged forwards, struggling and protesting. 'I'm one of you!' he cried. 'I was born here—'

'And yet you served in King Artos' court, and the regent who followed—'

'As a *servant*—'

The crowd's mood turned uglier still. Shouts of 'Liar!' and 'Spy!' rang out.

The speaker on the platform pointed dramatically at the subject of their vitriol. 'Another loyalist! No doubt there's more of them in our midst! Find anyone associated with this bastard! Friends, family, I want them all in custody! Let's see what lies they have spread!' The words rang out across the square, fuelling the already venomous atmosphere.

'Embervale, *move*,' Torj hissed, dragging Wren towards the gates—

But like a dam breaking, the crowd surged into the surrounding space at the speaker's bidding.

Torj shoved Wren behind him as they backtracked. They should never have stopped. Reports and supplies be damned, they should have taken their chances living off the ruined fields of Delmira. Torj's muscles coiled, ready to spring into combat, but his hammer . . . His fucking hammer was strapped to the saddlebags back at the edge of the forest.

Beside him, forks of lightning were already dancing across Wren's fingertips. Without thinking, he covered her hands with his. The power winked out at his touch, leaving a pulse of heat echoing across his palms.

'Without storm magic is best,' he cautioned. 'They already hate royals. If they find you here, using it against them . . . You'll only further their cause. Even as a Warsword and storm wielder, we cannot take on an entire town. We don't know what they have at their disposal.'

Wren's gaze was brimming with challenge.

'Please,' he added, not bothering to hide the desperation in his voice.

Wren pulled out of his grasp as though burned, but her expression was one of steel. 'I have other weapons in my arsenal.' She reached for her belt, where her potions and poisons were ready. 'Here.' She handed him several vials. 'If anyone gets close, hurl these as hard as you can at them.'

Torj nodded, gripping the glass vessels, noting how small they looked in his giant hands. As footsteps approached the alley, he tensed, slowly leaning in close to Wren. 'You can slip through the gap, into the square . . .'

Wren balked, looking from the small space to his towering frame. 'And leave you?'

'I'm touched that you care,' Torj said lightly. 'But I can buy you some time.'

'Not a chance, Bear Slayer. I don't give a shit who you are or what you did to me, I'd *never* leave someone behind. If you think I would, that's a bigger insult than everything that came before.'

'Wren . . .' he protested, her name bittersweet on his lips. 'We're cornered.'

'Are you a Warsword or not?' she hissed. 'Break the fucking wall!'

Somewhere along the main alley, angry voices grew louder. 'I saw something move! Down here—'

Torj pocketed the vials he'd been given and braced his hands on either side of the gap.

'Found them!' someone snarled.

Torj barely had time to turn and spot the torch hurtling towards them. He shoved Wren through the gap.

'You're mine to protect,' he murmured, before shielding her with his torso as all the debris in the alley caught fire.

Wren screamed, her hands reaching for him.

'Fuck.' He rammed his full strength against the sides of the gap, feeling stone crumble beneath his grasp. Behind him, flames licked up the walls. Smoke billowed, thick and choking. The heat intensified rapidly.

From the other side, Wren's eyes were wide with horror. 'Torj—'

Sweat poured down his face, stinging his eyes and mingling with the acrid smoke that threatened to choke him. But none of that mattered now. All that mattered was the wall before him, the last barrier between him and safety – between him and Wren.

He felt the first sear of flame across his back, the pain excruciating.

Torj's muscles bunched as he slammed his fist into the weathered stone. Pain shot through his hand, but he ignored it, striking again and again. The wall trembled, crumbling under his relentless assault. His knuckles split, leaving smears of blood on the rough surface.

'Torj!' Wren clawed at the stone too, though she had no Furies-given strength.

The heat bore down harder, scorching his flesh. Time was running out.

With a roar that came from the depths of his soul, Torj threw his entire body against the weakened section of wall. There was a moment of resistance, then a thunderous crack as the stones gave way. He tumbled through the opening in a shower of debris and dust, landing hard on the other side.

Flames engulfed the space where he had been just seconds before.

Wren's hands were on him, her voice cutting through the haze of pain as she hauled him to his feet.

'*Move*,' she commanded, her fingers lacing through his and pulling him into the fray. Beyond their hiding spot, Elmridge was in pandemonium, and they weren't the only ones fleeing the square. 'This way,' Wren ordered, still leading him by the hand through the chaos.

She twisted, throwing vials over her shoulder, the glass shattering behind them. Torj didn't look back to see what horror the poisoner had unleashed, but there was no blocking out the screams that followed.

Wren had their horses untied in seconds, her hands somehow steady. 'Here.' She shoved Torj's reins at him. 'Do you need a leg-up?'

The ludicrous image of Wren helping his hulking body up onto his stallion spurred Torj into action. His hands encircled her waist and he lifted her up into her saddle. He heard her breath catch, but she didn't protest. As soon as her boots were in the stirrups,

Torj swung himself up onto his stallion and urged him into a gallop.

The entrance gates were now ablaze, and, together, Torj and Wren rode away through the forest, leaving the encampment to burn.

CHAPTER 11

Wren

'A concoction of aloe vera will draw the heat from a burn and soothe the skin'

– *The Green Apothecary: A Guide to Medicinal Plants*

T HEY RODE UNTIL the plumes of smoke from the town were no longer visible behind them, until the rush of a river drowned out the screams still ringing in Wren's ears . . . until she saw that Torj was sliding from his saddle.

Wren leapt from her own mare just in time to break the Warsword's fall. She couldn't catch him completely, but with her body beneath his, she made sure he didn't hit the ground face first.

A grunt escaped her as the full weight of him hit her. Smoke tangled with that cedar-and-oakmoss scent she had loved as his hair fell across her face.

'Bear Slayer,' she wheezed, trying to wriggle out from under him. He didn't move.

'Torj!' she said loudly, shaking his shoulders.

A ragged gasp sounded, and suddenly Torj's upper half was braced over her, relieving her chest of his weight but not freeing her from the confines of his body completely.

'Embers . . .' he murmured, his voice thick with confusion, his sea-blue eyes searching her face. 'What—' He looked down to where their bodies were pressed together – to where he was cradled between her thighs.

He leapt off her, then stumbled with a wince.

'You fell off your horse,' she explained. 'I stupidly tried to catch you.'

'I don't fall off my horse,' he muttered.

Wren got to her feet, dusting off the dirt and grass from her skirts. 'All evidence points to the contrary, Warsword.'

But Torj was resting his brow against the side of his saddle, as though gathering his strength before hoisting himself back up.

'Don't even think about it,' Wren said, snatching his sleeve and leading him to a nearby fallen tree. There, she sat him down and took his wrist in her hand, feeling for his pulse. It was slower than she'd have liked. Next, she placed the back of her hand to his brow. Burning up, as she'd expected.

'Look at me,' she ordered, cupping his face and tilting his head to her. His movements were sluggish, and his pupils were huge.

She circled him, pausing at his back where his shirt had been singed off his skin and several burns were blistering.

'Shit,' she muttered, searching through her belt for the aloe vera she kept for such injuries. 'I know it's in here . . .' How many more scars would he bear because of her? She sorted through various herbs and tinctures, panic rising within her. He was hurt. And he'd been hurt protecting her, yet again.

Torj watched her, swaying. 'The kit you made me,' he said, voice hoarse. 'It should be in my saddlebag.'

For a moment, Wren simply stared at him. 'You kept it?'

Though his gaze was unfocused, Torj's throat bobbed. 'Yes.'

Wren didn't waste another second. She retrieved the kit she'd made him all those months ago and then positioned herself behind him, cutting the rest of his shirt away.

'Any excuse to take my clothes off . . .' he muttered.

'You're delirious with the pain.'

'I've had worse.'

Wren pushed away the tattered fabric, careful of where it stuck to his burnt skin. 'You will, if you don't shut up and let me work.'

His rough laugh sounded. 'Always patching me up, aren't you, Embers?'

'Don't call me that,' Wren told him through gritted teeth. Though she was holding on to her anger, seeing his back blistered like that hurt her. The burns weren't the worst she'd seen in her time learning the ropes as Farissa's apprentice back at Thezmarr, but they were gruesome to behold on someone she—

Wren shook her head, taking clean bandages from her own supplies and wetting them with the cold water from the river. She would have preferred clean, boiled water, but that wasn't an option. She'd have to cleanse the wounds properly with liquor later, but for now, she simply held the cool, wet cloth to Torj's heated skin.

She heard his breath whistle between his teeth at the contact, but then his shoulders sagged.

'Kipp and Dessa . . .' she ventured, rinsing the cloth in the river again and bringing the cold material back to Torj's skin. 'Do you think they were caught up in all of that as well?'

'Kipp's probably drunk on a tavern floor somewhere. I wouldn't be surprised if he and Dessa missed the whole damn thing,' Torj said roughly. 'Don't worry about it until you have to.'

Having cooled the burns and cleaned them as best she could, Wren applied the aloe vera paste with her fingers. She saw Torj's muscles tense beneath her touch, but he made no sound of complaint.

Despite everything that had happened between them, caring for him . . . It felt right. That emptiness that had hollowed her out inside eased at the closeness of him, something about him calming the storm that raged within. And yet . . . she had fought for him, and he'd ended it.

As she wrapped linen bandages around him, protecting the burns on his back, all her suppressed feelings rose to the surface.

'Only a fool would look at you and see anything less than perfection.'

Wren cleared her throat, wiping her hands on her apron. 'That's the best I can do for now.' The words came out harsher than she'd intended. She thrust a canteen of fresh water at the Warsword. 'You need to stay hydrated.'

Torj accepted it without a word, and she watched him like a hawk as he drank.

'Finish it,' she commanded when he made to pass it back to her.

He shook his head in mild disbelief. 'Bossy as ever,' he muttered.

'It's called being assertive,' Wren corrected him with a rush of irritation. 'And you'd do well to follow instructions if you want to be healthy enough to perform your Warsword duties.'

'Fair enough,' he replied, draining the flask.

Wren took it from him to refill from the river. She crouched on the damp bank among the tall grass and took a deep breath as she lowered the vessel into the cool current. She filled it and two others from her saddlebags, all the while feeling the Bear Slayer snatching glances at her.

'What?' she finally snapped.

'You're quiet. It's unlike you not to have something to say,' Torj ventured. 'It's disconcerting.'

'Perhaps I have nothing to say to you,' Wren replied flatly, twisting the caps back on the flasks and tying them to her horse.

'Since when? You've always got an opinion about something.'

Wren glared at him. 'What is it that you want? To exchange small talk on the road? I think we're a little past that, don't you, Bear Slayer?'

'You could tell me about the prophecy Queen Reyna made in the final weeks of the war,' he said slowly.

Wren shot him another incredulous look. 'What about it?'

'Why didn't you tell me that what happened to us at Thezmarr was foretold?' He tugged on his hair. 'That gold would turn to silver . . .'

Wren laughed darkly. 'Are you seriously sitting there lecturing me on withholding information? Did you hit your head in that alleyway as well?'

'Not that I recall.'

'No?' She took a step closer, folding her arms across her chest. 'Because that's the *only* reason you might have the balls to criticize my secret-keeping. Or are you about to divulge the real reason you left?'

She hated that she was the one bringing it up again, and in anger no less. It was the last thing she wanted to talk about, but the one thing that was constant, nagging her – especially with him so close; especially as she felt him track her every move and saw the heat in his stare.

Torj stood with a wince, towering over her. 'I told you why I ended things.'

'Right, because *you're a Warsword*,' she spat.

'That *is* what I am!'

'You've been a Warsword for as long as I've known you. That never stopped your pursuit before. Wilder and Thea have proven that it doesn't matter.' The words tumbled out of Wren before she could consider what she was saying, before she could strip away the vulnerable note of hurt in her voice. 'But I suppose I should be thanking you. It turns out one time was enough after all—'

'It was more than one time,' he growled.

Another derisive laugh escaped her. '*That's* your argument? A technicality on how many times you actually fucked me?'

He flinched at her coarse words. 'I'm here to protect *you*, not your feelings, Embervale.'

'Feelings? I have none of those left for you, Bear Slayer, beyond resentment that you're here at all.'

She hadn't realized how close they were standing, that she could feel the warmth radiating from his bare chest, that she was craning her neck to meet his furious stare. He was angry? Good. That made two of them, and she wasn't done.

'Perhaps this was all some big elaborate game to get under my skirts. To tell me one night wasn't enough, only to get exactly what you wanted. The famous ladies' man did exactly what he did best and then moved on.'

Torj's hand shot out, grabbing a fistful of her apron and pulling her close, so close she could almost taste him. 'Have I ever done *anything* to give you that impression? Did you truly think that fucking you once – or twice – or a thousand times, had I been so lucky – would make me want to fuck you less?'

Wren's chest heaved as her breath caught in her throat, her traitorous body responding to his closeness. She was grateful that he couldn't see her thighs squeezing together.

'I couldn't give a shit about what you want,' she said harshly.

In the distance, thunder cracked through the sky, but neither poisoner nor Warsword looked away from one another.

Anticipation and desire flooded Wren's senses while the rest of her became dangerously taut. For a moment, all she could do was stare into those deep-sea eyes, her words lodged in her throat as the intensity of him overwhelmed her.

A current sang between them, drawing them closer still. Gods, how was this fair? After everything, she still craved him. Still wanted him beyond reason. He had denied any sort of bond between them, and yet . . .

His gaze dipped to her mouth.

Wren sucked in a trembling breath.

'You should sit for a while,' she told him, pushing him away, her body still buzzing.

Seemingly stunned, the Bear Slayer took a step back, shaking his head. 'We need to get to the turn-off. Kipp and Dessa will be waiting. And the sooner you get what you need from Delmira, the better. We need to put a stop to all this madness before it gets any worse.'

With those words, Wren was catapulted back to where the weight of the world was on her shoulders. So far, she had failed to deliver what Drevenor and the midrealms had asked of her, and this . . .

this was her last chance to get it right before everything went to complete shit. Everything depended on what awaited her in Delmira . . . Scorched lands and endless stretches of nothing.

As though sensing her thoughts, the Warsword spoke. 'What was it like? Living there after the war?'

'Peaceful,' she lied.

'A strange description for a kingdom with a reputation dark enough to keep even the bravest folk away,' Torj said dryly.

'Superstition,' she shot back. 'I am no more damaged than I was when I arrived, and I spent five years there.' Wren inwardly cringed at her choice of words. She grew more damaged with every passing day.

'Didn't say I believed it,' he replied. 'But it's the reason no one crosses its borders. Everyone still believes that shadow magic curses its lands.'

A poisoned land for a poisoner, Wren thought. It was as fitting as it had ever been. Only now she wouldn't be crossing its plains alone, and it was not just her fate hanging in the balance.

She faltered. 'What if I can't find the plant I need?' How long ago had she harvested the sample she'd used in her experiments? Did she even remember the right spot? What if it wasn't by the cottage as she thought? She hadn't been in the best mental place back then, and Delmira was just one ruined indistinct patch of land after the next . . .

'Then you'll make it work some other way,' Torj told her, struggling to get his arms into a new shirt.

Wren clicked her tongue in frustration. 'Here.' She snatched the material from him and helped him into it from behind, her hands grazing the heated skin of his muscular arms as she did. Careful of his bandaged wounds, she lifted the fabric over his broad shoulders.

'I trust you can button it yourself,' she said, averting her eyes from his gloriously tattooed chest as she finished.

'I'll manage,' he replied roughly. The Bear Slayer had similarly avoided her eyes, and instead stared down at the ground.

With a sigh, she led Torj's stallion, Tucker, to the fallen tree, so the warrior could use it as a platform.

'I can mount my own horse,' Torj grumbled.

'Suit yourself. You'll only aggravate those burns,' Wren told him, returning to her mare.

But from the corner of her eye she saw the Bear Slayer reluctantly use the fallen tree to swing up into his saddle.

CHAPTER 12

Wren

'Desire can alter the mind as deeply as any poison'

— *The Poisoner's Handbook*

Once again, Wren found herself alone on the road with the Warsword who'd shattered her heart. To make matters worse, a violent storm had rolled in, and try as she might, Wren couldn't bring it to heel. She blamed him for that as well. There was no controlling the thick clouds swallowing up the sky, or the downpour of rain assaulting them.

'What's wrong with your magic?' Torj demanded from where he sat soaked in his saddle. The road had turned to a muddy river beneath their horses' hooves, and there was no reprieve in sight.

'Nothing,' Wren snapped.

'Then why can't you stop this?' he pressed.

'Perhaps I like seeing you suffer.'

Torj barked a laugh. 'Perhaps, but I can hear your teeth chattering from here. You're not exactly enjoying the monsoon.'

Wren clenched her jaw and tried to ignore him. She knew that everyone saw her as the most controlled Embervale sister, the most disciplined when it came to her storm magic . . . but here she was, drenched to the bone and shivering, unable to bend the storm to her will, unable to call it off.

'Seriously, Embervale,' Torj called over the roar of the rain. 'What's going on?'

'It's none of your business,' she said through gritted teeth.

'It's my business if something you once used for defence is no longer reliable.'

Wren urged her mare to quicken their pace. But after another hour of riding in the torrential deluge, her body aching from shivering so hard, she was relieved when Torj pointed to a dense copse of trees on the crest of a hill up ahead.

'We should take shelter there. The ground is high enough that I could pitch my tent. Keep a steady pace, though – we don't want to trigger a landslide.'

For once, Wren didn't argue.

The sky erupted with another deafening crack of thunder. She flinched. The storms had always been like kin to her, and now she was a stranger amid their chaos. Rain lashed down in angry sheets, stinging her exposed skin and plastering her clothes to her body.

Her mare gave a cry of distress, and Wren leaned forwards, stroking the horse's neck. 'Easy, girl,' she murmured, though her own heart raced.

Beside her, Torj's broad shoulders were hunched against the deluge, and Wren winced at the impact the rain must be having on his fresh wounds. His stallion plodded on stoically, head lowered against the wind.

They started the ascent to the hilltop, and Wren cast aside her concern at her lack of power and simply focused on controlling her skittish mount as best she could. Together, Warsword and poisoner urged the horses up the muddy incline, their hooves slipping on the sodden grass. As they reached the shelter of the trees, they guided their mounts to a halt. The canopy above provided some relief, but rain still found its way through, and Wren wondered whether she'd ever feel her toes again.

Torj swung down from his saddle with a grimace, the motion clearly pulling at his bandaged back. He moved around his stallion to help Wren dismount.

She eyed the puddles of water and muddy tracks on the ground, assessing the likelihood of landing on her arse. She hesitated a moment longer before accepting his outstretched hand. His fingers were cold, just as hers were, but familiar, strong. As she swung her leg over the saddle, her boot got caught in the stirrup, causing her to flail—

'I've got you,' Torj murmured in her ear, catching her against his chest. He had spoken those words to her before, and they had the same effect on her now. Despite everything he had done to hurt her, Wren's heartbeat quickened, and the urge to push her fingers through his wet hair and drag his mouth to hers overwhelmed her. For a second, she froze, staring up at him while his strong arms steadied her. Her palms rested against his rain-soaked shirt, feeling his heart pound beneath the material.

Then, as if burned, they both pulled away, Wren turning her back to him so she could compose herself.

'Thank you,' she muttered, looping her mare's reins around a low-hanging branch.

Torj was already moving to his saddlebags. He pulled out a rolled-up tent, the canvas heavy with water.

Wren tried to make herself useful, scouting for the highest, flattest patch of land. 'Here looks good,' she called.

Surveying the spot, the Bear Slayer nodded. 'It'll have to do.' He passed her a corner of canvas. 'Here. Lay this out.'

Their boots squelched in the mud as they worked together to spread out the canvas, careful not to touch one another again.

Torj used his war hammer to nail the pegs into the wet earth, while Wren threaded the poles through their respective loops. 'Do you think it'll hold?' she asked over the downpour.

'Once we're inside it should be fine,' Torj told her. 'Hold this corner for me.' He handed Wren a stake for the ground, their fingers grazing for a moment, sending an electrical current through Wren that made the storm above shudder.

Together, they wrestled with the tent in the howling wind. Wren couldn't stop her gaze from lingering on the Warsword's strong hands working over the ropes, securing them in place, his shirt completely plastered to his muscular torso.

'You alright?' he asked, wiping the rain from his eyes, spotting her labouring over a particularly stubborn knot in her own rope.

'I—'

But Torj was already moving behind her, reaching around to guide her hands. 'Like this.'

His breath was warm against her ear, and Wren felt a shiver that had nothing to do with the cold.

As the last peg was driven into the sodden earth, Torj motioned to the entrance of the tent. 'Get inside.'

Wren reached for the flap, but paused on the threshold. 'You're not coming in?'

'It's a two-man tent.'

'And we are two people.'

A flush crept up the Bear Slayer's neck. 'Uh . . .'

'You're really going to quibble over logistics in this?' Wren motioned to the relentless skies. 'Don't be an idiot. You'll catch your death.' She ducked under the flap and crawled into the shelter.

It was only when she was inside, with the sudden absence of wind and rain allowing her to think, that she realized what the Bear Slayer had been objecting to. It may have been a two-man tent, but the Warsword was bigger than the average man. *Much* bigger—

A pack was thrown in after her.

'There should be a dry blanket in there.' The Warsword's voice drifted inside, and then the warrior himself climbed through the tent entrance.

The small space felt so much more confined with Torj's huge frame inside, their shoulders already brushing as he fumbled with a small lantern, at last managing to light it and hang it from one of the poles across the top.

They both took a breath, and suddenly, Wren became all too aware of how her drenched gown clung to her skin. Her nipples were hard and sensitive against the rough fabric, and the way Torj was pointedly staring at the tent wall told her that he'd noticed the same thing.

Think of your opus, she told herself. *The clock is ticking. You need to find the silvertide rose and recreate the cure, not get caught up in* him *again.*

Wren steeled herself. 'We need to get out of these wet clothes,' she said, almost expecting him to protest.

Torj's voice was low and husky. 'I know.'

Wren's cheeks flamed. The thought of undressing in front of him . . . She was immediately brought back to their time in the meadow, where he'd sheathed himself inside her, where she'd come undone around his cock, pleasure rippling through her to the point of madness.

'I'll turn around,' Torj told her, shuffling on his knees, presenting his back to her. Wren could see the muscles bunching beneath his translucent shirt. For a moment, she simply stared, willing herself not to trace the corded sinew there. Then she remembered his burns, and worry speared through her – a practical concern; nothing more.

As though he could feel her eyes boring into him, Torj shifted. 'Embervale?'

'Don't look,' she warned him, her trembling fingers reaching for the ties of her apron. She wasn't sure if it was the cold or something else that had her shaking. Wincing as the icy air hit her wet skin, Wren began to peel off her soaked garments, hanging them as best she could from the poles within the tent. The sound of drenched fabric slapping against her as she wrangled it off seemed unnaturally loud in the confined space, and it was all the more heightened by Torj's presence.

When she'd removed the top half of her apron and gown, her

fingers struggled with the laces at the back of her skirts. Cursing, she pulled at them, only to find the wet knots tighter than before.

'Everything alright?' Torj asked quietly.

Wren let out a cry of frustration. 'No.' Her hands crept up to cover her breasts. 'I need your help with the laces . . .'

She heard his sharp inhale, and the sound of wet material rustling as he turned around. With her back to him, she couldn't see his expression, but she felt his warm breath ghost over her bare skin, his gentle fingers settling at the small of her back where the troublesome laces held her captive.

Only when she felt the tug of the fabric did she realize that Torj's fingers were trembling too. Every time they grazed her skin, she had to stop herself from arching into his touch, a touch she knew could set her alight. Every time his breath whispered along her spine, the ache between her legs intensified, her breasts growing heavy in her hands.

Wren had to bite her lip to keep a whimper contained.

Cold air kissed the base of her spine.

'There,' Torj said gruffly, turning his back to her once more.

Her voice was raw. 'Thank you.' She made quick work of removing her skirts, knowing they had little chance of drying by morning, but hanging them up anyway. As fast as she could, she slipped beneath the dry blanket and rolled onto her side, facing the wall, wincing at the cold seeping through the groundsheet.

'Your turn,' she told the Warsword.

The whole tent seemed to rock as Torj went about removing his soaked clothes, and Wren stared resolutely at the faded canvas, unable to stop her mind from wandering to the vivid picture the rustle of fabric painted for her.

Wren sucked in a breath as the blanket lifted and the Bear Slayer slid under it as well, careful not to touch her. But he didn't need to touch her to send that current of lightning rushing through her – the fact that he was mere inches away, completely nude, did that just fine.

Still shivering, she couldn't stop herself. She rolled to her other side to face him, holding the blanket high under her chin. His hair was messy, his cheeks flushed – with cold or exertion, she didn't know.

Devastating. That was how he looked, roughed up by the storm and naked beneath the blanket they shared. It was enough to make her heart quicken and fuel the pulse of need between her thighs.

'You're shaking like a leaf,' he observed as she bit her lower lip.

'Whoever said Warswords don't catch on quick?' she replied. Then, feeling bold, she added, 'We'd be warmer if we were closer...'

'I don't want that.'

'Fine. Then we'll freeze to death.'

'Embervale, I...' He trailed off.

'If you're happy chattering so hard you break a tooth, then so be it,' she snapped, unsure why she was arguing, why she was putting herself in this position. 'But for what it's worth, it wouldn't mean anything.'

The Bear Slayer muttered something to the Furies under his breath, before tilting his face to the roof. 'Fuck it.'

Solid arms enveloped her, drawing her flush against his naked form. A moan nearly slipped from her, and her hand brushed—

He was rock hard beneath the blanket, and hot, deliciously hot to the touch.

'According to your body, there's something here you very much want, Bear Slayer,' she teased, though it took all her willpower to draw her hand away.

Torj's grip tightened around her, almost crushing her to him. 'I'm a mortal, aren't I? No man could look at you without yearning for what doesn't belong to him...'

Despite the slickness that had gathered at her core, despite the primal need to rake her fingers down his body, the words were like a fine cut to the heart, and Wren had to swallow down the words, *I did belong to you, once.*

CHAPTER 13

Torj

'A poisoner's code should value simplicity: a single pinprick, a single drop, a single heartbeat between life and death'

— *An Encyclopaedia of Deadly Plants*

H E'D SAID THE wrong thing. He knew it as soon as the words left his lips and Wren's taunting ceased. Instead, she was still and quiet, her freezing feet warming between his calves.

Gods, he had dreamed of having her naked in his arms again, so many times. And now she was, but for all the wrong reasons. His cock was just about punching a hole through the blanket, yet he couldn't do anything about it. When her hand had grazed his shaft he'd nearly moaned at her touch, had nearly flipped her on her back and settled himself between her legs, where he belonged—

No. He had to stop thinking like that. He didn't belong with Wren. She certainly wasn't his to claim. He'd given up that right. And so he'd try to keep her warm in the night, nothing more. Though who could blame him for savouring the feel of her naked body against him for the last time?

He mentally traced every part where they were connected.

Feet to calves.

Thigh between thighs.

Her stomach to his side.

Her breasts to his chest.

Her hand resting over his ruined heart.

His hand on hers.

His arm curling beneath her, palm spread across the small of her back.

And her damp hair splayed across his shoulder.

Furies save me, he thought, staring up at the lantern he'd hung above.

He noticed immediately when Wren's breathing changed, her breasts rising and falling against him.

Small mercies, she was asleep.

The feel of her was addictive, so soft and warm against the hard planes of his body. He tried with all his might to keep himself leashed, but when her hands started roaming across his skin, he couldn't contain himself a moment longer.

'Fuck . . .' he groaned as her fingers traced over his nipples, and down to his navel. Another low, carnal sound escaped him as her lips pressed against the column of his throat and finally captured his mouth.

Wren's kiss felt like coming home.

Warm, wet, and wild.

Spearing his fingers through her hair, he took control, nipping at her lower lip, demanding entry. She opened for him and his tongue brushed hers, coaxing a whimper of need from her.

Gods, that sound would be the end of him.

He rolled her onto her back, not breaking their feverish kiss, but giving him access to her naked body beneath the blanket. He let his fingers trail down her neck and sternum. Wren arched and twisted, pushing her breast into his palm, her nipple hard beneath his touch.

'Torj,' she murmured into their kiss, rocking and grinding against the hard length of him until stars dotted his vision.

He circled her nipple with a featherlight, teasing touch, before he pinched hard, eliciting a gasp from her.

'Are you wet for me, Embers?' he practically growled, revelling in the way her body writhed for him, seeking the pleasure he promised.

'Yes,' she breathed.

'Show me,' he demanded.

The blanket shifted as Wren reached between her legs, her lashes fluttering against her flushed cheeks as she touched herself.

Torj was captivated, and had never been more aroused in his whole fucking life. Until her hand appeared above the blanket, her fingers glistening with her need.

With a moan rumbling through his chest, Torj snatched her wrist and brought those wet fingers to his mouth. Drunk on the taste of her, he licked them clean. But he was done playing with her. He braced himself over her, and Wren's legs fell open for him, allowing his cock to slide through her desire, coating him.

'Is this all for me?' he murmured, settling himself at her entrance.

'Yes . . .' she gasped, tilting her hips for him. 'Please . . .'

Torj slid his length over her clit, relishing how she bucked for more beneath him. She was so wet, so ready for him.

Her hands gripped his backside, hard enough that her fingernails dug into his flesh, the sting only adding to the sensation of being right on the edge of sliding home.

He kissed her, and positioned himself again, right where he knew she wanted him, ready to thrust his hips—

Torj jerked awake, a moan on his lips. Watery light filtered through the canvas, no thunder or rain to be heard.

A dream. It had been a dream. One he regretted waking from with every fibre of his being. Catching his breath, he came back to himself, the tent coming into sharper focus around him. But that feeling of longing lingered in his body, and he found himself as hard as granite.

With good reason.

Wren's hand was wrapped around his cock.

Without any more sudden movements, he turned his head, finding her fast asleep beside him. Even in slumber her brow was slightly furrowed, as though she were warring within her dream. Her lashes kissed the tops of her cheeks, and he noted how her new scar cut through her freckles.

The blanket had slipped slightly, revealing the smooth curve of her shoulder. But her grip on him was like iron. And every time he shifted, a bolt of pleasure rolled through him.

Furies save me. He stared up at the ceiling, wishing he had stayed asleep. The dream was a far more pleasant outcome than any he surmised would come to pass... To him, the possibilities were: Wren would wake and think him a complete pervert, or be completely mortified; she'd move in her sleep and he'd come all over them both; or she'd startle and yank his manhood clean from his body.

None of these options pleased him.

He resolved to try to move her hand, and if she woke, he'd simply have to explain. With a grimace, he reached down beneath the blanket and slowly tried to prize her fingers from him—

Wren startled with a gasp, and in a blur of movement, she was suddenly astride him, her hair loose and wild, her poison-tipped pin pressed against his throat.

'You've been practicing,' Torj managed, not daring to move, not when he was a hair's breadth away from deadly oblivion or being sheathed inside her. Pain bloomed in the wounds on his back, but he didn't give a fuck.

Wren was on top of him. Naked.

She seemed to realize it at the same time he did, and yet she did not yield. 'What were you doing?' she demanded, unabashed, the pin still held at his jugular.

Torj didn't move a muscle, even though he could feel the heat of her against him, the dampness there telling him she might have been having a similar dream. 'You had me in a compromising position,' he gritted out. 'I was trying to extricate myself.'

Her eyes narrowed. 'Oh?'

But Torj had let this go on long enough. With a hard strike of his hand, he knocked the poison-tipped pin aside, disarming Wren and flipping her onto her back, pinning her arms above her head and her body beneath his.

'Best keep practicing, Poisoner,' he murmured.

He heard her sharp intake of breath, noted how her back arched, pressing her bare breasts to his chest. And her eyes . . . Her eyes grew hooded with lust as her legs tangled with his.

Gods, he had to stop, had to get away from her, before all his restraint became nothing but dust in the wind.

But the way she was looking at him . . . He'd yearned to see that expression for weeks, to know that she still wanted him, despite everything he'd done—

Torj suddenly found himself being flipped onto his front, caught off guard by the swift twist of Wren's legs. What he'd mistaken for passionate entanglement was, in fact, a calculated move to gain the upper hand.

In one fluid motion, Wren straddled his hips from behind, her weight pressing him into the ground. She grabbed a fistful of his hair, yanking his head back sharply. The sudden pain elicited a gasp of surprise from Torj's lips.

Wren leaned in close, her breath hot against his ear. 'I've practised plenty,' she hissed.

Taking advantage of his stunned state, Wren snatched the blanket and her clothes. She rose in one graceful movement, leaving him naked and alone in the tent, his cock harder than ever.

CHAPTER 14

Wren

'Both Naarva and Delmira fell in the years leading up to the final conflict that would ultimately become known as the shadow war. However, the two kingdoms suffered different fates. While Naarva was overrun with wraiths and darkness, Delmira festered from within, its lands slowly dying, becoming barren'

– *The Midrealms Chronicles*

SHE HAD BEEN dreaming of the Bear Slayer moving between her thighs. It hadn't been the same lovemaking she'd experienced in the meadow. It hadn't even been fucking.

It had been *war*.

And for the first time, war felt *good*.

Rough, wild thrusts hitting that spot deep within had her calling out his name, clawing his back, biting his shoulder. She rode the waves of pleasure he offered, climbing higher and higher towards her climax.

'This means nothing,' she gasped between each pound of his hips. 'Less than nothing.'

He hauled her onto his lap, driving into her from underneath. 'Prove it,' he growled, reaching between them to circle her clit with his thumb. 'Fuck me like you hate me, Embers.'

Wren had woken to find her hand wrapped around Torj's cock, and her body wet and wanting – an ache she feared only the Warsword could sate.

Then he'd gone and overpowered her, a trick she wouldn't stand for, not after training so hard with Thea. Trying to forget the hard imprint of him against her core, she'd fled the tent, anger and arousal entwining to form something dangerous, something that might see her control slip.

Outside, Wren wrestled her damp clothes over her heated skin in the brisk morning air, cursing the Bear Slayer and his delectable warrior's body. Her mind wandered back to the conversation she'd had with Thea and now, more than ever, she longed to get her hands on that damn book her sister had revealed. When she was back at Drevenor, she'd go to the archives. She'd find a copy there and make sense of it all.

For now, she would pretend none of it had happened. *Denial. Always a healthy course of action*, she decided.

The storm had passed, and before her, the lands were carpeted in dew, sparkling beneath the sun's rays. The horses grazed happily nearby. Behind her, the canvas rustled, and Wren turned to see Torj emerging from the tent, his muscular form silhouetted against the greying fabric. He squinted against the day's brightness, one hand shielding his eyes, the other pushing back his tousled silver hair so that the morning light played across his chiselled features. His strong jaw was shadowed with stubble, and the uncertainty in his sea-blue eyes was quickly replaced with a hard expression. The thin shirt he'd hastily donned clung to his broad shoulders, hinting at the warrior's physique that she'd more than glimpsed just moments ago.

Wren caught herself staring and quickly averted her gaze, reminding herself of the fury that still simmered within her. Yet she couldn't entirely quash the traitorous flutter in her chest at the sight of him.

'Figured you'd want this back,' he said gruffly, holding something out to her.

Wren looked down to see her hairpin between his large fingers. Careful not to touch him, she took it, twisting her hair up from her nape and securing it in place.

When she was done, she turned back to him. 'I should check your wounds from yesterday. Clean them—'

'They're fine,' he grunted.

'Burns can get easily infected. Or if they don't heal properly, they can limit your range of movement,' she argued.

'I said they're fine.'

'Gods, you're a stubborn fool,' she muttered.

'Takes one to know one,' he replied without looking at her.

She rolled her eyes. 'If you're so *fine*, then we need to hurry,' she told him. 'The others will be waiting.'

'Hopefully.' Torj nodded. 'Go eat something. As soon as I pack the tent away, we'll be on the road.'

'I can help—'

Torj waved her off. 'Best if I do it myself.'

Wren didn't know if that meant it would be quicker without him having to instruct her, or if he simply couldn't stand her proximity.

That makes two of us, she thought bitterly.

They rode in silence for the entirety of the morning. The creak of saddles and the soft whinnies of the horses were the only sounds as they crossed field after field. Wren stole glances at the Bear Slayer, noting the muscle twitching in his jaw and the rigid set of his shoulders. She caught him returning the favour several times, his gaze lingering over her white-knuckled grip on her reins and the flush across the tops of her cheeks.

She couldn't help it. With those broad shoulders ahead of her, her mind took her back to when her nails had cut crescent moons into them as the weight of the Bear Slayer was braced above her.

The cool morning air did nothing to soothe the heat washing over her skin, and no matter how many potion ingredients she rattled off in her head, she couldn't stop certain images dancing before her.

Torj looked back sharply, just as a particularly erotic memory flooded her senses, and the blaze in his stare was like he could sense exactly what she was remembering . . . But as he twisted in the saddle, she saw the wince he failed to hide.

She urged her mare alongside his horse and reached for his reins, drawing them both to a halt.

'What do you think you're doing?' He gaped at her. 'You can't just—'

'I'll be seeing to your wounds now, Warsword,' she said, lacing her words with steel.

'Like fuck you will,' he bit back.

She raised a brow at him. 'You didn't retie the bandage. They're sticking to your shirt. It's an infection waiting to happen, and as much as your presence pains me, if you drop dead now it will delay my plans even further. Are you going to play nice, or do I have to use an incentive?'

Torj gaped at her in disbelief. 'You're not serious.'

But Wren held up a hand, calling what little lightning she could to her fingertips. If he feared her magic, then she'd damn well use it to her advantage. 'Deadly serious.'

'From what I witnessed last night,' Torj spluttered, 'you don't have it in you—'

She let a single burst of magic fly – a delicate bolt of electricity – and it hit him on the shoulder.

He jumped, shooting her a glare. 'Shit, Wren!'

'What were you saying?' she taunted with a sly smile; her day was suddenly looking up.

'What's the point in checking my wounds if you're just planning on injuring me further?' he muttered.

'If I recall correctly, you told me once that my lightning *tickled* . . .'

'I'm not doing this,' Torj replied, snatching his reins back and urging his stallion onwards.

Wren ground her teeth, the thought of his burns festering setting her on edge, but she forced a shrug. 'Don't come crying to me when you have to peel a layer of skin off with your shirt.'

By midday, the space between their horses had imperceptibly widened, and just when Wren thought she couldn't bear the silence, the tension any longer, she saw a familiar pair of horses on the horizon, and a long arm waving at them.

Her whole body sagged with relief – a feeling that lasted all of two minutes before they reached the road, and it was replaced with disbelief.

'Took you long enough,' Kipp said cheerfully, his mouth full of food.

'Is that a leg of ham?' Wren blurted, her eyes falling to the enormous slab of meat he was picking at.

On her horse beside him, Dessa gave Wren a resigned look. 'I wish I could say we didn't nearly die for it, but . . .'

'Nearly died?' Kipp interjected. 'It was *because* of the ham that we escaped that madness. It's been smoked and honeyed.'

Wren opened her mouth to ask more, but Torj beat her to it.

'Are you telling me that while Wren and I were nearly fucking burned alive, nearly run down by a mob of fanatics . . . you were off somewhere stealing a leg of ham?'

Kipp tore off a strip of meat and offered it to Torj. 'It's *really* good ham.'

Torj stared at him, and Wren swore the Warsword was going to reach across and throttle her friend with the aforementioned meat.

After another moment, the Bear Slayer shook his head and guided his stallion away, muttering, 'I'm too old for this shit.'

Wren tried to ignore the turn-off for the Mourner's Trail – the road that led to Thezmarr – as they passed it, but Dessa wouldn't let it lie.

'That's the way to the fortress?' she said, perking up and trying to peer down the road before turning back to Wren, Torj and Kipp. 'That's where the three of you met?'

Kipp nodded. 'The very place.'

'Perhaps one day you can show it to me—'

'I wouldn't bother,' Wren said flatly, squeezing her mare's sides to increase her pace. The more distance between her and that wretched place, the better.

To her dismay, Torj caught up with her. 'You're telling me you don't have a single decent memory from your time there?' he asked.

'None that haven't been overshadowed by everything else that happened there – or after,' she said pointedly.

'Not even patching up my sorry arse in the Bloodwoods the first time we met?' he pressed. 'You certainly weren't gentle with those stitches.'

And you weren't nearly as tough as you thought you were, she almost said. But instead, because she knew it irked him, she replied, 'I have no idea what you're talking about.'

Thankfully, it wasn't long before Wren found herself riding beside Dessa, with Kipp and Torj taking the lead ahead. Dessa, however, seemed distant, scanning the plains before them, saying nothing.

'Are you alright?' Wren asked her.

Dessa jolted in the saddle, turning to Wren as though surprised to find her there. 'Sorry?'

'I asked if you were alright,' Wren repeated.

'Oh. I'm fine. I've just . . . never really travelled like this,' she replied.

Wren hadn't considered that. She had done her fair share of travelling the midrealms, during both the shadow war and the five years she'd spent as the Poisoner. She was no stranger to spending hours on end on horseback or sleeping beneath the stars. Dessa, on the other hand, had remained in one place before coming to Drevenor.

'I'm sorry I haven't told you this earlier,' Wren started. 'But I'm grateful to have you here with me. I know it's not exactly luxury, and I know you're delaying work on your own opus . . . But I'm grateful. I want you to know that.'

Dessa gave her a sad smile. 'I know you are, Wren. I just can't help but wonder what my place is here . . . You, Torj and Kipp have done this a hundred times before. You know what you're doing out here when the road is rough and dangerous. Me? I belong in an alchemy workshop, or the archives . . . I don't know what I contribute here.'

'Dessa, do you think I'd stay sane with those two idiots if there wasn't another alchemist by my side? You contribute just as much as everyone else. I couldn't do this without you.'

'Yes, you could,' Dessa told her gently. 'You've done it before. And I'm not complaining, I'm not unhappy, I swear it. I suppose discovering that another of my teammates was a magic-wielding royal caught me off guard. And now I find myself on the road with a princess, a Warsword and a war strategist. It's natural that I feel a little out of my depth, isn't it?'

Wren cringed internally. 'I understand more than you know. During the war, I was the only alchemist on the road most of the time. Everyone else was a warrior, trained to slay monsters and protect the midrealms . . . I was just me.'

'There should be no 'just' in that sentence, Wren,' Dessa said.

'And I feel the same way about you,' Wren replied. 'I'll never tell you that your feelings aren't valid. You have the right to feel whatever it is you feel. But please know that from where I'm sitting, you're a vital piece of this team. We need you. *I* need you.'

Dessa smiled. 'Noted.'

'Good. Now can we talk about something other than war and Warswords? How is your opus progressing?'

They rode on for what felt like hours, slowly approaching the ruined kingdom Wren had left behind. The barren place that had honed her bleeding, grieving heart for half a decade. She was dreading seeing its scorched plains and lifeless lands.

Astride her mare, Wren crested the final hill, her heart pounding with anticipation and fear. She braced herself for the familiar sight of Delmira's desolation – the cracked earth and yellowed fields, the withered trees, the abandoned homesteads . . . The parched grasslands and the fading heather, and atop a plateau of cliffs, the skeletal remains of a city.

But that was not what she saw.

CHAPTER 15

Wren

'Knowledge is the victor over fate. The mind is a blade'

– *Drevenor Academy Handbook*

'THIS CAN'T BE . . .' Wren breathed, staring in disbelief. Where once she had wandered across dust and ruin, stretches of green stretched out before her. Many of the gentle slopes were blanketed in lush grass, swaying in the breeze like the waves of an emerald ocean. Dotting the landscape were wildflowers – splashes of purple and yellow among the heather.

Wren twisted in her saddle to face the others, waiting for someone to tell her she was hallucinating, that she'd finally gone and lost her mind. But Torj, Kipp and Dessa's expressions were etched with the same shock as her own.

'You said it was a wasteland,' Dessa said, shaking her head at the rolling verdant hills.

'It was,' Wren replied. 'Since its fall, it has always been considered dangerous, with shadow magic lingering beneath the surface. It's why no one ever ventures here . . . They didn't want the same curse afflicting them.'

Convinced they were in the wrong place, that they'd taken a

wrong turn and had ended up in some beautiful, wild part of Harenth, Wren checked their positioning. She looked for the landmarks that had so often guided her back to the cottage after she'd struck a name from her ledger, fully expecting to find them missing.

They were not. They were, however, much changed. The murky, swamp-like pond that had been her guiding point home many a time was exactly where she remembered it, only now . . . now it was a great, sapphire-blue lake. Still unable to believe her eyes, she looked to the north, where the ruins of the palace were meant to be. There they stood, untouched but for the grove of saplings that had sprung from the ground around the fallen stones.

All around, pockets of land were teeming with life. The very air seemed different – rich with the scent of earth and growing things, rather than the dust and despair she remembered.

'Embervale?' Torj prompted, bringing his stallion up alongside her. 'What's happened here?'

'It . . .' A startled laugh escaped her, and she shook her head. 'It wasn't like this when I left . . .'

'I second that. It was more like a graveyard,' Kipp offered.

Wren jumped down from her horse, brushing her fingers over the tall grass, half expecting it to crumble like ash at her touch. But it was *real*. Soft, full of vitality . . . Her mind reeled, trying to reconcile this growing paradise with the barren lands she had left behind. Six months ago, she would have sworn on her life that, like her, Delmira was beyond saving. But now? Now . . . she didn't know what to think.

Kneeling, she took a handful of earth from the ground, rolling the damp sediment between her fingers, feeling how different it was from the arid dust in which she'd once attempted to plant seedlings. It felt like a lifetime ago that she'd first come here alone, lost and broken, so full of rage that she'd punished the already ruined lands with her storms.

'Embervale.' Torj's husky voice cut through her thoughts again.

'Let's find this plant of yours, then we need to leave. This – development . . . It must be reported to Thezmarr.'

Wren wasn't sure why, but she didn't like the sound of that. Feeling strangely protective, she swung herself back up into her saddle and asked, 'Why does it need to be reported?'

'A ruined kingdom is one thing,' he told her. 'But fields of land that have prospered seemingly overnight is another.'

'He's right,' Kipp said, brow furrowed. Wren could count on one hand the number of times she had seen the strategist look so serious, and every single one of those occasions had been during the shadow war.

A knot of apprehension tightened in her gut. 'Alright,' she acquiesced, squeezing her mare's sides with her heels. 'This way.'

Wren urged her horse forwards, her companions following close behind. She was aware of Torj's gaze on her, on the land around them. She could feel him assessing every detail with a Warsword's keen eye.

The rhythmic thud of hooves on soft earth echoed her racing heartbeat. Every familiar landmark they passed left her more astounded – and more unsettled.

'See there?' she called out, pointing to a meandering stream, where she'd once broken down, sobbing uncontrollably as she grieved her friends and eldest sister. 'That was nothing but a dry riverbed when I left.'

The water sparkled in the sunlight, its banks lush with reeds and flowering plants. A heron stood motionless in the shallows. Wren wanted to revel in the joy that warmed her chest, but Torj and Kipp's reactions unfurled something else inside her – a cold tendril of worry, snaking through her stomach as she led them in the direction of her cottage. She hated it. At long last there was something good in this world, and it couldn't be celebrated?

A gust of wind carried the sweet scent of blossoms, and with it, a chilling realization.

As a barren territory, Delmira had been safe . . .

She glanced to her left, her gaze meeting eyes of striking sea-blue.

'You understand, don't you?' Torj said quietly.

Slowly, she took in the thriving parcels of land around them and nodded. 'No one wanted it before. But now . . .' she managed. 'Now it's a prize.'

Torj's voice was grim. 'Exactly.'

The prickling feeling of dread intensified as they crested a familiar hill. There, nestled in what had been a gnarled forest, stood her old home – the four walls that had housed her ruined soul for half a decade. The ramshackle cottage was still in disrepair with its sagging moss-covered roof, but now it was surrounded by a riot of wildflowers.

'This is where you lived?' Torj asked, swinging down from his stallion and taking in the potions lining the windowsill within.

'Yes,' Wren replied, not sure why she was suddenly feeling self-conscious.

Torj cupped his hands around his eyes to peer inside. 'It's very you . . .'

Wren balked. 'What? Messy and chaotic?'

'No.' The Bear Slayer shook his head, a hint of a smile playing across his lips. 'Wild and extraordinary.'

It was far from what she'd expected him to say, rendering her speechless. In the end, she chose not to respond at all. Instead, Wren dismounted and led her horse to the water trough, as she had done a hundred times before. Only this time it was different, for Torj was beside her, and Kipp and Dessa. For the first time, she was in her homeland, and she was not alone.

As though he sensed her conflicting emotions, Torj's hand found her shoulder. The fleeting warmth calmed her, offering a solace that she was yet to find elsewhere.

'Lead the way, Embervale,' he said, his voice dancing along her bones.

Putting some much-needed distance between them, Wren made

for the forest and wove through the dense trees, noting how even here, parts had flourished. Toadstools had sprung up from the ground, and wild geranium had bloomed, along with dog violet and bluebells. Before, this place had been cold, with a haunted feel about it. Every part of her mind was screaming that this couldn't be the same forest she'd roamed only six months earlier . . . but she couldn't deny the floral scents on the breeze, or the rustle of wildlife in the undergrowth.

On foot, Wren took her party deep into the forest, to where she had happened upon the bush all that time ago. Back then, it had been a mass of thorns and leaves. But now . . .

'Here it is,' she murmured, dropping to her knees before a tangled mass of verdant shrubbery. It was competing for space with dandelions with jagged leaves thrust skywards and several wild poppies, their scarlet heads nodding as she disturbed their patch.

Wren pushed the other flowers aside. Heart-shaped leaves, in a tapestry of green . . . Exactly as she'd left it. Only now it had blooms adorning its stems. Every petal bore the luminous quality of pearls, their edges ruffled like waves breaking on a midnight shore, guarded by thorns sharp enough to draw blood.

'I didn't misidentify it,' she muttered, reaching for the silvery-white flowers unfurling from the greenery, frowning. 'It *is* a silvertide rose . . .'

'Then what's the problem?' Kipp asked over her shoulder.

Wren sat back on her heels. 'I don't know. That's the problem.'

Dessa sat down beside her and unsheathed her own harvesting knife. 'What do you need?'

Still in shock, Wren let her friend's question ground her as she turned to her. 'See? What would I do without you?'

Dessa laughed. 'I'm sure you'd manage. But go on . . . Tell me how to help.'

Nodding, Wren pointed. 'Samples of everything. Those there: cut just above the root; don't damage the leaves. I want some whole from root to petal, some cuttings, and samples of the soil too.'

'Understood,' Dessa said. 'How are we transporting everything?'

From a narrow pocket in her satchel, Wren pulled out the special wrapping Farissa had given her. It was soft in her hands, with a pale silver hue to the shimmering fabric.

'Is that—'

'Silkspore, yes,' Wren told her.

'And for those of us not versed in weird alchemy?' Kipp quipped.

'Silkspore is what Master Alchemists use to transport living samples of plants,' Wren explained, carefully unfolding the material on the ground. 'It has preservation properties that maintain the perfect humidity and temperature for the wrapped specimen, while naturally repelling any insects or fungi.'

She took her own secateurs in hand, their familiar weight – not at all their sentimental value – grounding her. It was delicate work, and the forest seemed to hold its breath around them. The only sounds were the soft snip of their tools and the occasional rustle of leaves overhead, the Bear Slayer and Kipp saying nothing.

'We need to be careful not to overharvest,' Wren explained to Dessa in a hushed tone. She didn't know why she was whispering, only that the space seemed somehow sacred. 'Take only what we need and leave enough for the plant to recover and spread.' Her fingers ghosted over a cluster of tiny white flowers. 'See these? They're just beginning to bloom. In a few weeks, they'll turn to seed . . .'

Wren could still hardly believe what she was seeing: the silvertide rose spilling across the ground like a river, each bloom like a captured star. How had it flourished like this? How did it have an almost ethereal quality when the roses back at Drevenor did not?

Both she and Dessa worked quietly, and Wren was increasingly grateful for her friend's presence. 'Whenever I can repay the favour, Dessa, please let me know,' she said.

'Don't be ridiculous,' Dessa replied. 'It's not every day an alchemist can say that she helped an heir of Delmira save the midrealms.'

Wren laughed. 'Let's not get ahead of ourselves.'

The moment was short-lived, though, a curse bubbling from Wren's lips as she cut her finger on the rose's razor-sharp thorns.

Dessa grimaced on her behalf. 'They're like little daggers, aren't they?'

Wren nodded, sucking the blood welling at her thumb.

'How much more do you need?' Torj asked, scanning the silk-spore that was nearly at capacity and the jars of soil around them before lifting his gaze to the canopy to measure the dip of the sun.

'We're nearly done,' Wren told him, noting the shift in the dappled light herself.

Torj gave a nod. 'Good, because there's something we have to do before we return to Drevenor.'

Wren whirled to face him. 'What? What could possibly be more important than getting back to the academy and working on this cure?'

The Warsword looked uncomfortable. 'Farissa and Audra advised me that there is evidence to suggest that someone is leaking information to the People's Vanguard . . . details about Drevenor that no one should know.'

Dread washed over Wren. 'What of the oath of secrecy?'

'That doesn't prevent anyone from spilling secrets. It's merely the consequence if they're caught,' Torj replied. 'Farissa has released a series of false leads to those she suspects are working with the enemy. There's an event in Harenth hosted by one of these individuals who has known connections to the others. We've been tasked with infiltrating the party and searching the premises for anything that might implicate the host . . . Letters to allies, missives containing the incorrect information Farissa leaked . . .'

Frustration crackled alongside Wren's lightning. 'Surely there is someone else who can do this work? I need to get back—'

Kipp silenced her with a nudge. 'This might actually work in our favour,' he murmured. 'Regarding our other project?'

Wren pinned him with an indignant stare. 'This had better not be some ploy to stop at the Laughing Fox.'

Kipp had the audacity to look offended before turning back to the Bear Slayer. 'What kind of event are we attending, might I ask?'

'A formal one,' Torj replied. 'And in order to gain access and investigate, we need to be covert—'

'So we'll need formal attire,' Kipp said. 'I know just the place. Leave the disguises to me.'

'That's not happening.' The Warsword tilted his chin to the canopy, as though he were looking to the gods for strength. His exasperation brought Wren a small flicker of joy as Kipp addressed her and Dessa next.

'Who would you rather acquire gowns on your behalf? Yours truly, or . . . ?' He gave Torj's travel-worn garb a pointed look.

Dessa laughed. 'Given the covert nature of this assignment, I hardly think sending a Warsword into a dressmaker's shop is the way forward.'

Wren couldn't believe what was happening. She potentially had the answers she'd been searching for within her grasp, and now she was being diverted to Harenth of all places.

'I don't like this,' she muttered.

'For once we're in agreement, Embervale. But I have my orders, and your place is at my side until you're assigned another guard.'

Wren scoffed. 'Your place is by *my* side, Bear Slayer, much to my dismay. There's a difference—'

'We're going to Harenth whether you like it or not.'

Kipp elbowed him. 'Cheer up, Bear Slayer. A pint of mead in your hand and everything will be—'

Torj shoved Kipp aside with a glare before turning back to Wren and Dessa, who were shouldering their bulging satchels. 'Until we meet with Audra, this discovery about Delmira remains between us.'

'Anyone who strolls into Delmira will see it for themselves,' Kipp argued.

'Last time I checked, people rarely *strolled* into this kingdom, for fear of the darkness in its very marrow. It's also more than three days' ride to anything resembling a settlement.' Torj looked to Wren for confirmation.

She finished securing the samples in the silkspore, placing it carefully in her satchel. 'It's true,' she said, sheathing her secateurs in her belt and dusting her hands on her apron before starting back towards the cottage. 'In the five years I lived here, I didn't see another soul on this soil. Bar you, Kipp, when you came to see me.'

'Just because you didn't see them doesn't mean people didn't set foot in this territory,' the strategist commented.

'True,' Wren allowed.

Beside her, Torj made a noise of frustration. 'Can we just agree? No one speaks of what we found here. At least not until I've had the chance to talk to Audra.'

Kipp sketched a mock bow. 'As you wish, Bear Slayer.'

'What about Zavier?' Dessa asked.

Wren glanced across to see Torj warring with himself.

'He's the Prince of Naarva,' the Bear Slayer said at last as they reached the cottage and their horses.

'So?' Dessa's brow furrowed. 'He's our friend. We have to work together with him—'

Kipp reached out and squeezed Dessa's hand. 'Torj is right. He has conflicting interests as a monarch of the midrealms. I'm not saying we don't tell him. I'm saying we don't tell him straight away. Let the Bear Slayer talk to the Guild Master first.'

Wren fitted her boot to her mare's stirrup for what felt like the hundredth time, the motion now second nature to her, allowing her mind to spiral with a whirlwind of thoughts. She had come here, her stomach a pit of dread, simply hoping to find the plant she needed for her antidote. Instead, she'd uncovered something that would undoubtedly split her focus, that would set them on another unknown path.

What would Thea say, she wondered, to finding out after all this time that Delmira was not lost to the midrealms, but had been lying dormant all these years?

'Thea needs to know,' she said. 'It's her homeland too.'

'She will,' Torj assured her. 'But Audra needs to know first. There are many implications this sort of information could have . . . and we need to be ready.'

Reluctantly, Wren knew that Torj had a point. The unexplained rebirth of her kingdom was knowledge . . . and knowledge was power.

CHAPTER 16

Torj

'A Warsword will be for ever married to the
midrealms, and his duty to protect them'

— *The Warsword's Way*

As they rode south, Torj wasn't sure the alchemists understood just how much danger the new Delmira posed to them. He had been around long enough to spot a prize that could spark a conflict easily enough, and Wren's fallen kingdom was one of them.

While he trusted Wren and her friends to keep their word, who knew who else might have made the discovery already? His mind went to Silas the Kingsbane and how he'd left Queen Reyna to the Warswords so unexpectedly. Did the enemy already know? Torj would not risk a raven or messenger. The news would have to wait until they returned to Drevenor, and in the meantime, hopefully he'd learn more about whoever was leaking information from the academy.

Thankfully, the journey seemed quicker than their initial trek, but when they reached the fork in the road, Kipp veered his horse left, onto the route that led directly to the Laughing Fox in Harenth's capital.

'Snowden, I'll not have you jeopardize this trip, put Embervale in danger, for a fucking pint,' Torj snapped. 'I'll buy you one myself back at the Mortar and Pestle.'

'Easy, Bear Slayer. We need somewhere to wash and ready ourselves for the event, don't we? And you'll need to stay hidden until I can find appropriate disguises . . .' The strategist was failing to hide his glee, which only frustrated Torj further.

'Have you learned nothing in the past few weeks?' he demanded. 'The attack on Drevenor? The man following you from Settler's Port? The corpses hanging from trees? The fucking riot in Elmridge? The midrealms are not as they once were.'

'Which is why we need allies close,' Kipp said evenly, all traces of humour gone. 'The Fox is, and always will be, safe for us.'

'He's right.' Wren steered her horse after Kipp.

Gods, Torj missed dealing with shieldbearers at Thezmarr, where his orders were *followed*. 'I'm your guard. Your *protector*. I'll carry you to a damn safehouse if I have to.'

Fury blazed in Wren's gaze as it snapped to his. 'You lay a hand on me and see what happens, Bear Slayer. If I recall, you deemed my lightning a curse before. I have no qualms about cursing you all over again. I'll make the first time look like child's play.'

He stared at her. 'You threatening me now, Embervale?'

'Yes.' She lifted her chin in defiance. 'The midrealms were never safe, and I'll be damned if I live my life in fear. You're the one whose orders are delaying our return to Drevenor. You don't have to like the idea of getting ready at the Fox. You just have to come along – or don't.' She urged her horse forwards. 'See if I care.'

They rode through the night and into much of the next day, until Torj found himself staring at a familiar sign swaying in the wind. A laughing fox, its bushy tail curled around its body with a flourish.

Dessa, who was looking worriedly from strategist to Warsword, said, 'If we need somewhere to wait, I heard there's a lovely wine garden closer to the palace. It's a little . . . fancier . . . than this place. Perhaps we should take advantage now we're in a proper city?'

Despite his rage at the whole situation, Torj couldn't help but watch shock wash the mischievous grin from Kipp's face as he turned to Dessa and blinked slowly. 'Fancier?'

Dessa nodded enthusiastically. 'Yes, it's got beautiful outdoor day beds and—'

Kipp shook his head in disbelief, gaping at her as though she were a stranger. 'I think we should see other people,' he said flatly.

Behind him, Wren burst out laughing, the sound like notes of music to Torj's ears. How long had it been since he'd heard her laugh so freely? The fact that he couldn't remember hurt deeply. The fact that he wasn't the one to prompt it himself hurt more.

Kipp's expression remained deadpan, even as Dessa broke out in a fit of giggles. Torj doubted the strategist saw it as a laughing matter, and Torj himself was still too furious to enjoy the merriment at Kipp's expense. But Kipp simply pushed the door open and stepped inside.

The roar of enthusiasm that greeted the strategist was overwhelming, with patrons and staff alike welcoming him back into the fold like a long-lost hero. That was when Torj lost his patience entirely. He went in after Kipp, grabbing the younger man by the arm and hauling him to the side.

'What are you playing at?' he hissed. 'You're not twenty years old messing around as a shieldbearer any more, Kipp. You're putting people's lives at risk. You're putting *Wren's* life at risk.'

To his surprise, Kipp faced him, mirroring his anger. 'You don't know me well enough by now to know I would never do that?' he said. 'That I wouldn't bring us here if there wasn't an *actual* purpose?'

Torj narrowed his eyes. 'I know that you have a tendency to prioritize your own amusement over—'

'You are not the only one who cares for the midrealms. Or for Wren. You think because I don't wield a sword or a hammer that I can't contribute?'

'I didn't say that,' Torj replied, taken aback.

'People before you made the same error, Bear Slayer, and they didn't fare so well.'

The tips of Torj's ears burned with shame. He knew that before the war, Kipp had garnered a reputation for being a 'useless' shield-bearer at the fortress – someone who was often picked on by those on the brawnier side. But he'd more than proved himself during the final conflict, and his loyalty and devotion as a friend to those around him had never wavered.

'I'm sorry,' Torj said, hanging his head. 'I . . . I have a tendency to underestimate those around me, the people I want to protect.'

'Aww . . .' Kipp grinned. 'You want to protect me, Bear Slayer? How sweet.'

'Shut up.' Torj shifted on his feet. 'I said I'm sorry, alright?'

Kipp grasped his shoulder. 'Apology accepted. Now, let's find the rooms I've secured.'

'You've been in here all of two seconds, how have you—'

'The Son of the Fox has his ways, Bear Slayer,' Kipp replied slyly, before motioning to Wren and Dessa to join them.

To Torj's surprise, Wren pushed a foaming tankard into the strategist's hand.

'Wren!' Kipp beamed. 'Have I told you lately how much I love you?'

Torj wasn't expecting the impact of those words to hit him so hard – words he had once said to the poisoner himself.

Wren huffed a laugh. 'I don't believe you have—'

Kipp slung an arm over her shoulder. 'I *love* you. So much.'

Torj looked away. So this was to be his punishment for thinking he could ever have Wren Embervale as his, and for severing their soul bond without her knowledge. He would have to stand idly by and watch other men declare their love for her. Gods, he was jealous of *Kipp Snowden*, for fuck's sake. What was wrong with him? They were just friends, weren't they?

Even though he knew the answer, even though Dessa was standing happily beside the pair with an amused smile across her face, he hated it. He didn't like Kipp touching her, didn't like that she smiled for him. And he sure as fuck didn't like the words spewing from the strategist's mouth.

Torj cleared his throat. 'Thought you were taking us to some rooms, Snowden?'

'Right.' Kipp downed his drink. 'This way.'

He took them up the familiar stairs to the accommodations above the tavern and ushered them into a room with a roaring hearth.

'Am I right in thinking the event we need to infiltrate is the ball at Lord Hullet's manor?' Kipp asked Torj.

'How did you know that?' Torj asked.

Kipp grinned. 'There's only one significant gathering among the elite tonight, and I make it my business to know such things. It's vital if I'm to know what part we all need to play.'

'This isn't your task,' Torj objected.

'No, but I *am* the strategist of the group. Therefore, before I send for ballgowns and disguises, we need to get our roles settled.'

'And what part will the heir of Delmira be playing in your plot tonight?' Torj said, folding his arms over his chest.

He should have known it would be something outlandish by the glint in Kipp's eye, and the way he grinned before he said, 'Wren will be your wife.'

CHAPTER 17

Wren

'A bond between two magical beings is a dance of wills and fate'

– *Tethers and Magical Bonds Throughout History*

'WHAT?' WREN LOOKED from the Bear Slayer's flabbergasted expression to Kipp's smug smile.

'Warswords don't have wives,' Torj said between gritted teeth.

'You're not a Warsword tonight, my friend,' Kipp told him, shoving a pack into his chest. 'You said yourself that this assignment must be covert. I'm sure you'll make a fine nobleman, a handsome couple. Once you've bathed, that is. Right now, you both smell like horse.'

Wren didn't have the energy to argue. She simply slipped into the adjoining room with her things, hoping that the water waiting for her was hot and that Kipp's taste in women's clothing wasn't as scandalous as she feared.

The water was lukewarm, but it would do. As she washed herself, Wren's mind drifted to Delmira: the verdant stretches of grass, the wildflowers dancing in the wind, the glittering lake . . . The oncefallen kingdom was practically a haven. *How?* The question plagued her as much as the complications with the dark alchemy cure itself.

It seemed that every aspect of her life lately was a puzzle she couldn't solve.

Towelling herself dry, Wren reached inside her bag, only to pull out a small parcel of salted caramel delights. She'd taken the wrong pack. The Bear Slayer had a sweet tooth, alright.

His dagger came next. It was the one he'd insisted on her holding during that awful riot in Elmridge. It had never been his favoured weapon, she knew that much, but she'd seen it sheathed at his belt, and had watched him sharpen it several times over the years. Annoyed that she would have to return it to him to fetch her own belongings, she shoved it back into the pack—

Her knuckles hit something hard. Frowning, she pulled out something she didn't expect.

A *book*.

What in the midrealms was the Bear Slayer of all people doing carting a brick of a tome around on his travels? The man she knew was far more practical than that. Wren turned it over, her curiosity piqued.

Tethers and Magical Bonds Throughout History.

She froze, the words blurring before her eyes. This was the volume Thea had told her about. Wren had never imagined that the Bear Slayer might actually have it with him. Blinking the spots from her vision, she turned to the table of contents.

Parental and Inherited Magical Connections. Sibling Bonds. Animal Telepathy. Fated Enemies. Seers and Subjects. Bonds and Magical Objects. Alchemical Connections—

The door of her room burst inwards and Wren shoved the book beneath her discarded apron, heart hammering, clutching her towel to her chest. Kipp strode in with a garment bag.

'Disguises acquired!' he declared.

Wren's hand drifted to the scar on her throat. In certain circles it made her easily recognizable. But before she could point out the problem, Kipp opened the bag and presented her with a beautiful emerald-green gown.

'This comes with a choker piece that should do the trick,' he said with a wink. 'And a mask, if you fancy it.' His eyes fell to the open pack before her, the dagger's hilt peeking out. 'Did I mix up the bags again?'

'Seems that way,' Wren said as Kipp grabbed Torj's pack.

'Strange . . . It feels a tad lighter than it did,' he mused, a glint in his eye.

'Strange indeed,' Wren agreed, only just managing to keep a straight face.

Kipp motioned to the formal dress. 'Get ready. We need to leave soon.'

When the strategist had left, Wren took the volume in her hands once more, running her fingertips over the title.

Tethers and Magical Bonds Throughout History.

Gods, she was dying to open its pages and read the damn thing cover to cover. But there was no time. With regret bitter on her tongue, she got to her feet and slipped the tome beneath her pillow. There would be time enough for reading on the ship back to Drevenor. When it came to Torj Elderbrock, she had no intention of remaining in the dark.

She eyed the gown Kipp had selected and approached it, vowing that when she dressed, she would dress for war.

'You look beautiful,' Wren told Dessa, who was twirling before the full-length mirror in a strapless black gown, her tulle skirts swishing.

'As do you,' Dessa replied. 'But can I *please* paint your lips and line your eyes? You'll bring that Warsword to his damn knees.'

Wren chuckled. 'If you insist.'

Dessa swept kohl across her eyes and painted her lips with a soft, rosy colour. Wren hardly recognized herself. Gone was her stained apron and muddied hem; instead, she was resplendent in a ballgown of emerald-green and gold, with a dramatic choker piece to match. As Kipp promised, it covered the jagged line of her telltale scar well enough, and Dessa had taken care of the newer marred flesh on her cheek with cosmetics. Fine chains rested on her breasts, which had been pushed up by an unforgiving corset.

'Perfect!' Dessa declared.

'Thank you,' Wren said. 'I assume you and Kristopher will be getting up to no good this evening?'

Dessa shrugged. 'Potentially. I don't see why we can't work *and* play. Though between you and I . . . I suspect our time together has nearly run its course.'

Wren's brows shot up. 'Is that coming from you? Or him?'

Dessa sighed. 'Both? It was never going to be for ever, and right now, I think there are things bigger than us that need our attention.'

'Have you told him this?' Wren asked. She hadn't spoken to Kipp about Dessa; she had no idea where his head was at, but she didn't want to see either of them hurt.

'Not in so many words.'

'Perhaps it's time you did . . . ?' Wren ventured.

'Perhaps.' Dessa smiled. 'Not everyone is meant to stay together for ever, Wren. And I'm okay with that.'

'Well, if you need to talk—'

'I'll come find you,' Dessa replied with a wink. 'I'm going to get a drink downstairs before we leave. Do you need any more help?'

'I'm fine. Go and enjoy yourself while you can.'

There was no way Wren could get away with wearing her usual belt of potions and poisons, but that didn't mean she needed to attend the event unarmed. She took one of her more special vials and slid it down her cleavage, where it sat snugly. She treated her favourite hairpin to another dose of poison and secured her long tresses in place atop her head. And finally, she wrestled her skirts up and fastened a small dagger around her thigh.

'Glad you're not taking any chances,' said a familiar voice from the door.

Wren nearly jumped out of her skin. 'Have you ever heard of knocking—'

But the words faded on her tongue as she took in the man before her.

She had never seen him in anything other than Warsword attire, armed to the teeth, usually covered in dust from the road or blood from a fight ... Before her now stood not a battle-worn warrior, but a handsome nobleman. Half of his silver hair was swept back in a neat knot, the rest falling to his collarbones. His broad shoulders, usually obscured by bulky armour, cut a striking silhouette in a midnight-blue doublet embroidered with silver threads that matched his eyes and hair respectively. The fabric hugged his muscular frame, hinting at the strength she knew lay beneath.

Wren felt suddenly too hot, the gown too tight—

'You can laugh if you want,' Torj offered, the tips of his cheeks pink, his stance slightly stiff.

Wren opened her mouth to say something smart, but no retort came. 'You scrub up alright, Bear Slayer,' she managed, sliding her feet into the fine heeled slippers Kipp had provided.

Torj's mouth quirked to the side. 'You think?'

Wren shot a glare at him for good measure. 'Don't let it go to your head.'

'Too late,' the warrior quipped with a roguish grin.

Wren forced herself to look away. 'And how are your burns?'

'Better, thanks to you.' There was a smile in his voice that tugged at something inside her—

No. This flirting couldn't continue. They were not lovers. They were not friends. Not after what he'd said to her in the gardens.

'There is no 'always' for people like us.'

As devastating as she found him, as much as he affected her physically, she couldn't allow this. Armed with a beautiful gown and the title of the book he'd kept hidden, Wren steeled herself against his inquisitive gaze.

She took her cloak of black velvet off the hook and made for the door. 'Let's get this over with.'

Kipp and Dessa were waiting in the hall, dressed in similar finery, though looking significantly more cheerful.

Wren forced a smile to her lips as she nudged Dessa. 'You really do look beautiful,' she told her, because it was the truth. Her friend was utterly radiant with her voluminous skirts and blood-red lips.

Dessa gave a wicked grin as they followed Kipp down the back stairs and into an alley. 'A certain warrior can't keep his eyes off you.'

'Listen up, ladies,' Kipp said, drawing them into a huddle. 'When we leave here, we assume our pseudonyms. Wren, Torj – you are a wealthy, happily married couple from Aveum: Lord and Lady Hargrave. You are my honoured guests for the evening. Dessa, you were going to play the part of my sister, but I realize you can't keep your hands off me, so you'll be my intended bride from Tver, the Lady Kingsley. We'll be attending one of the most notable balls of the season, hosted by one of Harenth's most prestigious families. Honestly, I don't know how you would have managed this without my help.'

'Just fine,' the Warsword grumbled. 'I assume you can create enough of a distraction for Embervale and me to slip away and search for any evidence leading back to Drevenor?'

Kipp snorted. 'Have you met me?'

'Why us?' Wren asked. 'Why not Dessa—'

'*Because*,' Torj growled, 'you and I can play the part of the couple seeking a quiet reprieve, should we be questioned.'

'That's one word for it,' Dessa muttered, and Kipp barked a laugh.

'And you?' Wren asked her friend with a glare. 'Who are you meant to be?'

'Who do you think?' Kipp gave her an incredulous look as an ornate carriage pulled up at the end of the alley. 'I'm Kristopher fucking Snowden.'

'Furies save us all,' Torj muttered, striding towards the carriage.

The ride to the estate was short, but Kipp insisted that no nobles of their supposed standing would be caught dead wandering the streets in all their finery. *At least the carriage is large enough that we're not on top of one another*, Wren thought as it drew to a halt outside a grand manor house. But the musing conjured an image of herself and the Bear Slayer in that very position, and she had to borrow Dessa's fan.

Torj was the first to leave the carriage. With his back to her, Wren was allowed an unobserved moment to admire the way his black cape hung from his shoulders. The rich fabric swirled around him as he moved, so different from the practical, mud-stained cloak she was used to. Despite the noble trappings, she could still see the Warsword in him: the alertness of his stance, the subtle scanning of the entryway for threats, the power held in check beneath the fine fabrics.

It was a strange duality – the fierce protector and the handsome nobleman – and it heated her blood like nothing else.

Which was why when he turned and offered her his hand, she took it without thinking, his fingers warm around hers. As soon as her feet were on solid ground and she was sure she wasn't about to trip over her skirts, she snatched her hand back.

'*Happily* married couple,' Kipp reminded her, as he made for the grand stone steps leading into a brightly lit foyer. 'You're to dance, be merry while Dessa and I search the lower floors, then we'll swap and cause a diversion for you.'

Wren could already hear the music within – the soft melody of a lute, several fiddles accompanying in harmony. A strong hand slid around her waist, drawing her close as they headed into a crowd of nobility. Fingers unconsciously flexed across her hip, as though desperate to explore more of her.

'What are you doing?' she hissed at Torj, suddenly short of breath.

He didn't remove his hand. Instead, his thumb stroked over her gown deliberately, sending a shiver down her spine. It felt like forever since she'd been touched like this. Her body betrayed her, yearning for contact despite her rage.

And then, he leaned in.

'If you were my wife,' Torj said, his voice low and rough, 'I wouldn't let you go. So that's what I'm doing.'

She was speechless. His words seared into her like a brand, each syllable igniting a trail of fire across her skin. A maelstrom of desire surged through her veins, leaving her breathless and aching. He held her pressed to his side and she couldn't bring herself to pull away, the subtle touches sending sparks of awareness through her.

His familiar scent wrapped around her, and Wren let herself breathe it in, a delicious form of torture as they moved through the crowded foyer. Servants scurried about taking cloaks, and she found her shoulders bare.

Several eyes latched onto her as soon as her cloak was swept away by an attendant, scanning the opulent choker at her throat and the tops of her breasts as they rose and fell with each breath. Wren didn't care for their staring, but there was no denying that a certain kind of power was now in her grasp. She watched as a young nobleman started and stopped in her direction several times—

Soft lips pressed against her neck, right over her fluttering pulse.

Pleasure bloomed from that point through her whole body, causing her to clench her thighs together, feeling the dampness gathering there. A broad hand spread across her abdomen, the ultimate show of possession, pressing her flush against the muscular Warsword at her back. And without thinking, she arched into him, relishing the hard planes of his body against hers.

'Do you think I'd allow someone to approach my wife like that?' The rich timbre of Torj's voice went straight to her core.

She had to bite her lip to keep from whimpering, until she remembered herself. She needed to come from a position of strength if she was to interrogate him about the book she'd found. She refused to be a simpering fool at his mercy.

Together, they entered a grand ballroom. Its soaring ceilings were adorned with crystal chandeliers and ornate gilded mouldings that traced intricate patterns along the walls and archways. It reminded Wren of the places she'd been as the Poisoner, with all the trappings of unimaginable wealth. Enormous arched windows lined the entire far side of the room, their panes reflecting the flickering candlelight and revelry. This was exactly the sort of party the marks from her ledger had attended.

Noting that Kipp and Dessa had long since peeled away from them, Wren turned to the dancers twirling across the floor. There were various pairings: men and women, women and women, men and men, and no one batted an eye. A pang of grief struck Wren as she wished Ida could see the freedom here.

Women wore sweeping gowns of silk and velvet and were adorned with more jewels than Wren had ever seen. In another lifetime, this might have been all she'd ever known – a world of decadence and splendour, not plants and poisons; not battle and death.

As though sensing the change in her, Torj's thumb stroked the soft fabric at her waist: a small, intimate gesture, causing a wave of goosebumps to break out across her skin. Every nerve ending felt electrified, attuned to the Warsword's proximity and each tiny movement of his fingers against her. She only hoped he didn't notice the hitch in her breath.

To her surprise, he tugged her towards the dance floor, the music swelling and ebbing like a living thing through the crowd of couples. 'Come on, Lady Hargrave. Kipp told us to dance.'

'And you're always so accommodating of Kipp's requests, are you?' she said wryly. 'I thought this was *your* assignment?'

'It is. But we can't just barge in and ransack the private rooms, can we?'

He swept her into his arms, her long skirts swishing beneath them as they fell into step with the pairs around them. Torj's fingers laced through hers, warm and firm, his other hand holding her waist.

'Hand on my shoulder,' he murmured, his breath tickling her ear, his scent intoxicating.

Wren stared up at him, trying to find her footing. 'Here I was thinking the Bear Slayer didn't dance.'

'I didn't say I do it well,' he replied gruffly, brows knitting together in concentration. When he found his rhythm, he met her gaze. 'Though I'm not the Bear Slayer tonight – I'm your husband.'

She hated that those words found their way into her chest, causing her heart to flutter and her core to tighten in anticipation. It was dangerous, being so close to him. The force of him was overpowering, and she worried she might lose herself again.

The music picked up pace, and warm notes plucked on the lute punctuated the sweeping strings, guiding the dancers. Wren, however, had no idea what she was doing, and neither did Torj, by the way he fumbled through the steps.

'Don't you dare drop me,' Wren warned him, narrowly missing a collision with a woman whose dress was unnecessarily voluminous.

Torj peered down at her, and for the first time, she noticed flecks of gold amid the sea-blue of his eyes. How had she never seen them there before?

'I'd never let you fall,' he said, his gaze dropping to her mouth.

Despite everything, Wren wanted to kiss him, every part of her calling out for his touch.

She shoved those feelings deep down and replied in a cold, flat voice, 'But you're more than willing to walk away.'

CHAPTER 18

Wren

'In alchemy, balance is not merely desirable – it is the difference between transformation and destruction'

– *Arcane Alchemy: Unveiling the Mysteries of Matter*

TORJ'S HANDSOME FACE tensed with anguish. 'Embers, I—'

But Wren shook her head, the rage within unfurling fast. 'Enough.' She pulled back as much as the dance would allow. 'You think this is *fair*? What you're doing? That you're happy to touch and kiss me, to play pretend? After everything you said to me back at Drevenor?'

The Warsword flushed, dipping his head in shame. 'I'm sorry.'

Wren didn't care. The lingering looks, the nickname, claiming her as his wife . . . Was it all just a game to him? She wouldn't stand for it. 'I don't want your apologies. I want the truth.'

'The truth?' Torj missed a step, causing them to stumble.

'Do not tell me it's because you no longer want me. Every action, every look of yours contradicts that claim. There's something you're not telling me . . . Do you think I can't handle it? Do I not deserve to know?'

His hand tightened on her waist. 'Wren.' Her name on his lips was the height of injustice, the way it sounded in his husky voice, the nerve it hit inside her.

The Furies bestowed a small mercy, then. As the tempo of the music slowed, Wren guided them towards the edge of the dance floor, where they might step off without causing any disruptions—

She froze. Her halt was so sudden that Torj stepped on her toes.

'Sorry,' he blustered. 'I didn't mean—'

But Wren had barely felt it. Her gaze had fallen upon an older nobleman a few yards away. He wore a rich burgundy doublet and was lifting a silver goblet to his lips in one hand, while the other rested on a bejewelled golden cane.

The Poisoner's life collided with Wren's in that moment.

Perseus Graymoor.

A mark she'd never struck from her ledger.

A man who'd—

'You think I don't know who that is?' Torj's voice rumbled beside her, his grip on her tightening. 'Don't even think about it, wife.'

'I'm not your wife,' Wren hissed. 'And I have no idea what you mean.'

'Now is not the time or place to play assassin,' the Warsword murmured.

'Were it up to you, all those corrupt bastards I ended would still be walking free, spreading a different kind of poison throughout the midrealms.' Old rage resurfaced as she watched her mark reach for a fresh goblet of wine.

'Embervale,' Torj warned. 'Promise me you won't. I need you to promise me that you won't strike another name off your ledger. Not while you're in my charge.'

Wren tore her eyes away from Graymoor and faced Torj, her fury awakening the dormant lightning lingering beneath her skin. The audacity of this man . . .

'I owe you no promises,' she whispered fiercely, twisting out of his grasp. 'I owe you *nothing*. Now, let's do what we came here to do before I throttle you on this dance floor.'

Torj hesitated, but after a quick glance around, he looped her arm through his and escorted her away from the waltzing couples. When they reached the stairs, a trio of guards stopped them, politely informing them that the upper levels were for overnight guests only.

They found Dessa, who was on the edge of the ballroom with a group of noblewomen. Thankfully, she was observant and immediately extricated herself, coming to Wren's side.

'We need that distraction soon,' Wren murmured to her.

Dessa nodded. 'I hear there's a beautiful view of the lower city from the terrace.'

Trying to ignore the hulking warrior attached to her, Wren let her friend lead her through the throngs of silk and velvet, towards an open pair of gilded doors on the far side of the grand ballroom. Cool air kissed her face as she stepped out onto the balcony, a relief from the stifling heat of the dance floor and the Warsword who held her in his thrall.

Constructed of smooth, pale stone with intricate balustrades and a floor of mosaic tiles, the balcony was just as breathtaking as the interior of the manor. Wisteria wound its way up the pillars and gold lanterns illuminated an array of frescoes along the walls.

'Lord Hargrave,' Dessa said to Torj pointedly. 'The civilized thing to do would be to offer your wife and her friend refreshments.'

Torj's lips pressed together before he replied through gritted teeth, 'What would you and *my wife* like to drink?'

'Sparkling wine,' Dessa said with a casual wave towards the servers with trays behind him before tugging Wren to the edge of the terrace. There, they took in the view of the formal gardens and the glimmering city below.

'He's taking his role seriously,' Dessa commented, glancing back at the Warsword in all his finery.

'A little too seriously,' Wren added.

'That man burns for you, Wren. The sooner you both catch alight the better, lest you set the whole world ablaze.'

Wren thought of the way Torj had kissed her neck in the foyer at the mere approach of another man, her cheeks heating at the memory.

The Bear Slayer returned, holding out two flutes.

'You're too kind, Lord Hargrave,' Dessa said, batting her lashes.

Torj rolled his eyes and turned to face the view. Wren, however, followed Dessa's gaze across the crowd to a nobleman leaning against a pillar. He was tall and slender, and, though his clothes were simple, it didn't take a trained eye to know that they were of a fine make. He carried himself with the easy grace of a person born into wealth and power. The small circle of noblemen and women who surrounded him looked captivated by whatever tale he was telling, charmed by his confident smile, failing to identify the boredom in his eyes.

'Do you know him?' Wren asked her friend.

'I know *of* him... That's Lord Devereux. He owns several estates between here and the far reaches of Tver, and it's rumoured that he funds the entire Tverrian army as well. He's apparently one of the wealthiest men in the midrealms, if not *the* wealthiest.'

'Oh?' Wren had heard that family name somewhere; it was unique enough to leave an impression.

Dessa continued. 'From what I've heard here tonight, he also funded the rebuilding of King Leiko's castle after that first battle in Notos.'

Wren's brows shot up. 'I saw the state of that castle myself... His coffers must run deep indeed to have funded those repairs.'

Dessa nodded. 'He's been very generous.'

Wren didn't have the heart to tell Dessa that generosity like that rarely came without strings.

To her dismay, the man in question seemed to sense her attention. His eyes met hers across the balcony, and after a beat, he saluted her with his glass.

'Aren't you meant to be causing some sort of diversion?' Torj asked Dessa sharply.

'All in good time, Lord Hargrave.' She smiled sweetly and offered him two small pieces of parchment. 'You'll need these to get upstairs as overnight guests. Perhaps it's time you took your wife on a tour of the manor?'

CHAPTER 19

Torj

'Scholars still debate whether the centuries of rule in Tver were maintained more by their magic or their masterful political alliances with prominent families'

– *The Midrealms Chronicles*

WIFE... THE FURIES certainly had a wicked sense of humour tonight – or Kipp did, at the very least. Torj had never seriously considered what he was giving up by becoming a Warsword. The knowledge that Thezmarr's most elite warriors never took wives – or husbands – had seemed inconsequential back then; he had never wanted to settle down anyway. But as the word had left his lips on several occasions that evening... *Wife. My wife.* He'd realized he liked the sound of it, the taste of it.

But that future had never belonged to him. It had been a dream, nothing more.

It didn't stop him sliding an arm around Wren's waist and leading her from the terrace, or from admiring the elegant slope of her neck, wrapped in that striking choker.

'Farissa told me that Lord Hullet's study is on the third floor, by the library,' he told her, guiding her through the sea of opulence and finery.

Having shown their overnight passes to the guards, they ascended the sweeping staircase to the first floor, Torj noting several sentries stationed at the doors to various suites.

'Come on, Dessa . . .' he muttered as he felt a pair of eyes on them.

He paused to brush a lock of hair behind Wren's ear, hearing her sharp intake of breath at his touch. Gods, he was pathetic. He'd vowed to himself that he'd keep his distance, but at the flimsiest of excuses, he'd got as close to her as possible, driven mad by his need for her.

A loud crash sounded from below, and suddenly the guards were rushing to the balustrades, peering down.

'Pick me up,' Wren hissed.

'What?'

'Pick me up – make it look like you're taking me to bed,' she said with more urgency. 'We're lingering here too long.'

Torj swept her up in his arms, staring deep into her eyes. 'As you command, wife.'

'Stop calling me that.'

Hiding a smile, Torj made for the next flight of stairs, and the next. It wasn't hard to pretend he was utterly captivated by the woman he carried; it certainly wasn't hard to convince the guards they passed that he desperately wanted to take her to bed. Guards and guests alike gave them fleeting, knowing smiles as they passed, and Torj wished the night was heading in the direction they assumed.

However, as they reached the next landing, Wren practically leapt from his arms and stared at a pair of double doors before them. She blinked. 'This is the library?'

Torj pushed a door open. 'Apparently so.'

Wren gasped as she entered behind him, and even Torj had to admit it was an impressive sight. There were shelves of books as far as the eye could see, a private collection to rival that of Drevenor's archives.

'Unbelievable,' Wren muttered.

'The study is at the far end,' Torj told her. 'I hope you're still good at picking locks . . .'

'How do you know I can do that?'

Torj scoffed as they headed towards where Kipp had told him the study was. 'How many of your poisoned victims were found within a room locked from the inside?'

'I have no idea what you're talking about,' Wren replied, already twirling her hairpin between her fingers.

Torj suppressed a smile. For so long he had abhorred Wren's other life, had resented that she felt the need to take justice into her own hands, but there was something intoxicating about seeing her in her element.

When they reached the study door that matched Farissa's description, Wren took her hairpin and a thin piece of wire to the lock. It was a sight to behold – a beautiful woman dressed from head to toe in finery, crouching before a silver latch.

Torj heard the lock click, and a smug smile graced Wren's face as she pushed the door open.

'What are we looking for, exactly?' she asked, surveying the large oak desk. It was meticulously organized, unlike the workspace of someone else Torj knew.

'Anything that could indicate correspondence from Drevenor. A letter with an academy seal, a familiar name – even familiar handwriting,' he replied. 'No one outside of Drevenor is supposed to know what happened, and yet Audra received information that secrets were being sold here. If we find one of Farissa's false leads, it will confirm who the traitor is.'

Something rattled, and he looked up to see Wren testing the drawers. 'All of these are locked. Keep a lookout.' She was already brandishing her hairpin and wire.

Torj kept another smile to himself. Gods, he loved her confidence, her complete mastery of herself in situations like this, and how she was never afraid to give an order, even to a Warsword.

Glancing at the door, Torj rifled through books and pieces of parchment while Wren worked on the drawers.

'False bottoms,' she announced, not even looking up as she lifted the first layer of contents.

'There might be hidden compartments at the back as well,' Torj offered.

'This isn't my first break-in, Bear Slayer,' Wren huffed.

While he searched the shelves, pulling out volumes and testing for a secret passage, Wren continued rummaging through the desk.

'Here,' she called, setting something down for him to see.

Torj frowned. 'Royal ancestries?' Leafing through the sheets of parchment, he saw nothing special about the lines of succession listed. 'You can get these records anywhere . . .'

Wren pointed to something faded in the top corner of each page. 'But they didn't come from just anywhere.'

Torj held the parchment up to the light, where an imprint of Drevenor's sigil had been pressed, the lettering and design raised.

'It's not a seal,' Wren said. 'But it's as good as. This was made with an embossing stamp. My guess is that these documents were taken straight from the academy's archives.'

Torj tried to absorb the implications, but couldn't wrap his mind around why someone would risk revealing Drevenor's secrets by sending documents one could obtain at almost any library throughout the midrealms.

'Odd . . .' Wren murmured, pausing over the lineage for Naarva. 'Zavier's been left off this. It's incomplete.'

Torj peered over her shoulder, and sure enough, there were no heirs listed below King Mulder and Queen Yolena. 'It could mean anything.'

'It could,' Wren agreed. 'But it's a link to Drevenor at the very least.'

They continued their search, the atmosphere growing tense around them, every creak of the floorboards amplifying their urgency.

Torj's gaze snagged on something gold and gaudy in a hidden compartment. 'What's this?'

'A paperweight?' Wren took it from his hand, her fingers brushing his as she examined it herself. 'It's an ornament . . . of a laurel,' she said thoughtfully.

'Like what they used on the novices at the welcome gala?' Torj asked, remembering that night all too well.

'There are many types of laurel,' she replied. 'A bit of a stretch in terms of a connection to Drevenor. Bored noblemen have all sorts of useless shit. We can't take this or the documents with us.'

'No, we can't,' Torj agreed, scanning the desk again.

Wren moved with practised efficiency, deftly sorting through more drawers and cabinets. 'Did Farissa tell you what false lead to look for exactly?'

'She did. But I don't see anything close to its description here—'

Wren froze. 'There's someone in the library . . .' she murmured.

Torj felt it too, a shifting presence beyond the stacks of books outside.

'I'll go and distract them,' Wren told him. 'You finish here.'

She was gone before he could argue. Torj tried to finish their search thoroughly, but the scars on his chest were prickling. He couldn't focus on the task at hand when Wren was out there facing Furies knew who, trying to buy him time.

'Fuck this,' he muttered, glancing back to ensure they'd left no trace behind before navigating the maze of shelves. He rushed through the library towards Wren. When he turned the next corner, his eyes locked onto her immediately.

Beneath the towering bookcases, another man was holding Wren's hand, his lips brushing against her knuckles in a lingering kiss.

A searing bolt of jealousy ripped through Torj, setting his blood on fire, narrowing his vision. His body coiled with barely restrained anger. The muscles in his jaw ticked and a primal sound built up in his chest, threatening to tear free from his throat.

Every rational thought he'd had leading up to this moment vanished. The apologies, the reasoning – all of it was consumed by the overwhelming need to claim Wren as his own, to erase any trace of another man's touch from her skin.

He squared his shoulders, and the air around him seemed to crackle, a palpable energy that radiated from his frame as he moved towards Wren and her unwelcome companion. Torj made his footsteps heavy and purposeful, his eyes never leaving the offending man's face. His hand twitched at his side, instinctively reaching for his war hammer, which wasn't there.

Wren sensed him first, and when she glanced his way, there was no surprise on her features. Only cool detachment. The very expression he himself had failed to master only moments ago.

Nearly blinded by rage, Torj grabbed the front of the man's doublet and lifted him bodily from Wren, ramming his back into the wall. 'Take your hands off my wife.'

'That's hardly the way to greet an old friend,' the nobleman said, his silken voice carrying a note of amusement.

Torj almost faltered as he came eye to eye with someone he'd once known well.

Darian fucking Devereux.

Torj's grip only tightened. 'What the fuck are you doing here?'

'Come now, you used to call me brother,' Devereux replied, completely unfazed despite his current position, where his feet were dangling above the marble floor. The bastard was lucky he was still in one piece. He'd had his hands on her, his *lips* on her—

Torj was practically snarling. 'She's. My. Wife.' Each word was punctuated with rage, laced with a fierce, unyielding intensity. As he said those words again, he realized he nearly believed them, and how deeply he wanted them to be true. The air between him and Devereux was thick, threatening to ignite at any moment.

'Husband.' The word was a command on Wren's lips, one that had him releasing his captive with a flex of his fingers.

'Elderbrock,' Devereux said with a light laugh as he straightened his jacket. 'You and I both know you have far too much self-loathing to marry someone of her calibre.'

Though Devereux seemed to have inherited his awful father's talent for cutting remarks, Torj didn't flinch. The bastard was still within reach, and he could damn well throw Devereux through a wall if he fancied it. More than anything, though, Torj was conscious of Wren looking between them, gauging their familiarity and animosity.

'You two are friends?' she asked, brow furrowed. Torj could hardly blame her. Wren had known him for over twelve years and not once had she seen him with someone like Darian fucking Devereux.

Devereux gave her a charming smile. 'I doubt the Bear Slayer would see it that way—'

'Observant of you, as always,' Torj said flatly, turning to Wren. 'This is Darian Devereux, Lord of Larkwood Valley. Darian, I suspect you know who Wren is, or you wouldn't be here.'

'Observant of you,' Devereux chimed back before addressing Wren. 'It's a pleasure, though your choice of escort leaves a lot to be desired.'

'Enough,' Torj cut in.

'Ah, yes, we can't tarnish your pristine reputation, can we?' Devereux chuckled lightly. 'What do they call you now? Saviour? Lightning-kissed Bear Slayer?'

'And what do they call *you* these days, Darian?' Torj's words were poised to cut.

'All manner of names, I'm sure. But what's a few names against a vault of gold and an army at your back, eh?' Devereux winked, clearly enjoying himself immensely. 'I assume you got what you came for?'

Torj didn't think it was possible for him to get any tenser than he already was, but he was wrong. How did Devereux know they were after something? And why was he looking so pleased? Torj itched to wrap his hands around the nobleman's throat and squeeze the answers from him. He wouldn't be surprised if Devereux turned out to be the one pilfering secrets from Drevenor and selling them to the highest bidder.

'We came up here to fuck,' Wren said bluntly. 'So yes, I'd say so.'

Devereux gave her a sultry smile. 'I do love a foul mouth on a princess.'

Torj had the front of the man's doublet in his fist again. 'Go back to whatever festering hole you came from, Devereux. Before I send you through one of these windows.'

'I'm sure we'll be seeing each other again soon, old friend. And what a pleasure to meet you, Elwren. Next time, let's leave the warrior brute at home.'

Before Torj could tear his head from his shoulders, the arrogant prick walked off.

Torj's chest was heaving as he turned to face Wren and found her studying him. She pinned him with the same look she had when she was trying to solve a problem at her workbench, when she felt a calculation was just beyond her reach . . . but there was something else in her willow-green eyes, something darker and more complex swirling in their depths.

'What was that about?' she demanded, her voice tight.

'I told you,' Torj said hoarsely. 'I'd never let someone touch you if you were mine.' He noticed that her hair was unbound, framing her face with locks of burnished gold and bronze. And she was twirling her poison-tipped hairpin between her fingers.

'But I'm not yours,' she stated.

Torj swallowed the lump in his throat, clinging to his last shred of willpower to stop himself from reaching for her. 'You are tonight.'

Wren considered him for a moment, before she leaned back against the shelf behind her, lifting her chin in challenge. 'Then prove it.'

Torj closed the gap between them, trapping her. He saw her pulse flutter in her neck and her gaze grow hooded as she licked her lips. The tops of her breasts rose and fell with each breath against the confines of her corset, and it took every ounce of his restraint not to tear it down the middle.

Torj let his eyes drop to her mouth, and it was all he could do not to claim it with his. Instead, he braced himself over her, inhaling her addictive scent, wishing they were anywhere but here so that he might strip her bare and lick every inch of her. 'The thought of anyone else touching you . . . kissing you . . . It drives me mad.'

Wren's body reacted beneath his. He could feel the hitch in her breath, the subtle spreading of her legs beneath that beautiful gown. But her eyes . . . Her eyes were cold, calculated.

'And yet you won't tell me the truth.' She reached up and traced his jaw with her fingertips, a teasing, taunting touch. 'You think you're going mad now, Bear Slayer?'

She leaned in.

He thought he might die from the need for her.

Her words ghosted over his lips as she whispered, 'I'm not wearing any undergarments.'

CHAPTER 20

Wren

'A magical bond can take many forms, many of which we still do not understand'

– *Tethers and Magical Bonds Throughout History*

Hearing Torj use the word *wife* did something to her. At first, it was a thrill – a glimpse at a future that could have been, a word that tangled longing with the darker side of her, with that molten fury that always bubbled so close to the surface.

But how dare he? After everything they'd been through, after every horrible word that had left his lips back at Drevenor. How fucking *dare* he?

So she'd left him there. The shocked breath he had expelled as she whispered the words *'I'm not wearing any undergarments'* had been her reward.

He'd been about to kiss her, about to lose all that tightly leashed control. Wren wasn't about to give in so easily. The book was waiting for her back at the tavern, and she'd find out what the Warsword was hiding, one way or another. If it meant torturing the Bear Slayer until he cracked, so fucking be it. Wren was used to playing the long game.

Thankfully, when she left him, she ran straight into Kipp, who declared their business concluded, all the important people absent, and the party dull. Together, they went to the balcony to retrieve Dessa, who seemed to be the only one from their group enjoying herself.

As Wren looped her arm through her friend's, the nape of her neck prickled, and she turned to find a pair of dark eyes on her. Darian Devereux was watching her from where he stood holding court once again beneath the wisteria. His gaze held a glimmer of amusement, directed at Wren.

Dessa elbowed her. 'Looks like someone made an impression.'

Wren scoffed. 'I've got enough troubles, Dess.'

'I hope they're all as delectable as him,' Dessa said with a smirk.

Wren could only shake her head. 'You're incorrigible.'

Torj was waiting with their cloaks in the foyer. Wren took hers without a word, without so much as a glance at him. *Let him stew*, she thought bitterly as they made their way to their carriage. Luckily, she found herself at Kipp's side.

The strategist slipped a piece of folded parchment into her hand with a whispered aside. 'The location you requested, Your Queenliness.'

'What have I told you about calling me that?' she hissed. 'Besides, aren't I meant to be Lady Hargrave this evening?'

Kipp shrugged. 'Be whoever you want, Wren. It's of no consequence to me.'

Wren stopped in her tracks, yanking Kipp back as well. 'You mean to tell me there was no reason for me to pretend to be *married* to the Bear Slayer throughout that whole charade?'

Kipp gave a sly smile. 'Absolutely none. I suspected that the evidence Torj wanted was long gone already.'

'I could kill you,' Wren seethed.

'But then who would meddle in your terrible love life?' he asked sweetly.

'Dessa would give you a run for your coin,' Wren muttered. 'She's clearly been spending too much time with—'

A high-pitched scream cut through the night.

Wren's side was instantly warmed by the towering presence of the Bear Slayer, who was on high alert. Chaos ensued as a crowd gathered at the manor entrance. Wren tried to get a look at what had caused the outburst, but there were too many people.

Frozen with morbid curiosity, she and the others watched as at last, a body was brought out on a stretcher. There was just enough light from the torches lining the forecourt to illuminate the bejewelled golden cane resting beside the corpse.

Perseus Graymoor.

Torj's eyes snapped to hers, dark and dangerous, a silent accusation.

'Wasn't me,' she told him, producing the untouched vial of poison from her cleavage, showing him that not a drop had been used. 'Wish it had been, though,' she added. And with that, she accepted Kipp's assistance into the carriage.

Upon their return to the Laughing Fox, Wren wriggled out of her gown and into an oversized nightshirt with a sigh. It felt good to be back in her own clothes, where she was clearly Wren the alchemist, the poisoner – not a noblewoman whose moody husband couldn't keep his hands off her. While she was still fuming at Kipp for his prank and at Torj for being Torj, Wren couldn't wait any longer to read the book beneath her pillow. The magic beneath her skin was too alive, too restless for sleep, and it seemed to be reaching for answers as much as she was. There was no way she could sneak out of the room without the Warsword knowing, so with Dessa snoring lightly in their shared bed, Wren sat on the floor by the fire with the book in her lap.

Tethers and Magical Bonds Throughout History. For a moment, she simply stared at its cover, suddenly unsure of what she might find between its pages, scared of how it might change what was to come. Wren could pinpoint several times in her life when she had felt as though she were on the cusp of something momentous: when she had become Farissa's apprentice at Thezmarr, when she had sensed Thea's storm magic awakening, when she had shared her power with Torj . . . Tonight, with this strange book, felt much the same as all those occasions.

Taking a deep breath, Wren turned to the table of contents. It listed dozens of terms she had never heard, terms that no doubt came before the midrealms were formed as they were now – when magic was not found in royals and Warswords, but was freer throughout the lands.

As she scanned the words she felt dizzy, and familiar voices filled her head, distant but clear.

Torj's husky words came first. *'I feel like myself, only . . . more. In the years after the war, I felt it only occasionally. A thrum of power, like an echo left over from the battle, but . . . Since I saw Wren again, it's been different.'*

'Different how?' Thea demanded.

Wren couldn't see them, but their conversation bloomed in her mind, and somehow, she *knew* it was real – that it was one they'd had in the recent past.

'It's as though we're linked. I can sense her power, her emotions,' Torj said. *'We're . . . in tune with one another.'*

'I mean, has this link caused you pain? Do the scars ache?'

'No,' he said quietly. *'It has never hurt me.'*

Wren's hands warmed suddenly, and she had to stifle a gasp to keep from waking Dessa. She stared at the book in her hands.

'You kept saying you were linked. *That's not an injury – it's a connection . . .'* Thea supplied. *'I hate to break it to you, but you've been researching the wrong thing, Bear Slayer.'*

It was some kind of ancient magic that was allowing Wren to see another person's past, providing her with the connection, she could feel it in her bones. Her gaze trailed further down the list of contents, landing on two words just as Torj's voice came to her with a rush of feeling.

'Soul bonds . . .'

CHAPTER 21

Torj

'A Warsword's duty is bound to the will of the Guild Master of Thezmarr. Their word is law'

– *The Warsword's Way*

THE NEXT MORNING, the Laughing Fox was a hive of activity as the first rays of dawn crept through the grimy windows. Inside, the air was thick with the aroma of freshly baked bread and sizzling sausages, mingling with the tang of sour mead. Patrons crowded around tables, their voices a low rumble punctuated by occasional bursts of laughter or exclamations of disbelief. By the looks of things, some hadn't retired the night before and were simply carrying on into the day.

At the heart of the commotion was a single topic: the unexpected demise of Perseus Graymoor. Torj still wasn't sure it hadn't been at Wren's hands.

The poisoner was sitting in one of the corner booths and staring into her mug of tea. He knew he'd taken things too far last night, that he'd let that protective streak morph into something darker. It was impossible not to feel how he felt about her, but he'd made his bed, and now he had to lie in it. That was what he'd told himself over and over into the early hours of the morning. And yet he couldn't help but feel that something was wrong, something more than he realized. The discomfort only seemed to grow in his chest, like a weed taking over all else. That they hadn't found the evidence Farissa wanted was only part of the puzzle.

Rubbing the calluses on his fingers, Torj cleared his throat, but Wren didn't so much as glance up. In fact, she hadn't met his eyes since last night – not that anything good ever came from that these days.

As though sensing his distress, Wren stood abruptly and went to Dessa at the far side of the tavern.

As they prepared to leave, Kipp was unsurprisingly surrounded by a small crowd, his expression wistful as he talked animatedly with the bartender and several patrons. Dessa, who was now waiting by the door with Wren, sighed.

'Forget the rebel uprising,' she said with a note of amusement. 'Getting Kipp out of the Laughing Fox might prove to be our greatest challenge yet.'

Torj stole a glance at Wren, who didn't so much as smile.

When they were at last on their way to Settler's Port, Torj could feel Wren's eyes on him. She was studying him, albeit not very covertly. *Why?* When she wasn't looking at him, she was distant, gazing out at the road ahead, her expression blank, showing no emotion but for the crackle of magic he sensed around her.

After the events of last night, Torj had hoped for a quiet ride to the docks, but Kipp seemed intent on making the morning painful. 'So,' the strategist said, loud enough for the others to hear. 'Lord Devereux from the ball . . . I take it you know him?'

Torj silently cursed Kipp. How had he found out about their little run-in? What else did he know that he wasn't letting on?

'Unfortunately,' Torj allowed, adjusting his grip on his reins and urging Tucker into a faster pace.

'How?' Wren asked. It was the first word she'd spoken to him since the ball. And she still hadn't looked him in the eye.

Torj couldn't help himself. He signalled to an annoyed-looking

Kipp to fall back and positioned his stallion alongside Wren's horse as they rode out of the city. With Kipp and Dessa out of earshot, he said, 'A word of advice . . .'

Wren speared him with a look that told him the last thing she'd do was take advice from him, but his words spilled over anyway.

'Don't get mixed up with Darian,' he told her.

'I can get *mixed up* with whoever I like, Bear Slayer.'

'Not him.'

'Why?' she challenged. 'Are you jealous?'

Yes, he was fucking jealous. *Of course* he was jealous. Darian fucking Devereux had sought Wren out in the library. Darian fucking Devereux had kissed her hand. His filthy lips had touched her skin.

But before he could answer, Wren forged on. 'Or perhaps this is just another secret you intend to keep from me? You have plenty of those, don't you, Warsword?' She was tense in her saddle, her eyes scanning him rapidly, searching, assessing.

Torj didn't know what was going on with her, but if he wanted Wren to heed his warning, he had to be honest. He had to relive the past. 'Devereux and I have a complicated history.'

'That much was obvious.'

Torj raked his fingers through his hair, trying to gather himself before he delved back into things he'd rather forget. A small mercy was that Dessa and Kipp had well and truly fallen behind.

'We were childhood friends, alright?' He couldn't bring himself to look at Wren as he spoke, instead focusing on the road ahead. 'Darian was the son of a nobleman, and my mother was a maid in their manor.'

Torj's throat grew tight at the mention of his mother, the words heavy on his tongue. The memory of her sent a familiar ache through his chest, and he gripped the reins tighter, steadying himself. He had told Wren of her fate a few months ago, so she was aware of the darkness lingering there. She was the only person he'd ever told, and he felt her gaze on him at last, her silence urging him to continue.

'When my mother worked, she took me with her, so that I wasn't around my father. Darian was around the same age, and his mother insisted that I play with him. She said it was good for her son to meet people from all walks of life and that I may as well take advantage of his tutors. She was a good woman.' From the corner of his eye, he saw Wren's expression soften.

'So you grew up together . . .' she ventured softly, watching him closely.

Torj nodded, the memories flooding back. 'We explored the forests together as boys, took classes together, got into more scrapes than I can count . . . Darian was like a brother to me. It was thanks to the Devereux stable master that I arrived at Thezmarr knowing how to ride a horse.' Torj took a deep breath and swallowed hard. 'Despite our differences in social standing, we had very similar upbringings . . . Where my father used fists, Darian's father used words, and sometimes I don't know who bled more.'

He risked a glance at Wren, catching the sympathy in her eyes. It made his chest tighten in a way he wasn't ready to examine.

Her throat bobbed. 'I'm sorry,' she said.

Torj had told her once before he didn't want her pity. He forced a shrug. 'It's in the past now.'

'Then what happened to make you hate him?'

The question hung in the air between them, and Torj found himself torn between the desire to bare his soul to her and the instinct to guard his wounds and keep his distance. The road stretched out before them, a silent witness to his struggle. 'A number of things,' he said eventually. 'After I left for Thezmarr, he started to show his true colours. He stepped into the role of the powerful nobleman's son, and then became an influential figure in his own right . . . It was at his bidding that I was sent to deal with the cursed bears in Tver.'

Wren frowned. 'Why? And . . . is it a bad thing? You gained your moniker there. You became a living legend . . .'

'It was also when my grandmother went missing. Darian used

his influence to keep me away from Tver when there was a lot of unrest going on. Because of him, I lost my grandmother. Because of him, I wasn't there to protect her . . . He became more and more like his father. He had the women's shelter that helped my mother knocked down, the one that my grandmother worked at.'

Wren was watching him closely; he could feel her warring with herself.

'Like I said, it's in the past now,' he told her, eager to bring the topic to a close.

'Apparently not, if he's seeking you out.'

'It wasn't me he was seeking, Embervale,' he told her, trying to strip the frustration from his voice.

'What would he want with me?' she asked.

'I'm sure we'll find out soon enough.'

Wren stared at him then, and he couldn't for the life of him read the storm brewing in her eyes.

Torj swore he felt something flicker between them, the echo of what was once there. 'So you see? You can't get mixed up with Darian. I won't let you. You're mine to protect—'

Fury flashed as Wren protested. 'I'm not—'

'No matter what happened between us . . .' Torj had to get the words out, had to let her know. 'You'll *always* be mine to protect.'

CHAPTER 22

Wren

'The rare phenomenon of the soul bond has not been recorded for centuries'

– *Tethers and Magical Bonds Throughout History*

ABOARD *THE FURIES' WILL*, Wren watched as the Bear Slayer rested his elbows on the railing and looked out to the white-tipped waves on the horizon, the breeze dancing in his silver hair. He looked much more at ease in his warrior's garb than the nobleman's finery, his hammer finally secured across his back once more and that wicked dagger sheathed at his hip.

Gods, she was so fucking *angry* with him, and yet . . . when Torj had told her of his upbringing with Darian, her heart had broken for him. The thought of anyone raising a hand to a child made her see red, and for that child to be Torj . . . If he hadn't killed his father, she'd have put his name in her ledger herself.

Holding two steaming cups of tea, Wren took a deep breath, relishing the briny taste in the air, and went to stand beside him. Her arm brushed against his as she offered him one of the drinks. 'It's not poisoned.'

'Wouldn't blame you if it was,' he said, accepting the mug and cupping it between his large palms with a glance at her belt of potions.

For a moment, they stood there, sipping their tea and staring out at the dark waters as the ship set sail. The warmth of him seeped into Wren's side and it was all she could do not to lean into his strength, into the familiar scent of him.

With Kipp and Dessa 'occupied' below deck, Wren felt the distance between herself and Torj all the more keenly. There had been a brief pocket of time where they too might have been wrapped up in each other in one of the cabins downstairs. Despite her anger, Wren couldn't deny how much she *missed* him. They'd been happy together, once.

The Furies' Will hit a wave, rocking violently. Torj's hand closed over her arm, steadying her, not releasing her until she found her balance once more.

Years ago, she, Thea, Wilder, Cal, Kipp and Torj had boarded this very same ship, sailing from Harenth to the coast of Tver, to aid King Leiko in the defence of his castle. Even then, Torj had stayed close to her side, and for the most part, she'd been oblivious to his attentions or dismissed him as a shameless flirt. Now, she knew the Bear Slayer much more intimately – or so she had thought.

The rare phenomenon of the soul bond has not been recorded for centuries. She could see the small text of *Tethers and Magical Bonds Throughout History* blurring before her, recognition stirring within. But she had made mistakes before. Perhaps it was something she simply wanted to believe.

'I found the book in your pack . . .' she ventured, before silently cursing herself. It wasn't the most subtle segue.

Torj's body tensed; she felt the shift in him beside her. 'I—'

'Don't insult me with another lie.' Wren held her tea between her hands, but didn't drink. She suddenly found herself wishing for something far stronger. 'I found it. I've started reading it. I just wanted to give you the opportunity to tell me yourself. Thea told me to talk to you. She seems to think there's a decent, honest bone in your body, that there's a reason you did what you did . . .'

'There's nothing more to explain. We're not a good match. We never were.'

'Then you'll have no problem telling me about soul bonds.'

Soul bonded. That was what she had read about in that godsforsaken book. That was what she was trying to identify between herself and the Bear Slayer. But for all their supposed connection, there was no golden thread, no physical manifestation like the stupid volume had described. The text detailed an array of criteria, including intense physical attraction and a protective instinct. The author had clearly never met a Warsword in the flesh. All she had been left with were more questions than answers.

She watched a muscle feather in the Bear Slayer's jaw as he clenched his teeth, clearly opting for silence over any semblance of the truth.

'Are we bonded in such a way?' she pressed. 'Is it from that day in Thezmarr? From the final battle?'

She could practically hear Torj's thoughts whirring, struggling to find a decent lie to catch and present to her. 'War connects us all.'

The Furies' Will rocked beneath them as the wind caught in its sails.

'You were the only one who could get near me. The only one who wasn't thrown back by the lightning. No one else wielded my power for me,' she said tentatively. 'No one else could withstand it . . .'

'Some questions don't have answers, Embervale.' The sea spray caught in his silver hair, making it glisten.

'But this one does, doesn't it? I felt it then, and I feel it now. Something . . . different. When you're near, my magic feels . . .' The words tumbled out as she finally pinpointed the effect he had. 'More focused. Clearer. Like it knows you.'

'Magic responds to strength. I'm a Warsword. My strength is Furies-given. Perhaps you should try zapping Wilder or Cal and see what happens.' He took a long drink of his tea, not meeting her gaze.

'Then why do I not feel that way around them?' Her voice hardened and her cup creaked in her grip. 'Why did it feel like you'd taken a piece of me when you left?'

'We were close.' Torj tipped the dregs of his tea overboard. 'Of course it hurt.'

'You're still lying.' Wren's fingers sparked with frustrated energy. 'Even now, can't you feel it? The way my magic reaches for you?'

As if in response, a tendril of lightning danced between them, crackling with her anger.

Torj stepped back, breaking the connection, and the loss of it ached in Wren's chest. He closed his eyes for a moment, as though bracing himself against an onslaught of pain. 'It doesn't matter what I feel.'

'It matters to me.' Gods, she hated the way her voice threatened to crack, hated the hurt that seeped through. 'Whatever this is between us, whatever you're hiding . . . I deserve to know.'

He turned away, and the movement felt like a physical blow. What could be so terrible that he couldn't even look at her? 'Let it go, Wren. Please.'

'The truth is inevitable.' Despite her rising frustration, she kept her voice neutral, soft. 'As am I. If it's the last thing I do, I will find out why.'

The Bear Slayer passed a hand over his face. 'It was never going to work, Embervale.'

She knew he used her surname as a form of distancing and she wouldn't stand for it. 'You almost kissed me last night.'

'I know . . .'

Wren studied him: the fine lines at the corners of his eyes, the dark shadows beneath them, the conflict shimmering in the blue that matched the sea around them. 'And you would have done more than kiss me.'

'Yes,' he admitted, staring into his empty cup.

Wren reached out, capturing his chin with her thumb and

forefinger, forcing his gaze to hers. 'I will find out soon enough, Bear Slayer, and when I do . . . you will answer for it.'

His eyes met hers, and her storm magic crackled, like the power inside her recognized its counterpart. The sensation made her lightheaded for a moment.

Torj's next words came out low and sultry, making her toes curl in her boots. 'I don't break easily, Embervale.'

Wren lifted her chin, relishing the challenge. 'We'll see about that, Warsword.'

CHAPTER 23

Torj

'The midrealms are comprised of five kingdoms ruled by magic-wielding families: the Embervales of Delmira, the Fairmoores of Harenth, the Stallards of Tver, the Duforts of Aveum and the Terlings of Naarva. So it has always been'

— *The Midrealms Chronicles*

'I DON'T KNOW why I'm surprised,' Torj muttered as he entered the ship's galley and spotted Kipp kicking his feet over the side of a bench, peeling potatoes.

'What?' the strategist replied with a grin. 'I was born in a kitchen, Bear Slayer.'

'I know . . . at the Laughing Fox. You've told me more times than I – or anyone else, for that matter – can count.'

Kipp flicked a ribbon of potato skin at him. 'How can I help? If you're in need of romantic advice – which you clearly are – I'm afraid for once I'm at a loss myself.'

Torj frowned. 'You? Kristopher Snowden? With no witty anecdotes on love and women?'

Kipp shrugged. 'Not today, my hammer-wielding friend.'

'What's wrong?'

A dramatic sigh followed and Kipp handed a potato and peeler to Torj. 'Oh, I'm just trying to find a way to break it to dear Dessa that we're not on the road to "for ever", you know?'

Torj stared at him. 'Tell me this isn't because she didn't like the Laughing Fox.'

'Did she *say* she didn't like it?' Kipp looked mortified. He nodded to the dirt-coated potato in Torj's hand. 'That's not going to peel itself.'

Mystified, Torj didn't think there was anything to do but peel the damn vegetable.

'And no,' Kipp continued. 'In answer to your question, it's not because of that. Though it certainly didn't help. Imagine insulting a man's palace like that?'

Torj huffed a laugh.

As always, Kipp had the gall to look offended. 'So tell me, Warsword, if you're not here for love advice – which, again, you *sorely* need – what *are* you here for?'

It took Torj a moment to move past the fact that he was in the galley of a ship peeling potatoes with the man who'd once been the *worst* shieldbearer at Thezmarr, asking for help. 'There are a few things I don't understand, that I need to piece together.'

'Just a few?' Kipp tossed a potato into the massive pot at his feet, unnecessarily splashing water everywhere. The look on Torj's face had him raising his peeler in surrender. 'Alright, alright! Are you going to tell me what you found in the private study last night? Before the dashing Lord Devereux spoiled all our evenings?'

'How'd he spoil yours?' Torj asked.

'A matter that's neither here nor there.'

Torj ignored this. 'He was there, right outside the study. Like he knew to expect us, like he knew we were after something.'

'Interesting,' Kipp said.

'I thought so,' Torj agreed. 'Which makes me think that we didn't find anything he didn't want us to find . . .'

'Which was?'

'Nothing that Farissa detailed to me. But there was a binder containing all the ancestry of the royal families, dating back centuries. And an ornament of a gold leaf – a laurel, Wren said.'

'Riveting,' Kipp mused.

'They were hidden in a drawer with a false bottom,' Torj added.

Kipp paused. 'Well that makes things interesting at least.'

'So you think these things *are* relevant? Are they proof that there's a spy at Drevenor?'

Kipp made a non-committal noise. 'I'm not saying anything at the moment.'

'If there is, it's Darian fucking Devereux,' Torj said.

'And you think Devereux – what? Planted these items there in the hopes that a Warsword would somehow find them and come to all the conclusions he intended?'

'All I know is this . . . If there is power to be taken, Darian will take it.'

'You really hate the man, don't you?' Kipp observed. 'I do however, feel it's my responsibility to check . . .'

'What?'

'That you're not just jealous,' Kipp supplied.

Torj cut him a warning look. 'You're telling me that Kristopher Snowden, chief strategist of the shadow war, the man who's so well-connected he could get a tankard of sour mead in a desert, doesn't know about the Devereux family?'

Kipp offered a sly smile. 'Oh, I *absolutely* know about the Lords of Larkwood Valley, and all their dirty deeds. Doesn't change my question, though.'

'Piss off, Snowden,' Torj snapped. 'I don't want to talk about Wren.' It hurt just to say her name.

'Ah, yes, the king and queen of not talking about it.'

'As opposed to you, who wants to talk about everything under the damn sun?' Torj shot back. He unclenched his jaw. 'Have you heard from Cal?' he asked instead.

Kipp gave a nod of confirmation. 'Just before we left Drevenor he sent a raven from Ciraun. He introduced Zavier to Talemir and the shadow-touched folk who've been running the capital in his absence.'

'Did he say how they took the return of their heir?'

Finished peeling his last potato, Kipp jumped down from the bench and helped himself to a cask of wine on one of the far shelves. 'The response was mixed, from what I gather, as was to be expected. But as thick as Cal can be sometimes, he's not quite stupid enough to put too much detail into a message that could be intercepted.'

Torj supposed that was as much information as he was going to get. 'What are you doing down here, anyway? It's unlike you to hide yourself away.'

'Ah,' Kipp said sheepishly. 'I *may* have made a comment about the captain's daughter that he did not appreciate—'

Torj rolled his eyes. 'Kipp . . .'

But the strategist waved him off. 'It's fine, it's fine. I assure you, *she* didn't mind. But I thought it best to stay out of the way for an hour or so, get in the cook's good graces by peeling some potatoes—'

'And drinking his wine?'

'Never said I was a saint, Bear Slayer.' Kipp looked around with a sigh. 'Mainly, I needed somewhere quiet to think.'

'I know what you mean,' Torj replied. 'I still can't believe a Warsword is dead, and another is missing . . .'

Kipp made a noise of agreement. 'If I were Audra, I'd be ensuring the Warswords work in pairs from now on. And that those stationed in more remote regions be called back to Thezmarr.'

'It's going to keep happening,' Torj said. 'Even when I was fighting with Wilder, it wasn't an easy victory, not by a long shot. They're prepared. More than we realized.'

'We underestimated them,' Kipp agreed.

'We did.' Torj leaned back against the bench. 'Well, at least you got to visit home . . . How *did* you find returning to the Fox?'

'Different,' Kipp admitted, his face falling.

'Oh?' Torj was surprised. It had seemed to him that the strategist was having his usual whirlwind of a time.

'Harenth is different. Everywhere is different. Those damn posters are up everywhere, even in the Fox. According to Albert, people go there for a drink after rallies and protests and start fights. The Fox survived the shadow war, but this? I don't know. Bounties on strangers' heads? Public hangings? There are guards everywhere. My usual sources for ... things ... are going underground.'

Torj dropped the last potato in the bucket and wiped his hands on a rag. 'There was law and order before. There were systems and hierarchies. Designed for the protection of all those in the midrealms.'

The stairs to the galley creaked, and Wren's face peered down at them. 'Just because it's the way things have always been, doesn't mean it's the right way.'

'I didn't say that it was,' Torj replied evenly.

But Wren continued. 'Don't you ever wonder if all the trouble the midrealms have been through in recent years, with the shadow war and everything that came after, might have been prevented if we'd changed things sooner?'

Tossing the rag aside, Torj shook his head. 'People taking matters into their own hands never works out. Not like this.'

Wren scoffed. 'Is that what you really think, Bear Slayer?'

Torj tensed. Wren had done exactly that as the Poisoner – had broken the laws of the midrealms to deliver her own justice. 'Why don't you tell us what *you* really think, Embervale?'

'I think that societies that do not adapt or bend tend to break. Something is not working in the midrealms. It hasn't been working for a long time now. Until we acknowledge that, we are doomed.' Wren paused, her expression like a midnight storm. 'In short, I'm starting to think the rebels have a point.'

CHAPTER 24

Wren

'All transformation demands sacrifice. What is gained must first be paid for in equal measure'

— *Transformative Arts of Alchemy*

IN THE PAST, Wren had wondered fleetingly what it would be like to affect change throughout the midrealms. So often it was those with no notion of what life was like amid the mud who governed from their castles above the rest ... To her dismay, she found herself pondering the same question more frequently now: who was anyone to decide the fate of others? What made someone worthy of that kind of power? And who held *them* to account? Silas, who was resurrecting an evil they had defeated long ago, *needed* to be held to account.

Wren had never been so glad to see the wrought iron gates of Drevenor. The golden dusk light danced along the worn gravel road to the towering building at the heart of the grounds. Six months ago, she had arrived here as someone else entirely – the Poisoner, still thirsting for vengeance, still consumed by the shadows of the past ... but now another weight fell across her shoulders. The task of recreating a cure that could see her not only graduate to the rank of sage, but stop near-certain war from breaking out across the midrealms.

Beneath it all, another current ran deeper still. A current that found her slipping into someone else's dreams, someone else's memories . . .

Wren pushed the thought aside as she saw Cal and Zavier waiting for them in the academy foyer.

'You're back,' she choked out, hugging Cal. She turned to Zavier, unsure if they were at a point in their relationship where they embraced.

Zavier seemed to sense her hesitation and pulled her into his arms. 'You saved my life. I'll give you a damn hug if you want one.'

Wren laughed, drawing back as she surveyed him. 'No crown for you, Your Highness?'

'Oh, they tried,' Zavier replied darkly. 'Stupid thing near bruised my skull.'

'Probably because your head's too big,' Dessa quipped as she hugged him hello as well.

Zavier gave a huff of amusement. 'Delmirian air was good for you, then?'

Dessa blanched.

'So you met Talemir Starling?' Wren asked hurriedly.

'I did,' Zavier replied. 'It's thanks to him that I have a kingdom at all.'

Wren nodded. 'But you're here and not there?'

'I came back to submit my opus proposal. My council agreed that given the state of the midrealms, having another qualified alchemist on our side wouldn't go astray. I'll graduate to sage and then return to Ciraun.'

'What did you decide on for your opus, then?' Dessa asked.

Zavier paused before answering, 'A study on transmutation of sorts . . .'

Dessa's furrowed brow mirrored Wren's own confusion. 'That's an unexpected choice for you. Metals?'

'Not quite,' Zavier said evasively. 'But I'm late to meet Master Norlander. I'll see you both tomorrow?'

With another glance at Dessa, Wren nodded. 'Tomorrow.'

'Good to have you back, Zave!' Dessa called after him.

Wren watched him go with the distinct feeling that something had changed in the Prince of Naarva.

⁓

Wren slid her satchel onto the table by Farissa's bookshelves and sat down opposite her former mentor. 'What I'm about to say doesn't leave this room.'

Farissa glanced up at Wren and the Bear Slayer by her side, worry etched on her face. 'What happened?'

'Delmira is no longer barren,' Wren told her. 'When we arrived, there were parts that had flourished. Fresh green grasses, wildflowers, birds . . . It is not as it was when I left.'

'That ground has been poisoned for decades,' Farissa replied, frowning. 'I've seen it myself. I've tested many samples of soil . . . Nothing new grows there.'

Wren struggled to swallow the hard lump in her throat, bracing herself against the mounting pressure. She had tried to keep her concerns at bay during their travels, she had tried to tell herself that Farissa would know what to do, but now she was standing before her, she realized something: this was so much bigger than her, than Farissa . . . The effects of whatever happened here today would be felt across the midrealms for centuries to come.

She took a deep breath. 'It does now.'

Farissa picked at her nails, something Wren had never seen the alchemist do in all their years of working together. 'Who else knows?' she asked.

'Just us, plus Dessa and Kipp,' Wren replied. 'But it was plain as day as soon as we set foot into the territory. It won't remain secret for long.'

'I'll wager others know and have been keeping it to themselves,'

Torj added. 'The land there looks more fertile than any I've seen in years, like the old Delmira. It's kindling waiting for a spark.'

Dazed, Farissa rose from her chair. 'Audra must be informed at once.'

'Wait.' Wren reached for the buckle on her satchel. 'I brought the silvertide rose with me. I didn't misidentify it, not that I can tell. But I don't want to make any more mistakes or waste any more time.' She took out the silkspore and revealed the samples she'd collected in the forest. 'Could you confirm its identity? Then I can start work while you and Audra figure out what to do about Delmira.'

'Elwren, crown or not, Delmira is *your* kingdom. You should be involved in these discussions—' But Farissa's words died on her lips as she took in the sight of the plant Wren held out to her. It was perfectly preserved, the deadly thorns guarding silver-white petals as soft as morning mist, the foliage rich and green. It looked as though it had been freshly picked, not transported in a satchel for several days.

The older alchemist's hands trembled as she reached for the stem, tracing its heart-shaped, tooth-edged leaves, rolling the white flowers between her fingertips. The thorns were so sharp that blood welled on the pad of her thumb. 'Gods,' she murmured. 'This grew in Delmira?'

Unease churned low in Wren's gut as Farissa examined the plant with her mouth agape. 'It did.'

Farissa dropped the sample and fell back into her chair, as though she needed the extra support. 'Elwren . . .' she said quietly. 'I admit, I didn't quite believe it . . .'

'Nor did I, and I was standing before it myself,' Torj said from where he was leaning against the door.

'And there was more?' Farissa looked to Wren. 'More flowers? More plants?'

'More *life*,' Wren confirmed. 'Like all the land's prosperity has lain dormant for decades and suddenly awoken.'

Farissa stared at the rose on the table. 'You didn't misidentify it,' she said. 'It is indeed a silvertide rose. Perhaps there's a slight variation in its strain due to the different growing conditions, but yes . . . you were right. I hope you brought enough back with you to study and propagate?'

'I did. Soil samples too.'

Farissa's fingers hovered near the seemingly innocent bloom, not quite touching its petals. 'Kingdoms, rebel factions and midrealms guilds will vie for control over land like this,' she said quietly. 'Especially now, amid so much uncertainty . . .'

As Farissa's words washed over her, Wren's mind went strangely blank before it plummeted into a sea of images. Fire and ashes, scorched fields and thorns. A blend of what she'd seen in the past war and what might now loom close in the future. The promise of violence was thick, polluting her lungs after breathing in the fresh air of her homeland.

Wren desperately wanted someone to tell her that everything would be alright, that things weren't as bad as they seemed, but neither her former mentor nor the Bear Slayer said a thing. Breath shuddered out of her, her gaze meeting that of the Warsword who came to her side – the man who might be bound to her in a way she didn't yet fully comprehend.

'Delmira just became the most valuable asset in all the midrealms, didn't it?' she asked.

Torj dipped his head in confirmation. 'And you, the most valuable target.'

CHAPTER 25

Torj

'Though historically Warswords were trained to slay monsters alone, past battles have proven time and time again that they perform best within a unit'

— *The Warsword's Way*

As they returned to their adjoining rooms, Torj faltered. The fire had left the poisoner. He saw it in her sagging shoulders, in her absent anger, in her vacant stare.

Without saying a word, Wren waited by the door so he could enter and do his usual security sweep, which was unlike her. She usually protested, complained that he was breaching her privacy... Instead, she watched on with a blank expression, as though she barely noticed him there at all.

Her quarters were as chaotic as ever: her desk in disarray with dozens of pieces of alchemy paraphernalia scattered about, her bed unmade beneath the stained-glass window and several half-drunk cups of tea, the tannin leaving rings of brown along the ceramic. Kipp had ensured her pack and other supplies were delivered, and they sat neatly by the door. Torj checked the bathing chamber, beneath the bed and the latch on the window. He strode through to his room, which Thea had been occupying, and found it exactly as he'd left it.

'It's clear,' he called out to Wren.

'Good,' she said, her voice devoid of emotion. 'I have to get to work, so if you'll excuse me.'

'Let me help.' The words were out of his mouth before he could stop them.

For the first time since they'd arrived back at Drevenor, Wren looked at him – *truly* looked at him. 'You want to help?'

Torj found himself nodding, motioning to her workbench. 'I'm a soldier. Give me an order.'

'You want me to . . . order you about?'

It was only because he was desperate to see her feel something, to vanquish that dead look in her willow-green eyes, that he winked. 'You like the sound of that, do you, Embers?'

That anger flared back to life, and for once, he was glad for it. Anger was better than apathy. 'What have I told you about the name?'

'I seem to recall you enjoying it immensely . . .'

He hoped she'd come out swinging.

And she did.

'I wasn't the only one.' She stalked up to him, closing the gap between them until she was close – too close. Her words were a dark, sultry promise. 'I seem to recall you moaning that very name in my ear . . . I remember you telling me to go up in flames with you.'

With his cock already straining against his leathers, Torj yielded a step. Whose terrible idea had this been?

Wren closed the gap again, only a breath away. Gods, she hadn't been joking about driving him mad. He'd overplayed his hand, and now he was once more at the poisoner's mercy. Wasn't he always?

She gazed up at him through her thick lashes, her mouth slightly parted, her lips wet and tempting. 'Tell me about the soul bond, Bear Slayer.'

Had it only been days before that Wren had told him she had the book in her possession? Torj had no idea how much she'd managed to read, but he knew she was looking for evidence. Once she knew . . . He didn't know what was worse: that he'd lied to the woman he loved, or that he'd taken her choice away. Would she ever look at him the same way again? Or worse still, would she bind herself to him and risk her safety once again? Was that even possible after what he'd done?

He yielded another step, only to find his back against the wall. 'There's nothing to tell.'

Wren's fingertips dipped beneath the fabric of his shirt, tracing the outline of his scars. She watched the place where she touched him, as though she expected to see literal sparks fly. 'No? Why did you have the book, then? What's it about?'

'Didn't finish it,' he gritted out. 'I was bored shitless.'

Wren's fingers dipped lower, dragging over his shirt now, down his abdomen, tracing over every ridge there. She looked every bit as powerful as she did when she called a storm forth from the sky.

'You're a shitty liar, Warsword.' She tilted her face, so that if he dipped his head a mere few inches, he could kiss her. Gods, he wanted to. Every part of him was screaming to take her in his arms.

Her hand drifted south and his head hit the wall behind him. She was *testing* him. Trying to figure out what would make him crack. Whatever she'd read in that damn book had her research process well underway, and he was her experiment.

'Is this where you tell me you're not wearing undergarments again?' His breath caught in his throat at the pain of not being able to touch her.

'Wouldn't you like to know.' Wren stepped back, leaving him cold and wanting.

This woman would be the end of him, and she knew it.

But Torj had told no one of what he'd discovered. While Audra, Kipp, Thea, and Wilder suspected, he had never confirmed the soul bond's existence, nor had he told anyone that he'd severed the tether between them to save her life. Whenever he wavered, he thought of that moment – the moment where he'd seen the light leave her eyes – and resolve found him once more. He would do it all again to keep her safe. He would do it a hundred times over if it meant Wren still walked the midrealms, even if he couldn't walk beside her.

He straightened, adjusting himself. 'Tell me what to do, Embervale.' He could feel the sparks of storm magic crackling within her, a flurry of raw power that she seemed to struggle to control.

'You want an order, Bear Slayer?' she said sharply, thrusting her hand towards the corner of the room. 'Clean those pots over there. I need empty vessels to propagate the silvertide in.'

And then she was back at her desk, shoving aside the clutter and whipping out her notebook, as though she hadn't just had his heart beating in the palm of her hand.

Torj cleared his throat, hoping the action would somehow steel him against the utter turmoil roiling within. It did no such thing.

'Right,' was all he managed.

For the next hour, they worked in silence: Torj cleaning out small pots in the bathing chamber and bringing them back to her, Wren filling them with soil from a large sack at her feet. Torj didn't ask how or when she'd managed to obtain such a thing. He just did as he was told.

He watched as Wren planted a range of silvertide rose samples in the freshly potted soil. Her workbench was even messier than usual, covered in clumps of dirt and puddles of water, but she didn't seem to notice. Instead, she was intent on noting down the time of planting, how much water had been given, and where the soil had come from. He shouldn't have been surprised to find that there were, in fact, multiple bags of soil beneath her bench, from different parts of the academy grounds.

'I'm trying to determine where it might best grow. The soil consistency is different all over Drevenor,' she muttered, more to herself than to him.

Torj was more fascinated than he cared to admit as he glanced between the alchemist and the silvery blooms at her fingertips – their petals soft as whispers, their thorns sharp as broken glass.

Wren had dirt smudged across her scarred cheek and mud lining her short nails when she came to stand in the centre of the room, her hands on her hips. She looked from the floorboards to the stained-glass window, the crease between her brows deepening. 'They won't get enough light here.'

Before Torj knew it, she was barging through to his room, examining the angle of his window.

'The seedlings will have to live in here,' she declared. 'Your room gets more sun.'

Though Torj didn't particularly care, he asked, 'For how long?'

'No idea,' Wren replied. 'Some seeds can take as little as seven days, some up to two months . . . It depends on what conditions they find ideal.' She dusted her hands off on her apron. 'That will do for tonight. I'm going to bed.'

As she turned to leave, Torj couldn't stop himself; he caught her arm. 'Wait.' His voice was low, his heart pounding as his hand closed over her warm skin. 'You've got dirt on your cheek.'

His thumb gently brushed over the scar there, lingering a heartbeat too long. He had tended to that wound himself. He'd nursed her for weeks after the Gauntlet, washing the blood from her skin, treating her injuries with salves.

Their eyes locked, and for a moment the air crackled between them again, a familiar sensation stirring in his chest. Torj's heart stuttered. It was simply an echo of what had been, he told himself. There was no bond between them now. His own actions had ensured it.

With the dirt gone from Wren's cheek, he dropped his hand.

She, in turn, stepped back, looking slightly dazed. 'Tomorrow, then, Bear Slayer,' she said, heading to her room and closing the door between them, leaving Torj alone with the promise of tomorrow, and the lingering scent of soil and storm magic.

CHAPTER 26

Wren

'A soul bond is for life and whatever comes after'

— *Tethers and Magical Bonds Throughout History*

'A*LSO REFERRED TO as: soul bonded, bonded, fated pairing, twin flames, surge binding, soul ties . . .*' Wren murmured as she followed the line of text with her finger before dawn the next day. '*A magical bond that creates an intense connection between two individuals that goes beyond physical attraction and extends to emotional, mental and even spiritual planes, with the ability to transcend both time and distance . . .*'

Torj's gentle touch lingered on her cheek even now. He may as well have branded her for how keenly she could still feel his thumb brushing against her skin.

She continued reading. '*Those who are soul bonded can often experience an enhanced sense of empathy for each other, sharing emotions – be it joy or sorrow – as well as dreams and memories . . . Sometimes even the same physical sensations . . .*'

A breath shuddered out of her. She had meant to torture him, to lean into that caress and put him in a place of blue-ball agony. But the unresolved tension had nearly ruined her as well. Then the moment had been too intimate, too tender, and she'd found herself overwhelmed.

Did this book explain it? Was she truly soul bonded to the Warsword? And if she was . . . was it so terrible to be linked to her? Was that why he'd pushed her away?

Wren washed as quietly as she could in the shared bathing chamber, then set about her tasks. Crushing a handful of silvertide leaves in her mortar and pestle, she lost herself in the rhythm of work. The plant would have to dry in powdered form before she could use it in her cure, and after her absence, she would have to start several potions from scratch. But she relished the challenge. It forced her thoughts away from the devastating warrior in the next room and kept her worries about Delmira at bay. Her not-so-fallen kingdom's fate now lay with Farissa and Audra. They would know what to do, and they would see it through. Farissa had promised Wren she could inform Thea of the developments when the time was right, when it was safe to do so.

Wren consulted her notes and checked her supplies. She was running low on the enemy's alchemy for testing, and she would need to bleed herself again to trial her cure. Examining the silver-white petals of the rose, she wondered how the blooms themselves might interact with the rest of her concoction, or even the thorns. She ran her finger along one sharp point, hissing when it pricked her skin.

Blood swelled there, the same blood she spilled so freely trying to test her cure. A bead of it dripped from the thorn itself, the pad of her finger still stinging as she watched it.

The thorns . . . She hadn't explored them thoroughly. And the way her blood shimmered on the table's surface had her reaching for another silvertide rose, this one with more thorns than petals.

The first rays of morning light crept through her stained-glass window, creating a kaleidoscope of colour across the floorboards. Wren settled into her routine with practised efficiency, her hands moving from task to task with the certainty that came from years of training. She took stock of what herbs she needed, which tools required sharpening and oiling. It wasn't until a soft knock sounded at the adjoining door that she looked up.

The door swung inwards, revealing the Warsword she'd been desperately trying to forget. He was wearing his usual leathers and armour, his hammer strapped across his back and that curved blade sheathed at his belt. The warrior garb suited him far better than the nobleman's finery, she decided. But to her dismay, he was beautiful either way. Gods, she had to busy her hands, focus on something other than the broad globes of his shoulders and the thick muscles of his thighs.

'You've got a workshop with the Master of Warfare this morning,' Torj said by way of greeting, oblivious to her internal struggles. 'We'll go to the dining hall for first meal beforehand.'

Feigning a lack of interest, Wren waved him off, turning back to her bubbling crucible. 'I don't need anything—'

'It wasn't a question, Embervale.'

The soul bond often manifests as a protective instinct between the twin flames, varying in intensity from heroic deeds to simple acts of nurturing. The damn book was in her head again, and her gaze snapped to him, an argument poised on her lips. But her stomach betrayed her, giving a loud grumble instead. Gods, she hated that he was right. But it didn't mean they were soul bonded.

'Fine.' She wiped her hands on a damp rag and inspected her toolbelt. As she moved about the room cataloguing her samples, Wren felt the Bear Slayer's eyes on her. 'What?' she hissed at last, moving through the adjoining door to his room to check on the sun's exposure to the seedlings.

'I was just wondering what made you want to become an alchemist,' Torj said thoughtfully. 'I don't think I've ever asked you that.'

No one had ever asked her that, which gave her pause. Wren bought herself a moment to gather her thoughts by crouching beside the pots on the floor, positioning them so they could catch the best of the morning rays through the window.

'When I was a little girl, I saw an alchemist create a healing potion for Thea,' she told him, remembering the afternoon vividly. 'You can imagine what she was like when she was younger – she got into all manner of scrapes that needed tending. Even though she was the elder of us, I worried for her. This particular scrape of hers was bad. She'd brawled with one of the stable hands and managed to get a deep gash on her leg.'

'I can't imagine Audra being too happy with her,' Torj ventured.

'There was a lot that Audra didn't see back then,' Wren replied. 'I had patched Thea up on occasion, but this wound needed professional treatment, so I took her to Farissa. It was magic, the way she mixed the ingredients. I knew right then that I wanted to learn how to do that – to help people, especially people like Thea . . .'

Torj was still watching her, his expression soft. 'You've always had a big heart. It's one of the things I lo— admire most about you.'

Wren glanced up, seeing the Bear Slayer's cheeks tipped with pink, a panicked look in his sea-blue eyes.

Her storm magic suddenly awoke under her skin as though called, and Torj's gaze went straight to her fingertips, as if he could see the lightning coiled like a spring just beneath the surface.

Everything Wren had read that morning surged to the forefront of her mind, a glaring theory she could no longer simply dance around. But though his appearance betrayed nothing, Torj seemed distraught. Wren could feel it.

Taking pity on him, she returned to her room and picked up her oilskin satchel as though he hadn't said anything.

Opening the door, she turned to him. 'And you?' she heard herself ask. 'What made you want to be a Warsword?'

Torj locked the door behind them, and they started down the corridor. 'I wanted to defend those who couldn't defend themselves. Like my grandmother. But I think she saw a much bigger picture – that Thezmarr could offer a family, like the one I'd never had.'

Wren pictured Sam and Ida, and the room they'd shared with her and Thea for years. She remembered them laughing, playing

Dancing Alchemists, and gossiping about the boys and girls in the fortress. It brought an ache to her chest. She glanced at Torj. 'And did it?'

He dipped his head in confirmation. 'In the end.'

Her eyes flicked across to him as they took the stairs to the ground floor. 'You didn't have an abundance of friends from the start?'

'I know it's hard to imagine me as anything other than charming and popular,' he quipped with a sideways glance. 'But when I arrived at Thezmarr, I was no more than an angry, scrawny boy . . . When you want to punch anyone who talks to you, it's hard to make friends.'

Wren tried to picture the enormous man beside her as a teen, swinging his fists at anyone who approached, and found that she couldn't. To her, he'd always been the Warsword she saw now, even when she'd found him injured on the Mourner's Trail.

Her struggle must have been etched on her face, because a smile tugged at the corner of his mouth. 'Your disbelief flatters me, Embervale,' he said wryly.

'That's not my intention.' She rolled her eyes. 'So, what was the turning point for your supposed popularity?'

Torj huffed a laugh. 'Probably working under Talemir and Malik. Those two were like brothers . . . The two of them fighting together was unlike anything I'd ever seen. And outside of the fighting? They laughed. They laughed so much together it was ridiculous. Darian and I had already drifted apart, though it was before I knew who he'd really become. But I missed that sense of brotherhood.'

They crossed the foyer, beneath the great tree that reached up into the dome-capped ceiling and past the glass cylinders that held stones of black garnet to keep score for the various teams. Wren hardly paid attention; she was too distracted by thoughts of a younger Bear Slayer, trying to find his place in the world.

'So you befriended Wilder?' she pressed.

'I tried,' Torj said. 'We both had a lot to prove, or so we thought. We were intensely competitive, as the two standouts of our cohort.'

Wren snorted. 'So modest.'

Torj shrugged. 'I was going for honest.'

'Makes a nice change.' But there was no bite to Wren's words. She was dismayed to find that she was enjoying herself, that sinking into conversation with the Bear Slayer was *easy*. It felt like the most natural thing in the world to walk beside him, to ask about his life. Despite everything that had happened between them, she wanted to know him better. She hated that.

Torj ignored the jab. 'After Malik was hurt, Wilder was different. I tried to be there for him, but he blamed himself for what had happened. He went off on his own a lot after that.'

'And Talemir?' Wren asked.

'Tal . . . Well, not long after Malik was injured, Tal went to Naarva and didn't come back. But before he left, he told me to keep trying with people. To keep myself open. The advice served me well enough. I found myself with plenty of friends at the fortress and throughout the midrealms. People would come to me often for advice, for help . . .'

The image of him was becoming clearer to Wren now, and it made her chest ache. 'And who did *you* go to?'

'My grandmother was my constant, until she disappeared.'

'And after that?' Wren knew the answer. She had seen the Warsword before and after the war. He was the pillar upon which everyone else leaned; he was the ear that listened, the shoulder to cry on, the voice of reason.

'It doesn't matter,' he said as they reached the dining hall.

They entered together and made a beeline for Dessa, who was sitting beside a surly-looking Zavier. A few paces back was Cal. He gave Wren a small wave, but didn't approach the table, seeming content to guard his charge from the outskirts of the dining hall.

Wren's stomach gurgled at the sight of the spread before her: the table boasted several trays of food – eggs, rashers of bacon, pastries. She and Torj took up the space on the bench opposite Dessa and Zavier. Wren reached for the teapot—

Torj's hand grazed hers as his fingers grasped the handle.

A current surged between them and Wren drew back quickly, a silent gasp on her lips.

Magical resonance. More words from the book came to her. *A bonded pair possess a powerful synergy that resonates when they are together.*

Saying nothing, Torj lifted the pot and poured her a cup. He added sugar, exactly how she liked it, before sliding it across to her.

'Thank you,' she murmured, warming her palms against the hot ceramic.

Torj simply dipped his head in acknowledgement and made his own cup.

Suddenly, she was very conscious of Dessa watching them, smiling smugly. Keen to draw attention away from herself, Wren turned to Zavier. 'How did submitting your proposal go?'

Zavier's expression instantly darkened. 'Good morning to you too.'

Wren balked. 'It didn't go well?'

Her friend sighed. 'It's complicated.'

'I'm sure we can handle it,' Dessa said, pursing her lips in annoyance.

Wren lifted her cup to her lips and bit back a moan. There was nothing quite like that first sip in the morning. 'Come on, Zave, tell us.'

'I'm ironing out the finer details,' he replied. 'But the reception from the masters was mixed. The topic is a tad controversial.'

'What is it?' Wren pressed. 'Transmutation is one of alchemy's basic fundamentals . . .'

Zavier took a deep breath. 'I wanted to explore the possibilities of human transmutation.'

Wren's mouth fell open. 'What?'

'That was the response I got from Crawford, Tremaine and Mercer, too,' he said dryly.

Beside Wren, Torj cleared his throat. 'Does someone want to fill me in?'

Zavier sighed. 'Do you attend none of Wren's lessons?'

'Not if I can help it,' Torj replied.

'Human transmutation is hardly something that was covered in our novice lessons, anyway,' Wren chimed in. 'It's a particularly taboo area of alchemy. It involves attempting to bring the dead back to life.'

'That's impossible,' Torj blurted.

Zavier nodded. 'So many have said over the years. Which is why my proposed opus is entirely theory-based . . .'

Wren's skin crawled all the same. There was something deeply unsettling about the concept itself.

'Any particular reason for this area of study?' Dessa asked. 'You've never talked about it before.'

'Why does anyone want to raise the dead?' Zavier shrugged. 'I've lost family. Sometimes I like to picture a world where they're not gone.'

His words were like a punch to Wren's chest as the faces of her own beloved dead swam before her. For a moment, she imagined being here with Sam and Ida, wondering what subjects they'd choose for their opuses. She pictured Anya standing guard beside Cal, or joking with Kipp . . . The world would have been so different if they'd stayed in it.

Dessa was nodding. 'I suppose if we're to study something so deeply, it's almost a requirement that it's personal . . . I know I feel the same way about mine.'

'You're working on storing memory, yes?' Zavier asked, clearly desperate to change the direction of the conversation.

'Yes. For my father. He has ongoing memory loss – key moments in his life are just wiped away. I'm working on adapting the memory weave for a more positive effect on the world. Perhaps I can help the victims of the disease and their families from suffering what we have.' Dessa glanced around self-consciously. 'I realize it's not saving the midrealms or raising the dead, but . . .'

Wren reached for her instantly. 'It's just as important.'

'It's alright that it's not,' Dessa replied, her head hanging slightly.

Giving her a strange look, Zavier turned to Wren next. 'Dessa told me you got the samples you needed. Any other news from your fallen homeland?'

Wren busied herself with reaching for a pastry to buy herself a moment. She didn't like lying, not to her friends. 'Nothing of note.'

The way Zavier's gaze lingered on her made Wren question if Dessa had caved and told him about Delmira. He was waiting for her to elaborate, but what could she say? That they'd discovered the rebirth of her homeland? That the kingdom once thought cursed was now one of the most valuable places in the midrealms?

'Did we miss any announcements this morning?' Torj interjected. 'It was my fault we were late.' They hadn't been late, but Wren was grateful for the interruption.

Zavier looked to her again. 'Actually, a chronicler came looking for you.'

'What?' Wren blinked. 'Why?'

'Apparently there are some scholars here who are writing a historical account of the shadow war. They want to interview you.'

Wren's blood ran cold, the last corner of her pastry frozen halfway to her mouth. The last thing she wanted was to recount her experiences of the war with a stranger. Just the thought had her hands growing clammy, and for a second, she thought she could smell the acrid scent of burnt hair.

Torj's knee bumped against hers under the table.

Wren came back to herself. 'What did you tell them?'

'That you were too busy and important to talk to the lowly likes of them,' Zavier quipped.

'You didn't.'

'I did not,' Zavier admitted. 'I told them you were only just returned from a research trip abroad and I had no idea when you'd have time for such things.'

Wren loosed a breath, her whole body sagging with relief.

Zavier shot her a sympathetic look. 'I expect they'll find you soon enough, though,' he said with a note of apology. 'According to the new novices, the High Chancellor made a big speech about contributing to other disciplines only a few days ago . . . *Knowledge is the victor over fate* and all that . . .'

'It's an honour to be invited to contribute, you know,' Dessa said quietly. 'I'd be glad to do so if I was asked.'

Wren's breakfast turned sour in her gut. She knew Dessa didn't mean anything personal by it, that the comment was born of her own inner battles, but it still stung. She had relived her darkest memories over and over for the better part of half a decade already. She didn't want to keep doing so.

Wren nodded her thanks to Zavier, but she couldn't shake the feeling that her past was catching up to her and soon she'd have nowhere left to hide.

As they prepared to leave for their workshop, Wren caught Torj's gaze. The concern in his eyes made her heart flutter. She suppressed the urge to reach for his hand, something that, for a moment, felt like second nature. Instead, she shoved her hands into her apron pocket and averted her eyes. Even now, the force of him was overwhelming.

And that terrified her more than any interview ever could.

CHAPTER 27

Wren

'There are seven metals within the discipline of
alchemy, their properties studied at great length:
gold, silver, mercury, copper, lead, iron, and tin'

– *Alchemy Unbound*

WREN SAT BETWEEN Zavier and Dessa in the poisons dungeon, waiting for the Master of Warfare to arrive. The shelves on either side of the chamber were overflowing with ingredients, and several of the plants had grown considerably in Wren's absence, their vines curling over the edges of the shelves and dangling down. Workbenches filled the centre of the room, but several seats were empty. When they'd been here as novices, the room had been full. As adepts . . . things were different.

Wren knew that several from her original cohort had not made it through the Gauntlet, but her memory of the graduation ceremony that preceded the battle was hazy. She had stood with her teammates on the podium, but her gaze had been on the Bear Slayer, whose pride was written all over his handsome face as he watched her from the crowd. It was no wonder she had no recollection of who had joined the adept ranks with her, Dessa and Zavier.

Now, she realized just how much her cohort had dwindled after the Gauntlet. She scanned the faces of those entering the room, trying to recall who was missing.

'So few . . .' she murmured.

'Many didn't pass the loyalty test before the Gauntlet,' Zavier told her quietly. 'While you were gone I had the pleasure of witnessing the memory weave in use again.'

Wren blanched. 'No . . .'

'Unfortunately,' Zavier said grimly. 'Selene Tinsley, Kyros Sorrell . . . Their memories were removed, and they were sent back to where they came from.'

Wren shifted in her seat, unease washing over her. 'It doesn't seem right.'

'They used the memory weave?' Dessa asked, looking up from her sketches.

Zavier nodded.

To Wren's surprise, she gave a frustrated sigh. 'I would have liked to observe that again.'

Both Wren and Zavier stared at her.

'You *want* to see that?' Wren asked, sure that she had somehow misheard her friend.

Dessa looked thoughtful. 'Well, I'm not sure I'd say *want*, as such . . . But you know my opus is a memory device. It might have been useful to watch the process through an analytical lens . . .'

'I would have happily traded places with you,' Zavier muttered, pulling out his notebook and quill.

'Perhaps next time you could take notes,' Dessa offered helpfully.

Wren had to swallow a laugh at Zavier's expression as she turned to him. 'About the chronicler . . . Did they ask you to contribute?'

He shook his head. 'Why would they? I wasn't in the midrealms for the shadow war.'

His words made her pause. '*That's* something we haven't talked about yet . . . Where *were* you? What happened after the fall of Naarva?'

Zavier sighed. 'I knew this was going to come up sooner or later.'

Dessa reached over Wren and patted his arm. 'You don't have to—'

'Speak for yourself,' Wren cut her off. 'I want to know.'

Zavier pushed Dessa's comforting hand away. 'I've already had to go over this with the High Chancellor and Guild Master of Thezmarr a million times – one more won't kill me.' He cracked his knuckles on the desk. 'It was years before the war you fought in . . . But Naarva was on the brink of falling to the shadows, and we ran.'

'Who's we?' Wren asked.

For a moment, Zavier pressed his lips together, and then he answered, his voice softer than before. 'My parents, my brother and me . . . I was young, so I don't remember the specifics. I just remember there was a boat.'

'Where did you go?' Dessa breathed.

'Beyond the Veil.'

The Veil had fallen at the end of the shadow war, but before that, it had been a seemingly impenetrable wall of mist surrounding the midrealms. It was believed to have kept out monsters, a barrier between their kingdoms and the dark world beyond – a twisted lie whose origins were still unclear.

'What was it like? Where did you live? Did you know what was happening back home?' Wren had a dozen questions on the tip of her tongue, but she was interrupted by the entrance of the Master of Warfare.

Master Crawford swept into the chamber, wearing the same dark clothes and an assortment of rings on his fingers. 'Welcome back, adepts,' he said, taking his place behind the desk at the front and scanning the empty seats. 'I did warn you that all paths lead to the underworld, did I not?' It was a rhetorical question. He ran a hand over the scarring on his face. 'Today we will explore corrosive compounds . . . In the simplest sense: the creation and application of substances designed to break down materials.'

Wren straightened. During the war, she had experimented with a particular concoction of sun orchid essence that had been weaponized against shadow wraiths and reapers. Upon contact with their sinewy flesh, it had burned them, but she wasn't sure if it would be categorized as corrosive. Was flesh a material?

'For today,' Master Crawford continued, 'in groups, you will be given a specific material. You will need to create a compound that corrodes this material. Over the course of our next three lessons together, you will be required to present a formula, create the compound, develop delivery methods for said corrosive and specify safety measures for handling it.' The Master of Warfare pointed to each team. 'Oak. Granite. Copper. Birch. Ceramic.' He gestured to Wren, Dessa and Zavier. 'Iron.'

Wren tensed. Iron was arguably the hardest, and she suspected that Master Crawford had purposefully chosen the most challenging material for them.

'What are you waiting for?' he asked. 'Get to work.'

For the next two hours, Wren and her teammates stayed hunched over their workbench, Zavier sketching out potential formulas for metal-corroding agents, Dessa and Wren pointing out potential issues with control variables and safety hazards.

Zavier ran his fingers down the list, his hair falling into his eyes, his brow furrowing in concentration. 'We have oxidizers for rapid rusting of iron, and therefore steel . . . Several multi-phase solutions for if the iron is layered and time-released compounds for penetrating particularly thick structures . . .'

'Should we ask what the target might actually be?' Dessa asked.

Wren shook her head. 'If he wanted to give us specifics, he would have. I think we need to prepare a compound that can be adapted for several possibilities. We anticipate the additional step in the challenge and work accordingly.'

'Agreed,' Zavier said.

Dessa groaned. 'As if we don't have enough to do with our opuses.'

'Such is the life of an adept, Odessa,' Master Crawford said from behind her.

Dessa flushed bright red. 'I wasn't—'

'Complaining?' he finished for her. 'That's exactly what it sounded like.'

'I—'

But the Master Alchemist had already walked away.

They didn't get as far along as Wren would have liked, but by the time Master Crawford was dismissing them, her back was aching fiercely, and her eyes were tired and gritty.

The Bear Slayer was waiting for her outside, and Cal was waiting for Zavier.

'You know,' Dessa said thoughtfully, 'it just struck me that I'm rather unimportant next to two guarded royals all the time.'

Zavier shot her a contemptuous look. 'Again, I'd trade places with you any time.'

With the rest of the afternoon free to work on their opuses, Wren, Dessa and Zavier decided to go to the archives. As they walked through the academy, Wren noted the increase in guards at the entrance and several unfamiliar faces who looked out of place in the academic setting.

'Do they expect another attack on Drevenor?' she asked her friends in a low voice.

It was Torj who answered as they made their way up the stairs. 'Additional security measures have been taken at several key locations across the midrealms. Drevenor, being the potential birthplace of the cure for the weaponized alchemy, is being prioritized.'

'No pressure,' Wren muttered, rubbing the back of her neck. She was sore. Sore from being hunched over her workbench last night, sore from the uncomfortable chairs in the poisons dungeons. Her back ached, and no matter how many times she rolled or rubbed her shoulders, the pain persisted. She'd have to make a tonic when she returned to her room later.

When they reached the archives, Wren temporarily forgot the pain as she breathed in the comforting scent of parchment and leather. Having spent many of her formative years in Thezmarr with its tiny library of warrior and military books, every time she set foot in the archives was like a dream.

Then she remembered the last time she'd been here with Torj, and her face flushed hot.

'Did you miss me, Embers? Because I missed you . . . Shall I show you how much?'

He'd shown her. Thoroughly.

Wren barely registered moving through the stacks towards one of the private study rooms with her friends. She was too conscious of the Warsword at her back, the Warsword who had lifted her skirts around her hips and licked her until she saw stars.

'I could taste you a thousand times and it would never be enough.'

A storm vibrated beneath her skin, as though her magic remembered it too. And when she glanced behind her, the Bear Slayer's eyes were dark with desire, lost in that exact moment with her.

CHAPTER 28

Torj

'A soul bond goes beyond an intense physical attraction. It manifests as a soul-deep instinct, almost primal in nature – to protect, to touch, to claim'

– *Tethers and Magical Bonds Throughout History*

WITH ONE BACKWARDS glance, Wren nearly destroyed him. Her gaze was heated, her cheeks tipped with pink, a beautiful flush blossoming down her neck.

She was thinking of *him*. He could feel it.

As soon as her eyes met his, an ember caught alight. All the blood in his body rushed south as the images of what they'd done between these very shelves flashed before him. From her expression, she was picturing the same moment between them, and the urge to snatch her away from the others and throw her against the wall was almost overpowering. Only the discipline of a Warsword kept him in check – that and the fact that he didn't know if she'd return the sentiment or slap him across the face. Or both. He'd gladly take both, he decided, as she tore her eyes away from him and entered the private study room, closing the door after her teammates.

Torj and Cal stood watch shoulder-to-shoulder outside, and

though Torj didn't feel like talking, he needed to take his mind off his hardening cock. 'How's it been with Zavier?' he asked Cal, scanning the shelves, monitoring the occasional footsteps nearby.

'Intense,' Cal replied. 'We had endless meetings here with Audra and the High Chancellor before we rode to Ciraun for more meetings with Talemir and the shadow-touched. There was a lot of controversy about his return and what consequences he should face for keeping his identity hidden and not returning to the throne sooner.'

'What did Talemir have to say about it?'

Cal shrugged. 'That he never wanted the burden of leading a whole kingdom, and he was glad for the heir's return in any capacity.'

'And Zavier's handling it well?' Torj asked.

'*Well* might be a bit of a stretch. He barely sleeps, he's lost weight . . . and he's certainly more of a recluse than my last charge.'

'That might not be the world's worst thing,' Torj ventured. 'Definitely less drinking and tavern-hopping.'

Cal huffed a laugh. 'Probably for the best.'

'Speaking of – any clue where *Professor Vulpine* has got to?'

'None, which is surprising. I half expected him to barge into my quarters this morning and demand a visit to the Mortar and Pestle.'

'You know Kipp . . . He's always got several plates spinning at once.'

Cal made a noise of agreement. 'How were your travels?'

'The rescue mission went as well as could be expected. Hawthorne and I managed to get—'

'That's not the travel I was talking about,' Cal interrupted.

'Oh?'

The younger Warsword rolled his eyes. 'I meant once you met up with Wren. You really fucked things up there, didn't you?'

'So I've been told. Several times,' Torj replied testily.

'You said you wouldn't hurt her.' Cal's voice was soft, but accusatory.

Torj's mouth was suddenly dry. 'It wasn't what I wanted.'

'It's what happened.'

Torj felt his jaw tic as his temper rose. 'Stay out of it, Cal.'

He expected his former protégé to back off, as he would have done when he was an apprentice, but Cal fixed him with a hard look. 'No. I won't. What do you have to say for yourself? I saw the way you looked at her then, and I see it now. You love her. So why did you do what you did?'

'It wasn't that simple,' Torj ground out. He hadn't signed up to be interrogated. It was none of the Flaming Arrow's fucking business.

But Cal wasn't done pushing him. 'Then why did you come back? Why not go abroad like you intended?'

'You think I wanted this? You think that this isn't agony for me?' The words flew from his mouth in anger and it was too late to take them back.

'Then fucking do something about it,' Cal snapped.

'You have no idea what's coming, Cal.'

'You think I don't know unrest when I see it? You think I lived through the same war as you and came out the other side none the wiser? Whatever is coming, you're a fool if you don't realize you're stronger together than apart.'

But before Torj could open his mouth to retaliate, the door swung open behind them and Zavier strode out.

'Cal, I think we need to make a trip to the conservatory,' he said, with a curious glance at Torj.

Did he hear us? Torj worried. *Surely we weren't that loud . . .*

But Zavier didn't spare him another look. The long-lost Prince of Naarva simply waved goodbye to the two women inside and strode off with Cal in tow.

Moments later, Dessa made her excuses and bid them farewell, leaving Torj alone with his charge. He peered inside the study room to find Wren wincing as she rolled her shoulders.

'Are you hurt?' he asked, startling her as he stepped inside.

'You scared me!' she said with her hand over her heart. 'No. I'm fine.' She turned back to the book in front of her and rested her head in her hands with a sigh. 'I don't know if I'm going to be able to recreate the cure I used on Zavier,' she said softly.

Torj's chest seized for her. 'You got what you needed from Delmira. Why wouldn't it work this time?'

Wren rubbed her temples. 'I don't know if you've noticed, but things tend to not go to plan around here. If I don't succeed . . .'

'You will.' He said it firmly, with no room for compromise, and he believed it with every fibre of his being. He believed in her. He always had.

Wren fitted her hands to her hips and arched her back, stretching what were clearly aching muscles. Guilt lanced through Torj as his gaze dropped to her breasts, which were thrust forwards. She was in pain and he was ogling her. He truly was a bastard.

'Here.' He moved towards her without thinking – apparently, he was doing a lot of that lately – and rested his hands on her shoulders.

A slight gasp escaped Wren, and all he wanted to do was swallow that sound with a kiss, but instead he stood behind her and slowly started to knead her shoulders.

Wren melted into his touch. 'Oh.'

'You're made of knots,' he told her quietly, working his thumb over a particularly hard spot behind her shoulder blades. He could feel her skin heating beneath the fabric of her gown.

'I haven't been moving as much. I was stretching and training with Thea every morning before we left here—'

A moan broke from Wren's lips, her head tipping back slightly.

The sound went straight to Torj's cock. It was a miracle he was able to keep the same rhythm with his hands as he worked across her tight muscles.

The flush across the back of Wren's neck told him that she hadn't meant to be so vocal. Torj only just managed to bite back a comment about enjoying her noises.

She cleared her throat. 'The exercise was helping,' she continued, as though she hadn't made a sound. 'But since we returned I've moved from one workspace to another, and . . . Well, apparently my back isn't what it used to be.'

'I know what you mean,' Torj said with a soft smile. 'Can I get you something for the pain?'

'I'll survive.' But she leaned into his touch with a quiet sound of relief. 'Right . . . there.'

Torj had never been more aware of the intoxicating scent of her, finding himself dangerously close to inhaling that hint of spring rain and jasmine directly, like an addict.

'You could train with me,' he ventured, working down the length of her spine as much as her chair would allow.

There was that arch again. *Furies save me.*

His heart felt raw, as though he had freshly ripped that bond apart all over again. Sometimes he thought he could still see glimpses of it – glimmers of gold. But Wren had said nothing, hadn't seen it. And that meant there was still a chance to save her from him.

'Why are you being so nice to me?' she said suddenly, wrenching him from the fantasy he'd been having where, in the midst of a training session, Wren straddled him as she had in the tent during the storm.

Torj's hands stilled. 'I—'

Wren pulled away from him, gathering her books and getting to her feet. 'I think it's time I returned to my room. I have work to do.'

'You should rest—'

'Until I can present the cure as my opus to the masters, there will be no rest for me, Bear Slayer.'

CHAPTER 29

Torj

'A guardian's oath is written in footprints that must never be seen, in battles that must never be fought, in sacrifices that must never be known'

— *Mastering the Craft of Close Protection*

'HAVE YOU DROWNED in there?' Wren called through the bathing room door.

For hours, she had been working at her desk, barefoot and harried-looking, pointedly ignoring Torj as he cleaned his hammer in the chair by her bed. It was long past midnight, and watching her attempt to rub her own shoulders for the tenth time was the final straw for him. He'd ducked back through the adjoining door to his room, putting his hammer away, retrieving the pouch he'd asked Farissa for and shutting himself in the bathing chamber.

He opened the door on her side. 'Is that wishful thinking?'

'Perhaps,' she replied, her eyes narrowing as she tried to peer around him.

He stepped aside, revealing the wooden tub, nearly full to the brim with hot, steaming water. Instead of the oil lamp, he'd placed several thick candles around the room, and a fresh towel waited on the rail.

'Get in,' he told her.

She stared at the bath, and the purple florets floating atop the water, taking a step forwards. 'Is that lavender?'

Torj suddenly felt ridiculous, his cheeks flaming, but he was too far gone now. 'It's supposed to be good for sore muscles . . .'

Wren opened and closed her mouth.

Torj studied her carefully. She wasn't angry. In fact, her eyes were lined with silver. She went to the side of the tub and trailed her fingers across the water's surface, disturbing a few florets of lavender. She captured her lower lip between her teeth and gave a slight shake of the head, as though she couldn't believe the sight before her. Torj took that as a good sign.

'Go on,' he encouraged her. 'I'll leave you to it.'

But Wren's gaze was intense as it lifted from the water and locked on his, her hands drifting to the ties of her apron.

Torj was frozen in place as she pulled it over her head and dropped it to the tiled floor. Next, her fingers found the buttons at the front of her gown, and no amount of training or discipline could stop Torj from following the folds of fabric as they fell away from her, revealing a column of bare, perfect skin.

Torj inhaled sharply. There was no scar from the battle where Wren had borne the wound inflicted upon him by Lord Silas, their soul bond linking them in shared pain. Wren's chest had no marred flesh, no reminder of that horrific day.

She watched him, and her hand went to that very spot on her chest, the place where there should have been a mark. 'We're soul bonded, aren't we?' she asked. 'Whatever it is . . . I feel it too.'

Every nerve ending in Torj's body was on edge, his fingernails cutting into his palms as he clenched his fists. Gods, he wanted her. He wanted her to understand. He wanted to explain that he'd never stopped loving her, that he'd only done what he did to save her, to protect her. And if he had the choice, he'd do it all again; he'd endure it a million times over, to keep her safe. But the words didn't come to him. For if he told her, what then . . . ?

'Have it your way, then.' Wren's hands went to the hem of her skirt and she pulled her entire dress up and over her head.

Torj felt as though the wind had been knocked out of him. He couldn't breathe. Not as the most beautiful woman in the midrealms stood naked before him, every inch of skin completely bare.

'Guess you have your answer about the undergarments now,' she quipped, dropping her dress to the floor.

'Are you trying to kill me?' Torj managed, his voice hoarse. He couldn't tear his eyes away from her. He knew what those curves felt like beneath his touch, he knew the weight of her breasts in his palms, he knew the sound she would make if he were to close his mouth around her nipple. And gods, he knew the wet, tight heat of her when he slid inside.

He wasn't thinking. He simply moved, closing the gap between them, so he was close enough to see the goosebumps rising across her skin. Her nipples were hard, her breaths coming quicker, and her eyes . . . Her eyes were dark with want.

He licked his lips, wanting nothing more than to haul her mouth to his, his cock so hard it was painful. Desire coursed through him – a molten current, begging for touch, begging for release. 'You're not fighting fair . . .' he murmured, his hand closing around her hip.

'Never said I would,' Wren replied, watching as his thumb stroked the juncture there.

Torj thought his heart might punch right out of his chest. 'Get in the bath, Embers.' He heard the warning in his own voice and saw how it made Wren shiver in anticipation.

'Or what?' She was toying with him, playing with fire.

His grip tightened on her hip. 'Or I won't be held responsible for what I do next.'

'I'm sure I could handle it, Bear Slayer.' Wren's hands went to his belt, the outline of his erection clear beneath his leathers.

But Torj caught her by the wrists. 'You've been antagonizing me for days. Punishing me . . .' His voice was thick with restrained need. 'I get it. I deserve it. But I've reached the end of my tether, Embers.' He spun her around and bent her over the edge of the tub, so that her backside was on complete display, and he could see the arousal gleaming between her legs.

Wren whimpered as he nudged her feet apart and held her in place over the ledge. She was so fucking perfect, so exposed for him while he was still fully clothed. Capturing her wrists in one hand, he let his other trail down her spine, down over her backside.

'I've been hard for days on end. For weeks,' he growled in her ear as his fingers grazed between her thighs, just shy of where he knew she wanted him.

'Torj . . .' she moaned, her body writhing beneath his hold, her back arching as she sought the friction she was clearly desperate for.

He slid his fingers down her centre, groaning at the wetness he found there. Wren bucked her hips, and Torj allowed his touch to circle her entrance, teasing, dipping in a fraction before retreating to rub her clit.

'Tell me you haven't thought about it,' he murmured. 'Tell me you haven't been reliving how we fucked . . .'

She was panting now, rocking back into his hand, looking over her shoulder, craning her neck to watch what he was doing to her.

Torj traced her entrance again. 'Do you remember what it felt like when I was inside you?' he murmured against her ear. 'Do you remember how perfectly we fit?'

Wren tensed, as though she were recalling those very details, the very imprint of him.

Torj's cock was throbbing, desperate to be freed from the confines of his leathers and seated deep inside of Wren. But this wasn't about him. It was about the poisoner, who was on the brink of begging . . . A thought that pleased him to no end.

For a moment, he thought he saw gold spark between them, which was impossible. That connection between them was gone. He'd torn the damn thing apart himself. He'd *felt* it rip between them, had felt every ounce of pain.

But there was no pain now. Not as he kissed her shoulder, then the length of her spine, all while she ground herself against his hand, leaving his fingers soaking.

He slid two fingers inside her and she gasped.

'Do you remember, Embers?' he said, pumping them in and out of her in a torturously slow glide.

'Yes,' she moaned.

Gods, he wanted to be inside her. But this was about beating her at her own game. 'Embers . . .' he said between kisses along her neck, still fucking her with his fingers, drawing out her pleasure, increasing his rhythm.

'Yes?' she whimpered.

He leaned in close. 'If you're going to make me suffer, imagining you with no undergarments day in and day out . . .'

He stilled his hand and withdrew his fingers.

Wren made a sound of protest.

'Then you can suffer with me.'

Her voice trembled with unmet need. 'What?'

'You said we weren't fighting fair,' he told her, leaving her by the tub and making for his room. 'Two can play at that game.'

CHAPTER 30

Wren

'The alchemist's crucible does not replace the
healer's garden – it amplifies it'

– *The Green Apothecary: A Guide to Medicinal Plants*

THE BASTARD HAD left her aching for his touch, a need that could not be met by her own hand. No answers, no orgasms, which meant Wren was still fuming the next day when she found herself in the healer's workshop with the rest of her cohort. The irony was not lost on her that today their focus was the creation of contraceptive tonics. Wren had been brewing and taking this concoction since her teenage years, and as such, she was several steps ahead of Farissa's demonstration.

'The supply you are preparing today is for the women's shelter you visited in the city as novices,' Farissa told them. 'It's delicate, important work . . . Though I can see there are some of you who do not understand its value.'

Wren's gaze flicked to where two adepts – men, of course – were talking among themselves, ignoring Farissa's instructions. Wren had heard her former mentor's voice dip like that several times over the many years they'd known one another, and it only ever meant one thing.

Farissa stopped before the adepts' workstation. 'Leave.'

'But Master—'

'You sit here openly disrespecting my discipline, gentlemen. I will not stand for it. Leave. *Now*.'

Dessa exchanged a smirk with Wren as the two pricks gathered their things with narrowed eyes and left the workshop.

Farissa stared after them for a moment, shaking her head before she turned back to those who remained. 'As I was saying . . . One of the key ingredients is a tiny, icy-blue fruit called frostberry – usually found in high mountain regions. It's known for its cooling properties and ability to "freeze," or certainly slow, some of the body's natural processes. We infuse this with crushed ginger and sliced whisper root, allowing it to ferment over several days.'

Wren was already finely slicing the whisper root.

'How do you know all of this already?' Dessa hissed, studying Wren's work intensely.

'I used to make this a lot at Thezmarr, for the men and women there,' Wren said quietly. 'The younger women would come to me for such things . . . Farissa taught me to make it when I was twelve. She knew that many of the girls would be too embarrassed to ask her, so she helped me learn, showed me how to distribute it safely.'

Dessa's mouth hung open. 'Truly? No one spoke of these things in my hometown.'

Wren shrugged. 'Thezmarr is no place for infants, Dessa.'

'Can you show me?' her friend asked.

'Of course.'

Over the next hour, Wren showed Dessa – and Zavier – how to brew the contraceptive tonic. Farissa had prepared a batch of the fermented liquid earlier, so Wren was able to show them how to turn it into a tea to be taken monthly, and how to create a dose to be swallowed as a pill. As Farissa said, it was delicate work; the dosage of each ingredient was crucial to avoid nasty side effects like cramping or bleeding.

She glanced at Zavier, who was scribbling notes. 'I'm surprised you don't know this one, Zavier, particularly with your affinity for unique plants . . .'

He didn't look up from his notes. 'It wasn't something I ever needed.'

Dessa's mouth dropped open a second time. 'What do you mean?'

Wren shot her a look to silence her, but Dessa was oblivious.

'Do you mean that you've never . . .'

Zavier did look up then, his chin lifted in challenge. 'Never what?'

Dessa scanned the cohort and lowered her voice. 'Never had sex?'

Wren nearly dropped her head into her hands, fully expecting Zavier to snap at their curious friend—

But Zavier barked a laugh. It was the first real laugh Wren had heard from him in a long while.

'No, Dessa,' he wheezed, his eyes bright with amusement. 'There's no need to look so shocked. I've had *plenty* of sex. Just never with a woman. Hence not needing this particular brew. But from what Farissa says, it's a skill every alchemist should have . . . so if you'd be so kind as to continue?'

Wren smiled and went to do just that, but Dessa was shaking her head in disbelief.

'Zave . . .' she murmured, forlorn.

Wren tensed. She hadn't expected this from Dessa.

But Dessa grabbed Zavier's arm, her eyes full of accusation. 'I don't even know who your type is.'

An undignified noise escaped Zavier at that. 'You really want to know *that*?' he said, brows raised.

Wren watched as Dessa's expression morphed into one of offence, a tic she must have picked up from Kipp.

'*Of course* I want to know,' Dessa said.

Zavier gave a sly smile and nodded towards the workshop's glass doors, where two Warswords stood guard outside.

'Everyone's got a thing for the Bear Slayer,' Dessa declared with a shake of her head.

'Not him,' Zavier replied, his eyes on the leaner of the two warriors.

Wren's eyes bulged. 'Cal?'

Zavier shrugged with a smile. 'He's as straight as the arrows he shoots, but a man can dream, can't he?'

Her gaze catching on the broad expanse of Torj's shoulders, Wren muttered, 'Yes she can . . .'

Dessa dissolved into laughter.

As they continued to work, Wren's thoughts drifted from the Warsword to her homeland, and how desperate she was to send word to Thea. Her sister deserved to know, not only because it was her birthright, but because it had the power to change everything.

Wren was still thinking about it when the lesson concluded and Zavier nudged her with his elbow. 'You coming?' he asked, nodding to the emptying space.

Dazed, she got to her feet. 'Actually, no. I'd like a word with Farissa. Tell Torj I'll be a few more minutes.'

When the room had emptied, Farissa shut the door and motioned for Wren to sit. 'How are you?' she asked, leaning against her desk.

'Not making much progress, I'm afraid,' Wren started, but Farissa shook her head.

'I didn't ask about your work. I asked how *you* were.'

'Oh.' Wren didn't know why the question caught her off guard, or why she suddenly felt vulnerable. Embarrassingly, tears stung her eyes. 'I'm alright.'

'Are you?' Farissa pressed, not unkindly. 'I realize that you're under a lot of pressure . . .'

Wren nodded stiffly. 'Any word from Audra? Am I able to contact Thea about all this soon?'

'Nothing from Audra yet,' Farissa replied. 'You have to hold off on telling Thea a little longer. If word—'

'Farissa, I understand what's at stake here, but surely it's not a matter of *if* but *when* this gets out? And I'd rather tell Thea myself. It affects her too.'

'I'm in agreement with you, Elwren,' Farissa replied. 'But we *must* be careful. A time will come when that knowledge will be more impactful than the swing of a sword. Keep it to yourself until such a time.'

Wren gnawed at her lower lip. 'You're worried.'

Farissa pinched the bridge of her nose. 'I don't remember a time when I wasn't—'

Raised voices outside had both women turning to the door.

'—the fuck are you doing here?' Torj's voice boomed.

A second voice, unfamiliar to Wren, shouted back, 'Lay a finger on me, Warsword, and I'll see you removed from your station so fast that—'

There was a muffled thump followed by a louder crash, and Wren's eyes shot to Farissa. 'Whatever's going on out there, Torj is likely going to kill someone.'

They made for the door. Wren swung it open to find Torj in a rage like she'd never seen, and a nobleman walking briskly away towards the main building.

'Who was that—?'

'I see you caught up with my father,' a smooth voice said from the other direction.

Wren turned to see Darian Devereux, looking as stately as the last time she'd seen him. His attire was impeccable, a stark contrast to the rustic surroundings. High cheekbones, a strong jaw and lips curved in a perpetual hint of a smirk gave him an air of smug amusement. Oddly, he didn't look out of place in the academy grounds, but his eyes were fixed on the back of the man he'd called his father, a steely glint there.

Wren pushed past Torj, whose jaw was clenched, a muscle twitching visibly. His broad shoulders stiffened, and his hands gripped his hammer hard enough to make his knuckles bone-white.

With a grimace, Farissa bade Wren a quiet farewell before slipping away.

Wren turned to Darian. 'What are you doing here?'

'There's to be a gathering of influential figures of sorts,' Darian said, a slightly sour note to his tone. 'Hence the presence of Father dearest.'

Torj seemed to come back to himself, and he faced Darian. 'This is no place for your dealings, Devereux.'

'I can't say I'm thrilled to be here either, old friend, but since I am . . .' The nobleman's gaze flicked to Wren. 'I may as well make the most of it.'

A guttural sound of aggression came from Torj, unlike anything Wren had heard before.

But Darian sought her. 'I'd like a private audience with you, Elwren, if you'd allow it?'

'Over my dead body,' Torj growled.

'So dramatic,' Darian scoffed. 'Are you her keeper?'

'I'm her protector—'

Wren had had enough. 'I can speak for myself. Darian, I've got three minutes. We can talk in the healer's workshop.'

The vein pulsing in Torj's neck looked as though it was about to pop, but Wren closed the door between them and turned to Darian. He looked like he'd just stepped out of a royal court, but beneath the polished exterior, Wren sensed something dangerous lurking.

'You're deliberately antagonizing him,' she observed, not that she was one to talk.

Darian smiled. 'It's one of life's simpler pleasures.'

'Why? What happened between you?'

The nobleman's smile faded. 'I'm sure the Bear Slayer gave you his abridged version. The simpler one.'

'I wouldn't call it simple,' Wren replied.

'I suppose not . . . Nothing is when the Devereuxs are involved. You had the pleasure of hearing my father before. I'm sure you can imagine how many of those conversations go.'

Wren folded her arms over her chest. 'I couldn't say.'

'My father and I have played this game for as long as I can

remember, and we'll play until one of us doesn't walk away.' There was a note of bitterness there that was gone in a flash.

'Why are you here?' Wren asked bluntly.

Darian's sly smile was back. 'To make our warrior friend sweat. Though would you blame me if I said I enjoy the pleasure of your company?'

'Blame you?' Wren scoffed. 'No. Believe you? Also no. You want something. This is an academy for alchemy. We do important work here. It's not a drop-in spot for bored noblemen.'

'I'm well aware. And I'm not the only one,' he replied, his voice turning serious.

Wren narrowed her eyes. 'What do you mean?'

Darian made for the door, coming face to face with the enraged Bear Slayer on the other side. It didn't seem to faze him.

Now, he spoke to both of them. 'My father and I weren't the first to arrive here today. And we won't be the last.'

Darian's warning stayed with Wren long after she'd left the nobleman. Whatever the reason, Drevenor becoming a meeting point for influential figures of the midrealms couldn't be good. In her experience, men like them only hungered for one thing: power, which meant that it was changing hands as she walked the academy's very corridors.

Later, she was in the archives, palming the grit from her eyes as she pored over yet another history text on Delmira. She had been reading since after supper and the words were starting to blur together, the blocks of text taunting her. There was so much more to get through and so little time. She had no concept of the hour, only that it was late and all the private study rooms had emptied hours ago.

The Bear Slayer was leaning against the doorframe, looking out onto the rows of shelves, always watching, always guarding. But it allowed her the freedom to study the back of him unobserved: the broad expanse of his shoulders, the candlelight dancing across his silver hair, his tapered waist and muscular backside, his thick thighs—

'Are you even reading?' he asked, without looking back.

Wren's gaze shot back to her book. 'What else would I be doing?'

'You haven't turned a page in a while. You're usually a fast reader, so I thought maybe something else caught your attention.'

She kept her voice even. 'There's nothing else of note in here.'

That prompted the Warsword to turn. Resting his back against the doorframe, he looked at her with a lifted brow. 'You've never been a skilled liar, Embervale.'

'That makes two of us. What are you suggesting?'

He gave her an infuriating smirk. 'You tell me.'

'No idea what you're talking about,' she said, training her eyes on the pages before her.

'No? What's the chapter about, then?' Torj teased.

'The close allies of the Delmirian royal family,' she said quickly.

Torj was behind her in an instant, pinning the book open with a flattened palm. '*Historical events preceding the fall of Delmira,*' he read over her shoulder. 'I told you you're a terrible liar—'

A knock sounded at the door, and Torj was already blocking her from view.

A harried-looking man in tattered robes peered inside the room. 'Elwren Embervale?' he asked.

'Who's asking?' Torj replied, still shielding her with his huge frame.

'I'm Magnus Crane. Chronicler and Historian of Drevenor. I need to speak with Miss Embervale. It's a matter of great importance.'

Wren's heart sank. For weeks she had managed to avoid the chronicler by slipping out back doors and ducking for cover within the alcoves. Her friends had bought her time and caused distractions, all so she wouldn't have to recount the war to this stranger, but tonight she was out of luck.

'It's late,' Torj said, his voice full of warning.

'I have tried to see her during daylight hours, as you well know, Warsword Elderbrock. She is hindering the work of myself and several colleagues by not cooperating. We are working under the instruction of the High Chancellor.'

Torj folded his arms across his chest. 'Make a damn appointment.'

But the man persisted. 'I'd be happy to, if—'

'Alright,' Wren heard herself say. 'Let's get this over with.'

Torj whirled around to face her. 'You don't have to—'

'I do,' she said reluctantly. 'Historian Crane is right. I'm hindering their work. I need to contribute.'

Torj's eyes narrowed as he stepped aside, allowing the scholar inside the private study room. Wren motioned for the chronicler to take the seat opposite her.

Magnus Crane slid his books and parchment onto the table and sat down. 'At long last,' he sighed. 'I'm eager to hear your recounting of the final battles in particular. It's my understanding that you played a significant role in these violent affairs.'

Wren didn't dare let her gaze slide to Torj; she simply told him, 'You can wait outside, Bear Slayer.'

He looked surprised, if not a little hurt. 'As you wish,' was all he said, ducking outside the room and closing the door behind him.

Wren closed the book before her and clasped her hands atop its cover. 'Tell me, Historian Crane, how may I be of assistance to you and the academy?'

The chronicler took out a quill and inkpot, as well as a fresh piece of parchment. Poised to transcribe Wren's answers, he asked, 'What was your background prior to the shadow war, Miss Embervale?'

Wren loosed a breath between her teeth. This she could answer easily enough. 'I was an alchemist in training at Thezmarr.'

'Apprentice to Master Alchemist Farissa Tremaine, if I'm not mistaken?'

'That's right,' Wren replied with a nod.

'And back then you went by the name Elwren Zoltaire, not Embervale, correct?'

'That is correct. For many years that was what I believed my name to be. My sister Thea and I were raised at Thezmarr, given the name Zoltaire by our warden there. We didn't know we were Embervales until later.'

Crane scribbled away, his quill scratching against the parchment hurriedly, flicking spots of ink across the table. 'So you were not aware that you were the heirs to the Delmirian throne?'

'No.'

'And how did you discover your heritage?'

'I thought you wanted to talk about the war?' Wren countered, shifting uneasily in her chair.

'Do you believe that your heritage is irrelevant to the war?' Crane fired back. 'You are a storm wielder, yes?'

'Yes,' Wren replied through gritted teeth.

'And did that not play a role in the battles?'

'It did,' she admitted, moving her hands under the table so she could pick at the skin around her nails. She already didn't like where this was going, could already feel her magic growing restless and agitated beneath her skin, reminding her that she wasn't as in control as she should be.

'Farissa Tremaine has already accounted for much of your work for Thezmarr in the lead-up to the war. She said you were an integral part of weaponizing alchemy against the enemy. Would you say that's accurate?' Crane asked, changing tack.

'I suppose . . .' Wren replied slowly, trying to remember those earlier days before the real fighting had begun. They were a blur to her. She had been so worried for Thea most of the time that her own contributions were murky. 'I did a lot of work with sun orchid essence,' she supplied, recalling the golden flowers that were a natural deterrent to the shadow monsters.

'And you were in two battles? The battle of the Aveum plains and the final battle for Thezmarr?' he pressed.

'Three, actually,' she corrected him. 'I was also present for the battle of Notos. Farissa and I played a role there in attempting to seal the tear in the Veil.'

'And it was here that the Daughter of Darkness abducted you?'

Wren's hands trembled in her lap. 'Anya was no Daughter of Darkness. She was the leader of the rebel force, yes, but she died defending Thezmarr and the people of the midrealms . . .' Her voice quavered. 'You do know that the Daughter of Darkness was in fact Jasira Fairmoore, Princess of Harenth, daughter of King Artos?'

'Yes, I have heard that account. Though the recent history books refer to Anya by that moniker.'

'Then they're incorrect,' Wren said, her temper rising. 'Tell me that you're not referring to her as such in your texts?'

'It hasn't been decided.'

'There is nothing to decide,' Wren snapped. 'That's historically and factually inaccurate.'

'Let's return to your role in the shadow war . . . How would you define your position during the conflict years?'

'My position?' Wren blinked. 'I was apprentice to Farissa Tremaine, as you already stated. I held no other official title during the war.'

'And yet you partook in the battles? I have several first-hand accounts of you wielding both storm magic and alchemy in the heart of the conflict, both on the Aveum plains and at Thezmarr.'

A rush of goosebumps prickled across Wren's skin, her magic stirring once again in response. 'I fought alongside my friends and family.'

'And yet you have no military training . . .'

'I was raised at Thezmarr. We knew fighting better than the rest of the midrealms combined. What exactly are you asking, Historian Crane?'

'I simply want to portray the war accurately—'

'Could have fooled me,' Wren muttered, picking at her nails beneath the table.

The chronicler shot her an annoyed look and scratched something down on his parchment. 'Do you have any personal records, diaries, or documents from the time that you'd be willing to share?'

Wren balked. 'You want my . . .'

'Personal documents, yes.'

She shook her head. 'That won't be possible.'

'Are you intent on obstructing the progress of the war's written histories, Miss Embervale?' the chronicler chastised her.

She clenched her jaw. 'Many of my personal documents were destroyed in the battle of Thezmarr. If you recall, much of the fortress sustained irreparable damage.' She didn't mention the notes and observations she'd kept since then.

His eyes narrowed suspiciously. 'Very well. How about you tell me of Samra and Ida – the two alchemists whose heads were found on the spikes of—'

'Don't.' Wren's blood ran cold. 'Don't speak of them.'

The historian's quill paused mid-scratch across the parchment. 'Elwren, if I am to paint an accurate picture, I need to explore every perspective. It's my understanding that these young alchemists were captured at Thezmarr and tortured for information—'

Wren's hands flew from beneath the table and slammed down on the surface, lightning sparking across her fingers and knuckles. The chronicler's chair scraped back as he scrambled away in shock.

Images of her friends' severed heads flashed before her – their eyes missing from their sockets, their mouths agape, screams etched on their faces. 'I said, *don't*.'

Wren couldn't breathe. The High Chancellor had also implied that Sam and Ida had been tortured for information about Wren and her alchemy designs, that it might have been her friends who had given up the knowledge of her work on the magic-suppressing manacles to the people who became the new traitors to the midrealms—

'See here, Miss Embervale,' the chronicler panted, his hand on his chest. 'You said you would cooperate. I cannot record your version of events if I'm under threat.'

Wren reined in her panic. 'My apologies,' she murmured. 'Sam and Ida . . . They were friends of mine.'

'An account confirmed by several other interviewees,' Crane said, sitting back down warily. 'Which was why I thought you might be aware of why they were interrogated so thoroughly.'

Wren was going to be sick. Her magic roiled within her unchecked, unchallenged, and her heart was racing, pounding in her chest. The lightning that had crackled across her fingers was growing—

The door burst open, and Torj Elderbrock filled the frame. 'This interview is over,' he stated, moving to stand beside Wren and stare down the chronicler.

'You have no authority here, Warsword,' Crane argued, albeit with a paling complexion.

'No?' Torj challenged. 'Fucking try me.'

Crane's eyes scanned the towering warrior, and slowly, he began to gather his things. 'The High Chancellor will be hearing about this—'

A blur of movement followed as Torj snatched a handful of the historian's robes. 'You tell the High Chancellor that if you badger my charge again – in fact, if you so much as look in her direction – I'll finish what I started after the Gauntlet.'

Wren didn't remember standing, but now that she was, her knees were buckling beneath her. Torj and the chronicler were hazy as the Warsword dragged the latter towards the door.

Wren's lungs weren't taking in enough air, and the walls around her were closing in, inch by inch, ready to crush her. Sam and Ida had been tortured because of her, tortured to their deaths, their heads mounted on spikes for all to see.

My fault. It was all my fault. She couldn't breathe. Her vision was all white spots.

She heard Torj say something in the distance.

But it didn't matter, because she was falling.

CHAPTER 31

Torj

'To truly understand the past, one must study the historian as much as the history'

— *The Midrealms Chronicles*

'I SHOULD CRUSH your tiny skull,' Torj hissed at the chronicler, clutching a fistful of his robes. 'Come near her again, and I'll do just that.'

He was throwing the scholar out of the study room when he heard a thud. And the sound of glass fracturing.

'Wren!' He was back in the room and at her side in an instant, finding her unconscious.

She'd fainted. And some of the vials in her belt had shattered on impact with the hard floor.

Careful of the broken glass, he took her in his arms, so her back was against his chest. 'Wren, wake up . . . Talk to me, Embers . . .'

His heart was pounding. She looked so fragile, so small, and around her middle, blood was blooming across the linen of her gown and apron. She'd fallen right onto her belt of tinctures, breaking the glass with her fall.

He ran a thumb over her cheek, feeling the line of raised scar tissue there from the loyalty test she'd faced during the Gauntlet.

'Embers,' he murmured, pressing a kiss to the top of her head without thinking. He couldn't bear the thought of her hurting, and he hated that he'd been so busy delivering his version of justice that he'd let her fall. He cradled her, kissing her temple. 'Embers...'

Slowly, she came to. Her breaths came in quick and ragged, as though she were somewhere else in her mind.

Torj held her, stroking her hair. 'I've got you. I've got you.'

He stopped her from writhing and embedding any more glass in her midsection, waiting for her to ground herself in the present. He hated to think of what she might be reliving, even in the safety of his arms.

At last, she stilled, wincing with a hiss. 'What happened?' she asked, voice hoarse. She didn't pull away from his hold – that was a small victory in itself.

'You passed out,' he told her, eying the broken potions with his heart in his throat. 'Your belt... Was there anything in there that could hurt you?'

Dazed, Wren looked down. 'Oh.'

'Can any of this harm you? Do I need to take you to Farissa?' He couldn't keep the urgency, the worry, from his voice.

'No...' Wren said, reaching for a long shard of glass sticking out from her stomach. 'I'm immune to everything I keep in my belt.'

Torj batted her hand away. 'We'll treat this when you're back in your quarters. Or I could take you to a healer—'

'My quarters.' Wren grimaced again. The colour hadn't yet returned to her face.

'You're alright,' he told her. 'We'll get you fixed up.' The reassurance was more for him than her, he realized, but gods, he needed it. He had told her he'd never let her fall, and here she was—

'Torj?' she said softly, interrupting his thoughts. 'Can you help me up?'

He didn't need to be asked twice, but instead of planting her on her feet, he scooped her up behind the knees and carried her from the study room.

'The books—' she protested weakly.

'Fuck the books.'

He should have crushed the damn chronicler's skull. All it would have taken was a single flex of his hand. Standing outside the door, he had felt Wren's distress. He didn't know how else to describe it, but her magic had called to him, somehow signalling that she needed help. And then he hadn't thought twice; he'd simply burst in.

Wren might have put on a brave face, but the war was an open wound to her, and that moronic scholar had rubbed salt in it. Torj wouldn't stand for it. The prick was lucky he'd only been thrown from the room. Torj had wanted to do much worse.

He carried Wren to her quarters and sent the academy guard stationed at her door to collect the books she'd been reading. When they were inside, Torj laid her on the bed. Ignoring the ache in his chest at the sight of her in pain, he went to her workbench. There, he found a small steel tray and a small pair of tweezers among her tools, which he set down beside her, along with an additional lantern so he could see the lacerations in the light. With tender precision, he sat on the edge of the bed and sought those fine shards in her abdomen. Using the tweezers, he grasped the first fragment, feeling her sharp intake of breath beneath him.

'We're always patching each other up, it seems,' she murmured.

They didn't speak after that as Torj worked gently and methodically, each piece of glass yielding reluctantly beneath his ministrations. He dropped the fragments into the tray with a faint clatter and persisted, his focus unwavering, even as her discomfort seeped into him. As another shard surrendered, he exhaled, his heart heavy with each flicker of pain he had caused her.

'Thank you . . .' she said softly.

'I shouldn't have let him talk to you,' Torj ground out.

'It was my choice,' Wren countered, flinching as another piece of glass was removed.

Torj didn't reply. He was too busy berating himself for his error.

He'd made so many of those with Wren. He swept his hands lightly across her waist, searching for more shards.

'I'm not mortally wounded,' Wren said quietly after a moment, watching him with a strange expression. 'It's a few scratches. They'll scab over by tomorrow.'

'You're always getting hurt around me.' He heard the crack in his own voice and shut it down, clenching his jaw so hard he felt his teeth creak.

'The world's a dangerous place, Bear Slayer . . . You can't protect me from external threats *and* my own stupidity all at once.'

'I can damn well try,' he bit out.

'And try you do. Much to my dismay,' she added. Her small hand closed over his. 'At ease, Warsword. I can take it from here. But I think you'll need to help with the laces at the back of my dress again.'

Torj's cheeks went instantly hot.

'Nothing you haven't seen before,' Wren said with a small smile, swinging her legs over the side of the bed with another wince at the pain. After carefully removing her apron, she turned her back to him. 'I just need you to do the laces, please.'

It was her manners that nearly undid him. Where were her sharp tongue and slicing words? Torj was glad she couldn't see the tremor in his fingers as he reached for the laces that started at the base of her neck. It was intensely intimate, sitting on the edge of her bed with her, the ties of her gown unravelling beneath his touch. A glimpse of another, impossible life, where the woman before him was his wife, and helping her with her bodice was a nightly occurrence before they curled up together. A dream long lost.

The folds of Wren's dress fell away from her skin as he worked his way down her spine, and he could see her goosebumps as his fingertips brushed her bare back. She was soft and warm, and he wanted nothing more than to strip her completely and worship her—

She's injured, you selfish prick, he told himself, freeing the last of the laces.

'There,' he said, standing abruptly, needing the distance between them. 'You'll clean the cuts?'

'I think I can manage that, yes,' she replied, capturing her lower lip between her teeth.

He had to get out of there before he did something stupid. Well, *more* stupid than all the other things he'd done since returning as her guard.

Torj forced himself to move towards the door. 'Call out if you need me – anything – help.' He stammered over those last words like an awkward youth with a crush and turned on his heel before she could see that flush creeping back up his neck. Gods, he was losing sight of himself. He had sworn he would put their past behind him, he had sworn he'd protect her and no more, but nothing would quell the storm inside his chest – the storm that smelled like spring rain and jasmine, that had him in knots.

'I'm alright,' she reassured him from the bed. 'A few shallow cuts. No stitches needed. Nothing a little salve won't fix.'

'That's lucky,' he said stiffly.

'Lucky there was a great big Bear Slayer there to carry me back to my rooms and tend to me?' she quipped.

'I'm not sure my presence brings much luck these days.'

He found himself hesitating at the threshold between their two rooms. He had fought cursed bears, arachnes and shadow wraiths; he'd travelled the midrealms and led fucking armies. He'd closed a portal to a world of nothing but pain and darkness, and yet . . . it was the poisoner, the storm-wielding alchemist, who threatened to bring him to his knees. He had never been one to concern himself with what others thought, but when it came to Wren? It was all that mattered.

'Embervale?' he asked, not turning around in case she was undressed.

'What is it?'

He could tell by her voice that she was moving, tending to the cuts on her abdomen. But he needed to ask, needed to know . . .

Still facing his own quarters, with his back to her, he forced the words to form on his tongue. 'Am I a good man? Despite . . . despite everything?'

The question hung between them, leaving him naked and exposed in an entirely new way. He had well and truly shattered the thing between them the moment he'd torn their soul bond in half. He hated the silence, hated that it confirmed all his very worst fears about himself.

But then Wren was there, touching his arm, trying to turn him to face her. 'What do *you* think?'

He drew a trembling breath, not daring to look at her for fear of what he might say or what he might find written all over her beautiful face. 'I don't know any more,' he admitted hoarsely.

'Only a good man would say that,' she said, her hand still on his arm, her thumb stroking the muscles there.

He came alive beneath her touch, his breath shuddering out of him as a wave of emotions hit. He felt that familiar storm magic dancing across his skin, calling out to him like a dark promise.

'What I want to do to you isn't what a good man would do,' he murmured.

Wren's hand reached up, cupping his face and turning him to her, finally. And he stared at her. She was wearing a nightshirt that hit the tops of her thighs, the fabric thin enough that he could see the outline of her sinful curves beneath.

'Does that mean you want to do wicked things to me, Bear Slayer?' she whispered, her thumb now tracing his bottom lip.

'Wicked isn't the half of it, Embers.' He breathed her in like he'd been deprived of air, like he could fill his lungs with the very essence of her. His gaze travelled every inch of her, taking in the flush across her freckled cheeks, the curve in her parted lips, the heat in her stormy gaze.

The heir of Delmira would break him. He had known it from the moment he'd first kissed her, and long before. He reached for her, sliding his fingers along her jaw, scanning her face for any hesitancy.

There was none.

Instead, she was up on her tip-toes, pressing her mouth to his.

It was the whisper of a kiss, the promise of something far deeper.

They broke apart, staring at one another, their chests heaving with restrained desire.

'Torj—'

But he slanted his lips over hers, kissing her hard.

Gods, he'd been wanting to do it for a lifetime. Every little touch between them had been like a bolt of lightning, and now . . . they both moaned at the contact, and Torj gripped her hair at the roots as she opened for him, allowing his tongue to sweep in and explore. The taste of her, the *sounds* escaping her as they deepened the kiss – it was enough to make his knees buckle.

More. More. More. He had to have *more* of her. She was as intoxicating as ever, dragging the darkest want from his very being, turning him feral with need.

She bit his lower lip, the brief sting of pain causing a burst of pleasure, even as he tasted copper. Her cuts forgotten, Wren's hands were all over him, demanding, claiming – and Furies save him, he'd give her *exactly* what she wanted.

Her nightshirt slipped from her shoulder as she raked her fingers across his chest and down his abdomen, as she shoved him against the doorframe. She was everywhere, just as impassioned as he was. The wall between them had come crashing down and now they broke upon each other like waves in a storm.

And as Wren's breath flickered against his lips, as his desire nearly consumed him, he saw it . . .

That thread of gold linking them once more.

Wren was oblivious to it, her fists balled in his shirt, her mouth reclaiming his.

And then she broke away, as though sensing the jolt of shock that coursed through him.

The shimmer of gold vanished, and all Torj saw was her.

Running a thumb across her lips, she stepped back.

'What are you doing?' he managed, heart hammering. 'I—'

But Wren cupped her hand over his mouth, her gaze fierce. 'I'm going to leave before you say something to ruin this.' Her hand remained over his mouth. 'Let me have this, Bear Slayer. I don't want every intimate moment we've shared to be tarnished by your words of regret.'

Her request seared the open fracture in his heart. Regret? How could she think he regretted her? She was all he'd ever wanted. To have shared what they had was a privilege he'd never thought possible. His only regret was hurting her, not being good enough for her . . . But he said none of this. Instead, he nodded slowly.

Wren released him and pressed a soft, gentle kiss to his lips before nudging him towards his room.

'Goodnight, Torj,' she murmured, and the door clicked closed behind him.

On the other side, with waves of feeling mercilessly barrelling into him, Torj braced himself against the timber.

I love you.

CHAPTER 32

Wren

'Above all else, alchemists are seekers of the truth'

– *Alchemy Unbound*

There was no sound from the adjacent room, but three words came to Wren, echoing in her chest. They remained as she readied herself for bed, and they were with her when she awoke the next morning.

I love you.

She couldn't explain it, she didn't understand it, but somehow, in her bones, she knew it to be true. In spite of the brutal way he'd ended things, and all his protests and mixed signals since, the Bear Slayer *loved* her. He may not have said the words aloud, but she had felt them in his kiss.

The knowledge only added to her turmoil. It was yet another question she didn't know the answer to. Her gaze drifted to her windowsill, where her assassin's teapot – the Ladies' Luncheon – sat, a layer of dust coating it. She had been proud of it, once. An invention she'd used to deliver justice on more than one occasion. But now . . . now it was just another thing that could be used against her, against the people she cared about.

I should destroy it, she thought. *Like I should have destroyed those manacles after the war* . . . But when she reached for the dainty work of ceramic, she found that she couldn't cast it into the fire as she intended. Sam and Ida had brainstormed its design with her. Her friends had been by her side when she'd given Farissa the first successful demonstration. A part of them lived within the invention, so instead, she boxed it up and hid it away beneath her bed. She couldn't bear the thought of it hurting someone she loved.

One day I'll get rid of it, she vowed. *But not today.*

As the early sunlight filtered through her window, Wren cleaned her cuts and treated them with more salve, thinking of the Warsword on the other side of the wall. Now, more than ever, she was drawn to him, and against her will, the love she'd drowned so thoroughly in anger was rising to the surface once more.

She pressed her fingertips to her lips, still swollen with the passion of his kiss. Whatever he was keeping from her, she would crack him, eventually.

As if she'd summoned it, there was a gentle knock at the adjoining door.

'Come in,' she called, throwing her apron over her head and tying it at the back.

The door creaked open and Torj entered tentatively. 'Morning...'

The Bear Slayer, as handsome as he was, looked tired. There were dark shadows beneath his eyes, and his stubble was longer than usual.

'Couldn't sleep?' Wren asked, surveying him.

'Hard to sleep after a kiss like that,' he replied gruffly.

Wren's brows lifted. 'So we're not pretending it didn't happen?'

Torj pushed a loose lock of silver from his forehead. 'I can still feel the imprint of you like a brand, Embers, so no. No pretending.'

'Thank the gods for that,' she said.

'How are you? How are your wounds?' he asked, scanning her critically.

'No lasting damage.' She eyed her empty toolbelt on her workbench with a pang of regret. 'I'll have to go without that today, or I'll aggravate the cuts.'

Torj frowned. 'You never go anywhere without it . . .'

'No, I don't,' she replied. 'I suppose I'll have to rely on your burly presence to protect me after all.'

Torj went to her workbench, picking up the belt. 'Have you got more supplies for it?'

'I do.' Wren motioned to the spare vials held in a wooden frame. 'There.'

'Restock the belt,' he told her.

'Why? If I'm not wearing it—'

'I'll wear it.'

Wren blinked. 'What?'

'I'll wear the belt,' he repeated. 'I assume you'll be able to adjust it so it fits me?'

'Well, yes, but . . .'

'But what, Embers?' he challenged. 'Having your potions and poisons makes you feel safe. I realize it's not the same as possessing them yourself, but if having them within arm's reach helps alleviate any fear, then let me wear them.'

Wren's words caught in her throat. Of course Torj had noticed that she felt vulnerable without her tinctures. Her hands trembled as she went about replacing her supplies and adjusting the belt for his larger frame.

'Here.' Her voice cracked as she held it out for him.

To her surprise, instead of taking the belt, Torj stepped into her space, lifting his arms so she could loop it around his middle.

'Would you mind?' he asked. 'I'm paranoid that I'll break something and poison myself . . . We're not all immune.'

'You are.' The words were out before she could stop them, her fingers brushing his shirt as she fixed the belt around him, drawing it together at the buttons of his leathers. She could feel the heat of his gaze on her.

'What?' he asked.

Wren took a breath, wishing she hadn't opened her stupid mouth. 'You are immune,' she explained slowly. 'At least to the majority of things I use.'

Torj tensed beneath her touch. 'How can that be?'

Wren focused on threading the end of the belt through the buckle and securing it just above the bulge in Torj's leathers. 'I've been exposing you to each one little by little, to create immunity.'

'So what you're telling me is that you've been poisoning me bit by bit, every day?' There was a wry note to Torj's voice.

'Something like that.' Wren dropped her hands from the belt and put some much-needed space between them. 'I did the same for Thea growing up. And Cal and Kipp, to a lesser extent. I'm sorry, I should have—'

But Torj closed the gap between them once more and reached for her, tracing a featherlight line across her jaw. 'All this time . . . you've been protecting me?'

'Someone's got to,' she muttered.

Torj's gaze dropped to her mouth, a strange expression flickering across his face. 'Thank you.'

'You're welcome.' Wren broke away, dusting her hands unnecessarily on her apron. 'Shall we go?'

Torj hesitated. 'How ridiculous do I look?' He motioned to her belt of potions around his waist, in stark contrast to the hammer strapped across his shoulders and the curved knife sheathed at his side.

'Only a little. You may pull it off yet.' She couldn't help the smile that tugged at her lips. 'Apparently you're a Warsword of many talents.'

Torj made for the door with a backwards glance full of heat. 'You already knew that, Embers.'

Wren's cheeks flamed, but she threw up a hand in protest. 'Don't start, Bear Slayer.'

His answering grin was wicked.

That night, back in her room, Wren was bleeding herself again, refusing to admit that she felt faint. She didn't know how many times in the past few weeks she'd taken samples from her own veins, only that she needed more. Bruises had bloomed in the crook of each arm, the skin there tender, but she didn't care.

With Zavier and Dessa's help, she'd developed a cooling system to keep her vials at the right temperature so that the components of her blood weren't compromised, but there was another issue . . .

She was running out of the enemy's alchemy samples as well.

After the battle in Drevenor's hall, she had collected as much of the strange shimmering substance from the weapons of the dead as possible. At the time, it had seemed like more than she needed, given that in its presence her own magic shrank back. But now, having heated countless blades and arrow tips to loosen the alchemy from the steel and captured it in an array of glass vessels, she realized there wasn't enough. Not when she was burning through her ingredients and blood so quickly.

White dots swam in her vision, and she startled back to herself, red streaming down to her wrist, spilling over the shallow dish on her workbench.

'Shit,' she muttered, pressing a fresh linen cloth to her vein—

'What the fuck are you doing?' growled a familiar voice from the adjoining door.

Wren didn't turn around. Instead, she wrapped a bandage around her arm and hastily pulled her sleeve down. 'Don't you ever knock?'

'Not when I feel—' He cut himself off.

'Feel what?' Wren demanded.

'Nothing,' he bit out. 'It smells like blood in here.'

Another wave of dizziness washed over Wren, and she tried to subtly brace herself against the workbench. 'You don't say,' she replied dryly.

The Bear Slayer stalked towards her, taking in the crimson-filled vials. 'Furies save me, tell me this isn't all yours.'

'It's not all mine,' she echoed back without hesitation.

'Horseshit.' Torj shook his head, his eyes alight with fury as he turned to her. 'This must be, what – two pints?'

'Hardly—'

'Don't do that,' Torj snapped.

Wren blinked. They had argued countless times before, across the span of *years*, but there was a note in his voice now that was unfamiliar to her. 'What?'

'Be reckless with yourself,' he replied, his tone dark with anger. 'You are too valuable, too important to take risks like this—'

'It's part of my work,' she retorted, her own rage bubbling to the surface. 'What would you say if I told you not to fight monsters, not to wield that hammer of yours?'

'That's different.'

An exasperated noise escaped her, and had she not needed the support of her workstation, she'd have thrown her hands up in the air as she demanded, 'How?'

'It just is,' he said stubbornly.

'A stellar argument there, Warsword—'

'Don't push me,' he warned.

'Or what?' she taunted, folding her arms over her chest, trying not to wince as she brushed the tender spots at the crooks of her elbows. '*How is it different?*'

'Because I'm expendable!' he blurted.

Wren's mouth fell open and she stared at the man before her. 'Is that what you think?'

Torj shrugged, but the movement was forced. 'It's true. If something happened to me while I was performing my duties, there would be no lasting consequences for the world. There are more Warswords now, plenty of people to take my place. But you? If something happens to you while you're taking stupid risks with yourself . . .' He shook his head, cursing under his breath.

Wren's magic was restless beneath her skin like never before. It tended to flood to the surface when her emotions were high, when her mental energy was depleted and, most often, when Torj was near. She did her best to ignore it, to stamp it out. She couldn't afford to lose control; she couldn't afford another split in her focus – but his words . . . They broke her.

'You're not expendable,' she said quietly, her gaze meeting his. 'Not to me.'

It didn't matter how angry he made her. It didn't matter that he'd broken her heart, or that he was hiding things from her. Not in this moment. For a world without the Bear Slayer was a world she wasn't interested in.

She closed the gap between them, taking his hands in hers. 'Don't you *ever* think that,' she told him fiercely.

Torj's expression guttered. She recognized the grief as though it were her own. Something tugged inside her chest: an ache, a yearning that felt bone-deep, *soul*-deep. For a second, Wren thought she saw a flicker of gold in the air—

'Do you know what it's like to want someone so badly you can't breathe?'

The words were raw and desperate, bleeding with pain.

'And to know that no matter what, you can't have them? They can never be yours?'

Wren stared at him, shaking her head. 'And whose fault is that?'

It was only when Torj pulled his hands from her grasp as though burned, when he had walked away, that Wren realized . . .

He hadn't spoken those words aloud.

CHAPTER 33

Torj

'The culmination of a soul bond is much like death . . . inevitable'

— *Tethers and Magical Bonds Throughout History*

THE ADJOINING DOOR burst inwards after him, and Wren came charging in. 'Do you know what you just did? What *we* just did?'

Torj stared at her, still trying to recover from the storm that raged within.

Wren didn't back down. She never did. 'You spoke into my mind, Torj. Into my fucking mind. And I *heard* it.'

'What?' He blinked at her, certain that she was speaking a language he didn't understand for all the sense she was making.

But Wren was a living storm before him, power crackling all around her. 'You spoke into my mind,' she said again. 'And don't you dare tell me that you don't know how.'

Torj had to brace himself against the back of the chair at his desk. *Impossible*. The word vibrated through him. Panicking, he wondered if she could hear that too. But he *didn't* understand how. Not at all. Not when he'd destroyed the bond—

Suddenly, Wren was standing before him, close enough that he could scent the jasmine in her hair, could see the heat in her gaze, the certainty.

He drank in the sight of her, overwhelmed by the storm growing in his chest. 'Furies know I have tried to stay away. I have tried to protect you from this. But the force of it, the force of *you* . . .'

His body heaved, and something inside him snapped – the last remnants of his restraint.

He seized Wren, gripping her behind her thighs and shoving her up onto the desk. 'I can't take it any more. *I want you*, Wren. I want you so badly I can't breathe.'

'Why?' she demanded. 'Tell me why it's like this, Torj. Tell me why I can feel you in my blood, under my skin. Tell me why I can see your memories and share your dreams. Tell me why I can hear your thoughts. Just tell me why—'

'*Because we're fucking soul bonded,*' he roared.

Wren's expression was triumphant, a queen grasping her hard-won victory.

'At least . . . we were,' he said quietly.

'Were?' Wren echoed with a laugh. 'This doesn't feel like *were*.' She grabbed a fistful of his shirt. 'I'm not going anywhere. I know what you are to me . . . And what I am to you.'

Torj couldn't take it any more. Couldn't hold back all that he felt. 'You are everything to me.' And then he covered her mouth with his.

Torj cupped her face in his hands, threaded his fingers through the hair escaping her pin, tilting her to him for better access. She opened for him, allowing his tongue to sweep in and explore, to brush against hers and elicit a gasp of pleasure from her.

Her legs parted around him, and he eagerly closed the gap between their bodies, pressing his cock into the heat between her thighs. Wren arched her back, grinding against him, seeking friction before she dragged him to the floor.

His lips found her throat, sucking the sensitive skin there, licking over the hurt before moving over her mouth again. The kiss was hungry, desperate, and he couldn't get enough.

Wren's hands were in his shirt, tracing over his skin in a fever, and he was molten beneath her touch. He grabbed the hem of her skirt, drawing it up over her legs, bunching the fabric around her waist while Wren fumbled with his belt. She made a delicious noise of frustration that he covered with his mouth, a noise that turned into a moan as he brushed the centre of her with a single knuckle.

She spread herself wider, baring herself to him. 'I want to feel you inside me. I want to feel you dripping down my thighs.'

Her filthy words, the image she painted, sent a frisson of longing straight to Torj's cock, ricocheting up his spine. He licked his lips as he looked down at her, glistening and perfect. Together, they watched as he circled her clit with his thumb, as he pushed two fingers inside her, feeling her walls clench around him. He pumped the digits in and out, his cock begging to be freed from the confines of his leathers and sheathed inside of her, that hot, wet feel of her taunting him.

'Gods,' he murmured into the crook of her neck as she raised her hips to meet the thrusts of his fingers, her desire soaking his hand. Torj brought his mouth back to hers, stroking her tongue with his, coaxing desperate whimpers from her.

A deep, guttural moan escaped him, vibrating through his chest as her body collided with his. There were too many layers between them, too much fabric in the way.

But Wren was uninhibited, unapologetic. She tore at the buttons of his shirt, raking her nails down his exposed chest, over his nipples.

Astride him now, she ground herself against his cock, and Furies save him, he saw stars.

'Too many clothes,' Wren muttered against his lips, echoing his thoughts as she reached for his laces.

Torj finished shucking off his shirt, groaning as Wren palmed him through his leathers before tugging the wretched material down around his thighs.

'Fuck . . .'

His erection sprang free, and Wren rubbed against him, eliciting another primal sound from him as his cock hit bare, wet skin. He was practically pawing at her, sitting upright to rip her apron over her head.

'More fucking laces,' he grunted as his fingers fumbled with the back of her gown. The material fell away, baring her shoulders to him.

Deepening another kiss, Torj let his fingers tangle in her hair as he bucked beneath her. He was distantly aware that they were behaving like wildcats, grinding and clawing at each other on the floor, but as Wren writhed above him, bunching her skirts around her waist, that observation vanished.

Tracing the curve of her hips up to the swell of her breasts, he leaned in and took her nipple in his mouth, coaxing a whimper from her as he grazed the tight peak with his teeth.

'*Gods.*' Wren moved against the length of him, crying out as his cock hit her clit.

Torj swallowed the sound with a savage kiss, and rubbed the head of his shaft against her, white-hot need blinding him.

'Fuck me,' Wren whispered desperately. 'Fuck me hard, Bear Slayer.'

Her words set him on fire. Gripping her backside hard enough to bruise, he lifted her off him and had her on her back in seconds. Wren's legs fell open for him, and he was cradled between her thighs, the tip of his cock pressing against her—

Wren's eyes went wide. 'Wait.'

Torj froze, heart suddenly in his throat. 'Did I hurt you?'

Wren shook her head, catching her breath. 'No. I . . .' She seemed to take a moment to gather herself. 'Are you still taking the contraceptive tonic?'

Torj's stomach bottomed out, and he withdrew instantly. 'No,' he croaked. 'I stopped the day . . . The day of the battle. I knew I wouldn't need it.' He could feel her eyes boring into him, could feel the questions in her smouldering gaze. 'What about you?' he asked hoarsely.

'I still take it,' she replied evenly. 'But the tonic is most effective when both parties do.'

Torj speared a hand through his hair with a muttered curse, his cock still rock-hard, weeping at the tip, his heart still hammering wildly.

'I won't take that risk. Not even for you, Bear Slayer,' Wren told him.

That got his attention, and he lifted his head to meet her eyes. 'I would *never* ask you to.'

'Good,' she replied, her lips curving into a wicked smile. 'Then I suggest we find alternative options in the meantime . . .'

Torj didn't need telling twice.

He pushed her onto her back once more and dragged the dress bunched around her waist over her hips, tossing it aside at last, his own hunger reflected in her stormy eyes. Drinking in the sight of her, he mapped her throat with kisses before brushing his lips against hers.

'Where to start, Embers . . . Where to fucking start . . .'

CHAPTER 34

Wren

'In a union between twin flames, a gold thread often manifests, quite visible and tangible to the bonded pair. It symbolizes the fire between them, the light in the dark'

– *Tethers and Magical Bonds Throughout History*

THE BEAR SLAYER knew *exactly* where to start. His kiss became deep and dominating, as though he were trying to pour all the unspoken things between them into her. He slid himself between her legs, but didn't enter her. Instead, he rubbed the head of his cock across her clit until she was panting. Pleasure rippled through Wren and she grabbed his hair, moaning into his mouth before he broke away and dragged his teeth down her throat. Her body bowed beneath him, desperate for more.

Torj's hands were everywhere, cupping and squeezing her breasts as his mouth and tongue mapped her neck, her chest, her nipples. The pressure switched from light and teasing to rough and insistent, coaxing soft cries from her lips.

Her hands had a mind of their own as they traced his sculpted shoulders, his chest, his back. She drank in the shape and feel of him, wanting to remember every dip of sinew, every scar.

Wren was on fire, her skin hot and damp with the need for him, her hips rising to meet his as she silently cursed the line she'd drawn between them. The mere thought of him pushing inside her drove her wild; a slight shift from beneath him would have him at her entrance, and a tilt of her pelvis would have him sliding home, hitting that spot that made her head tip back in ecstasy.

'Don't tell me your restraint is wavering . . .' Torj murmured against her skin.

'Never,' she lied.

His answering chuckle made her toes curl.

And then, he stopped toying with her.

Two fingers pushed inside her and she cried out as he lowered himself down her body, sucking on her clit without mercy. Wren tried to reach for him, to wrap her hand around his cock, but he batted her away, seeming intent on focusing on her.

She let him.

The sensation was overwhelming, and the power of the climax building within was staggering. Torj pumped his fingers in time with the strokes of his tongue and Wren felt as though she were about to explode.

She forgot herself completely, grinding against his face, taking everything he gave her, demanding more. Every muscle in her body was taut, desire coiling tighter and tighter to the point where it was almost too much to bear. Almost.

He withdrew his fingers and she whimpered in protest, only for him to drive his tongue inside her and circle her clit with his thumb.

Wren's thighs trembled on either side of his head as he fucked her with his mouth. The moan that broke from her was feral, delirious, but just as she was about to crest that peak of no return, Torj slowed his efforts, drawing out her ascent to the point of madness.

'This isn't fair,' Wren panted, attempting to reach for him again. 'I want to make you feel good too . . .'

Torj moaned against her core before pulling back and gazing up at her, his blue eyes molten. 'You think this doesn't make me feel good, Embers? Feasting on the most beautiful woman in the midrealms? Making her moan my name? It's the best fucking feeling in the world.'

He sucked her clit again, and Wren bit back a scream, gripping his hair by the roots, chasing the high with her hips. 'Torj!'

Working her with his fingers, he hummed against her. 'What do you want? Name it and it's yours.'

'I want to taste you while you taste me,' Wren managed, as spirals of intoxicating sensation took hold.

'Then sit on my face, Embers, and suck my cock while you do it.'

His filthy words washed over her in a haze of desire, and Wren had never moved faster. She scrambled upright, flushing at the sight of Torj's wicked grin as she lowered herself over his mouth.

The first lick from the new angle had her trembling on her knees, but she was about to give as good as she got. Wren wrapped her hand around the hard length of her Bear Slayer and heard the sharp intake of breath beneath her.

Pumping his cock slowly, she circled the tip with her tongue—

'Fuck, Embers—' came the muffled shout beneath her, and she couldn't help but smile against him, couldn't help but revel in the power of it.

Then, she swallowed him down.

Torj's hips bucked beneath her, and he worked her in earnest, matching her rhythm on him with his fingers and tongue.

Wren felt him hit the back of her throat, the things he was doing to her only allowing her to take him deeper. She moaned around him and reached to cup his balls, drawing them into a gentle caress that had the Warsword cursing again.

His fingers pushed back inside her, his tongue swirling around her clit as Wren arched into him, her nipples hard and tight, brushing against his stomach as they moved together. She could feel her climax building from the base of her spine, rippling outwards throughout her entire body. He did that to her. Only him.

Torj's hands spread her wide from below and she had never felt so exposed, or so aroused. The pressure mounting within increased, rising higher and higher, spinning out of control.

'Torj,' she moaned around him, but words beyond his name were lost on her, and at last, Wren let herself go.

She attempted to cry out his name again as she tipped over the edge she'd kissed several times already, her orgasm crashing down around her in a wave of blinding white. His cock in her mouth muffled her scream, and as Wren came, so did he.

Torj spilled his release on her tongue, jerking beneath her with a carnal groan.

Still trembling as the aftershocks of her climax shuddered through her, Wren took him deep in her throat, stroking him through the final waves of his orgasm.

When she rolled off him and nestled herself against his side, the Bear Slayer shook his head in wonder. 'Holy fuck, Embers . . .'

And Wren laughed, as a glimmer of gold danced between them.

CHAPTER 35

Wren

'An alchemist must always trust in themself. Good instincts are vital for their own protection in what can often be a deadly art'

— *Drevenor Academy Handbook*

WREN LOOKED FROM the flecks of gold to the beautiful Warsword before her. 'How can you say we *were* soul bonded?' she asked in wonder. 'This is proof right here . . .'

Torj's throat bobbed, and he reached for the nearest piece of clothing, which caused unease to ripple through Wren. She pulled her dress over her head, suddenly feeling self-conscious.

When they were both dressed, she sat down on his bed, where she didn't fail to notice the little bundle of dried lavender on his windowsill, from when they'd harvested the herb during her novice training. Her heart seized.

I want you so badly I can't breathe.

Torj didn't sit. He paced the length of his room. Once, then twice, passing a hand over his face as though he needed to gather himself to get through this next part.

'I didn't believe it at first,' he murmured, his hand drifting to the scars on his chest. 'Even when I saw glimmers of it, even when I felt things between us that pointed right to that fucking book. Those who are soul bonded are drawn together, across time and distance. They can share dreams and visions. They can sense one another's emotions. It manifests as a gold thread, linking the pair . . .'

Though she knew it already, as Torj spoke the words, it was like a piece of a life-long puzzle was clicking into place. Wren felt the truth of it echoing in her bones, in the lightning that sang beneath her skin, that called out to her from the scars over Torj's heart.

She stared at him, her voice hoarse as she said, 'That's us . . .'

'It was.'

Wren gnawed on the inside of her cheek, a knot forming in her stomach. 'Why wouldn't you want to believe it? Was it so terrible? The thought of being connected to me in that way?' It came out as a whisper, a tremor of insecurity barely hidden.

Torj's gaze shot to her, realization dawning on his handsome face. He rushed to her, falling to his knees before her where she sat on the edge of his bed. 'No,' he murmured, brushing her hair behind her ear. 'Of course not.'

'Then why deny it? Why not tell me about it?' she asked, freezing beneath his touch, torn between the desire to lean into his warmth and the need to protect herself.

Torj closed his eyes, as though bracing himself. When he opened them, they were filled with a pain that mirrored her own. 'Because there are negative consequences to a connection like that. Consequences I didn't want to face, didn't want to force on you.'

'Force on me?' Wren echoed, her voice rising. 'I was already part of this, as much as you.'

'I was trying to protect you, Embers . . .' His voice was raw, pleading.

'What happened?' she demanded, her stomach turning to lead. 'What happened to the golden thread? What happened to our soul bond?'

'The day of the attack at Drevenor—' Torj took a trembling breath. 'I severed it.'

Wren blinked at him. She was sure she was missing something, that there was some part she hadn't understood. 'You did what . . . ?'

Torj clutched her hands in his. 'When I was wounded . . . we were connected. That pain you felt? That was *my* pain. You were bleeding because of me. You were dying because of me . . .' His voice broke. 'I had a warrior's second, a mere breath between life and death, to make that choice . . . to make my actions mean something.'

Wren remembered the lancing pain through her chest, as though she had been speared with a red-hot knife. She remembered not understanding, not knowing why there was crimson flowing from her breast or why she was screaming. When she had come to, there had been no mark. No evidence of that agony. An invisible lie.

Wren pushed his hands away. 'And you thought that instead of telling me all this, it was better to break my heart? Better to lie? Better to make me question everything we had felt for one another?'

'I was trying to save you.'

'You *did* save me. And then you lied. Again and again, Bear Slayer.' Wren stood, putting distance between them, her arms wrapping around herself as if to hold the pieces of her heart together. She used the name pointedly, for in that moment, she wanted to hurt him, wanted to put the distance between them that he'd created when he'd thrown those words at her in the gardens.

'You made me someone I'm not.'

'There is no 'always' for people like us.'

'It's a curse, *Embervale.'*

'How could you take that choice from me? Hide it from me?' she asked, her chest aching anew at the memories crashing back into her.

'If you had been in my position . . .' Torj shook his head, his eyes lined with silver, as if he too could see their past unfurling before him. 'If you knew what it was like to watch the light leaving your eyes . . . If you knew you could stop it, prevent it from happening again . . . Tell me you wouldn't make the same decision.'

Wren looked at him – really looked at him. At the man she loved, the man who had hurt her, the man who had tried to protect her in all the wrong ways. She saw the fear in his eyes, the regret, the love that still burned beneath it all.

'I can't,' she croaked, her anger giving way to a deep, aching grief. 'You took that choice away from me.'

'Wren . . .' Torj murmured, reaching for her again. 'I'm sorry. I'm so fucking sorry.' Still on his knees, the Warsword cradled her hands in his. 'Tell me how to fix this. Tell me how to make this right. I would do anything for you.'

'I know.' Wren's voice cracked again. 'But I don't know how . . . how to move past this.'

'Wren, please . . .'

Once again, she pulled her hands from his, letting her fingers drift to the scar at her throat, the wound he'd closed in those final moments of the war, her flesh searing beneath her own storm power at his guidance. *'I'm sorry . . . I'm so sorry,'* he had murmured then.

Now, he said those words again, his hands empty in his lap, as though he didn't know what to do without her touch. He looked younger in his devastation, in his pain.

Wren struggled to swallow the lump in her throat. 'I forgive you, Torj. I do.' The words surprised her as much as they did him, by the look on his face. 'But forgiveness doesn't erase what happened. It doesn't change that I can't fathom why you lied. Why you hurt me so deeply . . . How can I trust you? You didn't trust me.'

'I understand,' Torj said hoarsely. He bowed his head and stood, his shoulders caved in, despair lining his face. 'Where does this leave us, then?'

'I don't know.' Her voice was soft but steady. 'I know how you feel about me . . .'

She moved towards the door, pausing with her hand on the latch. Without turning back, she spoke one last time, her words hanging in the air between them like the remnants of their severed bond.

'But it isn't always enough, is it?'

CHAPTER 36

Torj

'A Warsword must never break. A Warsword is the unyielding shield upon which the darkness crashes'

– *The Warsword's Way*

'I*T ISN'T ALWAYS enough.*' Wren's words echoed long after she'd gone, becoming a chant in Torj's mind that morphed into something darker: *you're* not enough.

His room was too small to contain him and the grief that wracked his body. Torj desperately wanted to leave this place, this godsforsaken academy that had been the catalyst for so much brokenness. But it was a unique form of torture to be in love with – to be *soul bonded* to – the woman who no longer wanted you, the woman you were duty-bound to protect.

Torj couldn't leave. Instead, he took to the corridors outside, pacing the length of the hall, his gaze constantly flicking to Wren's door. Every tormented thing he'd ever felt surged to the surface, becoming poison in his blood.

You're not enough.

An echo of storm magic thrummed in his chest, warring with him, threatening to split his scar open anew. For the briefest of seconds, he wished it would. Physical pain he could understand;

his whole childhood had been governed by it. But this? This was a wound he couldn't fathom. His body was full of fire, and he didn't know how much longer he could take it—

A cloaked figure stopped outside Wren's door, and Torj was there in an instant.

'What the fuck are you doing here?' he snarled in Darian Devereux's face, shoving him roughly against the stone wall.

'I would have thought that was obvious,' Devereux replied, not a hair out of place, not a flicker of fear in his expression.

'You have no right to be here,' Torj said, refusing to loosen his grip.

Devereux's voice was silken. 'I have *every* right to be here. A nobleman of fine breeding and wealth, come to offer the Delmirian princess aid she doesn't even realize she needs. We both know I am more suited to a place by her side – or in her bed, for that matter – than you.'

A dark laugh escaped Torj. 'She'll poison you before you can so much as take off your boots.'

'Careful, now. You know how danger excites me.'

Torj was trembling. To him, Devereux weighed nothing. It would be easy to lift him from the ground so his feet were dangling, so he could be thrown across the corridor. Torj pictured it in his mind. 'If you lay so much as a finger on her . . .'

'I'd like to do more than that, I assure you. We've shared before, haven't we? We can share again if you wish, brother—'

Torj hurled Devereux across the hall, slamming him into the opposite wall, hard enough that the windows rattled. His body slid down the bricks, dust and fragments falling around him as he hit the floor. With a hoarse laugh, the nobleman collected himself, wiping blood from his chin.

'There you are,' he sneered, the expression distorting his otherwise handsome face. 'You are your father's son after all.'

Torj hated him. Hated him with every fibre of his being. Hated that Devereux knew the origin of the scars on his arms, knew which bones were weaker from multiple fractures . . . Knew the ugly truth of it all, and had still become the man before him.

Devereux continued as though nothing had happened. 'I really think you should be more generous with me after all I've done for you . . . Don't you agree, Bear Slayer?'

'All you've done for me?' Torj blinked, his fingers flexing at his sides, yearning to close around the bastard's throat.

Devereux spat blood on the ground. 'Yes. You wear that moniker because of me.'

'Becoming the Bear Slayer cost me my only family,' Torj managed, rooting himself to the spot before he broke bones.

'Did it?' Devereux mused. 'I thought it made you a legend.'

Torj shook his head in disbelief, hardly able to recognize his childhood friend in the monster staring back at him. 'No legend is worth that cost,' he replied.

'I wouldn't know,' Devereux said smoothly. 'Now, if you'll excuse me . . .' He gestured to Wren's door—

'What part didn't you understand?' Torj growled, blocking him. 'You're not seeing her.'

'Well, that's not your choice, is it, soldier? Why don't we ask the beautiful Elwren what it is that *she* wants? Or are you afraid of what she might say?'

Torj's fist was already swinging for Devereux's face, but a large pair of arms braced around his chest and hauled him back. He found himself being dragged away. Only a Warsword could stop him like that.

'Have you lost your fucking mind?' a familiar voice said.

'Cal, let me go.' Torj struggled against his former protégé's hold as Devereux approached Wren's door unhindered.

'Why? So you can kill one of the most influential figures in the entire midrealms? One who's funding a good portion of its efforts against the Vanguard?' Cal shoved him backwards. 'I don't fucking think so, Elderbrock.'

Torj was panting, his blood roaring in his ears, demanding an outlet, demanding that Devereux's smug face meet the justice of his fist—

'Now's not the time, Bear Slayer,' said a weak voice to his left.

Torj glanced sideways to see Zavier bracing himself against the wall, looking pale and tired, with Dessa hovering close by, her hand on his back.

'What's wrong with him?' Torj asked bluntly, surveying the green tinge to Zavier's face.

'Too much fire extract with Kipp,' Zavier muttered, swaying on his feet.

Cal gave Torj another shove, bringing his focus back to the matter at hand: Devereux was knocking on Wren's door.

'Can I trust that you're not going to maim any noblemen this evening?' Cal pressed. 'I've got to get Zavier back to his rooms.'

'No promises,' Torj growled, not taking his eyes off the door, which had opened a crack.

'What do you want?' came Wren's sharp voice from within. The flinty note in her demand made Torj's heart leap.

'Bear Slayer?' Cal snapped. 'No violence tonight.'

Torj released a shuddering breath. 'Not tonight,' he vowed.

That seemed to be enough for the younger Warsword, who wasted no time scooping his charge up in his arms and hurrying down the corridor.

Torj turned back just in time to hear the rest of the exchange between Wren and the noble-blooded prick.

'I only require a few moments of your time,' Devereux was saying.

'At this hour?' Wren asked.

'For you? Any hour.'

Light spilled from the room as she opened the door wider and Devereux slipped inside. Torj's chest seized.

Swallowing the lump in his throat, shoving down the devastation that threatened to burst from him, he took up his station.

He was her guard, nothing more.
The chant in his mind started anew.
Not enough. Not enough. Not enough.

CHAPTER 37

Wren

'Come winter the petals fall, but the thorns remain'

– From *Root to Petal: Understanding Plants and Their Properties*

'WHAT HAPPENED TO YOU?' Zavier demanded, staring at Wren's puffy eyes as they reviewed their work in the warfare dungeon the next day.

'I know I look like shit, but do you really need to draw attention to it?' Wren hissed, rubbing her aching temples.

'Depends,' Zavier replied. 'How bad is it?'

Despite the fact that Torj was currently stationed outside their lesson, she hadn't spoken to him since last night. She'd done nothing except stare at that damn book and wonder where the fuck they'd gone wrong.

Now, she surveyed Zavier in return. Her friend's skin was sallow, his hairline damp with sweat, his lips dry and cracked. 'Are you alright?' she asked, noting that he appeared to have lost weight as well.

'Why wouldn't I be?' he said defensively.

'You . . . you just don't look like yourself today.'

'I know I look like shit, but do you really need to draw attention to it?' he parroted.

Wren gave a tired laugh. 'Fair enough. I don't think any of us look like ourselves lately.' She looked around the workstations. 'Where's Dessa? She should be here by now.'

Zavier shrugged. 'I think she and Kipp ended things between them last night. Perhaps she's taken the morning to . . . deal with that.'

'She would have told me!' Wren exclaimed.

Another shrug. 'First time for everything, Poisoner.'

Wren's brow furrowed as she glanced at the door, waiting for Dessa to burst through at any moment.

'If you're this antsy, you may as well tell me what happened to get *you* in such a state,' Zavier said. 'Or are your secrets only good enough for Dessa's ears?'

Wren snorted. 'Since when are you interested?'

'Since I need something to make this lesson a tad less dull.'

Normally, Wren would have laughed, but the hollowness within her only widened. 'I'd keep that to yourself. Master Crawford has excellent hearing, if you recall . . .'

Zavier rolled his eyes. 'Dessa was careless, as usual.' He motioned to the vials of corrosive agent they had created. 'Her handwriting looks like a child's. How are we meant to read these labels, for Furies' sake?'

'It's not that bad.' Wren picked one up and pointed to the admittedly messy scrawl. 'That's the date, those are the ingredients . . .'

This time it was Zavier who looked to the door, clicking his tongue in annoyance. 'Alright, she's definitely late. We still need to test everything to ensure it can be reproduced, *and* we still need to develop application methods and safety measures. It'd be nice if she showed up to pull her weight.'

'Ease up,' Wren said with a note of warning. 'She's never let us down before.'

'First time for everything,' Zavier repeated darkly.

'You're in a mood today,' she observed. 'Why don't *you* tell *me* what happened? Is it something to do with your opus?'

Scoffing, Zavier shuffled his notes. 'Not even close. How about we both mind our own business?'

'It's called showing an interest in your friends' lives, Zavier . . . You might like to try it sometime.'

'I assure you, I would not. The only thing I'd like is to complete this damn task so I can get back to—'

The dungeon door swung open and in strode Torj and Cal, their expressions hardened.

'What is the meaning of this?' Master Crawford demanded. 'I was assured that there would be no disruption to my lessons.'

Cal had the audacity to shrug. 'Prince Zavier and Princess Elwren's presence is required by the Guild Master of Thezmarr and the High Chancellor. We're just following orders.'

Wren's gaze cut to Zavier, whose brows were raised.

'We're being summoned?' she asked, directing the question at Cal.

'It certainly seems that way,' Master Crawford snapped, motioning for them to leave. 'Get out before you disrupt any more of my lesson.'

Wren gathered her things quickly, hoping that Dessa would soon show up to pack away their work, and followed Zavier from the dungeon.

With Torj and Cal stationed outside, Wren and Zavier entered the High Chancellor's chambers to the sound of raised voices and the thudding of fists against a table. All eyes went to the pair as they approached, and Wren's hand drifted to her belt of vials, seeking the familiar comfort.

At an oval table before her were more than a dozen agitated faces, some familiar: Lady Liora, Queen Regent of Harenth; Audra, the Guild Master of Thezmarr; and King Leiko of Tver, who sat next to Darian Devereux, Lord Lucian and a handful of other noble figures. The Master Alchemists of Drevenor were also present, though they stood with their backs to the wall, not seated at the table. The only friendly face was Kipp's, but his expression was one of stone as he took stock of the room, his gaze lingering on the Devereux men.

'We were summoned?' Zavier said curtly.

'Yes,' King Leiko replied. 'We are here to discuss the threat that Silas the Kingsbane and the People's Vanguard pose to the midrealms. It's high time the Terlings and the Embervales contributed. Take a seat.'

Already, Wren didn't like his tone. King Leiko had tearfully thanked her at the end of the war, both for her heroics at the battle of Notos and for saving him from King Artos' empath control . . . Apparently the King of Tver had a short memory, for he looked at her now with contempt.

Saying nothing, Wren slid into the empty chair offered to her. She looked to Farissa across the room, but her former mentor's expression betrayed nothing.

'We were just discussing the People's Vanguard and how they are gathering numbers by the day,' King Leiko told them testily. 'It has been suggested by some sources that they are raising an army to march on each of the capital cities.'

Wren's blood ran cold. 'What—'

'What sources?' Zavier demanded, cutting her off.

'Trusted sources close to each of the crowns,' Lord Devereux Senior replied, his voice smooth, full of command.

Zavier eyed him suspiciously. 'Who are you?'

'Lord Lucian Devereux of Tver, Prince Zavier,' he replied with a bow of his head.

Wren glanced at Zavier, noting how his fists clenched beneath the table.

'Princess Elwren.' Lord Lucian bowed his head again, this time in her direction. 'Another of our lost monarchs returned to the fold.'

'Wren is fine,' she told him.

But the nobleman raised a brow. 'I would not so easily dismiss your status. You may be grasping for it before long.'

Wren's gaze swept around the room before narrowing on the older man. 'And what is your role here, Lord Lucian?'

His smile didn't reach his eyes. 'I am here to assist His Grace, King Leiko. In recent years I have taken a far more hands-on approach to my support for the Tverrian crown.'

'We were discussing the possibility of the rebels rallying an army,' Audra cut in, looking as severe as ever with her hair scraped back and her spectacles perched on the end of her nose.

'Indeed,' Lord Lucian replied. 'I was about to say that between my own private forces and the units I manage for His Majesty, we have the numbers to protect Tver.'

'Perhaps it's best we don't underestimate them, Father,' Darian said.

'Our men are the same calibre as those at Thezmarr,' Lord Lucian snapped. Wren had to stifle a scoff, but he continued, 'Our position is strong.'

'As you say, Father,' Darian replied, his face a mask of calm.

Wren glanced from father to son, her curiosity piquing as Darian's own words came back to her: *'My father and I have played this game for as long as I can remember, and we'll play until one of us doesn't walk away.'*

Like his sire, Darian wore an unreadable expression. Long gone were the roguish grin and flirtatious banter that infuriated the Bear Slayer. Here was someone cold and calculated.

'What news on Silas the Kingsbane?' the High Chancellor's voice rang out across the table. 'I have received no update since his attack on our grounds.'

Audra stood, clasping her hands behind her back. 'My Warswords have been tracking him across the midrealms. He has been travelling ever since.'

'And yet you haven't taken him down?' King Leiko's tone was accusatory.

'The situation is a delicate one—'

'Delicate?' the king spat. 'Delicate how? He attacked the rulers of the midrealms, *several times*. He destroyed a good portion of *this* academic institution and took the lives of a dozen people in that very hall. Furthermore, he goes about spreading treasonous propaganda throughout our lands. He needs to be dealt with.'

'Well said, my king.' Lord Lucian tapped his goblet on the table in solidarity. 'The Guild Master should be using the brute force of Thezmarr to bring him down, not following him about the kingdoms, taking notes.'

Only decades of knowing Audra allowed Wren to spot her tell – the flare of her nostrils. It was a subtle tic that belied her former warden's rage. Audra had spent many a year being told what to do by men; Wren knew she did not suffer it gladly now. She waited for the moment Audra would put them in her place. The Guild Master could flay a man with words just as easily as a blade.

But to Wren's surprise, the older woman said nothing. Instead, she scanned the table, seeming to catalogue everyone there, waiting and watching. That, more than anything, caused a chill to rake down Wren's spine. Audra had often done the same thing before and during the war, always assessing, always calculating her next move. It meant that there was more going on than the dick-measuring contest in front of them.

Wren glanced at Zavier, who was glaring daggers at the Devereux noblemen, while the masters around the perimeter of the room looked increasingly uncomfortable. The party at the table had broken out in hushed whispers, though Wren could make out none of their words exactly—

King Leiko slammed his fist on the table. 'I have another pressing matter that needs immediate attention.' The King of Tver motioned to his captain stationed by the heavy oak doors. 'There is a traitor in our midst.'

Wren's heart seized as the doors creaked open and Dessa stumbled into the room.

She barely kept her footing as a burly guard shoved her forwards. Wren shot to her feet. This couldn't be real. Dessa was good and decent. Dessa was her *friend*.

It was then that she noticed Dessa's face, usually alight with mischief, was a canvas of anguish. Tears carved glistening tracks down her cheeks; her lip was split, a trickle of dried blood stark against her skin.

Wren's fists clenched at her sides. 'What is the meaning of this?'

But Zavier was faster. From nowhere, he unsheathed a thin blade and pointed it at the guard whose meaty hand was bruising Dessa's arm. 'Unhand her,' the Prince of Naarva ordered. Kipp was on his feet too, his mouth open in outrage.

'Odessa Chamberlain is a traitor to the midrealms and all its crowns,' King Leiko declared.

'Release our student, Your Majesty,' the High Chancellor said, holding out a trembling hand as though to soothe a wild beast.

But the king did not relent, and in the presence of other threats, his guard had drawn a blade on Dessa. He held the wickedly sharp edge mere inches from her throat, a silent warning that made Wren's blood run cold. One wrong move, one act of defiance, and Dessa's life would be forfeit.

'What is she holding?' Lady Liora asked, her prim voice cutting through the promise of violence.

'*King Leiko*,' the High Chancellor interjected, an edge to his voice this time. 'Release Miss Chamberlain at once. She is a student of this academy and therefore under my care.'

'She's no longer a student. She is a traitor to the crowns, as His Majesty has clearly stated,' Lord Lucian declared. 'And Lady Liora asks a poignant question: *what is in her hand?*'

Wren's gaze went to Dessa's fists clenched at her sides. She couldn't see anything, but Dessa was trembling uncontrollably, refusing to meet her eye.

The room seemed to shrink, the air growing thick and oppressive. Wren's ears rang with the pounding of her own heart as she watched her friend dragged before the king, the blade still poised at her throat.

King Leiko's eyes flashed as he stood up suddenly, closing the distance between himself and Dessa. Wren's lungs constricted as he invaded her friend's space, his face mere inches from hers. With a sharp nod, he signalled the guard. The blade pressed harder against Dessa's throat, and Wren's rage surged as she saw a bead of crimson bloom where steel met flesh—

Lightning crackled, but King Leiko held up a hand of flame in her direction. 'Don't you dare.'

If Wren struck, she'd risk the blade slipping across Dessa's skin, or the king burning her. Beside her, Zavier seemed to come to the same conclusion; he gripped her wrist and pushed her hand back down.

King Leiko, incensed now, snatched Dessa's hand, where she was clutching something as hard as she could. Despite her trembling body, her jaw clenched in defiance, her lips pressing into a thin line.

Wren couldn't believe this was happening: that she was in a room of powerful people and no one was stopping the king – including herself.

'What is it?' Lady Liora demanded again. 'Would someone show us what she's holding, for Furies' sake?'

Wren's stomach turned to lead as she glimpsed a hint of green and silver-white between Dessa's knuckles.

No. It wasn't supposed to happen like this.

But King Leiko's patience snapped. He whirled to face the assembled nobles and masters, his eyes blazing. 'The question is not *what* she's holding. It's *where it's from*,' he spat. 'This woman has been keeping a secret, one that could turn the tides of our upcoming conflict.'

In one fluid motion, he grabbed Dessa's clenched fist and slammed it down on the table, causing her to cry out in pain. Wren caught a fleeting glimpse of something shimmering as it settled on the wooden surface before them all.

Wren's eyes widened as she stared at the fistful of delicate iridescent petals scattered across the polished wood. Their glow seemed to pulse in time with her racing heart.

'It looks to be a simple rose,' the Master of Lifelore observed, his weathered face wrinkling as he surveyed the plant. 'Silvertide, if I'm not mistaken.'

The silence that followed was deafening. But King Leiko rounded on Dessa once more, his fury palpable.

'I'll ask you one last time, girl,' he growled. 'Where did you get this? Tell them what you admitted to me. Tell them where it's from!'

Lady Liora, clearly confused by the reactions around her, spoke up hesitantly. 'For the love of the Furies, will someone answer him?'

The question hung in the air.

Wren's mind was racing. Her gaze locked with Dessa's, and in that moment, a thousand unspoken words passed between them. Her friend gave a subtle shake of her head.

But as Wren looked at Dessa – battered, bleeding, yet still protecting her – she knew there was only one choice.

A time will come when that knowledge will be more impactful than the swing of a sword.

Slowly, deliberately, Wren produced a sample of her own from one of the pouches her belt. All eyes turned to her with a mix of curiosity and suspicion as she held the bloom up for all to see. She took a deep breath, steeling herself for what was to come, knowing that nothing would ever be the same again.

'The Master of Lifelore is correct; it *is* a silvertide rose,' Wren said, her voice steadier than she felt. 'Only this particular specimen is from Delmira.'

CHAPTER 38

Wren

'After the deaths of King Soren and Queen Brigh, no heirs to the kingdom of Delmira came forwards to claim their throne of ruins. It has remained a wasteland ever since'

– *The Midrealms Chronicles*

TIME HUNG SUSPENDED, just for a moment, as all eyes fell to Wren. The weight of their stares was a crushing pressure that threatened to overwhelm her. She fought the urge to shrink back, to hide from the accusations and betrayal etched on every face.

Instead, she lifted her chin in defiance.

And then the room erupted.

Fists slammed atop the table, accompanied by a cacophony of raised voices; chairs were knocked backwards as people stood in outrage. King Leiko's expression morphed from surprise to fury, and he made a move towards Wren, scattering the papers that had been neatly piled before him.

'I wouldn't do that if I were you, Your Majesty,' said a familiar voice from the doorway.

Torj didn't shift an inch, didn't fall into his usual rhythm of brute strength and violence. His glimmering dark eyes said more than enough. Both he and Cal stood at the entrance now, their presence commanding the entire chamber.

'This doesn't concern you, Warswords,' Lord Lucian told them. 'Or perhaps you were in on this betrayal?'

Neither Torj nor Cal moved, but Torj's gaze slid to the nobleman. 'Though my current duty binds me to the heir of Delmira, I am a Warsword of Thezmarr. I do not answer to you.'

But Warswords or not, they could not save Wren from this. She looked to Farissa, to Audra, and both women gave her a nod of encouragement. There was no going back, no hiding this any more.

Wren swallowed hard, her throat suddenly dry. 'I discovered the rose on my recent research trip to Delmira,' she began.

'But Delmira is barren. Nothing grows there,' Master Norlander argued, not taking his eyes off the vibrant petals on the table.

'I thought so too,' Wren told him with a nod. 'In all the years that I lived there after the war, it barely supported the grasslands and the heather. The earth was cracked and dry, the fields yellowed . . .'

Beside her, she felt Zavier go rigid as he learned the extent of her and Dessa's secrecy. And she could sense Torj's eyes on her, his anguish for her. It was hitting her in waves.

Nevertheless, she forged on. 'But when I returned, I discovered that it is barren no longer. Kristopher Snowden, Odessa Chamberlain and Torj Elderbrock can attest to this. However, it was at my insistence that they kept this information secret.'

Torj stepped towards her. 'Wren—'

But she flung up a hand, silencing him.

'I went back to identify and source a plant that had helped me create the cure we used against the enemy's alchemy during my time as a novice. I didn't know that Delmira had changed; I didn't know what it had become,' she told them. 'I understand how this must look, but I didn't keep this from you with ill intent. I was trying to avoid more conflict—'

The Master of Lifelore stepped forwards, his usually calm demeanour shattered. 'You had no right to make that decision.'

'Did I not?' Wren shot back. 'I *am* one of the heirs of Delmira, after all.'

But she had never seen her teacher incensed like this. 'You don't know the half of it. Do you even know what Delmira was like before it fell?'

Wren suppressed the instinct to look to Farissa for guidance. Instead, she waited.

Master Norlander forged on. 'It was the crown jewel of the midrealms for agriculture. Naarva may have been the Kingdom of Gardens, but Delmira . . . If something grew there, it was better, richer, more potent in whatever properties it held. People would pay bags of gold for a simple sack of soil from the lands there. It was the most fertile, the most sought after.'

Wren faltered. 'How?'

'Well, *that* was the question. Generations of Embervales kept their secrets close to their chests, refusing to share their methods with the rest of the kingdoms, ensuring that theirs remained on top.' The Master of Lifelore shook his head as though he were personally offended. 'You should have informed us immediately.'

At last, Audra stood. 'And what? Alerted the entire midrealms to the rebirth of a dead kingdom before we've had a chance to secure it?'

King Leiko glared at her and then Wren with loathing. 'Delmira has no ruler. It is not governed or guarded. Anyone can march onto its lands and take what they want. We should have been informed. We are allies. This is a blatant disrespect for that supposed trust.'

As the cacophony of voices washed over Wren, the full weight of her decision crashed down upon her. She had tried to do the right thing, to maintain peace and order, to listen to her superiors, those who were wiser than herself . . . and yet before her, the past five years of peace wavered. Alliances and friendship forged in hardship were crumbling under the weight of this revelation.

And now, rage simmered in Wren once more.

Lightning pricked at her fingertips, and outside, thunder shook the sky.

Audra's eyes flashed in warning. But Wren wasn't in control. She couldn't help it as the power surged through her, as it demanded that she yield. She thought she had mastered it years ago; she had always shown more command over it than either of her sisters, and yet here she was, losing hold—

Torj was suddenly at her side, covering her hands with his, stopping the storm from breaking.

'Delmira needs to be protected,' King Leiko declared. 'I shall have my army march there at once.'

Audra's voice projected across the chamber, as steely and commanding as ever. 'Unless permitted by the rightful heir to the kingdom, to invade Delmira, ruler or not, is an *act of war*, an act against the peace accords of the midrealms. Thezmarr will answer accordingly.'

'Are you threatening the King of Tver, Guild Master?' Lord Lucian asked.

'I am reminding the King of Tver of his oaths,' Audra said coldly.

The king's gaze shifted to Wren, full of ire. 'Is there anything else Princess Elwren deigns to share with us?'

'I didn't know any of this until a few weeks ago. Our kingdom was *barren*, as far as I know.'

Lord Lucian sneered. 'So *now* it's *your* kingdom . . .'

Torj took a step towards the nobleman, bracing a hand on the wicked blade at his belt. 'You forget yourself, Devereux.'

'The truth of the matter is that Delmira is no longer barren. The kingdom belongs to the Embervales, as it has throughout history,' Audra proclaimed. 'If this is something you object to, you need to make it known. We will reconvene to continue this tomorrow morning at the eighth hour. Meeting adjourned.'

Wren didn't realize she was shaking until Torj pushed her gently back into her chair. He stood silently by her side as they watched the chamber empty, with countless glares shot in her direction.

The weight of everything was crushing. Somehow, she had wound up with the fate of a kingdom in her hands. Again.

She only looked up when the door clicked closed.

The faces that stared back were of those she cared for: Torj, Cal, Kipp, Dessa, Zavier, Farissa and Audra. And Wren couldn't bear it, couldn't bear the pity etched into their expressions.

She went to Dessa first, tilting her friend's head gently to the light so she could scan her for injuries. 'Are you alright?' she asked, noting where a trail of blood had dried on Dessa's neck. Wren reached for her kit, but Dessa batted her hands away.

'I'm fine, Wren. I swear. You have bigger things to worry about.'

Wren wanted to drop her head into her hands, to hide away from it all. But instead, she looked to Audra, whose mouth was set in a grim line.

'That won't be the last time such notions are voiced, Elwren,' the Guild Master told her. 'I can station warriors at Delmira's borders for the interim while we work out what to do, but I cannot give a rulerless kingdom a permanent guard. And I fear this will only get worse, especially once the People's Vanguard are made aware.'

Wren nodded slowly, then turned, seeking the keenest mind in the room.

Kipp's eyes locked onto hers in understanding. 'You know what you need to do?' he asked.

'It's time to call Thea back.' Wren took a trembling breath and rose to her feet. 'Delmira needs a queen.'

CHAPTER 39

Torj

'A magic wielder steeped in emotional turmoil is a dangerous thing. It is one of the many duties of a Warsword to protect the sovereigns of the midrealms, but also to protect the midrealms from its sovereigns'

— *The Warsword's Way*

TORJ DIDN'T KNOW how many minutes had passed in that chamber. Twenty? Thirty? So much could change in such a short expanse of time. So much had.

He saw the weight of the world fall on Wren's shoulders, and there was nothing he could do. A long time ago, he'd sworn he'd never be helpless again, and yet here he was. How could he protect her from this?

When at last they were alone in the council room, Torj turned to her, reached for her. 'Wren, I—'

'We're going to the rookery,' was all she said.

They were silent as they left the main academy building and started to climb a spiral staircase in one of the rear towers. Torj had used the rookery dozens of times during Wren's novice training to report back to Audra, sending missives when he was under the impression he had a magical wound that might send him into madness.

When they reached the top, he opened the heavy wooden door out onto the rooftop, where a dozen or so ravens squawked in their cages.

Wren peered over the ledge, out onto the grounds, a low whistle sounding between her lips. 'Everything looks so small from up here,' she said quietly. He could hear the heartbreak in her voice, and it damn near ruined him. He had done that to her, as had the midrealms she'd fought so hard to save.

But there was nothing for him to do but follow her gaze. Torj had never actually stopped to survey the lands from the rookery, always so intent on completing his task and getting back to the poisoner who stood beside him. Now, he looked out onto Drevenor's lands with her. Beyond the gardens and the greenhouses was Evermere Forest, and beyond that Torj could see a glimmer of sea.

Wren fumbled with her oilskin satchel, retrieving a quill, an inkpot and a piece of parchment, setting them down on the top of the wall.

'I never wanted to ask this of her,' she murmured as she stared at the blank page, her magic crackling around her. 'It's not fair . . . Not after everything she's done. And yet here I am, asking anyway.'

Torj didn't know what to say, so he stayed silent as the wind picked up around them and Wren put quill to parchment and wrote to her sister.

When she was done, Wren rolled the message into a scroll with shaking hands and surveyed the ravens in their cages, their home locations scrawled across the top of the bars. She selected a bird, tying the missive to its leg and coaxing it out of its cage.

There was something majestic about this woman, even in her simple gown and apron, as she walked to the ledge of the rooftop, a raven perched on her fingers . . . It was how she carried herself, her back straight, her chin lifted. But as the raven took flight, her legs seemed to buckle and Torj caught her by the waist.

The poisoner stepped away from his grasp, pressing a hand to her chest as the clouds above darkened. 'I need you to take me somewhere – a place I can . . .' She trailed off, wincing and clenching her fists. 'Somewhere safe – for me.'

Torj felt the power vibrating around her, fighting against whatever tentative hold she had, and he understood.

'Come with me.' He guided Wren from the rookery, her whole body shaking suddenly.

'Hurry,' she murmured, squeezing her eyes shut.

She was trusting him, he realized as he navigated the spiral steps once more. Her storm magic called out to him, as it always had, but he didn't let it lure him, didn't let himself get caught up in its song.

He took Wren across the grounds, half carrying her as she fought against the beast that raged within.

Torj wanted to tell her he was sorry that after everything she'd been through during the war, and everything since, she'd found herself in this position. She didn't deserve it. He wanted to tell her that it would be alright, that they had survived worse, but all those reassurances died on his tongue when he glanced at her.

A mask had slid into place. The mask she'd worn so well in the post-war years; the mask of the Poisoner. A mask that served as a wall, locking everything inside, and everyone else out.

'This way,' he told her softly. 'Not far now.'

They passed beneath wrought iron gates, through the gardens and beyond, where the more isolated meadow sprawled outwards.

He hadn't been here since . . . since everything. But with the power rolling off Wren in waves, he'd heeded her words: *somewhere safe for me.*

When she opened her eyes, she sank to her knees. As she tipped her head to the sky, a cry of relief escaped her lips, and suddenly, she unleashed her storm, a tempest of chaos and destruction.

Torj was blown back by the force of it, landing hard several yards away in the grass. He leapt to his feet, a silent cry for her on his lips as a wild gale tore up the flowers and earth around Wren. Near-deafening thunder boomed overhead, and flashes of brilliant white split the black clouds closing in.

A maelstrom surrounded Wren, lightning shooting from her hands into the wind while rain lashed down, violently hammering everything below.

It was a reckoning of grief, of sorrow. Pain poured from her, giving rise to the frenzied storm around her.

And through the deluge, Torj could see her sobbing.

He could stand it no longer. Fighting against the tempest with all his Furies-given strength, he moved towards her. The storm battled him with every step, but he refused to leave her alone in this. Debris hit him, slicing at his skin, knocking the breath from him as he grappled with her power and slowly closed the distance between them.

Wren's hair was loose and wild, caught up in the savage gale. Blue lightning flitted across her skin in a deadly dance.

With no thought for his own safety, Torj did the only thing that felt natural. He reached for her.

He felt no pain as his warm skin met hers, his arms wrapping around her and her magic. The storm continued to rage around them, but no lightning assaulted him, no force threatened to tear him away from her.

Torj had become what he was always meant to be: the shield between Wren and the world that had already taken too much.

CHAPTER 40

Wren

'Alchemy is often considered a lonely discipline, but what many novices and adepts fail to realize is the necessity for community, for lasting connections within the craft. The mind is a blade, but many minds make an army'

– *Alchemy Unbound*

WREN BARELY REMEMBERED how it had happened. One minute she'd been writing a desperate plea to Thea, overcome with guilt, and the next she'd been in the eye of a violent storm, with Torj's arms around her. He had held her so tightly, as though he could fight fate itself and anchor her to the world.

The Bear Slayer hadn't flinched at her power this time. Instead, he had embraced it, embraced *her*, while the feel of him flooded her senses, washing away the chaos within. He hadn't said a word; he had simply been there, pulling her back from the darkness.

Now, as he escorted her back to the main building, his cloak wrapped around her shoulders, Wren felt utterly raw and depleted . . . but an ember of something forgotten glowed in the otherwise hollow pit of her chest.

They didn't speak until they reached the residence halls and Wren brought them to a stop. 'I have to see Dessa,' she told the Warsword at her side.

'Wren . . .' he protested gently. 'I think you need to rest. You can talk to her tomorrow.'

Wren had already raised her fist to knock. 'They hurt her. *Because of me.* I have to make sure she's alright. I was distracted before – I didn't check properly. Not like I should have.'

Torj didn't protest again. She knew he understood.

With her heart in her throat, she pounded on the door. 'Dessa? Dessa, are you in there?' Panic gripped her in a way that usually had her hurtling back to the past, but she rooted herself in the present, in the rapping of her knuckles against the timber. 'Dessa!' she half-shouted.

Relief surged through her as the door opened a crack, a head of red hair peeking out. 'Wren?' The door widened, and Dessa stepped back, her face forlorn, her eyes red. The shallow cut at her throat from where the dagger had pressed was scabbed over, but the sight of it made Wren's stomach lurch.

With a brief look, she told Torj to stay outside as she swept into Dessa's room, the door clicking closed behind her.

'Wren, I-I . . .' Dessa stammered. 'I'm—'

But Wren swept her friend up in her arms, hugging her tightly. 'I'm so sorry, Dessa—'

'*You're* sorry?' Dessa choked into Wren's neck. '*I'm* the one who betrayed you. I'm the one who let the secret out.'

Wren grabbed her by the shoulders and held her at arm's length so she could double-check her for injuries. 'You did *no* such thing, you hear me? I put you in a terrible position, *your life was at risk*, and you still didn't say a word. This is on me. And I'm so sorry for it. I'm sorry for not being a better friend.'

Tears streamed down Dessa's cheeks and Wren wiped them away with her thumbs, cupping her face.

'Please forgive me?'

Dessa shook her head. 'There's nothing to forgive. I thought I let you down, that I ruined everything.'

'You didn't, on both counts,' Wren assured her. 'It was me who let you down.'

'No—'

'Yes,' Wren said firmly. 'And it won't happen again. That's not the kind of friend I want to be.'

'You're not.' Dessa smiled through her tears. 'I'm just sorry they found out. I know that's not what you wanted.'

'It wasn't going to be a secret for ever, Dess. It's too big. But what happened?'

Dessa sighed. 'I was in the conservatory working on my own opus, a few benches away from where you left your samples. Some of King Leiko's advisers were taking a tour of the grounds with some novices, but one of them . . . I think one of them was an alchemist. He stopped when he saw the roses. He started touching them, plucking at petals and examining the leaves, saying that he'd never seen a rose so perfect.'

Wren's skin crawled. 'And then what?'

'And then he found your notes—'

'That's not possible . . . I keep my notes locked away in my room. I—'

She saw Dessa's throat bob. 'It's my fault. The last time we worked together I took yours by mistake. I'd only found them among mine that morning. I put them on your desk with the roses so I'd remember to give them back to you and . . . he saw them. He saw the map of Delmira. And by then I'd come over to your station to make sure he wasn't tampering with your work, which gave me away. He shoved the map into my hand and dragged me before the king. The rest, you know.'

'Gods, Dessa. I'm so sorry. You didn't deserve that.'

'Neither did you. I should have been more careful.'

'Please don't blame yourself.' Wren hung her head, the next words tumbling from her mouth in a raw admission. 'I don't remember the last time I was sure about anything, the last time I felt like I wasn't on the edge of making some monumental mistake. What is going to become of alchemy as a discipline with a tyrant at the helm? What of Drevenor? Once more of this poison spills out into the world, there'll be no putting it back.'

Dessa was quiet for a moment before she nudged Wren. 'Do you want a cup of tea?'

A weak laugh bubbled from Wren's lips. 'What?'

Her friend went to where a small pot hung over the hearth. 'I say this with love, Wren, but . . . you look exhausted. A cup of tea won't solve all your problems, but it's a good place to start.'

Wren's whole body sagged with relief. 'I'd love that.'

The women sat cross-legged on Dessa's bed, steaming mugs of tea between their palms, and Wren sank into the warm comfort of female friendship once more. It was a balm like no other, she realized. She needed it.

When she'd settled in, Dessa told her about her progress with her own opus – the memory device to help her ailing father. She told her how much interest the masters had shown in it, how excited they were on her behalf.

'I'm worried I won't have enough time, though,' Dessa admitted. 'It's such intricate work, it can't be rushed . . . but our presentation day is so close now.'

Wren knew the feeling well. 'The pressure is mounting, isn't it?'

'Truly,' Dessa agreed. 'You'd think during this time of upheaval we'd be shown a bit of grace, but . . .'

'Knowledge is the victor over fate,' Wren replied.

Dessa huffed a dry laugh. 'And the mind is a blade . . . Drevenor stops for nothing, not even a possible war.'

'I think we're beyond the realm of *possible* now,' Wren said gently.

'I think you're right.' Dessa heaved a sigh. 'Shall we talk about something else?'

The conversation shifted to romance, as it tended to with Dessa at the helm – but for once, Wren wasn't the subject in question.

'Things are over between Kipp and me,' Dessa admitted, draining the rest of her tea.

'Zavier mentioned it. I'm sorry.'

Dessa sighed. 'It was fun while it lasted, but after we went with you to Delmira . . . I realized my priorities are with the academy. I want to put my work before all else, until I meet someone who feels like home . . . Does that sound ridiculous?'

'No,' Wren told her. 'It sounds wise.'

'Well, I have my moments.' Dessa poured them both a fresh cup. 'And you? Have you fixed things with your Bear Slayer?'

'No,' she admitted. 'It's not easy.'

'The good things never are, Wren.'

Wren let out a rueful chuckle. 'I'll say.'

The next morning, as the early light bled into the council room, Wren's head was already aching. She sat beside Zavier, who'd been strangely understanding about her keeping Delmira a secret, while Lord Lucian Devereux, King Leiko, and Lady Liora had graciously come to the conclusion that the Embervales were indeed the rightful heirs to the kingdom. The newfound state of said kingdom was another thing entirely, and the rulers raged and bickered about what to do with the information. Meanwhile, Darian Devereux watched everything unfold with a bored expression, and Kipp sat at the far end of the table, his auburn hair falling over his eyes as he scribbled away in a small notebook.

'If we keep this hidden from the common folk, it's more fodder for the People's Vanguard to use against us. They'll say we're hiding resources, that we're deliberately keeping them in the dark,' Lady Liora argued, her face flushed with passion.

'And if we announce it to the midrealms, people will flock to Delmira and ravage the lands,' Audra countered.

The dispute had gone on in circles like this for the better part of an hour, and to Wren's further dismay, the chronicler Magnus Crane sat in the corner, scribbling away on a roll of parchment, glaring at her whenever he got the chance. Apparently, history was being written in this very room, by a biased fool.

Rubbing her temples, Wren glanced at Kipp, who was still quiet on the outskirts of the room, sipping from a mug she suspected contained something stronger than tea. But the strategist's eyes were bright with interest, his brows knitted together as he followed the debate back and forth.

At last, he cleared his throat. 'Until there is a structure in place for the governing of the kingdom, we cannot let this information spread,' he told the seated party. 'If Delmira is as superior as claimed, whoever holds the kingdom has an advantage in the conflict ahead. The last thing we can afford is for the enemy to get their hands on more potent ingredients, or to win over more of the common folk with promises of land. The People's Vanguard nearly bested us in Drevenor's own halls. If they can enhance their concoctions, it will be over for us.'

'Kristopher is right,' Audra said. 'Currently, only the silvertide rose from Delmira has been effective in Wren's experiments against the dark alchemy. If they get wind of this, we'd be giving them the very blade that ends us all.'

'So what?' King Leiko interjected. 'We're to wait until the Embervale girls – who have previously rejected the crown, might I add – decide the fate of the whole midrealms?'

The way he spat the word *girls* had Wren's blood boiling, as though she and Thea were still teenagers running around Thezmarr. They were women – women who had defended the midrealms and nearly lost everything. She had listened to men talk about her as though she wasn't there for long enough, and she was *done*.

Wren got to her feet and stared down the King of Tver. 'I may not wear a crown, Your Majesty, but I deserve your respect – or have you forgotten my role in the war? How I saved you? How I brought you back from the brink of insanity?'

'That's hardly—'

'I'm still speaking.' Wren had learned from the women who came before her how to make her words sharp enough to cut glass. Audra. Farissa. Anya. Thea. She rarely used that tone, but the utter disrespect in this chamber called for it now. 'I have summoned my sister here, and as the only living heirs of Delmira, she and I will decide how to handle this development. I assure you, I have no intention of hiding resources or abusing power, but nor will I hand the enemy the best chance we have at defeating them. Unless you have any genuine questions or suggestions, I have work to do.'

Wren waited a moment, watching as the realization dawned on each face before her that they had no choice but to wait, or declare war on her homeland.

'Good,' she said curtly, before leaving the room.

Torj was waiting for her outside. 'That went well . . .'

'You heard?' she asked.

'I heard you put those pricks in their places.'

A smile curled Wren's lips. 'Someone had to.'

'Elwren!' a voice called after them, and Wren turned to see Audra hurrying towards her. 'I'd like a word with you in private,' the Guild Master said without preamble.

Before Wren could answer, Audra was leading her into an empty room, dismissing Torj with a wave. When the door clicked closed, Audra faced her.

'I have a list of Warswords for you to choose from,' she stated, producing a piece of parchment from the folds of her cloak.

Wren stared blankly at the yellowed square. 'What?'

'It was never my intention to break my word to you,' Audra continued, still holding out the list. 'I agreed that in exchange for you creating the cure, Elderbrock would no longer be in your service, that we would find you a suitable replacement once Thea returned to her regular duties. I have not forgotten my promise.'

Wren stared at the tally of names as Audra pushed the parchment into her waiting hand.

'I'll have your choice of guard here within the next two days, and I'll have the Bear Slayer removed by the end of the week,' the Guild Master told her.

'I don't want a replacement,' Wren blurted, pushing the list back.

Audra's brow furrowed. 'You don't?'

It was as though Wren were watching herself from a distance, a stranger to her own actions, her own words, even as they threatened to carve her open anew.

'I'm his to protect,' she said. 'And he's mine.'

CHAPTER 41

Torj

'Often among circles of those in close protection roles, there is a misconception that if a guard is skilled enough, there is no need for their charge to carry a weapon. However, it is a guard's duty to equip their principle with every possible asset for protection'

— *The Guardian's Handbook: Principles and Practises of Personal Protection*

WREN LOOKED SHAKEN as she returned from her brief meeting with Audra. The latter looked subtly pleased – a fair sign that schemes were afoot and playing out exactly how she wanted. But Wren held her head high as she strode down the corridor. Elwren Embervale had always been a force to be reckoned with, but hearing her stand up for herself in a room full of small-minded pricks was something else entirely.

It wasn't until they turned a corner towards the dining hall that Torj noticed the new addition to her belt of potions.

His dagger.

If he had felt pride before, he didn't know this new sensation blooming in his chest – it was something far more smug, far more primal. He wasn't about to let her know that, though.

'Do you even know how to use that?' he asked with a nod to the blade in question. 'Properly?'

Wren looked down, as though she'd forgotten it was there. 'It seems simple enough.'

'You realize that's like me telling you that alchemy is simple?'

Wren shrugged. 'I felt like wearing something a little more . . . *commanding* today.'

Torj nodded. 'It suits you.'

'You think?'

'So long as you're wearing it and not wielding it for the moment,' Torj quipped. 'I'll teach you.'

'I'll be giving it back, so that's hardly necessary.'

But Torj shook his head. He didn't want it back. He liked that she was wearing something of his for the world to see.

⁓

Later, in the dining hall, Wren sat down opposite Torj, next to Kipp. Immediately the pair huddled with their heads close together, talking inaudibly as the rest of the hall dug into their dinners. Torj knew plotting when he saw it, and those two were up to no good.

He leaned in a little closer, busying himself with pouring a tankard of mead.

'Are you going to do anything with the information I gave you?' Kipp was saying, stuffing his face with roast potatoes.

'I'm looking into it,' Wren said stiffly, clearly avoiding Torj's eye across the table.

Kipp shrugged and loaded his plate with more food. 'So long as you remember—'

'A deal's a deal, I know.'

Torj couldn't help himself then. He waited until Wren's eyes met his. 'What's that about?'

'Nothing that concerns you, Bear Slayer,' she said lightly, taking a sip from her goblet.

'If you're getting into debts with the Son of the Fox, I feel like your bodyguard should know about it,' he ventured, glancing at Kipp, who was now deep in conversation with Dessa.

'My bodyguard knows what he needs to know,' Wren replied.

'I *highly* doubt that, Embers—'

'A word, if you don't mind, Elwren?' came a smooth voice that made Torj's skin crawl.

Devereux appeared by their table, and it was all Torj could do not to block her completely from his view. The fat lip the nobleman wore brought him some measure of satisfaction, though.

'In private,' Devereux added with a sly look at Torj.

Torj knew he had to keep himself in check. This was no deserted corridor. This was the busy dining hall of Drevenor Academy. If he threw a nobleman around again, people would notice.

As Wren gave her consent and stood with the smarmy prick, he had no choice but to fall back and watch them move to the edge of the hall. He hated that they looked good together – the handsome nobleman in his fine clothes and the beautiful alchemist. Who knew what honeyed words that snake was whispering in her ear?

'If you're going to burst into flame, Bear Slayer, can you kindly put a bit of distance between us first?' Kipp commented.

'Why are you always so intent on irritating me?' Torj replied moodily.

'I think you're doing that all on your own,' Kipp told him, with a glance at Wren and Devereux. 'They're just talking.'

'It's never just talking with Darian.' From the looks of things, the nobleman hadn't changed a bit. He still dressed like a pampered prince, still laced his words with false charm.

'I have news from Thezmarr,' Kipp said, voice low.

'Go on,' Torj replied, not taking his eyes off his charge.

'Cahira has been laid to rest on the Plains of Orax. Farissa went to examine the body herself. It was definitely a variant of the dark alchemy Lord Silas is using.'

'We guessed as much, didn't we?'

Kipp nodded. 'The missing Warsword has also been found.'

'Alive?'

'Dead. Killed the same way as Cahira.'

'Shit,' Torj muttered, his heart sinking. The strength that had risen from the ashes of the shadow war was fading. 'Our Warsword numbers are dwindling... Does Audra know how many are ready to take the Great Rite the next time it presents itself?'

'She told me three, maybe four,' Kipp said. 'But what good will that do if the enemy has the ability to strip them of their Furies-given strength the moment they have it?'

'We don't need Warswords for this fight,' Torj told him. 'We need alchemists.'

He hadn't stopped watching Wren and Devereux across the hall, noting the subtle stiffness in Wren's shoulders, and how her hand rested on the grip of his dagger.

'He's had more than enough time to chat, wouldn't you agree?' Kipp mused.

'For once, Kristopher, yes, I would.'

Torj strode over to Wren and placed himself between her and the nobleman.

'Time's up, Devereux.'

Devereux gave Wren an infuriating smile, followed by an even more infuriating bow. 'Until next time, Princess.'

As he walked off, Torj realized that Wren was still gripping his dagger.

'I'm definitely teaching you how to use that,' he told her.

CHAPTER 42

Wren

'The fool draws water from an empty well, while the wise seek new springs'

– *Arcane Alchemy: Unveiling the Mysteries of Matter*

WREN WAS A woman obsessed. She spent hours, days, hunched over her workbench, her back constantly aching. It was akin to wading through mud, trying to understand the properties of the dark alchemy, as well as what made the Delmirian rose different to the rest. Even wearing gloves, she had pricked herself on more thorns than she could count, her blood dotting the workbench, along with dozens of severed thorns.

She had always thought she worked well in organized chaos, but in the early hours of yet another morning, the clutter simply reflected the state of her mind. Nearly every surface was covered: a small wooden rack held vials of royal blood and alchemical concoctions, a mortar and pestle housed crushed herbs, and several open books with her notes in the margins were scattered about.

Any day now, the High Chancellor would call upon the adepts to present their findings, and with every day that passed, Wren was less sure of her convictions.

Peering into a shallow glass dish, she used a dropper to deposit three beads of blood into the sample. Nothing. Her supplies from Delmira were already dwindling, and those she tried to propagate didn't have the same effect in her alchemy. She had studied the samples of Delmirian soil. All the masters had. None of them could discern what made it more fertile than any other.

Wren buried herself in work, because every waking moment that she didn't she worried for Delmira and for her sister. She wasn't sure when to expect Thea's arrival, but with every day that passed, she grew more anxious, more guilt-ridden.

And then there was Torj . . . The Bear Slayer hardly left her side, despite what had happened between them. Wren was too tired to be angry; she was simply heartbroken, for the both of them. She tried to understand the secrets, the choices made for her, but all she was left with was a hollow feeling in the pit of her stomach.

Wren didn't want to feel that way for ever. Glancing up, she took in the sight of the towering Warsword, who was pacing her quarters for the millionth time, his movements methodical and efficient, that tic in his jaw the only tell that he wasn't alright.

'Have a drink with me,' she heard herself say suddenly.

Torj whirled around. 'What?'

'Was I speaking the ancient tongue of the Furies without realizing?' she replied. 'I said, have a drink with me, Bear Slayer. Must I always promise not to poison it first?'

They were in a strange place, caught somewhere between her sorrow and his regret, that wall of secrets now rubble between them. And yet she couldn't help wanting to be near him. She couldn't help craving his touch or relishing the sound of his husky voice. She missed him – missed *them*.

As usual, the Mortar and Pestle was bustling with scholars and students alike, with Kipp holding court at the bar. Wren and Torj had taken a corner booth away from the noise, and Wren was currently staring into a tankard.

'I've summoned Thea right into a waiting ambush,' she told the Bear Slayer. Just because they weren't together, didn't mean she couldn't talk to him. He had always been there for her, had always been a friend.

'What do you mean?' he asked gently.

'She's a Warsword.' Wren took a deep drink. 'I don't need to tell *you* how much that means to her. The world is asking her to be a queen instead, to give up her totem and swords.'

'You think it's only a symbol and some steel that makes a warrior a Warsword?' Torj asked, motioning to the armband of three crossed swords around his bicep.

But Wren put her head in her hands, despair gnawing at her from within. 'Thea was happy. She gave everything in the war, and she was meant to live the days after it in peace – or hunting monsters abroad, which is her version of that. Now I've got her tangled in this mess.'

'This isn't your fault,' Torj told her. 'You didn't start a rebellion. You didn't attack a king or queen—'

'I may as well have,' Wren argued. 'They used my work as a foundation for their own evils. The alchemy I used on those manacles all those years ago . . . It had the ability to target certain properties, like the Furies-given strength that Warswords have. Silas took that and has been altering it – to weaken Warswords, to mute the magic of royals. It's my design, the alchemy that targets. My fault.' She sighed. 'Perhaps there was a certain comfort back then. When you faced a monster, you knew that danger and death awaited in fangs and talons, in the shadows lashing at you. But now . . . With the men of the midrealms, there's no telling what threats lurk beneath their jewels and fine clothes. No knowing what perils are threaded between their elegant speeches and formalities. Do you ever think that things seemed simpler in the shadow war? Monsters were bad, we were good . . . But now everything is in shades of grey.'

'*You* are good, Wren,' Torj said.

She gave a dark laugh, starting as he gripped her hands in his. They hadn't touched since that night when they'd laid it all out on the table.

'Oh?' was all she managed.

'You are good and decent, kind and loyal, clever and determined. There is no one else I would want by my side, whether it's wartime or not.'

His words made her ache. She drew her hands back out of his grasp and took another *long* drink.

'And yet I'm failing the task I was given,' she replied flatly.

'You haven't failed,' he told her.

'No? What's it called when you don't get a result?' she countered. 'I've tried so many versions of this.'

'It's called progress,' Torj said, his voice low and earnest. He moved closer, his eyes locked on hers. 'Every attempt, every failure, is a step forwards. You're mapping uncharted territory, Embers. No one has done this before.'

'And what if no one can?' She voiced the fears aloud, as she had done with him before. No matter what was happening between them, she seemed to always find herself opening up to him like she did with no one else. It was easy, confiding in him. It always had been.

He reached out, hesitating for a moment before taking her hand in his once more. 'If there's one thing I know about you, it's that you don't give up.'

There seemed to be a layered meaning to those words, an unsaid truth that pulsed between them.

'Perhaps it's time I did,' she said quietly.

But Torj shook his head. 'That's not who you are.'

'And you know me so well?' she challenged, suddenly realizing how close he was, his scent wrapping around her.

'Better than I know myself sometimes . . .'

Heat crept up Wren's neck. 'That's quite a claim.'

'The midrealms need your stubborn streak. So keep trying. Keep *failing*. It only brings you that much closer to your goal.'

'If you say so . . .'

'Has anyone ever told you that you're a morose drunk?' he asked.

Wren raised a brow and replied dryly, 'I'm usually a barrel of laughs.'

'Sure you are, Embers,' Torj teased. 'That's why we're nursing the same warm drinks, sitting here in the back, away from all the merriment.'

It felt both strange and natural to be here with him, joking as though there weren't a huge barrier between them. Wren wanted to sink into that old comfort, that blanket of normality and safety the Warsword had become. She peered over his shoulder to where Kipp was waving his arms about as he told yet another story, her lips quirking to the side before she downed her drink.

'You want to be in the heart of the party, Bear Slayer?' she asked, signalling for another round.

'Well, nothing crazy, I just thought—'

Wren cupped her hands around her mouth and shouted, 'Kipp!'

'Shit,' Torj muttered, twisting in his seat to see the strategist's face light up.

'How about one of your toasts for the Bear Slayer?' Wren called.

Torj groaned, his head dropping to the table.

Sure enough, there was a blur of movement, and Kipp was at their table in an instant.

Wren didn't leave it there. She needed fun. She needed escape. She needed to torment the Bear Slayer, just a little. So she knocked her fresh tankard against Kipp's with a grin. 'Torj was just saying how much he *loves* your toasts. Particularly when you're regaling tales of his heroics . . .'

Torj grunted. 'I was *not—*'

But Kipp was already hitting a fork to the side of his drink, the sound ringing out across the entire tavern, drawing everyone's attention. 'Ladies and gentlemen! Good folks of the Mortar and Pestle!'

Torj glared at Wren, and she noticed the tips of his ears turning red, a small tell that brought her a glimmer of joy amid the gloom.

'You're going to regret this, Embers,' he muttered.

Wren beamed. 'A bodyguard threatening his charge? That must break the handbook rules . . .'

'You're unbelievable,' he said between gritted teeth.

'I am indeed.'

Kipp's loud voice projected to the corners of the tavern. 'Among us tonight is a legend of Thezmarr,' he declared, raising his tankard high, foam slopping over the sides and onto his doublet. 'A true hero of the midrealms. Though he may prefer monsters to a cheering crowd, let's hear it for him anyway! To Torj Elderbrock—'

Wren grinned as Torj groaned, his face flaming.

'—may your ale never run dry, may your enemies always cower, and may you never run out of bears to slay!' Kipp shouted. 'To the Bear Slayer! The man, the myth, the legend!'

Wren joined in the cheering as the elated crowd swarmed the warrior. Torj's sea-blue gaze met hers, and she grinned, lifting her tankard in salute.

CHAPTER 43

Wren

'Observatory Hill is the single best location on the
eastern isle of Naarva for studies of astronomy, and
for alchemy that aligns with any phases of the moon'

– *Drevenor Academy Handbook*

'ENJOY THAT, DID you, Embers?' Torj's voice was low as he extricated himself from well-wishers and fawning women and rejoined Wren, who was sitting in their corner booth feeling smug.

'Immensely,' she replied, still grinning. 'Now who's a terrible drunk?'

'Drunk?' he scoffed. 'Not even close. You, on the other hand? That's a different story.'

Wren waved her glass at him. 'I've been drinking water for the past hour, Bear Slayer. While you are leaning a little far to the left.'

She watched as Torj looked down, taking stock of his body. 'Am I swaying? Or is that the bar?' he asked, blinking slowly.

'Come on, Warsword. Let's get you back to your room before Kipp calls for another toast.'

'That was your fault,' Torj slurred.

'So it was,' she said with a laugh.

'Gods, I love that sound . . .' he murmured, leaning closer.

Wren smiled, secretly loving this uninhibited version of the warrior. 'Is that so?'

Torj blinked at her again, as though he hadn't meant to say those words aloud. 'I'm going to kill Kipp,' he grumbled. 'I should throttle him for endangering my ability to perform my duties.'

'Perhaps tomorrow, Bear Slayer.' Wren was waiting beside him. 'Shall we?'

Torj stumbled, and Wren looped his muscled arm around her shoulders. She knew the sight must be ridiculous. If he fell, she had no hope of catching him. In fact, he'd take her with him. But she couldn't seem to pull away. She liked his closeness.

'Are you smelling my hair, Bear Slayer?' she asked as someone held the door open for them and she hauled him through.

He inhaled deeply. 'No.'

Wren laughed again as they staggered across the grounds. 'Oh, how the tables have turned . . . Last time it was you carrying me back to the room.'

'You're hardly carrying me, Embers,' Torj muttered, and he lifted her up off her feet.

'Put me down!' she shrieked, laughter still on her lips.

For a moment, she glimpsed the life she might have had: carefree, stumbling home with Torj, chasing each other through the dew-soaked grass. The easy conversation, the quiet moments in between. Gods, it made her chest ache.

She made a show of kicking her legs and he carefully set her down. When she peered up at him, she could sense the shift in his mood. But she wasn't ready for the fun to be over, not when there was so little of it these days. They deserved one night of laughter, didn't they? One night of stupidity?

Wren bumped her hip against his side. 'Do you remember how angry you were with Cal when he was drunk on duty?' she teased.

Torj snorted. 'I'm not drunk. I'm tipsy.'

Wren patted his arm, pulling him towards the doors to the main building. 'If you say so, Bear Slayer.'

'You know,' he declared, 'I hate it when you call me that.'

'Because?'

'Because it's not my name. Not to you.' He halted before the grand doors, as though he didn't want to cross the threshold. 'Are you cold?' he said suddenly, apparently seized by an idea.

'No. Why?' she asked. He was close enough that his body heat was radiating outwards, keeping the night's chilly air at bay.

'I want to stay out a little longer.' Torj tipped his chin to the sky. 'I want to see the stars.'

'Is that safe, bodyguard?' Wren quipped, mentally picking the best spot on the grounds for stargazing and debating the risks versus the reward.

'You're always safe with me,' he told her.

'It feels that way,' she admitted, keeping her arm linked through his and guiding him away from the building. 'But I'm not sure that's always the case.'

The Warsword nodded sadly. 'I've let you down in the past.'

'I know you'd never let anything happen to me.' She hadn't been talking about her physical safety, anyway; she'd been talking about her heart – bruised and broken by his words. But she didn't want to have this conversation. Not now. Not as she led him towards the best place to view the stars. 'Do you miss being on the road?' she asked instead.

'No,' he said. 'I miss *you*.'

Wren stopped walking and looked up at the man towering beside her.

His eyes were on her, clear and bright. 'It's *you* I miss,' he told her again, cupping her face in his hands. 'I miss talking with you. I miss your smile. I miss the weight of you in my arms. I miss . . . everything.' The words seemed to tumble from his lips, a broken dam of feeling.

Wren struggled to swallow the thick lump in her throat.

Torj dropped his hands and took a deep breath, as though measuring his next words. 'I thought you were taking me to see the stars, Embers . . .'

Wren hesitated, just for a moment. He sounded so lost, so broken, that she wanted to be a balm for those wounds, however briefly. As devastated as she was, she never wanted to see him hurting. She tugged on his sleeve. 'I am. Keep up.'

Dessa had told her about the place – Observatory Hill. An elevated grassy knoll on the very outskirts of the grounds, in a clearing in Evermere Forest, away from the lights and chimney smoke of the academy.

Together, they hiked to the summit. Wren's legs burned from the climb, but the ache was nothing compared to the flutter in her chest every time Torj's hand brushed against hers. When they finally reached the top, they lay on their backs, Wren flushed and suddenly nervous, the cool grass a stark contrast to her warm skin.

The night sky unfurled above them, a canvas of countless stars. Wren's heart caught in her throat. She'd seen the stars before, of course, but never like this – never with him this close.

She made a flourish with her hands. 'Here you go. Stars,' she said, as though she had made them herself.

'Thank you,' Torj replied roughly.

Wren dropped her hands by her sides, her fingers curling into the soft grass. She blinked up at the twinkling silver against the darkness. 'Why did you want to see them?' Her voice was barely a whisper, afraid to shatter the moment.

Warm fingers found hers, callused yet gentle. Wren's heart raced at the contact.

'Maybe because when I look up there, it doesn't all feel so impossible,' Torj murmured. His words seemed to vibrate through her, settling deep in her bones. 'During the years after the war, I'd look up at the night sky and find comfort in the thought that you might be looking up at the same time. I liked to think that life is made up of smaller moments, threads in a tapestry of something much bigger . . .'

Wren's heart seized, her fingers tightening around his. 'And what is it about these smaller moments?'

'They're what make the infinity bearable. Wren, I—'

She heard him swallow, hard. The vulnerability in his voice made her want to turn and look at him, but she was afraid of what she might see in his eyes – or what he might see in hers.

'The moments with you, anyway,' he went on. 'With you, every second feels important.'

Wren's throat tightened, tears burning at the corners of her eyes. 'When was the last time you lived in the moment?' she asked softly. The name *Bear Slayer* danced on the tip of her tongue, but she held it back. After what he'd admitted, the title seemed more like a burden than an honour.

'That night in the room . . .' he said, his voice low and husky. Memories of that night flooded Wren's senses – his touch, his scent, the look in his eyes, the heat of his body on hers. 'I forgot about consequences and duty. There was only you.'

Wren turned her head then, finally allowing herself to look at him. Torj's profile was etched against the starry backdrop, his features softened by starlight. She watched as he swallowed again, his throat bobbing, and felt an overwhelming urge to trace the line of his jaw with her fingertips.

'And now?' she whispered, her heart pounding so wildly she was sure he must be able to hear it. 'Are you living in the moment now, Torj?'

He turned to face her, their noses almost touching. His eyes, reflecting the starlight, were clear now. 'I'm trying,' he murmured, his breath warm against her cheek. 'Gods, Wren, I'm trying.'

Ever since the truth had come out about Delmira, Wren had felt as if she were standing on the edge of a precipice, the vast unknown before her utterly terrifying.

But here, under the infinite sky with Torj's hand in hers, she wondered if she'd be brave enough to fall again – or if she'd ever stopped falling at all.

CHAPTER 44

Torj

'The sense of responsibility a guard feels for his ward is prolific, even when circumstances go beyond their control, dedication, or skill'

– *Vigilance and Valour: Tactical Training for Professional Bodyguards*

'Kipp,' Torj groaned. 'Not so loud, for Furies' sake.'

His head was pounding. A fact made no better by Kipp's jovial recounting of the previous night's antics at the Mortar and Pestle over the breakfast table.

'I did warn you that you were overindulging,' Kipp said with an infuriating smirk.

'Horseshit. You practically poured the fire extract down my throat.'

Kipp scoffed. 'Let's be realistic, Bear Slayer. Could I, with my mere average mortal strength, actually force you to do anything?'

Torj simply grunted. 'I should throttle you anyway.'

'Drink this first,' Wren said from beside him, removing a spoon from a fresh cup of juice and pushing it towards him.

'If you're meaning to poison me, I think I did enough of that myself last night,' he muttered, taking the cup. 'Or perhaps you mean to put me out of my misery.'

'Has anyone ever told you you're a touch dramatic when you're hungover?' Wren asked, her lips quirking to the side.

'It's not dramatic if you're dying, Embers,' he replied gruffly, eyeing the offered drink suspiciously.

Wren pushed it closer to him. 'Who knew Warswords were such babies? It's a rehydration tonic,' she added.

'Where's mine?' Kipp blurted, looking hurt.

Wren laughed. 'I suspect any water in your poor body turned to sour mead long ago. You don't need one.'

Kipp turned to Dessa, pouting. 'You'll make me one, won't you, beautiful alchemist?'

Dessa snorted. 'You made your bed, Kristopher. Now you need to lie in it. Adepts don't have time to make fools hangover cures.'

Mouth agape, Kipp thrust a finger in Wren's direction. 'Wren did for Torj!'

Dessa smiled slyly at the Delmirian heir. 'She did indeed . . . Why is that, I wonder?'

Torj was too hungover for this shit, but he didn't miss the glare Wren sent Dessa's way, or the delicious blush that stained the tips of her cheeks.

He brought the cup to his lips and downed the lot. His eyes bulged, and he only just managed to keep the foul liquid in and not spray it across the table.

Chest heaving, he turned, horrified, to Wren. 'That was disgusting.'

'The price you pay for blowing off so much steam,' she said with a shrug.

The fact that she had recognized why he'd 'overindulged,' as Kipp put it, was a testament to how well she knew him. He'd typically have a few drinks here and there, but he never got caught up in the chaos, not since becoming her guard – with the exception of last night.

They'd watched the stars together.

He'd held her hand.

He'd memorized the constellation of freckles across her nose in the moonlight.

'Are you coming, Torj?' Her voice cut through the haze of his thoughts.

Torj.

Not Bear Slayer. Not Warsword.

Torj.

For the briefest of moments, he half expected that when he looked up, Wren would be holding out her hand, ready for him to lace his fingers through hers. He'd brush his thumb over her knuckles and then draw her close to his side, wrapping an arm around her shoulders for all to see.

But Wren wasn't holding out her hand. She was talking to Kipp, their voices hushed, their expressions unusually serious.

'What's going on?' he demanded, getting to his feet, pleasantly surprised to find that his head was no longer spinning.

'Nothing of note,' Wren said dismissively.

'Embers . . .' he warned. Kipp was always full of schemes, and if his charge was getting caught up in something dangerous, he needed to know.

'You had your secrets, and now I have mine,' she replied. 'Now hurry up. Zavier, Dessa and I have booked one of the workshop rooms.'

༄

'Another Warsword has gone missing,' Cal told him as the two warriors stood guard outside the alchemy workshop.

'What?' Torj whirled to face him. 'Who? When?'

'I got a letter from Thezmarr this morning . . .' Cal said slowly. 'It's Vernich.'

'Vernich?' Torj stared at his former protégé. 'Vernich's retired. He's been in some fishing village for years.'

Cal shrugged. 'I only know what I've been told. Apparently Esyllt keeps in touch with him and never heard back. When he sent some Guardians to investigate, they reported that his place was empty, and there were signs of a struggle . . .'

'Fuck,' Torj muttered. Vernich had always inspired controversy with his harsh brand of training methods and generally nasty demeanour, with Kipp bearing the brunt of his brutality as a shield-bearer. However, the war had shown everyone a different side of the older Warsword.

Torj pinched the bridge of his nose as shock rippled through him. Vernich Warner, the oldest of the three original Warswords from the shadow war, the warrior known as the Bloodletter, was *missing*.

Sighing, he said, 'I know you have a complicated history with Vernich, but . . .'

'He's one of us,' Cal finished with a nod. 'Kipp forgave him during the war, and if he could do that after what Vernich did to him, then who am I to hold a grudge?'

'Truth be told, I don't know who I feel sorrier for,' Torj replied. 'Vernich, or the morons who made the mistake of capturing him . . .'

Cal laughed at that. 'True. He's a hard bastard, that's for sure. Audra's got people out looking. I've never seen her so fucking angry. Apparently, she developed a soft spot for him over the years—'

A scream of rage pierced the air, cutting Cal off.

Both Warswords burst into the workshop, and Torj didn't know where to look first. Countless alchemy tools and bottles were suspended in the air, with Zavier standing in the middle, his face turned to the ceiling, his palms outstretched – *summoning magic*. On the far side of the room, Wren was shielding Dessa with her body, Torj's dagger in one hand, a ball of lightning crackling in the other—

'Zavier,' she called, a note of panic in her voice. 'Zavier, you have to calm down—'

But the Prince of Naarva gave another shout, and half the items in the air came crashing down. Glass splintered, flames burst into life in one corner—

'I can't save him,' Zavier choked out. 'Why can't I save him?'

Cal was at his side, trying to bring him out of whatever trance he was in, shaking him by the shoulders.

'I've failed them,' Zavier murmured, sending more paraphernalia flying across the room.

Torj was at Wren's side in a matter of strides, covering her body with his, blocking any flying debris from hitting her and Dessa.

'Cal . . .' he warned, as more glass shattered.

'He won't stop,' Cal called desperately. Even with Zavier's arms clamped to his sides with Furies-given strength, his summoning power raged on.

'We have to sedate him,' Dessa said from behind Wren. 'It's the only way.'

Wren was nodding, already reaching for her belt.

'I can't save him. I can't save him,' Zavier was still chanting.

Producing a vial, Wren tried to make a move for the prince—

'You're not going near him,' Torj told her, snatching the potion from her hands. 'Does he ingest this?'

For once, Wren didn't argue; she simply nodded.

Flipping a table to act as a barrier between Zavier and his fellow alchemists, Torj strode right for him. 'Get his mouth open,' he ordered Cal.

His former protégé did exactly that, holding his charge's nose until he gasped for air. Torj forced the small vial to Zavier's lips and emptied its contents into his mouth.

Everything suspended in the air around them fell as Zavier slumped to the floor in Cal's arms.

Torj didn't waste any time. He was back at Wren's side in seconds, scanning her for signs of injury.

'Are you alright? Did he hurt you?' he demanded.

Wren shook her head, dazed. 'He . . . he just lost it. One minute he was telling us how the work on his opus wasn't going to plan, and the next . . .' Her hands were trembling.

Torj looked to Dessa. 'Are you hurt?'

Wren's friend wore a similar expression of shock. 'I don't think so . . .'

'I'm taking him to Farissa,' Cal said from where he stood by the door, Zavier still unconscious in his arms. Cal's face was pale, stricken with the guilt that Torj knew all too well.

'You couldn't have done anything differently,' Torj told him.

Cal only shook his head.

'Tell Farissa we gave him valerian root essence,' Wren said, voice wavering. 'If she agrees, I think he should be sedated for the rest of the night.'

'I'll go with them,' Dessa announced, following as Cal carried Zavier from the workshop.

Torj watched Wren take in the destruction around them. 'Word of this can't get out,' she murmured. 'Both Zavier *and* me having trouble controlling our magic? The People's Vanguard would use it to unite the rest of the midrealms against us.' She crouched down in the mess, retrieving Torj's dagger with trembling fingers and offering it to him. 'I think it's time I gave this back to you.'

But Torj closed his hands over hers and pushed it back to her. 'No. I think it's time I taught you how to use it.'

CHAPTER 45

Torj

'Balance kept is ground never lost'

– *The Guardian's Handbook: Principles and Practises of Personal Protection*

'I TOLD YOU it wasn't designed for hands as small as yours,' Torj said, surveying Wren as she held his dagger. 'The weight and balance are wrong for you.'

'I thought you were going to *teach me*. Not stand here complaining,' Wren replied.

'I will, but you should really use a different dagger. We could get you one made.'

'I like *this* one.'

'Stubborn woman.' Torj shook his head. 'Show me your grip first, then.'

They stood in the grounds just beyond the greenhouses, in a clearing on the edge of Evermere Forest. Wren wore her usual simple gown, and while Torj had been tempted to tell her that trousers would be more practical, he decided that when it came to the poisoner, he had to pick his battles wisely.

Wren held the dagger out in her right hand, fingers curled around the grip. 'Like this?'

'Keep your hold firm, but not unyielding,' he told her, his callused hand enveloping hers as he adjusted her fingers on the hilt. The simple touch sent a familiar ache through his chest. 'Too tight and you'll compromise your own ability to move and adapt. Too loose . . .' He knocked the blade from her grasp easily, catching it by the tip with his free hand. 'And you're weaponless.'

The move brought him closer than Torj had intended, and her subtle intake of breath didn't escape his notice. He tried to ignore the intoxicating scent of her, his rough palm tingling where it pressed against hers as he returned the dagger. 'A dagger is good for when you're too close to throw your poisons and potions, and when you've already been physically overpowered.'

'Is my boot the best place to keep it?' she asked. 'You change between keeping it there or sheathed at your side.'

'It matters less for me,' he explained. 'People expect a Warsword to be armed to the teeth. If I have one in my belt, I likely also have one in my boot. You, however, have the element of surprise, the advantage of being underestimated . . .' He gestured to her skirts. 'Keep it where it's comfortable and within easy reach. In your boot or strapped to your thigh beneath your layers is usually best.'

Wren nodded. 'I'll get something fashioned.'

Torj loved watching her mind work. He could see the plans forming in the furrows of her brow. 'You're getting ahead of yourself there,' he told her, suppressing a smile. 'Show me your grip again.'

She did. Torj tried to knock the blade from her grasp again, but Wren held firm.

'Good!' He shifted and looked to her feet. 'Now your positioning. It's the same principles you've learned before, but everything flows from a solid foundation.' He nudged her stance wider with the toe of his boot.

Wren took to it easily. 'Thea drilled this one into me while you were gone.'

A tug of regret threatened to drag Torj under – that he hadn't been here for her, that someone else had taught her in his place – but he squashed those feelings down. 'Thea did a good job,' he said instead.

'I'd expect nothing else,' Wren replied. 'Now what?'

Torj guided her arm into a defensive position, hyper-aware of how she tensed at his touch. There was a time when she would have melted into him at such a moment. 'Have you ever heard of the warrior's second?' he asked.

'Only once. You mentioned it, when you talked about . . .' She trailed off.

'The soul bond?' he finished for her with a note of regret. 'Well, it's something we're taught as shieldbearers. When you're fighting for your life, there's a surreal moment, right before one opponent claims victory. It's the intake of breath before the slice of a blade, or the swing of a hammer . . . The warrior's second where we make our actions count, make them worthy of legend. I hope you never have to use your warrior's second, but if you do . . .' Torj demonstrated a sharp upwards motion. 'In a close fight, you'll likely be rivalled for strength, so it'll be rare that you're attacking from above. Mostly, you'll be wanting to use uppercut movements. Show me.'

When she lunged, he caught her wrist – gently, always gently with her. Instead of releasing her, his Warsword instincts took over and he pulled her closer. Suddenly she was pressed against him, her dagger arm trapped between them, and the familiar softness of her nearly broke his composure.

'This is why you need to be lighter on your feet.' His voice came out rougher than intended as he tried desperately to focus on the lesson rather than how right she felt against him.

But he'd lost the privilege to let his touch linger. He stepped around to face her, missing her warmth immediately.

'Try again, and remember to avoid striking bone where you can. The blade can get stuck, and if you don't have the strength to pull it out, you've just lost your weapon. Not to mention – really pissed someone off.'

Wren laughed, and the sound lifted the weight on Torj's chest, if only for a moment.

'Mirror me,' he told her, leading her through a series of simple movements, watching her determination build with each repetition. She'd always been a fast learner; it was one of the countless things he admired about her. As good a teacher as he was, he wished he could be half as efficient at mending what he'd broken between them.

'You're better than I expected,' he admitted. 'You weren't with Thea *that* long.'

Wren smiled sadly. 'I guess I never told you about Dancing Alchemists, then?'

'Dancing *what*?' Torj asked, stepping back and pausing their lesson for a moment. Another laugh escaped Wren, and he found himself smiling back at her.

'It was a game Thea, Ida, Sam and I used to play back at Thezmarr when we were younger,' she explained. 'It basically involved throwing knives at each other's feet and jumping out of the way.'

'What in the midrealms was the point of that?' he blurted.

Wren grinned. 'To avoid losing a toe?'

Torj chuckled. 'Good to know the alchemists of Thezmarr were just as foolhardy as the shieldbearers.'

'It was Thea's idea,' Wren offered with a shrug.

'I don't doubt it.'

Torj showed her all the basic techniques with a dagger – blocks, strikes, footwork patterns. But with each exchange, the air between them grew heavier with unspoken tension. Every correction became an excuse for contact, every demonstration a dance of desire that simmered just below the surface, despite the hurt that was buried beneath Wren's determination – the hurt that *he* had put there.

Torj forced himself to swallow the lump in his throat. 'In close quarters like this, your enemy's sword is useless. But a blade like this . . .' He guided the dagger in her hand in an upwards motion that could pierce between an opponent's ribs. 'That's dangerous.'

Like the way you're looking at me now, he thought as Wren's stormy eyes met his.

'When you fight with a dagger, you need to be efficient. Every movement should have a purpose, no wasted motion,' he told her. Unable to resist, he closed the short distance between them in two fluid steps. One hand caught her blade while the other settled at the small of her back. His traitorous heart raced. 'Like that.'

Her breath hitched. 'Very efficient.'

'Do you want to try?' he asked, using every ounce of willpower he had not to pull her into his arms.

'No,' she said, stepping away, allowing the cold to sweep in. 'I think I've got the hang of it for now.'

Torj hated the distance, hated the pain still lacing her words. 'Are you sure?'

'I'm sure,' she told him firmly, handing his dagger back. 'We're done here.'

CHAPTER 46

Wren

'The thicket's thorns ask no permission to protect what blooms within'

— *Elwren Embervale's notes and observations*

WREN WAS SITTING on her bed, having stared at the same page of her textbook for over an hour. Zavier was still in the infirmary. When he had woken from the initial dose of valerian root, he had had another episode, resulting in a healer being injured. Farissa had told Wren they would keep him sedated until he was no longer a threat to others or himself.

Dessa had been withdrawn ever since, and Torj . . . Torj still made her heart hurt. Wren winced as she tried to palm the grit from her bloodshot, puffy eyes. She was so tired of crying. So tired of feeling broken. Her head was throbbing, and she was considering making up a sleeping draft when her door creaked open.

With her vision somewhat blurred, she sent her poison-tipped hairpin hurling at her uninvited guest.

'Fuck!' Thea shouted, jumping several feet in the air from where the weapon in question had embedded itself between her feet. 'You haven't lost your touch, Wren.'

At the sight of her sister's familiar grin, Wren couldn't help it; she fell apart. Fresh tears tracked down her face and she let out a sob.

'Wren . . .' Thea murmured, her grin fading instantly as she rushed to the bedside. 'What's wrong? What happened? Who do I need to kill?'

Wren threw her arms around Thea's neck. 'It's good to see you, Thee.'

Thea squeezed her tightly, and despite the armour she was wearing, Wren felt the warmth of her, felt the gentle hand cradling the back of her head and stroking her hair.

Wren was usually the first to break away from an embrace. Sometimes the contact became too much, made her feel too vulnerable, like she might crack if she was given the support to do so. But she had already cracked, had already broken, and Thea was here to see her in all her messy glory. And so Wren clung to her sister for a few moments longer, the tears still falling.

At last, she peeled herself away and palmed at the wet tracks on her face. 'You're here.'

Thea surveyed her, gaze lingering on the dark circles Wren knew shadowed her eyes, and the swollen red tip of her nose. But her sister didn't ask, not yet. Instead, she nodded. 'I would have been here sooner were it not for Queen Reyna. She's been a royal pain in my arse ever since I met up with her and Wilder. I practically had to drag her here.'

'Thank you for coming,' Wren said, her voice threatening to crack again. 'I . . . I need you.'

Thea made a show of looking her over again. 'Clearly.'

A hoarse laugh bubbled out of Wren at that.

Thea pushed a pile of books off the bed, the tomes thudding to the ground. She settled herself on the other end of the mattress, shoving a few pillows behind her and looking to Wren with surprise. 'You must be out of sorts if you didn't round on me for not treating the books with respect.'

Wren motioned to her blotchy face. 'Clearly,' she echoed back.

Thea stretched out her legs, crossing them at the ankle, and pinned Wren with a knowing look. 'I'm guessing this isn't about Delmira and the political nightmare unfolding around us.'

'No.'

'The Bear Slayer?' Thea guessed. 'He's standing guard out there like the midrealms' moodiest statue. Hardly said two words to me. Do you want to talk about it?'

The thing between Wren and the Warsword was beautiful, like the rose she had been so desperately trying to propagate . . . But it was not without its thorns, and it had left them both bleeding more times than she could count.

'Eventually,' Wren told her. She got up and went to the washroom. After splashing cold water on her face, she returned to Thea. 'It's been a while since I sparred properly.'

Thea grinned. 'Then say no more, sister. Let's go.'

Wren rummaged through her trunk of clothes and found some leggings and a form-fitting shirt. She made quick work of stripping out of her dress and apron and into the new garb while Thea perused her workbench. When she had laced her boots and fastened her cloak, she reached for the door. 'Coming?'

Thea surged forwards, and Wren soon realized it was to place herself between Wren and Torj, who was indeed standing guard outside. He was as handsome as ever, even with the dark smudges beneath his eyes and his broad shoulders caving slightly forwards.

'You've got the night off, Bear Slayer,' Thea declared, slinging an arm around Wren. 'Don't wait up.'

'Thea,' Torj implored. 'That's not how this works. I don't—'

'She's got her Warsword guard,' Thea countered. 'I protected her before; I'll protect her tonight. End of story.'

Thea was already tugging her towards the stairs, and Wren's heart warmed. She'd missed her sister's rebellious spirit.

'*Thea*.' Torj's voice was firmer now as he started after them. 'You can't—'

'Know when to pick your battles, brother,' a familiar voice sounded from the other side of the corridor.

Wilder Hawthorne looked the same as he always had: an imposing figure wrapped in black leather, his two swords peeking from behind his back. He wore a resigned expression on his dark features.

Wilder lifted the bottle of wine he was holding towards Torj. 'Drink?'

Wren felt Torj's gaze on her, but she didn't meet it. Instead, she let Thea guide her down the hall, leaving the men in their wake.

The hour was late, so thankfully, the gymnasium was empty. As Wren pushed open the heavy wooden doors, the familiar scent of leather and sweat enveloped her. In the open space, with its high, vaulted ceilings and expanse of uninterrupted floor, Wren felt as though she could breathe again.

With that relief came perspective. Wren had spent the past two days thinking of nothing but the Warsword she'd just left behind. Despite the myriad of greater issues that demanded her attention, she hadn't been able to cast the Bear Slayer and what he'd told her from her mind. But now that Thea was here, solid and real before her, she could not ignore those greater issues any longer.

As Thea stripped off the bulk of her armour, the metallic clanks echoing in the empty space, Wren studied her sister. Thea's movements were fluid, her warrior's body honed by years of training and constant practise. Wren felt a pang of guilt as she realized how much she'd neglected her own physical conditioning lately. The burning pain she often felt in her back as she worked was a direct result of that neglect. Even now, she could feel the tightness in her muscles as she rolled her shoulders. The endless hours of crying hadn't helped.

'Ready?' Thea asked, raising an eyebrow.

Wren nodded, forcing a small smile. They fell easily back into the routine Thea had created for them when she'd been Wren's temporary bodyguard. As they moved through the familiar stretches, Wren felt some of the tension begin to leave her body.

The rhythmic sound of their breathing and the occasional pop of her joints filling the silence was oddly comforting.

'You haven't been training as much,' Thea observed as Wren dabbed the sweat from her brow with her sleeve. There was no judgement in her tone, only concern.

Wren avoided eye contact, focusing instead on a scuff mark on the floor. 'Things have been a little chaotic here.'

'Don't forget that moving your body helps,' Thea said gently, reaching out to correct Wren's form. 'It's the thing that houses that brilliant mind of yours. You've got to take care of it.'

'I know,' Wren sighed, the weight of everything she'd been carrying suddenly feeling impossibly heavy. 'It's been hard, Thee.'

The fact that she was admitting it told Wren just how much she'd been struggling. Usually she was a grit-her-teeth-and-get-through-it kind of woman; to admit hardship, even to Thea, meant that things were worse than she feared. The realization sent a shiver down her spine, despite the warmth of exertion.

The way Thea's celadon gaze softened told Wren her sister had come to the same conclusion, that she saw past the steel exterior Wren so often presented to the world.

'You're allowed to buckle sometimes, you know,' Thea said softly.

Wren gave a rough laugh. 'I feel like that's all I've been doing.' She followed Thea's lead through the next round of stretches, holding her elbow above her head and feeling the pull through her entire side. 'I don't know how you do it,' she muttered.

Thea frowned. 'Do what?'

'Stay so strong. During the war, after the war. You're a powerhouse. You never falter.'

Thea dropped her arms and stared at Wren. 'Is that what you think?'

'It's true,' Wren said, letting her arms fall to her sides and waiting for the next exercise.

But Thea didn't move on. 'Wren . . . I hate to break it to you, but I think you're forgetting a few key moments.'

Wren scoffed.

Thea's eyes didn't leave hers. 'You don't remember me crying on the clifftops about the stupid stable boy?'

'You were a teenager—'

'I'm not done,' Thea replied sharply. 'You don't remember the year I couldn't use my storm magic? The entire year I was so convinced that Wilder had betrayed me that I nearly ruined myself? What about when we thought we lost Kipp? Or when Anya died? Or when we saw Sam and Ida on those spikes? You think I didn't falter then? You think I didn't despair?'

Wren stared at her sister.

Thea cursed under her breath. 'I thought I made it clear when we were first training together, after whatever happened between you and Torj, that you could talk to me. That I *wanted* you to talk to me. That I'm *here*, even when I'm not.'

Thea shifted into another set of stretches, and Wren followed her lead, feeling the burn in her thighs, her calves.

'It's . . .' She trailed off.

'Not that easy, I know,' Thea said. 'But it's not about staying or looking strong. It's about getting through it in whatever way you can.'

Wren wrung her hands, still not quite comfortable with so much outwards emotion. Thea's sincerity and concern was forming a knot under her ribs. 'I appreciate it, I really do, but . . . right now, there are bigger things to worry about than me,' Wren told her, fighting the quaver in her voice. 'Thea . . . what's happening with Delmira—'

'I know,' Thea murmured. 'It's bad. Audra filled me in when I arrived.'

The missive Wren had sent her sister by raven had been vague for fear of it being intercepted, but she was glad the Guild Master had seen to the details. She wasn't sure she had the energy to rehash the politics.

Thea shook out her arms and legs, her muscles rippling. She

met Wren's gaze, her eyes dark with concern. 'Someone will make a play for the throne,' she said, confirming what Wren already knew.

Wren nodded. 'I think there are several plots already in motion,' she replied, her voice low. She leaned against a nearby pillar, its cool stone a stark contrast to her heated skin. 'I've been talking with Kipp between classes. He has several theories about which parties are putting their chess pieces in place.'

Thea's jaw clenched. 'So you and I need to talk about what *we* want.'

Wren pushed the loose hair from her face, her fingers lingering at her temples where her headache was worsening. She spoke the words she'd dreaded saying since she'd set foot on Delmirian soil again: 'I don't think it's about what *we* want any more, Thee . . .'

Thea tipped her face to the ceiling, closing her eyes as though she could block out reality. The torchlight flickered across her face, highlighting the sharp angles of her cheekbones. 'Fuck.'

The curse echoed in the empty gymnasium. When Thea opened her eyes again and grimaced, Wren mirrored her expression. 'Agreed.'

'Then we need to be honest with each other,' Thea told her, stepping closer. 'Completely transparent about everything, about what we see for our homeland.'

Wren folded her arms over her chest. 'You go first.'

'Fine,' Thea replied. 'I'm fucking terrified.'

A broken laugh escaped Wren, followed by a small wave of relief. 'I'm glad I'm not the only one.'

Thea flicked her braid over her shoulder. 'It was so much easier to dismiss our heritage when Delmira was nothing but a wasteland . . . No one demanding answers, no looming conflict over the land and its resources.'

'But that's changed,' Wren said gently. 'It's only a matter of time before someone stakes a claim, or plunders its fertile soil. If it falls into the wrong hands, Thea . . . we're—'

'Fucked, I know.' Thea drew a shaky breath. Her eyes, usually so confident, now held a vulnerability that made Wren's heart ache. 'I never thought this would happen. The life I'm leading now . . . It's one of adventure, of freedom. Isn't that what we fought for in the war? Isn't that the victory we won?'

'I thought so,' Wren replied, reaching out to squeeze Thea's arm. 'None of us could have seen this coming.'

Thea snorted. 'For all the prophecies floating around the midrealms, you'd think one would come in handy every now and then.'

'You'd think,' Wren agreed, a wry smile tugging at her lips.

Thea patted her hand and started to pace, footsteps echoing in the cavernous space. 'The question is . . . if not a true heir of Delmira, then who? Like you said, if Delmira itself falls to someone false, what happens? What will become of the midrealms? Of the peace we nearly died for?'

Wren watched her sister, noting the tension in her shoulders, the way her hands clenched and unclenched at her sides. 'I don't know,' she admitted. 'Do you believe it's true? That our parents and ancestors hoarded resources? Refused to share their agricultural secrets to keep power in their favour?'

'I'm not sure we'll ever know.' Thea rubbed the back of her neck. 'There are written accounts and histories, of course, but we've already seen how they can be skewed with an agenda. Do you know how many times I've had to correct someone about Anya? About the fact that she was a hero, not the Daughter of Darkness?'

Wren nodded. 'It's been the same here. A place of learning still intent on creating a false narrative.'

'So if this is what things are like now, what will they become if we don't take control?'

'What does Wilder say?' Wren asked, knowing there was no way her sister hadn't discussed this with the Hand of Death.

Thea's steps faltered at the mention of Wilder's name. 'He says he'll be by my side, no matter what . . .' She sighed, and Wren felt the weight of it in her own heart. 'For the sake of the midrealms, I'd do it,' she said softly. 'I would take the throne, stake my claim.'

Her words broke Wren apart. For she had known them already – had known that the moment there was a greater threat to the midrealms, her sister wouldn't stand for it, no matter what her own heart desired. Wren wished that she could be so noble, so ready to set aside her own path, to put duty before all else – but she pushed the thought away, the taste of injustice bitter on her tongue.

'I know.' She grabbed Thea's hand. 'What do we do now?'

'We take the time we've been given, and we tell no one. You show me what you found in Delmira and we'll see if we can make sense of it. But right now?' Thea squeezed her hand back. 'Right now, we spar. Elbows up, feet apart, sister.'

CHAPTER 47

Torj

'The wisest defence is the one that need not ever be used'

– *Mastering the Craft of Close Protection*

THE LAST THING Torj wanted to do was talk shit with Wilder all night. He knew it was only a matter of time until his fellow Warsword started interrogating him about Wren. The thought made his chest tighten, a mixture of anticipation and dread settling in his gut.

The only good news was that Wilder was happy to set up camp in his rooms rather than drag him down to the Mortar and Pestle. *Small mercies*, Torj thought, grateful to avoid the prying eyes and roaring noise of the tavern.

With a resigned sigh, he stoked the fire back to life in the hearth. The flames crackled and danced, casting flickering shadows across the stone walls of his quarters. The warm glow did little to ease the tension in his shoulders as he returned to his chair.

Wilder, lounging in the chair opposite, pushed a cup of wine towards him. The scratching of metal against the rough wooden table between them seemed unnaturally loud in the quiet room.

'Marise had this imported,' Wilder said, taking a long appreciative sip from his own cup.

Torj raised an eyebrow, peering at the dark ruby liquid. The rich aroma wafted up: hints of dark fruit and oak. 'How in the midrealms have you managed to see Marise amid all this madness?' Marise was a wine merchant from Harenth they'd all known for years, who had a reputation for the best wine connections in the midrealms and his infamous 'Dead Red' parties – all three of which Torj had attended, but had no recollection of.

'He was visiting Aveum,' Wilder replied, settling back in his chair. The leather creaked softly under his weight. 'Apparently he regularly provides Queen Reyna with consultations on her cellar.'

A hint of amusement broke through Torj's sombre mood. 'Of course he does.' Curiosity getting the better of him, he asked, 'How is the queen? Has her magic returned?'

Wilder swirled his cup, the wine catching the firelight. His expression grew serious, brow furrowing slightly. 'From what Thea tells me, Reyna hasn't had a full vision since the attack. She says that her magic is muted . . . Still there, but as though there is some sort of blanket over it.'

'She told you all that?' Torj was surprised. During their travels, the queen hadn't seemed like one to open up.

'Thea wrangled it from her, eventually.' There was a note of pride in Wilder's voice. 'She can be very persuasive.'

'No shit,' Torj said. He'd seen Thea's tenacity in action many a time. 'You've both been in Aveum all this time, then? Guarding the queen?'

Wilder shook his head. 'One of the newer Warswords took over after I was injured. I've been tracking the enemy across the midrealms.'

An icy shiver raked down Torj's spine. 'Then why are you here? Thea was summoned, I know that much, but you? Surely Audra would have you continue your mission regardless . . . ?'

'You know the evidence you searched for at that ball in Harenth?

'We found it,' Wilder said grimly. 'It led straight to Highguard, and it definitely came from someone at Drevenor.'

Torj mulled it over. What had they missed in Lord Hullet's study? 'Do you know who?'

'Farissa suspects but won't say. Apparently the High Chancellor is refusing to believe it, despite Silas's affinity for alchemy and the complex resources, tools and equipment he seems to have at his disposal. Much of which can only be found within these walls.' Wilder sipped his wine. 'All we know for certain is that they have a location in the city and a contact here who's helping. You know that Farissa has been feeding out incorrect information for weeks? It's managed to make its way into the People's Vanguard. Everything points to a traitor in the academy.'

Torj studied his friend for a moment: the relaxed way he was lounging in his chair, the gentle tapping of his finger around his cup, the gleam in his silver eyes.

'You're not meant to be telling me any of this, are you?' Torj guessed.

'Nope.'

Throughout their years of training and fighting together, both he and Wilder had always been steadfastly loyal to the guild, had always carried out their orders ... but that didn't mean they didn't bend the rules on occasion.

'Then why are you?' he asked at last.

'We'll get to that.' Wilder frowned at Torj's untouched cup. 'You only drinking fire extract these days, Bear Slayer?'

Deciding to go with it, Torj grimaced. 'Gods, no. Kipp made sure I can't smell the stuff without my stomach rolling for a good few weeks more.'

Wilder laughed. 'He has that effect on people.'

'That he does,' Torj agreed, finally lifting his wine to his lips. He took a small sip, letting the flavours roll over his tongue. It was good, damn good, but it did little to settle the unease in his gut.

'What about you?' he asked, desperate to keep the conversation away from dangerous territory. 'Are you all healed up?'

Wilder waved a dismissive hand. 'I'm fine. It was never as bad as you made out.'

Torj scoffed. He hadn't forgotten the blood spilling down his friend's arm . . . or how he'd imagined breaking the news to Thea.

'Please,' Wilder scoffed, leaning forwards. His eyes, sharp and knowing, fixed on Torj's face. 'You wanted an excuse to get back to Wren and I let you have it, because I wanted to be back with Thea.'

The truth hung heavy in the air between them. Torj's jaw clenched. He knew the conversation he'd been dreading was now inevitable. He took another sip of wine, suddenly wishing it was fire extract, bracing himself for what was to come.

'Let's have it, then,' he challenged. 'Say what you've gotta say, Hawthorne.'

Wilder surveyed him thoughtfully – and said something he did not expect: 'I've never seen Wren cry.'

'What?'

'In all the years I've known her – during the war, after it – I've never seen that kind of emotion from her. And when I showed up here and Thea was hauling her away, she'd been crying.'

Torj rubbed the back of his neck. 'As if I don't feel bad enough, Hawthorne . . .'

'I'm not trying to make you feel bad,' Wilder replied, reaching for the wine and topping up their cups. 'I don't really know what I'm trying to do. I guess, maybe make you see that you broke through that exterior. You.'

'And caused her pain.'

'No one goes through life unscathed, Bear Slayer,' his fellow Warsword told him.

Torj drank again and slid his cup back onto the table with a heavy sigh. 'I never wanted to be the one to hurt her. That's the last thing I wanted.'

'Did you finally talk to her?' Wilder asked.

Torj nodded. 'Two days ago. I told her everything. Told her why I ended it, that I was trying to protect her.'

Wilder groaned, dropping his head into his hands.

Torj's gaze shot to his friend. 'What?'

'You're forgetting I'm in love with an Embervale sister too,' Wilder said. 'If I recall, Wren didn't ask for your protection. In fact, she flat out refused it.'

'That's not the point.'

'No, it's not. But tell me, did you take a choice from her? Did you decide on her behalf?'

'I . . .'

'I'll take that as a yes.' Wilder shook his head. 'You idiot.'

Torj folded his arms over his chest, rocking back onto the rear legs of his chair. 'I don't remember you being fucking perfect with Thea during the war years.'

Wilder barked a laugh. 'That's why I thought you might have learned a thing or two from my mistakes.'

'Think again,' Torj muttered bitterly.

'Torj, *you* were the one who told *me* to be strong for Thea when she was about to walk into the Great Rite . . .'

'And I listened to you as Wren partook in the Gauntlet. I let her—'

'You don't *let* an Embervale sister do anything, Torj,' Wilder said gently.

'I know.' He forced himself to look at his friend. 'I made a decision in a desperate moment – one I'm not sure I'd make any differently, were I to face it again . . . But I broke her trust. And I can't get it back.'

Wilder reached across and gripped his shoulder. 'That's where you're wrong, brother.'

'Oh?'

'I hear Wren has run out of samples of the enemy's alchemy for her tests?' Wilder said, a wicked smile gracing his lips.

Torj felt a grin break out across his own face. 'Do you have a location in Highguard?'

'I do. In the old part of town, near the pleasure house.'

Torj got to his feet and reached for his hammer. 'Then what are we waiting for?'

CHAPTER 48

Wren

'Mark not the thorns, but rather what they've kept
safe through the ages'

— An Encyclopaedia of Deadly Plants

THE EMBERVALE SISTERS stood in the quiet conservatory, which was empty but for Dessa working on her own opus nearby. The redhead was so consumed with her project that she hadn't looked their way since she'd arrived, her eyes fixed on the parchment she was scribbling away on.

Thea stood with her arms folded over her chest as she surveyed the potted plants before her. 'Which ones are from Delmira?' she asked.

Wren pointed to a pair, their silver-white petals gleaming in the morning light that poured into the conservatory. Vibrant green leaves stretched towards the glass ceiling; their edges seemed to pulse with life.

'Those two are full specimens, from the soil they're in to the plant itself – all transported from Delmira.' She pointed to a different pot. 'That silvertide was transplanted to local soil, the most nourishing that the Master of Lifelore had to offer from his personal supplies.'

Thea's brow crinkled. 'It doesn't look as . . . *perky* as the ones from Delmira, does it?'

So far, they had managed to keep Thea's arrival hidden from the eager council, and Wren had never been more grateful to have her sister by her side. They had talked about Delmira at length, with Thea openly airing her fears and concerns about what taking on the crown might mean for her, for Wilder, for the future they'd envisioned together.

Wren had always thought of Thea as reckless and impulsive, but her talk of securing funding and defences was measured and considered. Wren suspected she had managed to get some time in with their strategist friend as well, for her observations were laced with calculation and long-term planning.

Wren had slowly begun to share what she'd learned about the underworld of the midrealms throughout her years as the Poisoner, and what they might encounter from certain highborns of each kingdom. Wren didn't like where the discussions had taken them, didn't for one second accept that there was only one way to solve their dilemma – but it felt good to talk, and for the first time in a long while, she felt as though she wasn't alone.

Sharing her work with her sister was another unexpected joy, and she found Thea waiting for her response expectantly, a far cry from the girl who used to skip lessons with Farissa.

'At first I thought perhaps the transplanted specimen was in shock from being moved,' she explained. 'They often need some time to recover, but its leaves are still curling, see? And some parts are wilting . . .' She moved along the bench, gesturing to another set of planters. 'These were propagated from cuttings. And these over here? From seeds . . .'

Toying with the end of her braid, Thea paced down the length of the bench, contemplating Wren's work.

Wren led her to another table. 'Everything here is the same species of rose from various locations across the midrealms: our gardens here in Drevenor, greenhouses in Ciraun, florists in Aveum, farms in Tver . . . We've sourced samples from everywhere.'

'So you're saying it's all about the Delmirian soil?' Thea asked, a note of uncertainty in her voice. 'Not the plant itself?'

'We thought that at first,' Wren ventured. 'But we've sent other alchemists in secret to bring back more samples, and there have been mixed results. In some soil, it doesn't matter how you try to cultivate the silvertide – seeds, cuttings, repotting the whole thing – they all flourish. But in other soil, still from Delmira, they flounder. They don't have the same effect in the cure I'm trying to replicate.'

'And that's why you're struggling with it?' Thea asked.

'That's the theory. But I feel like I'm hitting a wall with this research. Every lead I chase down just brings me to dead ends or more questions. I can't work it out. I can't make it right . . .'

Thea scanned her tormented expression and called to Dessa, 'I think we may need an *actual* alchemist's help here.'

As Dessa looked up from her tools, Wren noted the dark circles beneath her eyes, her unwashed hair.

'It's fine,' Wren said, offering her friend an understanding smile. 'Dessa has her own opus to work on. We're all under a lot of pressure.'

But Dessa shook her head and approached them. 'I'm sorry I haven't been around as much. This thing with Zavier has really shaken me up . . .'

'Me too,' Wren admitted. 'Please don't apologize.'

Dessa turned to Wren's work instead. 'For what it's worth, you're doing everything you can, Wren. This is a complex problem and it's not going to be solved overnight.'

'It's been months, Dessa. I can't help feeling like I'm letting everyone down. Like I'm not working hard enough or fast enough.'

'You were always going to feel that way,' Thea interjected. 'You're a perfectionist. You're too hard on yourself.'

Dessa nodded. 'She's right. You've been working yourself to the bone. We've all seen how you're tearing yourself apart over this. But why don't we try to look at it with fresh eyes . . .'

Wren laughed. 'My eyes are far from fresh, Dessa.'

'Well, that's why Thea and I are here,' she said simply. 'Tell us about the silvertide that has flourished.'

'I just went through all of that,' Wren replied, trying to quash her frustration.

Dessa smiled. 'No, you told Thea about the different samples and methods of cultivating. I'm asking you to talk us through the roses that are thriving.'

Wren examined her work, the numerous pots and blooming white buds. 'Well, it's obvious that Delmiran soil has something to do with it, as the masters told us in our *many* meetings . . .'

'So that's the common denominator of the successful attempts. What of the less prosperous samples that are also from Delmira? Obviously there are variations in soil across a kingdom due to landscape, altitude, minerals and salts, temperature and water, but beyond that . . .' Dessa finally drew a breath before ploughing ahead. 'Is there another point of difference between the Delmirian samples we haven't factored in?'

Thea hopped up onto one of the tables, dangling her legs over the side while she shrugged at Wren. 'Consider me out of my depth, sister. This is all you.'

Wren smoothed down her apron and stood before the cluttered benches, scanning each of their labels where the origin locations were listed.

She traced over them with her finger. There were her own contributions: *Cottage Garden, Forest near Cottage, Northern Side of Swamp, Thezmarr Border, Northeastern Route to Tver* . . . Then she turned to the samples that had been brought back by other alchemists in secret. Their locations were specified by coordinates.

'I need a map,' she said.

'Over there.' Dessa pointed to a large easel, where a map of the midrealms had been pinned.

'That's someone else's project,' Wren objected.

'Wren, you might be saving the world,' Thea laughed. 'I *think* that justifies borrowing someone's map.'

Wren found herself before the large expanse of parchment, admiring the scope of the topographical detailing. Dozens of pins lay in the tray of the easel, and she reached for one. 'Dessa, can you read the coordinates for me?'

As Dessa called out the longitudes and latitudes of where the samples had been taken, Wren located them on the map and pushed pins into the parchment. By the time they reached the last coordinates, Wren's stomach was sinking.

She stepped back and reviewed her findings. Dessa and Thea came to her side and stared at the locations dotted across the parchment.

'Well? What do you see?' Dessa asked.

Wren closed her eyes, bracing herself against more disappointment. 'I don't know,' she said at last.

'What do you mean, you don't know?' Thea pressed, scowling at the map.

'I mean I don't know what the point of differences might be between these locations and the others,' she admitted. 'I've never been to these places. I'm not familiar with any of them.'

'That's alright!' Dessa waved off her concern. 'You could always ask the alchemists who retrieved them—'

'Wait.' Thea held up a closed fist – a warrior's signal to stop. She stared hard at the pins. 'You've never been to *any* of these places?'

Wren shook her head. 'Not that I can recall. And if I did, it was nothing more than passing through.'

Thea pointed back at the tables, to the labels written in Wren's own hand. 'But you've been to all of *those* locations?'

'Well, yes. I gathered those samples myself.'

'That's not what I mean,' Thea said. 'You've been there *before*? When it was barren? That's how you discovered all this?'

Wren's skin prickled. 'Yes . . .'

'So that's the point of difference!' Thea grabbed her shoulder. 'Everywhere *you've* been, something has flourished!'

Wren shook her head with a sad smile. 'I've been lots of places, Thee. Not everywhere produces thriving plants.'

But Thea hadn't released her shoulder; in fact, she was only squeezing harder, motioning with her other hand to Wren's silver-tide samples. 'Then what is it about *those* locations that's special?'

Wren faltered. 'I . . .'

Slowly, she walked back to her workbench and looked to the labels again, her heart rate increasing. *Cottage Garden, Forest near Cottage, Northern Side of Swamp, Thezmarr Border, Northeastern Route to Tver . . .*

She pictured herself in each and every barren place, not as she was now, but as she had been back then, in the wake of the shadow war. Her skin prickled once more, and this time, a whisper of power flickered beneath it.

Wren turned to Thea and Dessa. 'Come with me.'

With her heart in her throat, she shouldered her satchel and left the conservatory, crossing the grounds with long, purposeful strides. She paid no heed to the greenhouses or the manicured gardens. She passed through the iron gates, hardly realizing that she'd broken into a run—

'Wren!' Dessa called from behind. 'Wait!'

But Thea was racing right alongside her, the two sisters running in tandem, the trees and buildings blurring together as the wind whipped through their hair.

Only when they reached the edge of the meadow did Wren skid to a stop, a cry on her lips.

In the place where she had unleashed her storm, where Torj had shielded her from herself, there was a sea of wildflowers, more vibrant, more resplendent than ever. It was as though the meadow had been holding its breath before, and now it flourished in reckless celebration, painting the world, as wild and untameable as Wren's magic.

Lightning sang in her veins, and the scent of rain danced in the wind. As she gazed at the meadow's wild beauty, an unbidden image of the silvertide rose flashed in her mind – its silver petals unfurling despite the thorns that guarded them, just as her magic had finally broken free of its constraints. She understood it now: the thorns were not meant to cage, but to strengthen.

Dessa gasped when she caught up with them, staring at the blaze of colours, shaking her head. She turned to Wren in wonder. 'It's not the Delmirian soil that will complete the cure, or end this battle . . .' she murmured. 'It's *you*.'

CHAPTER 49

Torj

'When fate draws its blade, time offers a single, perfect dance'

– *The Warsword's Way*

'THIS IS IT?' Torj asked dubiously as they stood in front of what appeared to be an empty cobbler's shop. He cupped his hands around his eyes to shield them from the sun's glare and peered through the grimy window. 'There's nothing in there . . .'

Wilder frowned, checking a scrap of parchment. 'This is the location our source cited.'

They were in the heart of Old Town, where the buildings were peeling away from their foundations and the scent of ale and smoke was thick in the air. Only a few doors down was the pleasure house that Torj had followed Wren into in her early days at Drevenor.

'Sorry, Bear Slayer,' Wilder said, looking down the alley. 'We must have got some bad information.'

But Torj's nape prickled. He went to the door and rattled the handle. It was locked.

Wilder clapped him on the shoulder. 'Come on, I'll buy you a breakfast pastry.'

'Wait.' Torj stood back, surveying the weathered facade of

the door, then the polished silver of its handle. 'The lock's new.' He went back to the window, peering inside more intently this time.

Along the walls, the shelves were empty. The cobbler's workbench was bare, no tools in sight. But the rug that lay in the centre of the room . . . There was a clear path worn through its weave, and one of its corners was turned up.

'It's here,' Torj said, suddenly certain. He gripped the door handle once more, this time using his Furies-given strength to break it. The lock gave way, and the door swung inwards.

Inside, Torj could see more telltale signs of frequent use: bootprints of varying sizes in the layer of dust on the floor, a lack of cobwebs above the door when there were plenty in the other corners of the shop. And then there were the scuff marks . . . right in front of a large cabinet.

'Wilder,' he hissed, pointing to the black scrapes in the timber floorboards and unstrapping his hammer from his back. 'It's a hidden entrance.'

Wilder unsheathed his swords and nodded.

Torj pulled the cabinet aside, revealing stone steps descending to a lower level. A soft, eerie glow emanated from below, the greenish light casting long shadows across the worn stairs.

'What's the plan, Bear Slayer?' Wilder asked, peering over his shoulder.

'Get in, get samples for Wren, get out.'

'Sophisticated,' Wilder quipped. 'I like it.'

Torj adjusted his grip on his war hammer and started the descent. The faint light from below did little to illuminate the steep, uneven steps that spiralled down, and similarly to the towers at Drevenor, he and Wilder had to move in single file down the narrow path.

As they moved further towards the bottom of the stairs, the air grew cooler and damper around them. Torj could hear the occasional scurry of unseen rodents, but nothing more.

When they reached the bottom of the steps, they found

themselves in an antechamber, where shelves and hooks housed aprons, gloves, and other protective wear, as well as a basin.

'Shouldn't there be guards?' Wilder murmured, brow furrowing.

'Depends if they've got the manpower or not. This is a well-hidden space . . .' But Torj felt uneasy all the same. If this was the chief location for the enemy's alchemy work, he would have thought no expense would be spared when it came to security. 'You think it's a trap?'

'Could be . . . Do we care?' Wilder challenged.

'Wouldn't mind an excuse to hit something,' Torj muttered.

'Then let's go.'

There were two doors. The first they tried led to a storage room, where floor-to-ceiling shelves were brimming with jars of powders, liquids and parts of dead creatures. But there was no one inside.

The second door creaked loudly as Torj opened it with a wince. Inside was a circular workshop with several smaller adjacent rooms. A stone table stood in the middle, covered in an array of glass alembics, retorts, and copper stills. He recognized several tools that Wren had on her workbench in her quarters. There was also a complex network of glass tubing connecting various vessels, and the faint hiss of escaping vapour.

There was no sign of the People's Vanguard, or anyone at all, for that matter.

'Do you think they got all this equipment from Drevenor?' Torj asked, stepping further into the workroom and noting a large furnace at the back with multiple layers for different heat intensities. The air shimmered around it, and the glow of the coals illuminated tongs, crucibles and moulds on the nearby workspace.

'They couldn't have taken all this without it going unnoticed,' Wilder replied, examining an herb rack where several types of plants and mushrooms were hanging to dry.

Torj stopped in his tracks. 'Shit . . .' he muttered.

Wilder was at his side a second later. 'What?'

Torj pointed to the tiny, unassuming vial sitting in a wooden rack. Its contents drifted within the confines of the glass.

'Fuck,' Wilder hissed, staring at the black ribbons swirling within. 'I haven't seen it in years . . . And I'd hoped I never would again.'

Torj grunted in agreement. 'You and me both, brother. But here it is. Shadow magic, in the flesh.'

'We knew they were using it in some form . . . but it's different, seeing it for yourself,' Wilder said slowly.

'Should we take it with us?' Torj considered the bottle. He didn't want to touch the damn thing. He'd dealt with enough darkness to last a lifetime. 'We don't know how volatile it is . . .'

Wilder seemed transfixed by the substance. 'It's too dangerous to leave here. I'll take it to Audra as soon as we're back.' He wrapped the glass in a discarded rag and pocketed it, before turning to survey the rest of the laboratory. 'What are we looking for, exactly? Let's get it and go.'

Torj rubbed the back of his neck. 'I've never seen it in a vessel,' he admitted. 'Only what it looks like when it's been used on weapons. But it's got a strange shimmer to it, and it smells like oranges.'

Wilder stared at him for a moment. 'Smells like oranges? Got it.'

Torj continued his exploration of the workroom, rifling through piles of parchment for clues, noticing that one of the crucibles was still warm to the touch. 'They can't have left here too long ago,' he said to Wilder.

'I'd come to the same conclusion,' his friend replied, passing his hand over a stove. 'The furnace is still hot.'

Carefully, they navigated the landscape of ongoing experiments, careful not to trigger any reactions. Scouring the clutter, Torj wondered if working in chaos was an alchemist trait in general. He was picturing Wren hunched over her bench when he detected the faintest hint of citrus in the air.

Following his nose like a hound, he reached the back of the workroom, where a greying sheet covered something. He reached for the fabric—

'Elderbrock?' Wilder called, a note of alarm in his voice.

Torj whirled around. 'What is it?'

Wilder was pointing to the ceiling, where vapour was billowing from the vents. 'Time to go, I think.'

Torj ripped the sheet away from what turned out to be a crate of vials. He recognized the substance instantly. 'This is it—'

'We gotta go,' Wilder called, not taking his eyes off the increasing clouds of vapour pouring from the vents.

Torj wrenched the lid from the crate and, shouldering his hammer, grabbed as many vials as he could, stuffing them in his pockets.

'Torj! Now!'

Torj launched into action, sprinting towards the door with his friend. They wove through the various stations, not caring about disturbing the equipment this time, knocking over several cauldrons in the process.

'Fuck,' Wilder shouted. 'I can feel that stuff on my skin. I—'

A thunderous sound shook the whole room.

And Torj looked up in time to see the solid iron door to the antechamber crash closed.

CHAPTER 50

Wren

'Between the storm and silence lies the breath that changes the world'

– A Recent History of the Shadow War

In her entire life, Wren had never seen Farissa smoke. But when she, Dessa and Thea finished explaining their theory, her former mentor stuck a pipe between her teeth, lit whatever was in its bowl, and inhaled deeply. Farissa braced herself against the mantle above the hearth and closed her eyes, exhaling a stream of smoke before she faced them.

'To be clear, you believe that it's not Delmira as a place, nor a particular strain of plant that made your original cure work, Elwren?' she asked.

'No.'

'You believe that Delmira's rebirth and your inconsistent results with the counter-alchemy are a result of storm magic?'

'Yes,' Wren answered, Thea and Dessa both echoing the sentiment behind her.

Farissa chewed on the end of her pipe thoughtfully. 'It's possible,' she ventured.

'It explains everything,' Wren said. 'When I first arrived in

Delmira after the war, it was all yellowed lands and little life but for some greying heather and a few trees. Everything else seemed like a wasteland.'

'And you were there for five years, correct?' Farissa asked.

'Yes. And nothing grew there, I swear it. I would have written to you, I would have—'

'You are not on trial, Elwren,' Farissa said gently. 'I'm merely thinking aloud.'

'Nothing changed in that time,' Wren reiterated.

'I'm not sure that's true . . .'

Wren's gaze shot to her former mentor. 'What?'

Farissa gave her a sad smile. '*You* changed, Elwren, and that is just as significant. However, what I'm interested in is the rate of growth. For five years after you first used storm magic in Delmira, nothing changed, nothing grew. And yet the meadow here, past the gardens . . . You used your magic there only days ago and already you have seen its impact?'

Dessa stepped forwards, her voice eager. 'We think Wren's storm power has grown stronger over the years, so its effects are more intense – accelerated, even.'

Farissa nodded. 'It has been known to happen. As a wielder matures, so does their magic.'

'I have another theory,' Thea said, twirling one of her star-shaped blades between her fingers.

'You do?' Wren asked, turning to her in surprise.

Her sister grinned. 'Perhaps the effects of your magic can also be more powerful when the place in question has some sort of significance to you.'

Wren's face flushed, and she silently swore she'd never tell Thea another thing.

But Farissa looked thoughtful. 'Also possible . . . Thea, what about your magic? Have you seen any similar results?'

'I usually leave a trail of torn-out monster hearts in my wake, not flowers,' the Warsword answered. 'So no, not that I can recall.'

'Then you should—'

'We already got her to use her magic on some nearby land,' Wren assured her. 'If it's anything like mine apparently is, we should know within a day or so.'

Farissa refilled her pipe and lit it once more. 'Then, Elwren, I believe you have work to do?'

Wren nodded, her mind already racing as she reached for the door.

'I'll gather the masters,' Farissa said. 'They'll be ready when you are.'

For the first time in months, Wren knew *exactly* what she was doing. Dessa and Thea helped her gather everything she needed from the conservatory and bring it to her room. One of the academy workshops would have been preferable, but she couldn't risk prying eyes or interruptions. Once she was settled, she consulted her notes on the variant that had saved Zavier's life and organized her equipment: crucibles, vials of blood, shallow dishes containing the dark alchemy she wished to counter. She harvested tooth-edged leaves from the Delmirian silvertide rose and ground them up in her mortar and pestle, her mind flitting from one possibility to the next. It hadn't been a single plant her storm magic had affected. If she could enhance the other natural components of the cure . . . there was no telling how powerful it would be against the enemy.

While she worked, Dessa and Thea played cards on her bed. The quiet hum of their presence didn't distract her, but served as a reminder of their support, their love. While it made her heart ache for Ida and Sam, it also made her grateful that she'd known them, and that even without them, all was not lost.

The nape of Wren's neck prickled.

She looked up, expecting to see someone watching her, but Dessa and Thea were immersed in their game.

Turning back to her workbench with a frown, Wren checked the crucible she had over a small burner. The concoction within was simmering, just as it should—

A shiver raked down Wren's spine and she startled, whirling around.

Dessa was laughing gleefully at the hand she had just played, but Thea, with her warrior instincts, had noticed and was looking around suspiciously.

'What is it?' she asked, getting up to check the doors.

'I . . . I just had a strange feeling,' Wren murmured. Her fingers tightened around the vial she held, her earlier ease evaporating. The prickling at her nape intensified, spreading across her shoulders and arms. She shifted at her bench, eyes darting around the room, searching for the source of her disquiet.

'Strange how?' Thea pressed, her eyes bright with concern.

'I . . .' Wren's voice trailed off as a new sensation overtook her. A faint golden glow began to emanate from her skin, visible only in the shadows cast by her sleeves. She clenched her fist, trying to quell the light, but it pulsed stronger, in time with her quickening heartbeat.

'What are you doing, Wren?' Thea asked.

Wren glanced from the gilded glow across her skin to her sister. Thea's blank expression told Wren that she couldn't see it, which made Wren wonder if she was finally losing her mind . . .

A golden thread. That was the description of a soul bond manifesting. But . . . Torj had destroyed it. He had told her himself. And she had *felt it* – every agonizing second of it – when he had.

Still, the magic crept across her body, tugging something inside her, something familiar. Wren opened her mouth to respond to Thea, but instead, a gasp escaped her lips as a vision flashed before her eyes.

Dark stone walls. The acrid scent of chemicals. A feeling of suffocation – and Torj's face, contorted in pain.

'*Wren*,' Thea said, more loudly this time. 'Tell me what's going on.'

'It's Torj,' Wren heard herself say, her voice tight. 'Something's happened.'

Thea's expression hardened instantly. She didn't question how Wren knew. She simply gathered her swords. 'Where?'

Wren's legs were unsteady as she stepped away from her work, the cure forgotten. As she took a step, she felt it – an invisible thread tugging at her chest, pulling her towards the door. 'I don't know exactly, but I can feel it. This way.' She turned back to call to her friend, 'Dessa? Can you please watch over these potions?'

'Of course.'

'Thank you. In another thirty minutes you can take them off the flames and let them rest. Don't let anyone in here. Don't let anyone else touch anything.'

Dessa nodded. 'Consider it done.'

The Embervale sisters left the academy. Feeling panicked as the foreign sensation grew stronger and more gold flickered in her vision, Wren turned to Thea.

'I think we need to go to Highguard. We're going to need a horse.'

'Luckily I have one of those,' Thea replied. 'And he's the fastest Tverrian stallion there is.'

Thea wasn't boasting; her mount, ridiculously named Pancake, streaked across the grounds and onto the road to the city with both women in his saddle. Wren clung to her sister for dear life, unable to remember the last time she had ridden at a speed this terrifying.

Neither storm wielder spoke as the stallion hurtled towards Highguard. The scenery was nothing but a dark blur either side of them, the crisp night air stinging Wren's cheeks.

At last, the torchlight of the city came into view, and Thea guided them through the gates. 'Now where?' she asked.

The cord grew taut within Wren. 'Follow the road to Old Town.'

Highguard's underbelly was as she remembered it, with its neglected buildings and dark side streets. Raucous noise from various taverns spilled out across the cobbles.

'On foot from here,' Wren said.

They dismounted Thea's stallion and the Warsword tied his reins to a tethering post outside the Happy Harpy.

'You're not worried he'll get stolen?' Wren asked.

Thea simply scoffed. 'I'd like to see someone try.'

As they moved down the street, the taverns' noise seemed to fade, replaced by a strange, hollow ringing in Wren's ears. The pulling sensation grew stronger with each step, urging her to move faster.

'Wren,' Thea murmured, a note of worry escaping. 'Is Wilder with him?'

'I don't know,' Wren replied, following that strange tug to the left, past several storefronts. 'Stay close.'

'I always do,' Thea replied, gripping the pommel of the sword at her belt.

As they hurried down the winding street, the glow on Wren's skin intensified, and she felt her connection to Torj growing stronger.

This was it – the thing he had supposedly destroyed, guiding her to him. Soul to soul. It didn't matter how it had survived or returned. All that mattered was that it helped her save him.

Flashes of his surroundings flooded her mind as she followed. Crucibles and moulds; a furnace and a drying rack for herbs. It was an *alchemy* workshop . . . but *here*?

She drew to a stop outside a rundown cobbler's shop – the door was open, and it was empty.

'Wren?' Thea asked from the doorway.

Wren found herself standing at the top of a stone staircase that spiralled deep underground. A cabinet had been pushed aside to reveal the secret entrance, and she knew in her bones that Torj was somewhere beyond.

Thea made to take the lead, but Wren thrust out a hand. 'Wait.' She rummaged through her satchel and pulled out two masks, handing one to her sister. 'Wear this.'

Both women tied the fabric around the lower half of their faces, and Wren checked the supplies in her belt.

'Ready?' Thea asked.

Wren nodded. The invisible force was insistent, drawing her closer, guiding her to Torj. 'Downstairs.'

Heart pounding with a mixture of anticipation and dread, Wren allowed Thea to lead. She wasn't so proud that she didn't recognize the value of having a Warsword in her arsenal.

As they descended the stone steps, the acrid smell of chemicals grew stronger, mingling with the damp, musty air. Shouting echoed from below, and there was a distant sound of shattering glass. Wren unsheathed her poison-tipped dagger and clutched a bottle of wild draketail in her other hand.

The clang of steel rang out, reverberating up the stairwell. When Thea and Wren burst into the antechamber below, they were met with chaos.

An iron door lay twisted on the floor, torn from its hinges by either a Warsword or an alchemical explosion. There was too much smoke and madness to know for sure. Fighting had spilled out from a laboratory. Plumes of vapour evaporated as they touched the fresh air of the antechamber.

Thea threw herself into the fray at once, her blade a blur of motion, but Wren saw it instantly: though it should have been an easy fight, the alchemists' knowledge of the space gave them a deadly advantage. Vats of acid were flying in the direction of Wilder, Thea and Torj – the latter cursing as liquid splashed across his boot and ate through the leather with a hiss.

The smell of burnt hair threatened to drag Wren back into the past, to a different battle. Her throat closed up, her stomach churning as that familiar panic set in—

'Embers!'

That name was her anchor to him, and she followed it up to the surface.

Wren darted out from her cover, her mind racing through the

contents of her belt. She threw her own concoctions with practised precision. A vial of widow's ash smashed against the wall, releasing a cloud of concentrated spores that had a masked man screaming and scratching at his exposed arms, raw and red with an instant rash. Parcels of soot root powder flew from her hand, a dark mass blooming, temporarily blocking the Warswords from sight so they could advance.

When she got close enough, Wren unleashed a dusting of brugmansia powder, reduced to its hallucinogenic properties. An enemy alchemist inhaled it and staggered, his eyes going wide as he began swatting at invisible assailants.

Where the Warswords couldn't swing their blades for fear of knocking the lethal potions and experiments, Wren wielded weapons of her own making. And she wielded them *well*. The coughing and shrieks around her were all the confirmation she needed that she was hitting her marks, that she was a worthy player in this fight.

Another band of masked alchemists swarmed in, alerted by their comrades. A glass sphere went hurtling towards Torj from across the room.

Wren didn't think. She flung her hand out, lightning shooting from her fingertips, knocking the projectile from Torj's path. Something shattered in the distance—

Wren's heart seized as she watched it unfold. Her lightning was encased by the strange, shimmering substance that had spilled across the floor. A silvery, fluid-like essence began to separate from the rest, moving with an almost sentient quality. It started to glow faintly, pulsing in a rhythm that reminded her of a heartbeat.

Realization hit her like a blow.

The silvery essence represented pure magical energy, distinct from any royal blood itself. The enemy's alchemy didn't target the blood directly, but rather the magic intertwined with it. It was happening before her very eyes, penetrating the magical element, showing her just how her cure worked against it.

Wren threw another small bolt of lightning, watching the alchemy react. It wasn't built on royal blood and bloodlines. It was built on the very fabric of magic itself.

Seeing what she was discovering, some of their opponents attempted to shatter the surrounding equipment and work.

'We can't let them destroy the workshop any further,' she shouted, noting the array of volatile potions bubbling in crucibles. She couldn't stand by and watch it destroyed, not when she needed it—

A lanky alchemist with a shock of white hair caught her eye. He was working furiously at a table, mixing reagents with trembling hands. Whatever he was concocting, Wren knew it couldn't be good.

'Thea!' she called out, gesturing towards the white-haired enemy. 'Cover me!'

As Thea nodded and moved to intercept anyone who might interfere, Wren sprinted towards the table. The alchemist looked up, his eyes widening in recognition. He reached for a beaker of swirling, opalescent liquid.

Time seemed to slow.

Wren threw her dagger.

It caught the man in the neck.

Blood sprayed, and suddenly the Bear Slayer was at her side. Not shielding her with his body as he had done so many times before, but fighting with her, a partner, an equal.

Together, with iron and alchemy, with Furies-given strength and lightning, they brought the last of the enemy down. Wren felt Torj's power surging through her as he swung his hammer and she cast bolts of lightning in its wake, more in control of her magic than she'd ever been.

At last, when the chaos around them waned, Wren saw it.

The gold thread.

The soul bond that linked her to Torj Elderbrock.

His pain was her pain, and hers was his.

The bond was still there. Still intact. She understood why he'd tried to sever it. Understood why he'd done what he'd done.

But that wasn't the only way . . . She saw it so clearly now.

Instead of tearing away from the bond, Wren clung to it, watching as its shimmering cord became more solid beneath her touch, as the connection between them grew anew. She poured all her love for the Warsword into every one of its fibres, and they shared strength and power as one.

Everything else faded away.

Wren went to his side and pulled the mask from her face. 'We were always stronger together.'

CHAPTER 51

Torj

'Magic knows its mirror – in resonance, two powers become one song'

– *Tethers and Magical Bonds Throughout History*

'WE WERE ALWAYS *stronger together.*'

The words settled in Torj's chest, a fragment that had been missing all his life sliding into place.

He looked at the woman who stood at his side, where she belonged – where she had always belonged. Radiant, beautiful, fearless.

Their soul bond gilded them, a ribbon of gold entwining around them.

Nothing else existed for him at that moment.

There was only her.

Their gazes locked, and Torj saw those willow-green eyes brimming with understanding, with forgiveness, with . . . love.

He reached for her, his fingers brushing over her fluttering pulse before cupping the back of her head, threading through her hair.

And then he crushed his mouth to hers.

His knees buckled beneath the force of it. Wren's lips scorched his in a fiery kiss, and Torj lifted her from the ground, wrapping her legs around his middle, not caring who else was there.

Wren was everything. Everything he'd ever wanted. Everything he'd ever needed.

He kissed her hard enough to bruise, until her fingers were digging into his shoulders and her tongue was stroking his in a fever.

Every kiss was a brand, a claim. For she belonged to him, and he to her.

Torj took her to the wall. He needed to be inside her, needed to—

Someone cleared their throat loudly.

He and Wren broke apart, panting.

Thea and Wilder were both waiting by the door. 'We'll leave you to it, shall we?' Thea said with a grin, winking at her sister. 'We'll take the supplies back to Drevenor.'

Wilder patted his pocket carefully. 'I've got to talk to Audra as well.'

Wren nudged Torj. 'Put me down,' she hissed.

'Not a chance, Embers,' he replied, before addressing the two Warswords. 'See you back at the academy.'

Wilder was shaking his head, a wry smile on his face. 'Take your time, brother.'

'Oh, I intend to.'

Wren hit him with the flat of her hand. 'Torj!'

But he caught her by the wrist and covered her mouth with his once more. He turned his back to where Thea and Wilder had just left. He didn't give a fuck that they were in an illegal alchemy workshop, surrounded by gods knew what. All he cared about was that Wren was here, with him.

At last, he took her to the wall, caging her against the stone, lost in the taste, in the feel of her.

Soul bonded.

Wren gripped his hair at the roots, demanding more access to his mouth, grinding against the massive erection he was pressing between her thighs.

This was where he belonged. With her, always.

Molten desire thrummed through him, pooling at the base of his spine, in his throbbing cock. The feel of Wren in his arms threatened to undo him. He'd thought of this moment so many times, dreamed of them finding their way back to one another, with no secrets between them, no hurt.

He could feel her heart pounding against his, that gold thread coiling around them, and he could hold it in no longer.

'I love you,' he murmured against her lips, grazing her throat with his teeth. 'Gods, I love you.'

Wren kissed him back just as fiercely. 'I love you too,' she said breathlessly, bunching her skirts up around them. She was as desperate as he was, arching into his touch, begging for more.

Torj glanced between them and swore at the naked perfection he found there. 'Do you *ever* wear undergarments?'

'Not lately. I grew fond of tormenting a certain Warsword. Are you complaining?' she challenged.

'Gods, no,' he said, fusing his mouth back to hers.

They were a mess of teeth and tongues, of pawing hands. Torj moaned, deep and guttural when Wren freed his cock from his leathers and licked her lips at the sight of the glistening tip.

'I need you inside me, Torj. Now,' she said, her voice thick with heated desperation.

'I started taking the tonic again,' he assured her.

'Fuck me, Bear Slayer,' she commanded. The title slipped from her mouth before she could stop it, but the low groan from the warrior in question told her that perhaps in this context, the name was acceptable.

Torj reached between them and dragged the head of his cock over her clit, notching himself to her entrance, moaning at the wetness he found there.

'Torj,' Wren cried out.

And then he sheathed himself inside her.

Elwren Embervale was *made for him*. Nothing had ever felt so good, so *right*. Tight, wet heat engulfed him, sending spirals of pleasure from his balls through his shaft with such force that he wanted to unleash himself then and there.

Wren's legs tightened around him, and he braced her more firmly against the wall to get better leverage as he pulled out and rammed back inside of her. Each stroke was more intoxicating than the last – addictive, maddening . . . Together, they were insatiable.

'I missed this,' Wren panted against his lips, moving with each one of his thrusts. 'I missed you.'

Missed her didn't even cover what Torj had felt in her absence. It was more like she'd taken a piece of him with her that he could never recover, no matter what he tried. He had dreamed of her, had smelled jasmine and rain even when she wasn't there . . . The world had been bleak and grey, a mindless drag from one day into the next.

'Never again,' he vowed, driving himself into her, finding that sensitive spot within.

'Never,' Wren moaned. As she did, her walls clamped around his cock and his vision blacked out for a moment.

'Gods,' he blurted, using every ounce of willpower to keep himself from spilling inside her. He wasn't done. Not by a long shot.

Holding her with one arm, he reached between them with his other hand, finding her clit with his thumb, circling.

'Torj,' she cried again, her hips bucking. 'Harder.'

He loved the sound of his name on her lips, loved that he could worship her the way she deserved. Applying more pressure to her clit, he did as she commanded, thrusting over and over again until her words became garbled, and she was shaking with need.

Wren's hand crept to his throat, squeezing gently. 'You're going to make me—'

He didn't stop. 'Come for me, Embers. Come all over my cock.'

'Fuck—'

Wren came around him with a moan he felt in his balls, tightening around him, riding him until he saw stars.

It was the final whimper in his ear that sent him hurtling over the edge after her. His climax hit so hard he nearly staggered as he spilled himself inside her, each wave drawing a low, carnal sound from his throat.

Wren swallowed it with another kiss, which was just as well, because the otherworldly experience had rendered him fucking speechless.

When their lips broke apart at last, Torj's eyes fluttered open to a vision of gold.

A gold thread, solid and real, laced around them both.

And Wren was smiling.

Soul bonded.

His soul bonded.

CHAPTER 52

Wren

'When twin flames dance, time itself bows to watch'

— *Tethers and Magical Bonds Throughout History*

How had she lived without his kiss, his touch? The feel of his skin against hers was like an answer to a long-forgotten question.

The gold thread of their soul bond shone brightly, in defiance of all they had withstood together. She felt that bond thrumming in her chest, connecting her to the Warsword who held her. His essence was in her blood, in her bones, in the very fabric of her existence somehow.

Still inside her, Torj kissed her slowly, thoroughly, as though they had all the time in the world. As though they weren't standing in the ruins of the enemy's alchemy workshop.

Wren deepened the kiss, revelling in the taste of him, in the knowledge that he was hers. Her fingers tangled in his hair.

Gold will turn to silver.

She banished the words from her mind, losing herself in Torj as their kiss evolved into a frenzy of fresh desire. Wet with his release, she could feel him hardening again inside her and she rolled her hips experimentally.

Torj groaned. 'You have no idea how much I want to stay here and fuck you senseless . . .'

Wren brushed the loose lock of silver from his brow. 'But . . . ?'

'It's not safe. They'll have reported the attack by now. We need to get out of here so we can have a force lying in wait. Wilder will have put it in motion already.' Torj lifted her off him, placing her carefully on the ground. He didn't release her completely, though, holding her steady while she regained feeling in her legs and cleaned herself up.

Around them, the golden thread dissipated.

Wren reached out to touch the final fading remnants, but her fingers hit only air. 'I still don't fully understand it . . .' she murmured, looking up at Torj in wonder. 'I thought you severed it?'

'I did.' There was regret in Torj's sea-blue gaze. 'Perhaps some bonds can't be broken.'

Wren cupped his face. 'I'm glad.'

Torj placed a hand over hers, pressing his brow to hers. With such reverence, he said, 'I love you.'

'I love you, too.' Wren's cheeks ached. Had it been so long since she'd smiled like this?

Torj traced a thumb over her lips. 'There's nothing more beautiful . . .'

Wren's eyes burned. But the tears that threatened to fall were foreign to her, unlocked by something other than grief and rage.

Happiness.

Was *this* what that felt like?

Torj laced his fingers through hers, pulling her towards the stairs. 'Let's go, Embers.'

When they emerged from the abandoned cobbler's shop, Wren was startled to find that it was daylight outside. It felt as though weeks had passed; so much had changed.

'Should we wait for Roderick?' she said with a glance at the clock tower looming above the underbelly of Old Town. 'He should be passing through on the next hour.'

Torj laughed. 'We're not sitting in the back of some cart. I've left Tucker at the stables. You're riding with me, Embers.'

※

The city passed them by. Sharing the saddle with Torj was different this time. Wren sat between the cradle of his muscular thighs with joy sparking in her heart. The press of his chest against her back was solid, reassuring, and he held the reins loosely with one hand, the other free to roam her body.

'I can't get enough of you,' he murmured, brushing his lips against the side of her neck.

'I can see that,' Wren replied, leaning into his touch. 'But perhaps we should wait until we're not in such a crowded place?'

'I don't give a fuck where we are,' he growled, cupping her over her skirts.

Desire unfurled at the base of her spine, spreading to all her extremities, pooling at her core. Torj had always been passionate, but the soul bond had unleashed him. And she loved it.

But as they passed beneath the Highguard gates and started down the road back to Drevenor, reality came sweeping in like a tide. For now, Wren had everything to lose.

She must have stiffened in the saddle, because Torj's grip around her tightened, his large palm spanning her abdomen, pulling her closer to him. But it was more than that.

'You can sense my emotions, can't you?' she asked, covering his hand with her own.

'Sometimes,' he said. 'I don't think I realized it until now, but sometimes I see your dreams too . . . On the way to Drevenor for the first time? I saw that nightmare you had as if it were my own.'

Wren remembered the way his eyes had darted to the exact place the shadows had been in her mind. It had been there, right from the beginning . . .

'And when we were in that tent during the storm?' he continued. 'I think we shared the same dream then . . .'

Wren's cheeks heated. She had woken with his cock in her hand and her thighs slick with need. Torture. It had been utter torture to have him so close and to deny herself his touch. Gods, the man was in her blood.

The hand at her stomach lifted, fingers stroking her throat. 'I dreamed I was kissing you here,' he told her, before his caress descended to her collarbone. 'And here . . .' His fingers moved lower, tracing the fabric of her bodice, her breasts. 'And here . . .' Warm lips grazed her neck, moving in time with his words, and a soft cry escaped her as he sucked gently on the sensitive skin there.

Torj shifted his hips behind her, the rock-hard length of him undeniable against her backside.

'You were grinding against me, and so wet, Wren . . . You were so wet for me.'

Wren hadn't realized that she was grinding against him now. She blinked, suddenly dazed. 'I dreamed the same . . .' she murmured, arching as Torj squeezed her breast.

'I know,' he replied with a low chuckle. 'I woke up with your hand on my cock, remember?'

'I remember.' Her breath hitched as his hand reached for the hem of her skirts. 'What are you doing?'

'I have to touch you,' he groaned.

She wished she could see his face, the pained expression of need she knew was there. 'You *are* touching me.'

'Not nearly enough,' he told her, pausing as her skirts slid up one thigh. 'Can I make you come again?'

The road before them was empty, the canopy joining overhead shrouding them in dappled shade – a false sense of privacy. Were anyone to join the trail, there would be no hiding themselves. Wren didn't care.

'Yes, Bear Slayer. Make me come.'

His hand slipped beneath her skirts, teasing her by drawing circles over her inner thigh, each movement bringing him closer to where she wanted him, only to deny her.

She made a noise of frustration, wriggling in the saddle, seeking what only he could give her.

A laugh rumbled against her back. 'So impatient,' he murmured, continuing his torture.

'These shared experiences . . . This bond,' she said breathlessly. 'Do you think . . . Do you think it makes us—'

His knuckle trailed down the centre of her. 'Makes us what, Embers?' he said, voice low.

His touch was agonizingly light, barely a whisper, but fanning the flames of her need into an inferno.

'More in tune with one another?' she rasped.

Torj's fingers slid through the wetness between her legs and plunged inside her. 'Shall we find out?'

Wren moaned, loud enough that the sparrows in the trees fled from their branches.

Torj laughed, grinding the heel of his hand against her clit as he fucked her with his fingers. 'Good thing no one's around to hear you screaming my name.'

Wren was too hot, her clothes too tight on her sensitive skin. She wanted to rake her nails across him, wanted to feel the thick length of him filling her again. She reached behind her, fumbling for his belt.

But Torj stopped her. 'Bond or not, your pleasure is my pleasure, Embers,' he said, slowly pumping her with his fingers.

She surrendered to him, tilting her hips to give him better access, allowing the pressure to start building. Every curl of his fingers, every brush against her clit had her writhing. Torj would let her climb the peak of climax, higher and higher until she was panting, and then change his rhythm, slowing down to teasing, luxurious strokes, edging her closer and closer to madness.

'It feels . . .' But she didn't know what it felt like, because it felt like nothing else she'd ever known: a pull between them, stealing the air from her lungs, lighting a fire within.

'I know,' he murmured.

Gods, her body came alive in his presence, calling out for his touch, his kiss. She forgot they were on horseback, that she was rocking in the saddle. She forgot they were on a public road, where anyone might pass by.

Wren forgot everything but him.

Her nails dug into the thick muscles of Torj's thighs, and her head tilted back, leaning against him as he drew out every ripple of pleasure.

The bond flared between them again, gold thread entwining around them once more.

It was beautiful.

And when Wren came apart on his hand, crying out his name, he held her tightly.

CHAPTER 53

Torj

'What fate has forged, even the Furies cannot sever'

– *Tethers and Magical Bonds Throughout History*

TORJ KNEW THAT they were riding back into the chaos of Drevenor. He knew that the midrealms were on the brink of conflict once more. Yet he couldn't contain the joy blossoming within. Wren was in his arms. Wren was *his*. And nothing in the world could stop that from feeling *right*.

She sagged against him in the saddle, wrapping him in her scent as the soul bond flickered between them, at last dissipating as it had before.

'No one can know,' he said quietly. 'About the soul bond. I don't want it used against us.'

'Do you think Silas realized?' she asked, drawing circles on his exposed forearms as he adjusted his grip on the reins. 'When he attacked the hall?'

'I don't know . . . Possibly.' He let out a breath. 'But with an informant inside the academy walls . . . I think we need to keep it a secret for as long as we can.'

Wren shifted against him. 'The bond, or us being together?'

From behind, he tucked her hair around her ear. 'What do you think, Embers?'

Her whole body rose and fell with her sigh. 'The bond . . . We actively hide it. In general, though? I think anyone with half a brain could figure out we're together. But it's not wise to flaunt it. That would be like lighting a beacon to our weaknesses. We keep things quiet. With all the political unrest now, with . . .'

'The Delmirian throne in question?' he finished for her. He had seen her battling with it for weeks. Wilder had filled him in on what Thea had planned: the storm-wielding Warsword was going to take the crown. Thea was going to shoulder the burden she'd dismissed time and time again over the years, and Torj knew that it wasn't sitting right with Wren. The anguish in her voice confirmed it.

'Yes,' she whispered. 'That.'

Even though she was sitting flush against him, Torj needed her closer. He wrapped an arm around her waist and held her to him. 'Whatever you need, Embers. Just know that keeping us secret isn't born of shame, or fear. I'd sing it from the rooftops if you'd allow it.'

Wren huffed a laugh. 'Now *that* I'd pay to see.'

'Maybe one day.' He nuzzled her neck, still marvelling at the fact that he was able to touch her so freely at last. 'But so long as you know that I love you and I want to be with you, that's enough for me.'

'The feeling is mutual, Bear Slayer.'

He smiled into her hair. 'Why do I suddenly like that name again?'

'Because it makes you feel like a king when I'm screaming it as I come on your cock,' she quipped.

The cock in question twitched in his leathers, still hard from their fun in the saddle. 'Such filthy words from a princess.'

'You haven't heard anything yet.'

He gave her a squeeze. 'Is that so? I'll be sure to wring every last word from your lips . . .'

The laugh that bubbled from her was like magic.

Torj knew it was short-sighted, that there were challenges to come. But with Wren in his arms, he could only feel contentment – and a flicker of disbelief that they had reached this point. He remembered the other times they'd shared the saddle, all sharp words and taunts. Now, he didn't want the ride to end.

But end it did, with Drevenor's wrought iron gates coming into view, the academy standing tall beyond the curling ivy.

He felt Wren tense between his legs, felt the tightness in her chest as though it were right there in his own.

'It's not going to be easy,' she warned, her voice no more than a whisper.

'I never said I needed easy,' he told her. 'I needed *you*.'

CHAPTER 54

Wren

'Some threads in destiny's tapestry cannot be cut –
they simply weave new patterns through time'

– *Tethers and Magical Bonds Throughout History*

THERE WAS NOTHING Wren wanted more than to sink into a hot bath with Torj and forget the midrealms existed. But that was not the life she led, and the Bear Slayer understood that. He had told her of the shadow magic he and Wilder had discovered in the enemy laboratory, which only fuelled her need to finish the cure, to stop Silas.

She thanked Dessa profusely for guarding her work in her absence and promised to update her as soon as she could. While Wren washed quickly, Torj retrieved the supplies Thea and Wilder had brought back from the enemy's workshop. When she emerged from the bathing chamber, she was touched to find that everything was set up for her at her bench. There was also a fresh pot of tea and some biscuits.

She glanced to where he waited in the adjoining doorway. 'You did all of this?'

His answering smile had her melting. 'There's nothing I wouldn't do for you.'

Wren bit her lip, warring with herself. Gods, she wanted to go to him; she wanted him close. After so long apart, after all they had missed together . . . Now they had no time.

Another smile, this one full of understanding. 'Do the work, Embers,' he said softly. 'I'll be here when you finish.'

Wren did go to him then, and brushed a kiss to his lips, a promise of what was to come when she finished her opus. 'Thank you,' she told him.

And then, she returned to the cure.

For months she had been working under the assumption that the alchemy attacked blood itself, and in that respect, the earlier cure she'd used on Zavier *had* been a fluke of sorts. But from what she'd seen in the laboratory beneath the cobbler's workshop, the alchemy – or curse – wasn't attacking royal blood; it was attacking the very fibre of the magic in their systems. The substance didn't just attack magical properties and fester, it multiplied upon contact with power . . . and now, armed with that knowledge and the knowledge about her own storm magic, she had to know, once and for all, if it would work.

Wren's hands shook as she set up her samples and the last of the Delmirian rose. If she managed to recreate the counter-alchemy, it would shift the tides of the upcoming conflict.

As afternoon turned into evening and evening turned into night, Wren called for Thea. Her sister gave her a fresh sample of royal blood to work with and promised to retrieve some from Zavier as soon as he was well enough, so Wren could be sure that whatever she created didn't simply work on her alone.

Seeing her focus, Thea didn't linger. Wren simply thanked her and continued her work.

At some point, Torj brought her more food. The Warsword didn't speak, didn't fracture her concentration; he simply stood by her side until she'd finished her bowl of stew and then took it away. When he was gone, his scent lingered, and she found herself moving towards the adjoining door before she stopped herself.

'Do the work, Embers. I'll be here when you finish.'

She turned back to her crucibles and powders, and continued.

Wren had no notion of the hour when there was a soft knock at the main door. She opened it to find Farissa on the other side.

'May I come in?' her former mentor asked.

Wren stepped aside. 'What time is it?'

'Nearly the third hour,' Farissa replied as she entered the room, taking in the chaos across every surface. 'I knew you'd be awake.'

When Wren had been Farissa's apprentice, they had always started their mornings before daybreak. Back then, Wren had found it invigorating, always something new to learn on the horizon. She thought the war had taken that joy from her, but Drevenor, even with all its faults, had given it back.

'I'd offer you some tea, but I'm afraid it's gone cold,' she said, closing the door and turning to face the older woman.

Farissa dismissed this with a wave. Her gaze roamed over the shallow glass dishes of blood, over the mortar and pestle that held the last remnants of the powdered rose leaves. 'You're ready, then? To present to the masters?'

'As I'll ever be,' Wren told her, palming the grit from her eyes. 'This is not a simple academic body of work, Farissa. The sooner the midrealms has this in their hands, the better it will be for all of us. I need to present it to the masters before the next council meeting. Before . . .' She trailed off. She couldn't bring herself to say the words.

'Before Thea declares she is taking the Delmirian throne?' Farissa finished for her.

'Yes.' Wren wrung her hands. 'I think it will be . . . *impactful* to announce the counter-alchemy at the same time. And for that to happen, I must pass the presentation.'

Farissa bowed her head. 'Be ready at dusk tomorrow.'

'Thank you.'

She thought Farissa would leave after that, but instead, the older woman closed the distance between them and wrapped her arms around Wren.

Farissa's body was hard and lean, but her embrace was warm. Wren could count on one hand how many times they had hugged in the decades they'd known one another, but she didn't break away.

'I'm proud of you, Elwren,' Farissa told her quietly. 'You have come so far in this past year alone. You are becoming the alchemist I knew you could be.'

Wren felt her lip quiver, and she didn't trust herself to speak. Instead, she simply nodded and patted Farissa on the back, at last pulling away.

'You did the right thing,' she blurted. 'Denying me a letter of recommendation for all those years. I would have . . .' She didn't know what she would or wouldn't have done, and that was what scared her. 'You did the right thing,' she said again.

Farissa smiled. 'I know. Get some rest, Elwren. You're going to need it.'

As the door clicked closed behind her, Wren stared at what countless hours of literal blood, sweat, and tears had produced: three small vials of a brilliant midnight-blue liquid that would either damn them, or save them all.

The adjoining door creaked open. 'You're finished?' Torj's voice danced along her very bones.

'I'm done,' Wren replied, her voice hoarse.

He crossed the room and wrapped his arms around her from behind. 'Does that mean I can take you to bed now?'

Wren laughed, turning around to face him. She studied the silver of his hair, the sharp line of his stubble-covered jaw, the white scar through his dark brow and the smile tugging at his lips.

'Have you been waiting up all night for me, Bear Slayer?' she asked.

'I waited years for you, Embers.' Torj brushed a heated kiss to her mouth. 'What was a few more hours?'

CHAPTER 55

Wren

'No boundary remains between what was once separate and what is now eternal'

— *Tethers and Magical Bonds Throughout History*

THE MAN BETWEEN her legs was a god. Wren gripped Torj's hair by the roots as he pinned her thighs open and devoured her. Grabbing the headboard above with her other hand, she writhed beneath his wicked tongue, admiring the way his broad golden shoulders rippled and tensed.

He had told her to sleep, that she needed to rest. But with his powerful body beside hers, rest was the last thing she wanted. Wren had slipped her hand beneath the sheets and around his cock – and that was all it had taken for the Warsword to unleash himself on her.

The noises escaping her now were incoherent, desperate pleas—

And then the room was tilting, with Torj suddenly beneath her, her legs astride his head as he licked her from below. He was a man starved for her, ravenous, and Wren loved every second of it. She couldn't get enough of him, had never felt this free, this uninhibited. She was riding his gods-damned face, for fuck's sake.

She cried out as he slipped a finger inside her, curling it to hit that spot that made her see stars. Sweat dripped between her breasts as she moved with him, panting at the pressure that was building and building.

When he reached up and pinched her nipple, she moaned, the sensation bordering on the delicious line between pain and pleasure.

'Torj,' she demanded, not afraid to tell him what she wanted – all of him. Now. 'Fuck me from behind.'

With a growl of approval, Torj circled her waist with his large hands, and she found herself being lifted from his mouth and turned around. On her knees, she faced the wall, the mattress sinking around her as he crowded her. He traced her curves from her waist to her breasts, lingering there, toying with her nipples, biting her neck, the hard length of his cock resting above her backside.

Wren ground against him, but her Bear Slayer seemed to be in no rush. He circled one nipple with a featherlight touch, teasing and taunting the tight peak until Wren was chasing the contact, the high that he offered. But his hands left her aching breasts, trailing down her arms where he laced his fingers through hers. Then, he positioned her grip back on the edge of the headboard.

'You're going to want to hang on tight, Embers . . .'

And then he slid inside her from behind in one punishing glide.

'Fuck,' he moaned, the sound echoing in Wren's bones as he forced her legs further apart and slammed into her again. And again.

'Harder,' she commanded. 'I need it harder.'

She felt his smile against her shoulder before his palm flattened against her back and pushed her down, giving him better access.

Torj pounded into her, the bed rattling around them and Wren hanging onto the headboard for dear life. She felt herself stretching around him, his cock filling every inch of her, the sensation so intoxicating it was almost overwhelming.

The wet slide of him, the heat of his skin, the slap of their bodies together had her begging for more as he frayed every nerve ending she had, the sensation mounting as he drove his cock into her. She was unravelling, losing herself to the utter frenzy between them.

'I'm not done with you yet,' he muttered, the words themselves threatening to send her over the edge. But the Warsword knew her body better than she knew it herself, and he slowed his pace, taking her back from the brink, drawing out each stroke, his grip still near-bruising. Wren's toes curled at the thought. She wanted his marks on her.

Then they were moving again, her body almost boneless as he drew her back up against him, manoeuvring them so he was seated at the edge of the bed with her in his lap, her back flush with his chest. His Furies-given strength was wasted on the battlefield, she thought distantly. This . . . *this* was what Warswords were made for.

She was straddling his thighs, the new position leaving his hands free to explore every part of her while she lowered herself onto his shaft and rode him. Torj groaned as she did just that, meeting her movements with thrusts of his own from beneath.

When his hand dipped between her legs, dragging the wetness from where they were joined to circle her clit, Wren's head dropped back against his shoulder with a cry.

'That's it, Embers . . .' he murmured, nipping at her throat, increasing the pressure and pace of his fingers between her legs.

Wren lost herself to the ecstasy coiling tighter and tighter inside her, lost herself to the fullness of him. He was everywhere, driving her to the edge of oblivion again and again.

Just when she thought she could take no more, he was shifting her once again. She made a brief noise of protest as he withdrew from her body and stood—

'I want to see your face when you come,' he told her, his voice low and husky with desire. Hooking his hands under her thighs, he lifted her as though she weighed nothing. But he didn't throw her on the bed as she expected . . .

He took her to the fucking wall.

Wren's back hit the cool stone, and then he was inside her again.

With her nails clawing at his shoulders, his back, Wren let go as Torj fucked her hard and deep. Every thrust, every slide of his cock coaxed bursts of pleasure from her, each one more damning than the last.

He captured her mouth with his. The kiss was as demanding as his fucking. He gave her everything, and Wren took it gladly, drinking in the taste, the scent, the feel of him, as though it could make up for all the time they had lost.

A frame on the wall toppled from its hook and shattered on the floor, but Torj didn't stop. He moved inside her like a man possessed, a man undone. With her legs wrapped around him, he pinned her to the wall, fucking her mercilessly and reaching for her clit. He timed the brush of his thumb with the moment he hit that spot deep inside her, and Wren nearly blacked out.

The climax that he'd been edging her towards for what felt like hours finally hit her.

Her vision blurred as her orgasm tore through her, and she clenched around his cock with a cry. Torj's gaze didn't leave her face, the heat in his eyes smouldering as she rode the waves of bliss he'd created.

And then he shuddered inside her.

The carnal noise that ripped from his throat made Wren's thighs tighten around him as she felt him pulse, felt him spill his own release. They were both panting, both damp with sweat.

And that thread of gold danced around them.

Wren wanted to say something, something that captured the momentous thing between them, the life-altering bond that she felt deep in her bones. She searched for the right words, the words to do justice to the man before her and the thing they shared. Torj rested his brow against hers and beat her to it. *Fuck, I love you.*

CHAPTER 56

Wren

'History bears witness to the undeniable power of prophecy across the midrealms...'

— *The Midrealms Chronicles*

*F*UCK, *I LOVE you*. Torj had spoken into her mind. His rich, husky tone had skittered along her bones, as real as if he'd spoken the words into the shell of her ear.

Wren clung to those words the next day as she gathered her things in her room. Her hands moved through the familiar motions of packing, but her mind raced with all the ways her presentation could go wrong. One miscalculation, one trembling hand during the demonstration, and she could lose everything she'd worked for.

Dusk was upon her all too soon, and she was meticulous as she prepared the vials of counter-alchemy and shuffled her notes together. She was as prepared as she'd ever be, and Torj grounded her like no one else. So she shouldered her satchel and held her head high.

The Bear Slayer was waiting outside her room. 'You're ready,' he said. It wasn't a question. It was a statement, and there was no quaver in his voice, no room for doubt.

'Yes.'

They didn't speak as they made their way to the lecture hall. It was as though Torj could sense that she needed to centre herself, to find the calm within. They crossed the foyer, beneath the great tree that reached up through the levels, and when they arrived at the door to the hall, Torj stopped.

Wren's breath caught as his lips brushed over hers. It was a whisper of a kiss, but she felt his love for her as though he'd poured it directly into her veins.

'You can do this,' he told her, and opened the door.

Wren entered alone, as she'd been instructed, and the vast lecture hall swallowed her footsteps. Torches cast pools of amber light down the tiered rows of empty seats – hundreds of them, all facing the demonstration space like a silent audience. The air held the sharp tang of cleaning solution beneath more subtle notes of aged wood and chalk dust. The auditorium was empty but for the five seats occupied at the front. There sat Master Crawford, Master Norlander, Master Mercer, Farissa and the High Chancellor.

Taking a steadying breath, Wren approached and stood before them. The polished wooden floor gleamed beneath her feet, worn smooth by countless students who had stood in the very same spot. From somewhere high in the rafters came the soft flutter of wings – several sparrows had found their way inside. The sound made the space feel even larger, even more hollow.

'What is the opus you present to us today, Elwren?' Master Norlander asked, clasping his hands in front of him.

Her palms grew damp, and she resisted the urge to wipe them on her apron as she noted the familiar faces now sharp with scrutiny.

'I chose to create a counter-alchemy to that which has been used by the enemies of the midrealms to mute and eradicate royal magic.' Wren placed her satchel on the table that had been set up for her and unpacked the things she needed. 'If you'd like to come forward to view my demonstration?'

Her fingers trembled slightly as she laid out the shallow dishes, each clearly labelled with whose blood it contained. The glass clinked softly against the wooden table, its surface etched with tiny marks and stains from past experiments. Wren distantly wondered how many had succeeded and how many had failed. But the familiar scent of her alchemy equipment – clean glass, cork stoppers and the metallic tang of blood – helped steady her nerves. This was her domain.

When the masters and High Chancellor stood before her table, peering down at her alchemy equipment, Wren started to speak.

'In these dishes are samples of the blood of magic wielders.' She pointed. 'This is mine. This is Althea Embervale's. And this is Zavier Terling's. Three samples of different royal blood.'

'Would you not argue that you only have two samples?' Master Norlander asked. 'Given that you and your sister share the same blood?'

'I have reason to suspect they are different in nature,' Wren said. 'But for now, the blood is untainted, taken straight from the vein.' She uncorked another vial. 'This is the substance the enemy has been using on their weapons. It is also the alchemy they forced Queen Reyna to drink, subduing much of her power.'

Wren poured the enemy's concoction into each sample. The reaction was immediate and violent – the blood didn't just shrink away; it writhed like a living thing. Where the two substances met, tiny sparks of magic crackled and died, leaving behind a residue that looked like tarnished silver.

'See how the blood shrinks away?' She pointed to where the blood was moving in the dishes, as though trying to escape the alchemy. 'I know from personal experience with this creation that the magic of the wielder retreats from this alchemy's touch, that it burrows deep inside the host to escape it.'

'Very well, Elwren,' Master Mercer said. 'And your counter-alchemy?'

Wren uncorked another vial. The cork came free with a soft hiss, releasing a scent like burnt metal and oranges. The liquid inside seemed to bend the light around it unnaturally. 'I broke the dark alchemy down into its numerous elements.' She gestured to her notes, where complex diagrams showed the various structures she'd discovered through countless hours of observation. Each component had been carefully isolated and tested; the results meticulously documented, and so she forged on. 'One part of lifelore that has always fascinated me is that the antidote to a poison often contains traces of the poison itself. I applied this logic to my methods here. I arrived at the perfect balance to disengage the active ingredients within the dark alchemy. See for yourself . . .'

She tapped several drops from the vial into each sample dish and watched as it took effect. Her creation was almost luminescent as it made contact with the corrupted blood, spreading like sunlight breaking through storm clouds. Her cure drew the dark alchemy away from the blood and seemed to absorb it, the reaction causing a gentle hiss and a ribbon of steam to rise, producing tiny specks that danced in the air before dissipating.

'Fascinating . . .' Master Norlander said, peering into the dishes.

'Indeed.' The High Chancellor nodded. 'Though have you tested on a live subject?'

Wren nodded. 'Several mice. The Prince of Naarva, at the end of the attack after the Gauntlet. And myself.'

'Given the nature of this opus, and its importance to the current conflict, I think it prudent to witness a live test for ourselves . . .' Master Crawford motioned to someone at the far side of the hall.

The click of boots echoed off the curved stone walls, heavy with urgency as two healers entered, holding up a slumped figure between them.

Queen Reyna.

Suddenly, the stakes of her demonstration crystallized with terrifying clarity. This wasn't just about Wren's opus. It wasn't even about the queen herself. It was about the fate that awaited the midrealms should she fail. *That* was what hung in the balance. The

Queen of Aveum was a shell of her former self. She looked frailer than she had when Wren had seen her after the death of her husband in the shadow war.

'Your Majesty,' Wren murmured, rushing to her side.

The queen's voice was raw and throaty as she spoke. 'They forced me to drink it when I was captured. Poured it down my throat.'

'And this happened?' Wren asked. 'You became sick?'

Queen Reyna shook her head. 'I felt my magic retreat, become muted . . . But beyond that, the effects were not so physical. I was able to ride to Aveum with the Warswords. I was in my palace for a time before I started to feel ill.'

Wren's mind was racing. 'A delayed reaction . . .' she said to herself. 'They wanted you to think you were well, only to have you fall ill later.'

The winter queen dipped her head in confirmation, the healers still holding her up on either side. 'Elwren, I cannot see the future any more. I cannot feel a trace of my magic.'

'She becomes weaker every day,' one of the healers said.

'I suspect that the aim was to use me as a scare tactic for the other royals,' Queen Reyna rasped. 'It's why Silas let me go with the Warswords. In the hopes I'd be taken right back here to incite panic, to show the rulers the fate that awaits them if they do not comply with his regime. I tried to go back to Aveum. I tried to stay away . . .'

Her words sent a chill through Wren. As far as she knew, Silas was yet to make any demands. He had spread his poisonous words across the midrealms like a disease, had provoked death and violence in the name of liberation . . . but he hadn't announced any ultimatums. Not yet.

One problem at a time, she told herself. The first step was to cure Queen Reyna. Then, and only then, could she deal with everything else.

Forgetting that the masters were there, Wren examined the queen. Her skin was cold to the touch, and beneath it, Wren could sense the corrupted magic moving like sluggish ink through her veins. Her heartbeat was slow, her complexion grey, and there was a blue tint to her lips, her fingernails . . . A slow poisoning of dark alchemy indeed.

'And usual healing methods?' Wren asked. 'Have they been effective for any kind of relief?'

'No. They simply result in the acceleration of previous symptoms. They make things worse.'

Sometimes, in the presence of other magic wielders, Wren could feel their power, but with the fragile queen in her arms, she felt nothing.

'I trust you, Elwren,' Queen Reyna wheezed. 'I entrust my magic, my life, to you.'

The healers lay her down on the ground, and suddenly Wren was keenly aware of all the masters crowding around her, their eyes boring holes in her back.

Gods, what if Reyna lost her magic for good? What if she *died*? The questions echoed in her mind with increasing urgency, each heartbeat bringing a new potential catastrophe to the surface. Her fingers felt numb as they gripped the vial, and for a terrifying moment, she feared she might drop it. Wren pushed the voices aside. The only thing that mattered now was that the cure *worked*.

Swiping another vial of antidote from the table and lifting the queen's head into her lap, she tilted Reyna's chin up so that the potion could slide down her throat.

'You're alright, Your Majesty,' she murmured. 'You're going to be alright.'

The queen's pupils dilated, and she stilled in Wren's arms. The silence in the hall became absolute, pressing against Wren's ears like a physical force. Even the usual creaks and settling sounds of the old building seemed to hold their breath. A drop of sweat rolled down Wren's temple as she saw an array of possible futures branching out before her, all of them balanced on the edge of a blade – her mind. The masters' presence faded away until there was nothing but her, the queen and the desperate prayer that her cure would work.

As the minutes ticked by, the healers panicked, shoving her aside so they could check Queen Reyna's pulse, her breathing, in a flurry of nervous movements—

'Give her a moment,' Wren hissed, watching with her heart in her throat.

A garbled noise escaped the queen, and she started to squirm against the healers' grips. Wren surged forwards, helping her sit up, and peered into Reyna's eyes as her pupils returned to normal size, as she caught her breath.

'How do you feel, Your Majesty?' Wren asked gently, still holding her trembling hand.

'I feel . . .' the queen rasped, taking in the eager stares of the masters gathered around them. 'I feel . . . like myself, albeit still a little weak . . .'

Wren nodded. 'That's a start. Your body will need time to recover, as with usual illness—'

'And what of your magic, Your Majesty?' Master Crawford demanded. 'Have your seer abilities returned?'

Wren cursed him silently, hating his impatience and insensitivity. The queen had been close to death – did she not deserve a moment to gather herself?

But Queen Reyna seemed to be testing herself, her brow furrowed. 'Seer magic is not like lightning and fire to be summoned.'

'But can you feel its presence? As you could before?' Farissa asked softly.

Slowly, Reyna nodded. 'I can.'

Master Norlander's eyes narrowed. 'Perhaps it's still depleted. Maybe Elwren hasn't perfected the—'

Queen Reyna gasped suddenly, her hand shooting out to clamp over Wren's. 'Gold will turn to silver in a blaze of iron and embers,' she said, her grip almost bone-breaking. 'Giving rise to ancient power long forgotten . . .'

Wren's heart sank, her shoulders caving. Gods, she wished the masters weren't here to see this failure. And Farissa, after all the support she'd given Wren, only to be let down so publicly.

She bowed her head. 'That is a prophecy from the past, Your Majesty. It has already happened . . .'

But Queen Reyna placed a finger beneath her chin, lifting it with a knowing smile. 'Has it?'

CHAPTER 57

Wren

'The sweetest peace blooms in gardens
guarded by thorns'

– Elwren Embervale's notes and observations

'I THINK WE have seen enough, yes?' Farissa failed to hide her smile as she turned to the other masters.

Wren's heart was still pounding, and it was only Queen Reyna's hand sliding from hers that brought her back to the judgment she now awaited. 'Thank you,' the queen said as the healers helped her from the stage.

There was a general murmuring of consent before the High Chancellor addressed Wren. 'Thank you for sharing your work with us, Elwren. Do you have the written report?'

Wren nodded, retrieving the carefully bound pieces of parchment in her satchel and offering them to the High Chancellor.

'If this result can be replicated across all those impacted, then you have just changed the tide of the war,' he told her. 'For now, you may go.'

Gathering her things with trembling hands, Wren practically fled the theatre, where her sister and two more Warswords were waiting in the foyer.

Warmth wrapped around Wren as the Bear Slayer encircled her with his arms, kissing the top of her head. Wren breathed in the familiar scent of him and grinned into his chest.

'It worked . . .'

'Of course it did,' Torj told her with a wide smile. 'You made it.'

Wren savoured his touch for a moment longer before she pulled away, aware that they were in the middle of the foyer for anyone to see.

Torj's arms dropped from around her and she turned to Thea, who was beaming.

'If I'm not mistaken, Wren just defeated dark alchemy and earned her spot as a sage at Drevenor. We need to celebrate. Let's go to that tavern Kipp's always on about.'

'That's a bit premature, don't you think, Thee?' Wren said, leaning back towards Torj to whisper, 'and I can think of other ways I'd like to celebrate.'

He went rigid beside her.

'We're busy,' he blurted out. 'Wren's got work for the academy—'

'I don't think so, Bear Slayer,' Thea replied with a knowing grin. 'We've handed the shadow magic over to Audra who's looking into it, and now our hands are tied while we wait for Wren's results. One drink at this tavern. Then my sister can do her "work".'

Torj laughed and gave Wren a shrug. 'I tried.'

'It was a poor effort,' Wren told him, but she couldn't help the smile tugging at her lips.

'It was,' Torj admitted. 'But perhaps you should see it as an opportunity.'

Wren raised a brow. 'Oh?'

Torj answered with a wicked grin. 'A drink, something to eat . . . You'll need your strength for what I have in mind for you.'

'Is that right?' Wren had to stop herself from leaning in, from pressing her lips to his.

'That's right.'

'Were we that insufferable?' Thea cut in, looking to Wilder for confirmation.

'Yes,' Wren and Torj replied in unison.

Wilder laughed and threw an arm around Thea's shoulders, pressing a kiss to her temple and leading her towards the academy doors. 'I'm afraid so, Princess.'

Wren watched them, her heart full. Gods, she was glad her sister had that happiness. After all they'd been through during the war, it was one of the things that eased her sorrows. Thea deserved that love.

Wren was jolted from her thoughts by a warm hand turning her body. She stared up to find Torj watching her, a soft smile playing on his lips.

'I think we should join them,' he said. 'Just for a while. It's not often you get to see Thea, and with what's to come . . . We could all use the distraction. Thea more than anyone.'

Wren found herself nodding. 'I love that about you,' she said quietly as they started after the two Warswords.

'What?' Torj looked genuinely confused.

'You're always thinking of others. And I love that you care for my sister.'

'She's my friend,' Torj said. 'They both are. I don't imagine a day when they won't be.'

Wren gave his hand a squeeze before dropping it quickly. 'That makes me happy, Bear Slayer.'

Torj leaned in, their sides brushing against one another as they walked. 'That's all I want from this life.'

'Not more Warsword glory and heroic adventures?' she teased.

Torj laughed, and Wren savoured the sound. He didn't laugh enough, she decided, and she would do everything within her power to change that.

'I've had enough glory and adventure for several lifetimes over,' he replied.

The evening was unusually warm, and the revelry had spilled

from the tavern to the grounds outside. Tables and chairs had been set up beneath the stars, and several fires illuminated the makeshift garden party. It was no surprise to see Kipp greeting Thea and Wilder warmly, thrusting drinks into their hands as he held court at a table with Cal and Dessa.

Wren glanced at Torj as they made their way towards the merriment. 'What do you see for yourself?' she asked. 'When . . . when peace is restored?'

Torj's fingers brushed hers. 'I've never really let myself think that far ahead. Being a warrior, a protector . . . It's all I've ever known.'

'But if you could do anything, be anything . . . what would it be?' Wren pressed.

He faltered, tugging her to a stop so they remained out of earshot of the crowd. 'Honestly? All I want is a life with you, Embers. A life where we're not constantly fighting battles or chasing prophecies or cures. Just . . . a simple life. With you.'

Wren swallowed the lump in her throat. 'And if I can't give that to you?'

'Then I'll take whatever you can offer and thank the Furies every day for it,' he told her fiercely.

Tears stung Wren's eyes. 'I love you,' she murmured, wishing she could press her lips to his.

Torj loosed a shaky breath. 'I have dreamed of the day you would say that to me so freely . . .' His voice was low and hoarse. 'It still doesn't feel real.'

'It's real, Bear Slayer.' She brushed her fingers against his again, entwining them briefly. 'I love you.'

'And I love you.'

'Good.' Wren smiled, swiping at her falling tears.

'What about you?' the Warsword asked. 'What do you see for yourself?'

'I want the same thing, only with one minor addition,' she replied. 'I want a cat.'

Torj made a noise of protest. 'Surely you can be convinced of a dog instead?'

'Not a chance.' She squeezed his hand. 'Shall we go and join our friends?'

'If we must,' Torj sighed, clicking his tongue in mock frustration. 'Whose idea was this anyway?'

With warmth blooming through her chest, Wren laughed and tugged her Warsword towards the revelry.

CHAPTER 58

Torj

'When a pair is soul bonded, it is the creation of something entirely new, like dawn born from the marriage of night and day'

— *Tethers and Magical Bonds Throughout History*

Torj thought he'd known happiness when Wren had told him that she loved him. But watching her beautiful face light up with joy, watching as tears of laughter streamed down her cheeks, was something else entirely.

He studied her with a sense of wonder. That this woman, who had walked through shadow and fire, who had faced her own darkest monsters, was here with a smile on her lips.

He knew Wren and Dessa were worried about Zavier, who remained sedated in the infirmary, but he was glad they were here. The women celebrated Wren's triumph together, and that was exactly how it should be.

Torj sat beside Wren at the wooden table beneath the stars, the grass growing wet with dew around them as the night wore on. He couldn't stop himself touching her: a fleeting squeeze of her thigh beneath the table, a brush of his leg against hers. Every graze of contact sent lightning singing through his veins. He could feel

Wren's power thrumming inside him, and as the hour grew late, he was practically vibrating with need for her.

'Something wrong, Bear Slayer?' she teased, her gaze dropping to the bulge he was adjusting in his leathers.

'Nothing I can't handle,' he murmured.

'Is it something *I* could handle?' she asked coyly, glancing around at their drunk, distracted friends and wetting her lips.

'You're playing with fire, Embers . . .' he warned.

'Am I?'

He sucked in a sharp breath as her hand slid into his lap beneath the table, and another as she brushed over his hard cock, squeezing him through the layers.

'You're forgetting how much I like to go up in flames,' she whispered in his ear.

Desire swept through Torj like a current, and he clenched his fists so suddenly he nearly upset his drink.

'Alas,' she said. 'I need to speak with Wilder.'

'That is *not* the name I want to hear on your lips right now,' Torj grumbled.

To his dismay, Wren looked delighted. 'I didn't take you for a jealous Warsword . . .'

'Only when my woman drives me to the point of madness under the table and then—'

'Your woman?' Wren echoed, grinning.

'Yes,' Torj replied, studying her expression for any signs of objection. 'My woman.'

Wren was all smiles. 'Well, your woman needs to speak to Wilder alone, without Thea. Can you occupy her while we get another round of drinks?'

'Anything for you, Embers . . .'

'Do I already have you wrapped around my finger so thoroughly?'

'That's been the case since the first day I met you,' he said warmly, spotting Thea standing hand-in-hand with Wilder at the far side of their table, deep in conversation with Kipp.

He squeezed Wren's knee before he got to his feet and approached her sister.

'A word?' he said to the older Embervale.

Thea flashed him a smile. 'Can't say I didn't see this coming . . . Alright, Bear Slayer, lead the way.'

Not sure what Thea was talking about, Torj led her away from the curious looks of the others, hoping he'd be able to stall her long enough to give Wren the time she needed with Wilder.

Thea folded her arms over her chest and smirked. 'So . . . you and my sister.'

'Yes,' Torj said simply. There was no point in denying it, not to Thea, who had seen them kissing in the alchemy workshop, who suspected – if not knew – about the soul bond.

'And you've patched things up properly?' Thea pressed.

'We have.'

Thea nodded. 'I'm glad to hear it, Bear Slayer. Wren was . . . not herself after the attack. I didn't like seeing her like that.'

'Nor did I.'

'Good. Because if she ends up in that state again, you'll have me to answer to.' Thea's words were light, but the storm in her eyes revealed the threat beneath them.

'I love her,' Torj told her.

'Of course you do.' Thea laughed. 'You've loved her for years. Good of you to finally catch up. Now, what is it you wanted to discuss?'

For a moment, Torj blinked, until he remembered that *he* had asked Thea for a private word. He recovered clumsily. 'I just wanted to explain. About Wren.'

Thea raised her brows. 'So, it had nothing to do with Wren wanting to talk to Wilder without me?'

'Uh . . .'

Just in time, Wilder and Wren appeared from the tavern, each carrying a fresh tray of drinks.

Thea clapped a hand on Torj's shoulder. 'No matter, Bear Slayer. Just remember . . . Hurt my sister again, and I'll end you.'

He huffed a laugh. 'Noted.'

She waved over her shoulder and strode back to Wilder.

'What was that about?' Wren asked, staring after her.

'Just Thea threatening my life,' Torj replied. 'Did you have enough time to talk with Hawthorne?'

'Yes. Thank you for that.'

'Are you going to tell me what it was about?'

Wren sighed. 'Not yet. Is that alright?'

Torj studied her as she seemed to gather herself, smoothing her palms over her apron and redoing her bun with her hairpin. Gods, she was beautiful. He admired the gentle slope of her neck, the slight flush of her freckled cheeks.

'You'll tell me when you're ready?' he asked.

'I will.'

'Then it's alright.'

He led her back to the table, where Kipp was trying to convince everyone to play a drinking game.

'Not on your life, Kristopher,' Torj told him as Kipp tried to push a cup of fire extract towards him.

Wren laughed. 'A wise move, Bear Slayer. You were a tad pathetic the next day.'

'I learned my lesson,' he replied, wishing he could pull her closer to him.

Kipp threw his hands up in surrender. 'Fine, fine. I'll have to ask my *real* friends.'

'May the Furies take pity on them,' Torj called after the strategist as he made a beeline for Dessa.

As they found themselves alone, Wren turned to him with a wicked grin, the very sight making his cock twitch. With a quick glance around, she ran her hand over him beneath the table and he swore under his breath. He'd have to untuck his damn shirt to hide the full outline of his cock straining against his leathers. Wren watched him do exactly that, smiling at him smugly.

'You're pleased with yourself, aren't you?' he ground out.

'Very,' she replied sweetly, rubbing his shaft again.

He covered her hand with his, giving it a warning squeeze over the length of him before releasing her hand back into her lap. 'Time to go,' he said, adjusting himself and standing abruptly. They'd done enough socializing for one night, he decided.

'So soon?' Wren asked innocently.

'You'd already be halfway up that hill if you knew what was good for you, Embers,' he replied darkly.

His body hummed with barely contained restraint as he bid the others goodbye and waited for Wren on the outskirts of the gathering. Her eyes were bright with mischief as she rejoined him. They walked along the stone pavers towards the academy. Torj waited until they were out of sight before he pounced.

She squealed as he swept her up in his arms and pulled her into a shadowed alcove behind a statue. 'You've been playing a dangerous game tonight,' he murmured, leaning in to breathe in the addictive scent of her, his nose grazing the delicate column of her throat.

'What are you going to do about it, Warsword?' she taunted, licking her lips as she stared up at him.

Torj captured her mouth with his. 'Everything.'

CHAPTER 59

Torj

'Scholars documented rare cases of soul-bonded pairs whose senses transcended mortal limits. What one perceived, the other knew – not through conscious sharing, but as naturally as breathing'

– *Tethers and Magical Bonds Throughout History*

WREN MOANED AGAINST him, the sound vibrating straight down into his cock. He knew she'd worked herself up just as much as him by the way her body arched for him. He cupped her breast over her gown and relished the whimper that escaped her, swallowing it with another kiss.

Wedging his knee between hers, Torj let his hands slip around her waist and drop to her backside, squeezing hard.

'This arse, Embers . . .' he groaned, kneading the soft flesh there. 'I can't get enough of it.' Still gripping her behind, he brought her forwards, so her core rubbed on his thigh.

'Torj . . .' Wren's voice was needy and breathless.

Smiling against her lips, he rocked her against his leg, feeling the heat of her through their layers. 'Not so smug now, are you?'

Wren rolled her hips, grinding against him as she fused her mouth back to his.

Longing ripped through Torj like a storm, and he matched her ferocity, tangling his tongue with hers, exploring every inch of her mouth. He felt every kiss in his blood, molten with the need to touch her, to feel her bare skin.

Wren reached down between them and palmed him through his leathers. A low groan broke from him, the friction deliciously torturous. More. He needed more of her. He needed her crying out his name as she shattered on his tongue.

Pleasure bloomed at the base of his spine, spreading to his tightening balls and his throbbing cock. Gods, if he didn't do something soon, he'd come in his leathers. He focused on the feel of Wren, inching her skirts up behind her.

She gasped as the cool night air hit her skin and Torj slid his hands over the bare curve of her rear. He knew he was being reckless, but he couldn't stop, not with her panting against him and rubbing herself on his leg.

He manoeuvred them deeper into the shadows, so they were covered by the huge plinth of the statue, and turned Wren so her back was flush with his chest, her skirts still rucked up behind her.

Torj dropped to his knees.

'What are you doing?' Wren whispered, sounding alarmed.

He kissed the base of her spine, down one curved cheek, biting gently. 'Do you want me to stop?' He bit the other side, moaning against her warm skin.

Wren's breathing hitched. 'No . . .'

'Then bend over for me, Embers. Hold on to the stone.'

'Torj . . .'

'Say the word and I stop,' he murmured, dipping his hand between her legs and cursing at the wetness he found there.

'Don't stop,' Wren whimpered, bending at the waist, baring herself completely to him.

'Fuck . . .' He parted her further and took in the view like a starved man, the nearby torches illuminating her glistening skin just enough that he almost lost control. 'Need to taste you,' he groaned.

And then he put his mouth on her.

Her legs trembled beneath his hold as he worked her with his tongue. He moaned at the taste of her as he devoured her, building her up to her climax, increasing his pace and keeping his rhythm steady.

'Furies – fuck,' Wren rasped, gripping the edge of the stone plinth.

Torj smiled against her as he swirled his tongue and sucked on her clit.

When he slid a finger inside her, she let out a strangled cry. He loved seeing her like this, quaking with pleasure, cursing and begging with his name on her lips.

'More,' she gasped, rocking back against his face in earnest now, any vulnerability long gone.

Torj obliged her, adding a second finger, his cock leaking at how good she felt, how good she tasted, imagining sheathing himself inside that addictive heat. He was losing his damn mind with desire for her, his cock ready to spill right into his trousers. Every time he thought his attraction to Wren couldn't get any more intense, he was proven wrong.

'Torj, I'm going to—' She cut herself off with a cry.

'Ride my face, Embers,' he groaned against her skin.

Torj felt her contract around his fingers, and he sucked her clit through the throes of her release as she shuddered around him.

He nearly came at the sound of her orgasm alone.

Wren's legs buckled and he extricated himself smoothly, holding her up, holding her close. But Wren twisted to face him, her hands at his belt.

'I want to feel you, all of you, inside me,' she murmured, buttons popping free beneath her fingers.

'We should get back to our rooms,' Torj managed, his breath stolen as a warm hand closed around his cock.

'I think that ship has sailed, Bear Slayer,' Wren said wryly.

She pumped him slowly, his whole body tensing in anticipation of the next stroke. Her hand worked him over until he was groaning into the crook of her neck, his balls tightening.

'Need to fuck you,' he growled, his hands sliding down to her backside again.

'So fuck me, Warsword,' she challenged.

He didn't need telling twice. He picked her up and propped her against the plinth as she pulled her skirts up around her waist.

Torj aligned the head of his cock with her entrance, holding his breath, tensing his body so he didn't lose control too soon.

Wren arched her hips towards him, and the tip of him slipped inside.

'Fuck,' he groaned, watching the crown of his cock disappear inside her. 'Embers,' he rasped. 'Look at this view . . . See how well you take me . . .'

There was nothing more erotic than watching Wren's eyes widen at the sight.

'Give me more,' she panted.

Torj gave her another inch, slowly, savouring the tight heat of her around his cock. 'Like this?'

'Stop toying with me, Bear Slayer.'

At her command, he slid home, watching as she took every inch, watching as her head tipped back in ecstasy with a gasp.

Torj gripped her hips and thrust inside her again and again, curses spilling from his lips as he gave himself over to her. Sweat beaded on his brow as he moved, his muscles trembling with restraint while she pulsed around his shaft.

Wren freed her breasts from the top of her gown, cupping them with her hands and pinching her nipples.

'Fuck,' Torj muttered at the sight, feeling his climax build. Gods, she was perfect. So fucking perfect. He reached between them and stroked Wren's clit until she was bucking against him, demanding more.

'Torj,' she cried out. 'I'm going up in flames—'

'Me too, Embers.'

Her walls contracting around him set him alight, and he erupted with a carnal moan. Pleasure rippled through him, a powerful tidal wave as he spilled himself inside her.

'Furies fucking save me,' he panted against her chest. 'You're going to kill me.'

She brushed a damp lock of hair from his eyes. 'I'm not nearly done with you.'

He huffed a hoarse laugh as he slid himself free, and helped Wren steady herself as he let her down, tucking his cock back into his leathers with a grimace at the mess.

Wren fixed herself as well, and they both paused behind the plinth, listening for any sign of life beyond. All was quiet, which only made Torj cringe at how loud they might have been, how their moans might have echoed across the academy grounds.

'That was reckless of us,' Wren said lightly, peering out at the stone pavers.

'I blame you and your wandering hands at the tavern,' Torj quipped, nuzzling her neck, dropping a kiss to the sensitive spot there.

Wren leaned into his touch. 'Perhaps next time we can fuck in a bed?'

Torj kissed her, hard. 'I'll fuck you wherever you want, Embers.'

CHAPTER 60

Wren

'Most concerning in the limited study of soul
bonds is not what has been discovered,
but what remains hidden'

— *Tethers and Magical Bonds Throughout History*

TORJ *DID* FUCK her in a bed that night. His, to be precise. He also fucked her on his desk and on the floor, and once in the bath.

The man was ravenous, and so was she.

Wren had never known a man like him, had never felt desire so all-consuming. It was only as he wrung another orgasm from her with his tongue the next morning that she held him at arm's length and panted, 'No more . . . I can't take any more.'

He gave her a roguish grin. 'I'll wager that you can—'

She hit his chest with the back of her hand. 'You *fiend*. I'll never walk straight again.'

Another smirk tugged at his lips and he winked, echoing her words from the previous night: 'I think that ship has sailed, Embers . . .'

Even as she shook her head in disbelief, she was smiling. Gods, her cheeks ached from smiling so much. When was the last time she'd experienced that sensation?

A knock at the door sounded and Torj groaned, pulling a pillow over his head.

'Just some food sent from Warsword Embervale,' the guard's voice called through the door.

Wren leapt to her feet, tugging Torj's shirt over her head and retrieving the tray. The guard blushed at her dishevelled state.

She closed the door, biting her lip to keep from laughing. 'So much for being subtle about us . . .'

Torj gave her a lazy grin from the bed, stretching out in all his naked glory. 'Embers, that poor bastard has been standing guard outside since we got back. These walls aren't soundproof.'

Wren waited for the wave of embarrassment to hit, but it never came. She simply didn't care. She'd spent the night fucking the Bear Slayer senseless, and gods, had it made her *happy*.

Just as she was about to bring the tray to bed, she saw a scrap of parchment poking out from beneath the bowl of bread. She recognized Thea's handwriting at once, wondering what sort of lewd comment her sister had made.

Her breath caught as she scanned Thea's words, the note ending with a hastily drawn lightning bolt.

'What is it?' Torj asked, brow furrowed.

But Wren wasn't ready to end their night together. Instead, she shook her head. 'Just Thea telling us we need our sustenance.'

Torj scoffed and helped her with the tray. 'She's hardly one to talk.'

They settled on the bed with the food and a flagon of wine between them, Wren still wearing his shirt, Torj still nude. Wren couldn't stop her gaze from lingering on him. It was unfair, really, that the gods had made him so perfect. He looked like a god himself, splayed out on the bed beside her . . .

When she met Torj's eye, he gave her a cocky grin. 'Not before you've regained your strength, Embers.'

She threw a piece of cheese at him.

Together, they ate and passed the wine back and forth. Wren

hadn't realized how hungry she was until she'd eaten more than half her share and found Torj smiling at her again.

'I knew I wasn't feeding you enough,' he said, pushing the rest towards her.

'It's not your job to feed me,' Wren replied, taking another bite of bread and washing it down with some wine.

'It most certainly is.'

When they finished eating, amid the rumpled sheets, he drew her to his chest and she melted into him, the soul bond flickering in bursts of gold around them once more.

'How is it that it still exists?' Wren wondered aloud as the sparks danced between her fingers.

'I don't know,' Torj replied, sounding equally mystified. 'I tore it in two with my bare hands. I truly thought it was gone for ever . . . What does the book say?'

Wren reluctantly peeled herself away from the warrior and retrieved the tome from her room. Dropping it on the mattress beside Torj, she turned to the relevant chapter. She had read it a dozen times over, and there was no mention of severing a soul bond.

'Try the index,' Torj said softly, drawing circles on her bare thigh as she scanned the text.

'Since when are you the scholar out of the two of us?' she quipped.

'Since you're distracted by my wandering fingers . . .'

Wren hid her smile and turned to the back of the book, where the major topics and events were listed in alphabetical order.

Breaking of bonds. Page 476.

Wren hurriedly found the page. It wasn't in the chapter on soul bonds, which was why she hadn't found it. She skimmed the paragraphs for the relevant phrase.

'*Certain magical bonds, like familial connections, end in death. Others, such as soul bonds, can only truly be severed if both parties agree,*' she read aloud. '*While a soul bond can be broken temporarily, it will repair in time if the love between the pair remains . . .*'

'That was why I could still see it . . .' Torj murmured. 'Even though I tore it apart, I still loved you . . . I never stopped.'

'Neither did I . . . Even when I was furious with you.' Wren reread the pages. 'That's it. That's the only mention of it.'

Torj peered over her shoulder. 'Then we have our answer . . .'

'Perhaps when this fight is done, we can sink into some deep research of the phenomena, maybe even pen our own contribution about our experience, but for now . . .' Wren closed the volume.

'For now?' Torj continued to draw patterns across her naked skin.

Wren smiled. 'For now, I say we just enjoy the benefits.'

'I can get on board with that.' The Bear Slayer kissed her soundly. 'Let's stay in this room for ever,' he murmured against her damp skin.

Even now, the huskiness in his voice curled her toes. 'For ever?'

'Mmm . . .' The sound rumbled beneath her and she smiled against his chest, admiring the ink there. Besides where his lightning scars broke the design, it was a beautiful piece – a canvas of golden skin and dark whorls that extended from the tops of his shoulders and down over his pectoral muscles.

She traced the lines with her fingertips, relishing the rush of goosebumps that washed over him, his nipples hardening at her touch.

'When did you get this?' she asked, continuing to trail her fingers over the swirls of ink.

Torj tucked a hand beneath his head and glanced down, his muscled abdomen rippling with the movement. 'After I became a Warsword,' he replied. 'I'd always wanted some sort of tattoo, but knew I'd fill out a lot more if I passed the Great Rite, so I waited.'

'You were confident,' she said with a laugh.

'You don't pass the Great Rite by being humble, Embers,' he replied, his mouth quirking to the side.

'What does it mean, then?'

'Something about the shifting sands of time . . .'

'Really?'

Torj snorted. 'No. I wish I could tell you there's some deeper meaning. But I'm a simple man, Embers. I just liked the design.'

Wren burst out laughing. 'You just *liked the design*?'

'Yep.'

Shaking her head, she asked, 'Do you think that's why Cal's got a laughing fox on his arse? He liked the design?'

Torj raised a brow. 'I don't *love* that you've seen Callahan's naked backside . . .'

Wren simply grinned.

'But no,' Torj laughed. 'I can attest to the fact that Cal was seeing double at that point, and Kipp gave the artist an extra piece of silver to copy the fox emblem from his kerchief.'

Wren muffled her snort with Torj's pillow.

'There's something I've been meaning to ask you,' he said.

'Oh?'

'What happened to Perseus Graymoor?' Torj pulled the pillow away. 'You can tell me now. You poisoned him, right?'

'No. I told you – it wasn't me.' Wren couldn't help the note of amusement in her voice. 'I was with my possessive husband the entire time.'

Torj chuckled. 'Then who did it? Who killed him?'

'Someone with excellent instincts,' Wren replied. 'I suppose it'll remain a mystery.'

As they lay there together, she pretended this was her new reality, that every morning could start just as they were now. But as the very first rays of dawn caught her eye, she remembered Thea's note on the desk.

She sighed, tracing the hard line of Torj's jaw with her fingertips. 'Do you think we wasted all those years?' she asked.

'Wasted?' Torj cupped her face in his hands. 'I think it happened exactly the way it needed to, Embers. I don't regret a moment of it. Not if we stand here together at the end of it all.'

'You'd do it all again?' she pressed.

'A hundred times over if it meant you were mine.'

She rested her brow against his. 'Then there's something I have to tell you,' she said.

He kissed her gently, pulling back to peer into her eyes. 'Embers, I already know.'

She stared at him, wondering how that was possible when she had decided for certain only moments ago herself.

'*I know you*,' he said. 'Sometimes I think I know you better than I know myself. I know there's something you have to do. I just hope you know *me* well enough by now to understand that I'm with you no matter what. With you 'til the very end.'

She nodded. The time for savouring one another was coming to a close. The outside world was calling.

'What did the note say?' he asked, propping himself up on his elbows.

Wren looked up, not managing to hide her surprise.

'You think I didn't see you hide that scrap of parchment beneath the tray?' he said with a smile.

And that only made it harder.

'Whatever it is, we'll face it together . . .' he murmured, brushing the hair from her face.

Wren gathered herself and nodded again. 'It was a message from Thea. There is to be a meeting in an hour. The People's Vanguard has marched on Delmira. And Silas the Kingsbane has laid claim to the throne.'

CHAPTER 61

Wren

'Beware the fury of a patient Delmirian'

– *Malik the Shieldbreaker,
former Warsword of Thezmarr*

THE MOOD WAS sombre in the makeshift council room as rulers and influential figures gathered around the table. Audra sat at the head, her Warswords lining the perimeter of the room, with several chroniclers and historians – including Magnus Crane – already scribbling notes on their pieces of parchment.

Torj's hand rested briefly on Wren's shoulder before he stepped into place beside Wilder, while Wren took her place beside Thea. Zavier's usual chair was empty, and Wren felt a pang of regret as she pictured him lying in the infirmary, his opus having driven him to the point of needing to be sedated. Naarva needed its prince, now more than ever.

'Our hand has been forced,' Audra announced without preamble. 'The rebel force known as the People's Vanguard has marched into Delmira. Their leader, Silas the Kingsbane – the same man who attacked this academy's very halls – has declared himself the new king. My sources report that they will reach the ruins of the capital by nightfall.'

The room erupted. Fingers were thrust across the table, faces reddening in anger, harsh words flung carelessly.

'This is the Delmirians' fault. If they hadn't delayed—'

'How do we still not know who this bastard is?'

'I can have our forces at our borders by dawn tomorrow—'

Wren had seen this before. The blame. The festering resentment. All of it boiling over into an uncontainable mess, one that poisoned the minds and hearts of men. Her gaze went to Farissa, then back to Audra, who was watching Thea expectantly.

Wren felt her sister shudder beside her, her expression ashen as her hand drifted absent-mindedly to where she once wore the fate stone that had spelled her death, or so she had thought.

They had discussed it at length since Thea's arrival at Drevenor. There was a line of succession; there was an armed force threatening the midrealms. Who better to lead their defence than a Warsword of Thezmarr?

Wren saw Thea's hands clench on the table as she stared at the grain of the wood. The shouting had grown louder, the raised voices adding to the pressure building in Wren's chest and the panic in Thea's eyes.

'What say you?' King Leiko demanded, his face ruddy, spit landing on the table. 'Will the princesses of Delmira finally make their choice? We need someone to oppose this tyrant already plundering your lands. We need someone to step up.' He flung a hand at Audra. 'Guild Master, do something!'

Audra's face was lined with regret as she turned to Thea. 'We cannot delay a moment longer. We need to know: what do you propose we do about the usurper who has claimed the kingdom for his own?'

Thea's mouth opened and she moved to stand—

Wren covered her hand with her own and squeezed it. As she rose, she whispered in her sister's ear, 'I claim this burden as my own, Thee. And you will let me have it.'

She heard the shuddering breath that left Thea, but Wren

straightened, pushing her shoulders back and lifting her chin as those gathered stared at her.

'The false king will be unseated,' she announced, her voice as clear as day. 'Delmira already has a queen.'

Stunned silence fell across the room and Wren waited.

'You're not the next in line,' King Leiko blurted.

'The law of the midrealms states that should the heir of any kingdom wish to abdicate their throne, they have the right to do so, with the next-born heir to take their place,' Wren replied calmly. She turned to Thea. 'Do you wish to abdicate your throne?'

Thea was still pale, and she paused, seeming to search Wren's face for any sign of doubt. Wren ensured that she saw none.

'I do,' Thea said at last.

Wren turned to the shocked faces before her. 'And I therefore take up that responsibility.'

'This is unprecedented,' Lady Liora declared from her seat.

'As are the times, Lady Liora,' Wren replied.

Lord Lucian's voice echoed down the table. 'The enemy has already infiltrated your kingdom, has likely already plundered the only resource you had . . . You have no funding, no army. How do you expect to win back your kingdom?'

Lightning threatened to spill from Wren's fingertips; she could feel it begging to be unleashed, could feel Thea's magic raging beside her as well. But Wren managed to keep it under control. Instead, she used words.

'We have already had one war of blood and steel, and there will be no shortage of those again. But this battle is a different beast. We must fight alchemy with alchemy, which is a skill I very much have in my arsenal, Lord Lucian.' She stared down at him. 'As for the flourishing state of Delmira, I have an answer for that too: it was storm magic that brought it back to life. *My* storm magic.' Wren glanced down at her sister, regretting that she hadn't been able to share the addition to that discovery in private first. 'We tested Thea's magic for the same capabilities and have since learned that it is an attribute unique to my own power.'

She had only just managed to slip away to the meadow before the meeting to confirm what she had suspected. The patch of grass that Thea had poured her own storm magic into had remained unchanged, whereas the small parcel Wren had treated that same day was already sprouting more wildflowers.

Thea didn't look surprised.

'So you're saying that your magic is the key to Delmira being the most fertile lands in all the kingdoms?' King Leiko asked, eyes narrowed. 'This was the secret your ancestors kept from the midrealms for centuries?'

'I believe so,' Wren allowed. 'And now I am sharing it with you, as a show of good faith for the kind of ruler I will be.'

They stared. They stared and stared at her, but Wren did not fidget; she did not waver beneath the eyes that threatened to bore holes through her.

'If there are no objections, I will consult with my counsel and devise a strategy to present to you shortly.'

Wren was trembling as she pushed her chair back, but she met Audra's gaze from across the room and was shocked to see the Guild Master dip her head in respect.

Wren surveyed those gathered around the table once more. 'You asked for a queen,' she said. 'Now you have one.'

CHAPTER 62

Torj

'For decades, the kingdom of Delmira has been
without a reigning sovereign, until now'

– Current Chronicling of the Midrealms

'YOU REALLY DID know what I was going to do, didn't you?' Wren looked at Torj in wonder, her hands trembling at her sides as they stood in the corridor outside.

'Of course I knew,' he replied, taking her hands in his, trying to absorb her fear. 'I knew the moment Thea offered herself up to take the throne. Before even that, really.'

'But . . .' She blinked up at him. 'I didn't know myself.'

'You did,' he told her. 'You just needed time.'

Her bottom lip quivered. 'I'm sorry . . . I'm so sorry—'

Torj took her chin between his thumb and forefinger, forcing her eyes to remain on his. 'You have *nothing* to be sorry for. Do you hear me? *Nothing*. With the weight of the whole fucking world on your shoulders, you have done what feels right to you, and that's all anyone can ask. Delmira is your family's kingdom. Your birthright.'

'I don't know what this means for us,' she said hoarsely. 'Is that wrong? That in the face of yet another war, all I can think of is the fact that I might lose you?'

Torj kissed her, claiming her fiercely. She opened for him, moaning into his mouth, her lips moving over his desperately.

He broke away, pressing his brow to hers. 'We survived one war,' he told her. 'We'll survive this one too.'

He remembered when he'd first met Wren as a beautiful young alchemist in the Bloodwoods, the hem of her skirts muddied, dirt lining her fingernails . . . It wasn't until years later that he'd discovered who she truly was – not only a fiery woman of Thezmarr, but a princess of the midrealms.

And now?

Now he was soul bonded to the future Queen of Delmira.

Torj peered into her willow-green eyes, watching as the dark shadows of grief morphed into determination.

'Tell me what you need, Embers,' he murmured.

She squeezed his hands. 'I need Kipp.'

CHAPTER 63

Wren

'The dichotomy of the crown is that it shows a man everything he could become, while slowly taking away all that he is'

— *The Midrealms Chronicles*

'You have me,' came a voice from behind them.

Kristopher Snowden approached with a wry grin on his face.

'And the rest of the gang,' he added, motioning to Thea and Wilder, who were striding after him. 'Cal is guarding Zavier, or he'd be right here too.'

Wren's mouth fell open. 'I . . .'

'You didn't think you'd be doing this alone, did you, Embers?' Torj's words rumbled against her side.

'I thought . . .' But Wren *had* thought exactly that. For the longest time, that was how she'd operated. For years it had been just her against the world.

As though reading her thoughts, Torj leaned in. 'You're not on your own any more.'

Tears threatened to spill, and she distantly recognized the strange feeling drifting over her . . . Relief.

Thea pushed past Torj and flung an arm around her shoulders, looking more herself than she had in days. 'You couldn't have given me the heads-up?' she demanded.

Wren shook her head. 'You'd never have agreed to it.'

Thea whirled around to face Wilder. 'And you? Pushing me back down in my chair? I suppose you were in on this?'

Wilder shrugged. 'You were forged with blood and steel, whereas Wren . . .'

'Came straight from the fire itself,' Thea replied with a grin.

Kipp cleared his throat. 'May I suggest we take this party somewhere more official?'

Wren realized with a start that they were all gathered in the corridor. 'Let's take one of the private study rooms in the archives.'

Kipp sketched a bow. 'As the queen wishes.'

Wren tried not to flinch at the title.

It was a snug fit, with three armed Warswords, a strategist and an alchemist, but they took their seats in one of the bigger private rooms in the archives. It was a circular room with wall-to-wall bookshelves, complete with a sliding ladder that reached to the higher shelves, but as they gathered around a large table, Wren couldn't pause to appreciate it.

She tried not to shrink away from the expectant looks cast her way and the countless challenges ahead etching lines of worry on each of their faces. A usurper had marched on Delmira and claimed it as his own. Lord Silas possessed alchemy that targeted magic wielders and Warswords alike. Wren had no army, no funding to obtain one and no people to rally to her banner.

Nor did she even have a fucking banner.

She allowed the flood of worries to wash over her, acknowledging each and every one before letting them dissipate around her. Despite the onslaught of problems she now faced, she knew her first point of action.

She turned to Kipp and said without preamble, 'I would like to offer you the position of royal advisor.'

The strategist leaned back in his chair, scratching his chin. 'What's the pay like?'

'Dreadful,' she replied.

'And the hours?' Kipp asked.

'Even worse.'

Kipp snorted. 'Dare I ask about the chances of success in this venture?'

Wren's lips twitched. 'Somewhere between slim and none.'

'Excellent.' He grinned, rubbing his hands together. 'When do I start?'

'Yesterday.'

Kipp's grin widened. 'Then it's a good thing I began working on this weeks ago.'

'How?' Thea demanded from across the table. 'All you've done lately is drink yourself stupid.'

'It's all part of the process,' Kipp declared, tapping his temple before he faced Wren again. 'I've already sent ravens to any noble houses with former ties to Delmira. When your kingdom fell, its people didn't simply vanish. They spread throughout the midrealms and beyond. Wherever they are, their oaths are still tied to the Embervale family. If there is honour among them, they will answer a call to arms.'

'What did you tell them?' Wren asked. She couldn't believe it. Long ago she'd learned that Kipp was always a few steps ahead, but this . . . ?

'I told them that the midrealms were under threat once more, and that the war hero heir of Delmira was claiming her crown in order to stand against tyranny and terror.'

Wren faltered. 'So they'll be expecting Thea, then . . .'

'No.' Kipp's brow furrowed. 'They are expecting Elwren Embervale. War hero of Thezmarr.'

'But—'

Thea cut her off. 'You are no less a war hero than any one of us,' she said sharply. 'The rest of the midrealms knows it. It's time you knew it too.'

Wren blinked. Yes, she had fought alongside them. But she had always felt on the outskirts of it all, with her potions and poisons instead of shield and sword.

The faces gazing back at her now told a different story.

With a knowing smile, Kipp continued. 'The law of the midrealms states that should a kingdom fall during war, the surviving kingdoms are obligated to share resources and help rebuild. It is a law that has been in action with Naarva since the end of the shadow war, and now with the emergence of a new queen, we will ensure that its benefits are extended to Delmira as well.'

Wren wrung her hands in front of her. 'But it's not enough.'

'No,' Kipp agreed. 'The very infrastructure of Delmira is in tatters. I am looking into any offshore coffers the Embervales might have had, but for now, you are a penniless player on a board of kings. Not only do you need to rebuild an entire kingdom, you need to defend it.'

The room was silent for a moment, the extent of the uphill battle ahead utterly overwhelming.

'You have two cards to play,' Kipp said slowly.

'Delmira . . .' Wren breathed.

Kipp nodded. 'Delmira was once the most prosperous land in the midrealms. More valuable than gold. As you are the only person who can make it that way again, you hold more power than you know. Not to mention that if your magic proves as effective in other kingdoms . . . you will be in high demand.'

'And the other card?' Torj asked, his husky voice heavy with dread.

It was then that Wren understood. She locked eyes with Kipp and he gave her a sombre nod.

'My hand in marriage,' she said.

CHAPTER 64

Wren

'The deepest silence falls just before the world tears itself apart, where fate balances on the edge of a blade, choosing which way to fall'

— *Elwren Embervale's notes and observations*

'WHAT?' THEA ALMOST upturned the table.

'You can't be serious,' Wilder said, looking from Wren to Kipp and crossing his arms over his chest. 'There's got to be another option.'

Only Torj was silent. Only Torj understood.

Wren's hand slid to his beneath the table, finding his palm cold and clammy against hers.

Kipp forged on. 'By the time we leave this room, you'll already have several offers. I know of four that were in discussion shortly after the last war. Queen Reyna has a nephew that she'll no doubt put forwards. Lady Liora has a son.'

'King Leiko will no doubt offer his own hand,' Thea said with disgust.

'I suspect so as well,' Kipp agreed with a grim nod. 'But I want to propose an alternative . . .'

Wren was rigid in her chair, her heart pounding against her ribs, her grip on Torj's hand tightening. 'Go on.'

It was the first time Kipp had looked uncomfortable, and he grimaced as he glanced between Wren and her Bear Slayer. 'Prince Zavier.'

'What?' Wren blurted.

Kipp gave her an apologetic look. 'You're friends. He's already taken back a working kingdom. Although Naarva was a fallen kingdom before, its absence from the last war means it's in better shape than the rest in terms of its infrastructure . . .'

Wren shook her head. 'Zavier would never agree to this.'

'He already has,' Kipp said. 'Were he not currently in the infirmary, he'd tell you himself. The advantage here is that he knows you and Torj—'

Torj stiffened beside Wren, but Kipp forged on.

'Zavier has agreed to marry in name only. You can lead separate lives. A marriage of alliance in the truest sense. He doesn't have much in the way of gold or defence forces, but the union of two royal families will carry a lot of weight with the people.'

'I can't believe we're talking about this,' Thea muttered, her head falling into her hands.

Nor could Wren. She had known it wouldn't be easy. She had known she would have to sacrifice part of herself. Her place at Drevenor. Her dream of becoming a Master Alchemist. She had given those up in the name of the greater good. But this?

'I need to speak to Torj alone,' she heard herself say.

The others didn't need telling twice. Thea, Wilder, and Kipp all hurried to their feet, the door clicking closed behind them.

Wren rose, turning the lock before she faced the Bear Slayer. 'Look at me,' she said softly.

When Torj's eyes met hers, Wren's resolve nearly fractured, for the deep-sea blue that locked on her was full of understanding, full of determination.

'I meant what I said before,' he told her. 'I'm with you no matter what, Embers. With you 'til the very end.'

'Even through this?' Wren's voice broke.

Torj's words were raw as he stood, closing the gap between them and taking her in his arms. 'Through anything.'

'This wasn't the future I imagined for us,' she whispered.

'Nor I . . . I wanted you to be free,' he murmured. 'But if it's the price of peace in the midrealms . . .'

'Then we have to pay it,' Wren finished for him.

Torj swept his thumb along her jaw and tilted her chin to his. 'I love you.'

'I love you too.'

Wren didn't know who moved first, but suddenly she was wrapped around Torj, her mouth fused to his in a searing kiss.

He carried her to the ladder against the shelf and slid her onto a rung to free his hands. His touch was a brand on her skin, and she memorized every brush of his fingertips, every imprint of him upon her, every sound that broke from his lips. She kissed him as though he were the answer to every question she'd ever had, trailing her hands over the hard planes of his body, committing every rippling muscle to memory.

Torj's belt buckle clicked open, and Wren tugged the laces of his leathers apart. 'I need you.'

His teeth dragged down the column of her throat, his fists bunching her skirts at her hips. 'I'm yours,' he growled against her skin.

With fumbling, shaking hands, Wren reached between them. She pulled her undergarments to the side and fitted him to her entrance, tears burning at the corners of her eyes. Tears she refused to shed when she had her soul-bonded here and now.

'Prove it, Bear Slayer. Fuck me like I'm yours. Fuck me so I feel you for days.'

Torj's gaze met hers, dark and unyielding. He clapped a hand over her mouth before he drove deep inside her. His palm smothered her scream, her whole body arching beneath his.

Wren held the rails of the ladder either side of her, clamping her legs around Torj's middle as he fucked her hard and fast. She could feel her back bruising against the rungs of the rattling ladder, but she didn't care. All she cared about was the man hitting that sensitive spot deep inside her, the man who had become everything to her.

Torj's lips scorched hers, setting fire to all her senses, coaxing ripples of longing to spread down her spine and right to her core. His body slapped against hers as he thrust inside, again and again, his rhythm punishing.

Heat flared between Wren's thighs as his pelvis hit her clit. She tilted her hips towards him, and Torj's cock sank even deeper inside her.

A low, rumbling sound of need escaped him, and Wren clapped her own hand over his mouth, his stubble prickling her palm. The sound of his desire, his desperation, lit an inferno inside her, and she held on to the ladder for dear life with her other hand as Torj's resolve shattered.

With each other's palms muffling their moans, they climbed the peak together, Wren clenching around Torj's cock as he fucked her harder than he ever had. He released her mouth only to reach between them, pinching her clit between his fingers—

Wren bit down on his shoulder as her climax barrelled into her. Stars erupted through her entire being, wave after wave crashing around Torj's relentless strokes.

'Wren,' he groaned, tensing over her, sinking deep inside her, his cock pulsing as his own orgasm hit and he spilled his release.

Wren blinked the room back into focus, panting as she locked eyes with the Warsword between her legs.

A thread of gold shone between them.

Tell me this isn't goodbye. Torj's voice echoed in her mind as the soul bond danced between them.

I could never tell you goodbye.

Wren's nape prickled, the glimmering gold vanishing.

A second later, a key turned in the door's lock.

Wren and Torj fumbled—

But the door opened.

Lord Lucian Devereux slipped inside the room, his gaze falling to where Wren's naked legs were wrapped around the Bear Slayer, her skirts barely covering where they were still joined.

Wren's face burned as Torj yanked her skirts down around them, slipping from her and turning his back to the Lord of Larkwood Valley to fix himself.

But the damage was done.

The nobleman studied her with a curled lip. 'Princess Elwren,' he tutted. 'Found rutting with another man while her hand in marriage is being discussed in the very same building . . .'

'It's Queen Elwren,' Torj growled.

'She's not queen until she is crowned, and a lot can happen between now and then.'

Wren's skin crawled. Lucian Devereux was holding himself like a snake coiled and waiting to strike.

'That door was locked,' she said slowly, stepping down from the ladder, adjusting her undergarments and skirts and trying not to crumple in shame.

'Gold and silver are powerful motivators,' he replied. 'I had a key made the moment I got here.'

'What do you want?' Torj demanded, standing protectively at Wren's side.

Lucian gave the warrior an icy glare. 'To speak with the heir alone.'

'Not going to happen.'

But Wren's skin was prickling, her lightning flickering in her veins in warning. 'Torj . . .' she said softly.

He turned to her. *Don't ask me to leave you.*

Never for long, my love. Wren kept her mask in place. 'I need you to find Kipp and bring him to me.'

Torj's eyes widened in disbelief. 'I—'

'Her first royal command,' the nobleman said dryly. 'You'd better run along, boy.'

Wren saw the Warsword's fists clench at his sides and she placed a hand on his arm. 'Please.'

Torj's eyes narrowed for a moment before he strode to the door and left. When it swung closed behind him, Wren turned her attention back to Lucian and folded her arms over her chest.

'You realize how reckless your little dalliance is?' he sneered. 'No one wants a princess broken in by a Warsword.'

Wren hated that she flinched at the coarse words. 'Why are you here? What do you want?'

'Surely you can guess, Elwren. Aren't you meant to be a promising student? One of the brightest within your rank?'

Wren's magic grew hot beneath her skin. 'Why would I give you anything?'

'Because,' Lucian said, his voice dripping slow and steady as poison, 'I have the thing you need most in the world.'

Alone in the private study room, the walls began to close in. Wren fought to keep her breathing even, ground her teeth to keep the flashbacks and panic at bay. Everything had changed. Whichever way she studied her position, she was trapped, with Lucian Devereux's words echoing in her mind, a drum beating a death-march rhythm. All that she'd imagined for herself, for Torj, evaporated, leaving the fates before them dark. Wren had to brace herself against the table to keep her knees from buckling, had to grip the edge to anchor herself to the present.

I have the thing you need most in the world. The thing she hadn't even known she needed.

A knock sounded at the door, startling her. 'Wren?' Kipp called from the other side.

Trying to hide the tremor in her hands, Wren opened the door and greeted both Kipp and Torj, who were peering at her expectantly. Torj scanned the room behind her, his jaw clenched.

But Wren stopped him from entering. 'I need to speak with Kipp alone.'

Torj's eyes narrowed with suspicion. 'What did that bastard say to you?'

'I'll tell you later,' she said. 'Can you please wait outside?'

Torj looked like he was going to argue, and Wren hated herself for it, but there was nothing to be done.

When at last Wren was alone with Kipp, she told him everything.

Her friend listened carefully, never interrupting, waiting patiently as she gathered herself between breaths, passing her his kerchief when her tears tracked down her face.

And when she finished, he straightened in his chair. 'Let me get this straight . . .' he said slowly. 'You're asking me to put aside my personal concern for your happiness and wellbeing?'

'Yes. I need an army. I need funding. I need resources. I need *time*.'

'And you want me to strategize as though this is some cold, unfeeling decision?' he asked, peering into her face as though searching for signs of madness.

'No,' Wren told him. 'I want you to strategize like this is war.'

CHAPTER 65

Wren

'A Master Alchemist knows the crucible merely completes
what careful preparation begins. Perfection or poison –
both are determined before the first spark ignites'

— *Transformative Arts of Alchemy*

THE ACADEMY INFIRMARY was quiet, with only a handful of beds occupied. Wren knew which belonged to Zavier immediately – it was the only one with the curtains drawn and a Warsword stationed outside.

Cal gave her a grim smile as she approached, Torj towering in her wake.

'It's time we woke the Prince of Naarva,' she told Cal. 'We have need of him.'

'Is that safe? For him? For us?' Cal asked, his brow furrowed with worry.

'Farissa has cleared it,' Wren replied, slipping behind the curtains, the Warswords following.

Zavier had wasted away. His face was gaunt and thin, lined with grief even in unconsciousness, his usual surly expression softened. He looked small in the infirmary bed, more childlike than Wren had ever seen him.

'We tried to bring him round to get him to eat,' Cal explained with a grimace. 'But he was too upset. He kept screaming about saving someone and failing them. Farissa always ended up giving him something to make him go back to sleep.'

'I see,' Wren said. It was much the same as when he'd had his first episode in the workshop. 'Do you know who he's been talking about?'

'His family?' Cal guessed.

Wren reached for the jar of peppered broadleaf that Farissa had left for her on the table by the bed. 'These act as smelling salts,' she told the warriors behind her. 'He'll come around quite quickly and suddenly. You may need to hold him down while I talk to him, and administer a calming draft if need be. Are you ready?'

Both Warswords nodded in confirmation.

Steeling herself, Wren removed the cork from the jar and waved the herbs under her friend's nose. A bitter aroma wafted up from the glass—

Zavier bolted upright with a gasp, his eyes flying open, wild and unfocused. The sudden movement sent the metal bed frame scraping against the stone floor, the harsh sound echoing in the confined space behind the curtains. His chest heaved beneath the thin infirmary shirt, damp with sweat.

Wren took a swift step back, letting Torj and Cal move into position. They gripped Zavier's shoulders, but he thrashed against their hold, his movements desperate but weak from days without proper food.

'Breathe,' Wren commanded, though her voice softened at the sight of his terror. 'You're in Drevenor's infirmary.' She held his stare, willing him to recognize her. 'I need you to breathe, and I need you to listen to me, otherwise we'll have to sedate you again.'

Zavier's eyes darted between her face and the Warswords restraining him. The afternoon light filtering through the curtains cast strange shadows across his hollow cheeks while his fingers clutched at the sheets until his knuckles turned white.

'I couldn't do it,' he rasped, his voice breaking. He swallowed hard, throat bobbing. 'I couldn't save—' He choked on the words, his whole body trembling.

'Who?' Wren asked gently, moving to retrieve Farissa's supplies. The glass bottles clinked together as her hands shook slightly. 'Instead of smashing everything in the room, why don't you tell us who you couldn't save?'

She lit the oil burner, and the warm glow of the candle flame cast dancing shadows on the curtains around them. The scent of lavender began to drift through the air, but Zavier's breathing remained ragged.

'My brother,' he finally croaked. His eyes grew distant, focused on something none of them could see. A tear slid down his cheek, but he didn't seem to notice.

'Zavier,' Wren started, perching carefully on the edge of his bed. The mattress dipped beneath her weight, and he flinched at her proximity. 'How recent was your brother's death?'

'He's . . .' His hands twisted in the sheets. 'He's not dead. But he's lost . . .' His voice trailed off, and he pressed his lips together as if physically holding back words.

Wren glanced at Torj, whose grip on Zavier's shoulder remained, but had loosened. The Warsword's expression was dark.

'What do you mean?' Torj demanded.

Zavier's shoulders caved, making him look even smaller in the bed. 'I've been trying so hard to reach him, to make him understand . . .'

The candle flame wavered, casting strange shadows across his face as he spoke, the scent of lavender drifting through the air but calming no one. Something in his tone made the hair on the back of Wren's neck stand up. Zavier's eyes met hers, and the raw pain she saw there made her want to look away. But she held his gaze as he drew a shuddering breath.

'My brother . . .' he murmured again, and the words seemed to hang in the air between them, heavy with unspoken fear. The infirmary fell so silent they could hear voices drifting in from the courtyard outside, oddly cheerful against the weight of Zavier's confession.

Wren realized she was staring, but she couldn't help it. 'So he's not dead? But you couldn't save him . . . ? I don't understand . . .'

His laugh was hollow, almost hysterical. 'No, you wouldn't. None of you would.' He ran a trembling hand through his unkempt hair. 'I thought—' His voice cracked, and he had to start again. 'I thought if I could prove his theory, or at least show him what was possible with human transmutation, then he'd . . .'

Cal's hand tightened on Zavier's shoulder. 'He'd what?'

'He'd be different.' The words burst from him like they'd been torn from his throat, his breath rattling in his chest. 'I thought that if I knew what he knew, I could reason with him. I thought if I could bring our mother back, I could bring *him* back . . . That I could save them both.'

The oil burner sputtered, startling Wren. None of it made sense to her, but dread was building in her stomach, a cold weight that grew heavier with each word.

'The whole reason I came to Drevenor was to understand him.' Zavier's hands were shaking now, and he clasped them together to still them.

'He's an alchemist?' Torj interrupted, his voice sharp with sudden understanding. 'Was he a student here?'

'He wanted to be.' Zavier's words came faster now, tumbling over each other like he couldn't hold them back any more. 'He was the real alchemist of the two of us. But I realized that if I couldn't save him . . .' His voice hardened. 'I had to be better than him, skilled enough to beat him.'

The cold weight in Wren's stomach turned to ice. 'Zavier . . .' She fought to keep her voice steady. 'Why hasn't he returned to Naarva? He has a crown waiting for him.'

Zavier's laugh was bitter this time. 'It's not the Naarvian crown he wants.' His eyes met hers, filled with such profound sorrow that she knew what he would say before the words left his mouth. 'It's yours.'

The candle guttered.

'Zavier,' Torj said, his voice dangerously quiet. '*Who* is your brother?'

The prince seemed to shrink further into himself, but his eyes never left Wren's face. 'His name was Andor Terling,' he answered, each word falling like a stone into still water. 'But he goes by Silas the Kingsbane now.'

CHAPTER 66

Torj

'When the birds stop singing and the wind dies midbreath, the Warswords know: this is not peace – it is the world drawing back from what approaches'

– *A History of Thezmarr*

IT WAS THE second time in as many weeks that Cal had to physically restrain Torj. He was ready to throttle the Naarvian prince.

'How long have you known?' he demanded. 'How long have you let people die, knowing who was at the helm?'

'I was only certain during the battle after the Gauntlet,' Zavier replied weakly. 'I felt his magic then. Before that it had been a theory, nothing more—'

'Gods, *that's* why his voice was so familiar. He has the same accent as *you* from beyond the Veil! And you didn't think to *share* this theory with anyone?'

Zavier shook his head. 'No one was supposed to know who I was . . .'

'People *died*,' Torj spat. 'Warswords *died*.'

Zavier threw the sheets back and swayed on his feet as he stood. '*I know*. I've been trying to stop him. Trying to—'

'Enough,' Wren said quietly, silencing them both. 'This is not the time nor place for this conversation. Zavier, are you able to leave the grounds? You won't risk hurting anyone with your magic?'

Zavier straightened. 'I can leave. Though I might need something to eat first.'

Wren nodded. 'Dessa's already fetching you something from the kitchens, and Kipp will come by to fill you in on everything.'

Torj watched her closely. 'What's going on, Embers?' he asked.

'Thea is coming by to get me,' she said slowly. 'I have somewhere I need to be—'

'Not without me you don't,' Torj countered.

To his immense frustration, Wren ignored this. Instead, she took his hands in hers. 'For now, I need you to promise me something . . .'

Torj waited.

'Promise me that whatever happens this afternoon, you'll wait. That you will not kill anyone, and that you will meet me in the gardens at dusk.'

Torj shifted from foot to foot. 'Wren . . . I don't like where this is going.'

'Promise me: *wait*. Kill no one. Meet me at dusk. No matter what.'

Torj took a deep breath. 'I promise.'

'No matter what,' she repeated.

He bowed his head. 'No matter what.'

When Thea arrived, her stance was rigid, her eyes steely. 'An assembly has been called at Highguard's town hall, and Wren needs to prepare,' she told them, tugging her sister away.

Torj made to follow. 'Of course—'

A fleeting look of regret passed over Thea's face before her voice became stern. 'You'll meet her in the gardens once it's done.'

'Once *what* is done?' he demanded.

But the Embervale sisters left without answering.

The corridors of Drevenor echoed with frantic whispers and hurried footsteps. News of the usurper's march on Delmira had spread like wildfire, igniting fear and speculation among students and faculty alike.

Torj stood amid the chaos, his heart pounding – not from the looming conflict or what they had learned from Zavier, but from the ache of Wren's sudden absence.

Her urgent exit from the infirmary had left Torj reeling, questions burning on his tongue. He had no idea what the bastard had said to Wren in the archives, or how Zavier factored into her plans, but something was *wrong*. The lightning scars over his heart prickled with unease.

In the lower levels of the academy, Torj got swept up in the madness as students made their way outside, determined to get to the city before the assembly. He fought his way to the front, where he could see Wilder and Cal guarding the other royals.

'Do you know what the fuck is going on?' he asked, scanning the surging crowd.

'Not a clue,' Wilder called back. 'But we've got to get this lot to Highguard.'

With Wren's absence like an open wound across his flesh, Torj sought to lose himself in the logistics of getting a bunch of rulers to the city.

'This is a terrible idea,' he muttered as he and Wilder oversaw the appointment of guards to the carriages.

'I'll say,' Wilder agreed. 'But Drevenor still isn't common knowledge to the people of the midrealms, and they need to make this announcement publicly, so Highguard is the closest option.'

A stable hand brought their horses ready and saddled, and Torj accompanied the party of rulers to the city, missing the beautiful alchemist at his side.

Torj had had no reason before now to visit the Highguard town hall, and he barely took in the details as he burst through its thick wooden doors, scanning the throngs of people for a messy bun of bronze hair.

What he saw instead was a regal woman waiting in the wings of the stage, resplendent in a gown of gold.

As though sensing his stare, she looked up, her gaze meeting his before it darted away, leaving a stab of hurt in his chest.

I'm with you no matter what, Embers. With you 'til the very end, he'd told her . . . What if it wasn't enough? What if *he* wasn't enough? What had changed?

Torj pushed his way through the common folk of Highguard, reaching the front of the hall, just below the stage.

A hush fell across the crowd as Zavier Terling took to the lectern. It was hard to believe that only hours ago, the prince had been unconscious in the academy infirmary. He'd been fed and bathed and looked every bit the pampered prince the midrealms expected him to be. Dessa had clearly used cosmetics to hide the dark circles beneath his eyes, though there was no solution to the hollowness of his cheeks. He wore an emerald-green doublet and a crown Torj had never seen before.

Pain lanced through his heart. He was staring at Wren's future husband. The man who would stand by her side through life, the man who would wear her ring, who would echo her vows of enduring partnership . . . Dread slid into Torj's gut. Was Zavier going to announce his engagement to Wren so soon? After what they'd just learned about his brother?

'People of Highguard. People of Naarva,' the prince called out. 'Earlier today, we received word that there is a pretender laying siege to the broken kingdom of Delmira as we speak.'

Gasps echoed around the hall.

'This usurper is no stranger to us. He is the leader of the rebel force, the People's Vanguard – the very one that has been terrorizing the midrealms for months.'

Stunned silence followed.

'But from this terrible situation, a wondrous thing has bloomed. Elwren Embervale, war hero of Thezmarr, heir of Delmira, has come forth to claim her throne.'

He motioned to where Wren was emerging from the side of the stage, her head held high, her back straight as she approached the Prince of Naarva.

She looked like royalty, and it made Torj's warrior heart ache.

Wren addressed the gathered crowd. 'Prince Zavier speaks the truth. I will be taking my kingdom back from its usurpers. And I will do so as Queen of Delmira.'

Hushed murmurs broke out across the crowd.

'But I will not do it alone,' Wren called. She gestured to another standing in the wings, and Torj's blood ran cold as the last person he expected strode across the stage, taking her hand in his.

Torj felt the moment his heart fractured.

He heard the rattling gasp leave his lips as his lungs constricted painfully.

The word *betrothed* rang out across the hall.

And an arrogant smirk found him in the crowd.

Darian fucking Devereux.

CHAPTER 67

Torj

'The lone flame flickers, but a fire blazing bright has the power to rewrite fate'

— *Tethers and Magical Bonds Throughout History*

TORJ FLED HIGHGUARD on his stallion, tearing through the city gates so fast that tears streamed from his eyes. Wind whipped through his hair and stung his cheeks, but he had to get out of there, had to leave that rotten place behind. He rode blindly towards Drevenor, his heart racing, nausea swirling low in his gut. He'd gather his things and get back to the port. He could board a ship. He could sail beyond the Veil border.

Darian Devereux . . . After everything Torj had told her. Why *him*? The man was a fucking monster, a blight upon the midrealms.

Kipp had outlined the plan. A marriage of alliance to Zavier – her friend, who they could trust; a fellow magic wielder, a smart match with resources of his own. Torj had hated the thought of Wren wearing anyone else's ring, but he'd told himself he could live with it. That if it meant peace in the midrealms, he'd stomach being the Queen of Delmira's secret lover. But Devereux? The man was poison.

Torj could barely remember the ride from the city by the time he got back to the academy. He didn't recall climbing the stairs or unlocking the door to his room. He stumbled inside, thoughts of Wren consuming him.

I could never tell you goodbye. She had said those words into his very mind, allowing them to burrow inside his heart as her soul connected with his.

She was everywhere. The spring rain and jasmine scent that lingered in the air; the bushel of dried lavender that still sat on the windowsill; the strands of bronze hair on his pillow, and the apron she'd discarded over the back of his chair. He could feel the echo of her storm magic too, ghosting across his skin, his lips . . .

With an anguished shout, he swept his forearm across the desk, sending books, parchment and a glass clattering to the floor. His thoughts were chaotic, panicked. One second, he was sure there must be an explanation, some plan he wasn't privy to, and the next . . .

Devereux. She chose Devereux.

He had told her he would stick by her through anything. That he would be with her until the very end, but this?

He looked to his pack. He could leave. Right now. He could be on the open seas within hours. He could . . .

His eyes fell to something else.

The dagger. The dagger he had taught her how to use, the dagger he'd secretly had altered just this week to fit her smaller hand . . . In the final rays of sun streaming through the window, the inscription he'd had engraved along its blade glittered back at him.

Iron & Embers.

He sank to the floor, his back against the bed, head in his hands. Devereux . . . For her to marry Darian fucking Devereux . . . How could she—

But still he heard her voice. *Meet me at dusk. No matter what.*

Breaking apart at the seams, Torj watched the shadows lengthen across the room. Dusk was approaching . . . and with it came a reckoning.

The sky turned blood red as Torj passed beneath the garden gates. He realized his hands were trembling. Whatever awaited him now, he both dreaded and desperately needed *answers*.

The rolling hills so full of wildflowers somehow seemed empty, like the cavernous space inside his chest, hollow and aching.

He had broken her heart here. Now she was doing the same to him.

A heart for a heart.

He supposed there was a brutal sense of justice in that.

And so he kept his vow. He waited.

Torj felt her before he saw her. A song calling out to him, the melody his soul knew. Wren was still wearing the gold dress as she approached, the same shade as the bond between them.

'You came,' she said softly.

He tried to swallow the lump in his throat. 'I gave you my word.'

'You did. And there's nothing I wouldn't give for you,' she told him fiercely, her gaze full of fire. 'Nothing.'

But Torj's eyes fell to the large jewel now adorning her fourth finger, recognizing it instantly: the late Lady Devereux's engagement ring. 'Then . . . what have you done? Did you ask me here for a morbid farewell?' His voice was hoarse, broken.

'No.' Wren's expression was steely. 'I told you I would never say goodbye.'

Torj stared at her. 'Then what, Wren? What reason could you possibly have for choosing *him*? For doing this?'

'It was the only way to save you,' she said. 'And I know that's something you can understand, because *you* made the same choice not all that long ago.'

'Wren . . . What are you talking about?'

Her mask of composure slipped for a moment, and she took his hands in hers. 'You have been *poisoned*, my Bear Slayer. *That* is what Lucian Devereux told me in the archives. You were targeted when you rescued Queen Reyna.'

'What?' Torj started. 'You can't believe a word that bastard says. He's lying.'

She shook her head sadly. 'He's not. I tested your blood for toxins myself.'

'*When?*' he demanded, incredulous.

'After he told me. I had your blood under my fingernails from when we . . . it doesn't matter. It's the truth. You need to trust me on that. *Please.*'

The desperate note in her voice stopped him from protesting. Instead, Torj tried to think about it rationally. 'If that's the case, you've created the cure. You saved Reyna. Why can't you use that potion on me?'

'This is a different poison entirely.' Wren's voice wavered. 'Whatever it's made of, it was designed specifically for you.'

Torj thought back to the queen's rescue . . . he remembered the chaos of the vapour, and the blue-grey smoke billowing from the broken vial beneath the enemy's boot. Searching his memory for more detail, he jolted. *The darts.* He'd shielded Reyna with his own body. He'd barely felt the things prick his skin . . . and with everything else going on, he'd thought no more of it. 'But I feel fine . . .' he told Wren, the blurry images still flashing in his mind, as though they had happened to someone else. 'That was months ago now. Surely I'd have some sort of reaction or symptoms if it were true?'

Wren squeezed his hands. 'It's been in your blood ever since. Perhaps it was even dormant for a time, but it's a slow-release toxin and eventually . . . it will kill you. But I'm not going to let that happen.'

Torj shook his head in disbelief, his mind reeling. 'How does Lucian know? And what's his role in all of this?'

'He has spies in the People's Vanguard who report back to him,' Wren answered. 'And Lucian wants what all men like him want: power. He thinks that by marrying his son into the Embervale family, he will gain more than he has ever had before. A storm-wielding daughter-in-law, storm-wielding grandchildren – not to mention access to the newly discovered prosperity Delmira now offers. He wants it all, and he's using you to force my hand.'

Torj's gut twisted as though a knife were embedded there.

Wren linked her fingers through his, stroking his callused skin with her thumb. 'Lucian thinks I'm caving to his will, that he has me over a barrel, but the engagement to Darian buys us *time* – time to find an antidote and more resources to defend Delmira.'

A hollow laugh bubbled from his lips. 'How did we fucking get here? *Darian*, Wren?'

'It's part of a much bigger plan. And it had to look believable,' she said softly. 'Everyone knew we were together, Torj. We might have hidden the soul bond, but our love? There was no denying that, and so the end of us . . . it had to be public, and your reaction had to be genuine. All the powerful figures had to see it for themselves. They needed to be convinced that we are over, and that my engagement to Darian is genuine.'

As her words washed over him, Torj felt as though he were standing on the precipice of something monumental, something that he didn't yet quite understand, but that could change the course of the future.

'It was the only way to reset the chessboard. To figure out who we can trust,' Wren continued, pain gleaming in her stormy gaze. 'I'm sorry to have done that to you, to have hurt you . . . But I did this to save you, Torj. To save the midrealms. All I can do is play the hand I've been given.'

Another shaky breath escaped him, and he hardly dared to believe it. 'It's a shitty hand,' he croaked.

'Terrible,' Wren agreed, her mouth quirking to the side. 'But do you remember telling me about the warrior's second? *This* is ours. The breath before the slice of a blade. The moment to make the swing of a hammer count, to make our actions worthy of legend . . .'

Gold flickered once more between them.

I love you, her voice bloomed in his mind, loud and clear, strong and unyielding. *I have always loved you.*

The green eyes that locked on his were full of passion, a storm of power. The soul bond shimmered to life between them, the gold more solid than ever before.

I love you, he echoed back silently.

And Wren smiled.

'I take it you have a plan?' Torj heard himself ask, his heart still raw but hope sparking in his chest.

She nodded. 'I have a plan.'

With trembling hands, Torj took hers in his as he knelt, pressing his lips to her knuckles before looking up at her.

He lay his war hammer at her feet and unsheathed the dagger he'd had altered, offering it, and his whole heart, to her. 'Then tell me how to serve you, my queen.'

'You stand at my side.' Wren's fingers closed over his, gold and lightning joining them as one. 'And we destroy them all. Together.'

Acknowledgements

This past year has been a rollercoaster, to say the least – a journey of stark contrasts and unexpected turns. I often felt as though I had whiplash from how quickly things changed. There have been plenty of highs, but there were also valleys so deep I wondered if I'd ever find my way back to the surface. Some days, the simple act of opening my laptop felt like scaling a mountain. Yet here we are, with a completed book in hand once again, and as always, it certainly didn't come together on its own.

First, to Gary. Thank you for being my safe harbour during the storm, for always championing me and my work, and for providing much-needed perspective. I'm so grateful for the beautiful life we're building together.

To C.A. Wright, fellow author, editor, and most importantly, friend . . . You've been a part of this wild career since the very beginning, and I couldn't imagine doing it without you. Thank you for your endless support.

Thank you to my incredible PA and friend, Anne. I honestly don't know how I managed before you came along. Thank you for being the buffer between me and the world when I need it most, and for being the ultimate hype woman.

Mum, thank you for proofing these pages, and for all your support and love of literature over the years.

All my love and thanks to the rest of the Scheuerer fam back home in Sydney.

Thank you to my wonderful friends who always support me in numerous ways: Eva, Lisy, Aleesha, Ben, Hannah, Natalia, Fay, Erin, Phoebe, Maria, and Joe.

Thank you to fellow authors Sacha Black, Meg Cowley, Morgan Bridges, Angelina J. Steffort, Tay Rose, V.B. Lacey, Penn Cole, Kara Douglas, Nicole Platania, Emilia Jae, and Sheila Masterson, for being amazing friends and sounding boards.

Thank you to my agents, Ezra and Ethan, for all your hard work.

To Gillian Green and the rest of the team at Tor Bramble UK and Pan Macmillan Australia, thank you for believing in this series and for helping me make such a splash.

A massive thank you to my street team, both past and present. I appreciate each and every one of you. Your efforts are inspired, and the conversations in Discord bring me so much joy from afar. Thank you, thank you.

Last but never least, thank *you*, dear reader, for continuing to give my books a chance. It's been a wild ride, and I can't wait to share the epic finale of this chapter with you.

Much love,
Helen

ABOUT THE AUTHOR

Helen Scheuerer is the author of the bestselling fantasy series The Oremere Chronicles, the Curse of the Cyren Queen quartet, The Legends of Thezmarr and The Ashes of Thezmarr. Her work has been highly praised for its strong, flawed female characters and its action-packed plots. Helen's love of writing and books led her to pursue a creative writing degree and a Master's in Publishing. She has been a full-time author since 2018 and now lives among the mountains in New Zealand, where she is constantly dreaming up new stories.